D0828434

REMOTE
CONTROL

REMOTE CONTROL

KOTARO ISAKA

Translated by Stephen Snyder

KODANSHA INTERNATIONAL
Tokyo · New York · London

Publication of this book was assisted by a grant from the Japan Foundation.

Originally published in Japanese in 2007 by Shinchosha Publishing Co., Ltd., Tokyo, under the title *Golden Slumber*.

Distributed in the United States by Kodansha America, LLC, and in the United Kingdom and continental Europe by Kodansha Europe Ltd.

Published by Kodansha International Ltd., 17-14 Otowa 1-chome, Bunkyo-ku, Tokyo 112-8652.

On pages 88, 90, 167, 219, 285, and 297, lyric excerpts of "Golden Slumbers" by John Lennon and Paul McCartney.

JASRAC 出1008870–001

Library of Congress Cataloging-in-Publication Data

Isaka, Kotaro, 1971-
  [Goruden suranba. English]
  Remote control / Kotaro Isaka ; translated by Stephen Snyder.
    p. cm.
"Originally published in Japanese in 2007 by Shinchosha Publishing Co., Ltd., Tokyo, under the title Golden Slumber"—T.p. verso.
  ISBN 978-4-7700-3108-2
  I. Snyder, Stephen, 1957- II. Title.
PL871.5.S25G6713 2010
  895.6'35—dc22
                          2010028485

Jacket design by Andrew Lee.

www.kodansha-intl.com

CONTENTS

PART

ONE

THE BEGINNING

Haruko Higuchi

Haruko Higuchi had arranged to meet Akira Hirano for lunch at a soba shop. Akira arrived late and, though they hadn't seen each other in four years, sat down without apologizing. "Some things never change," she said. Then, to the cook in his white smock behind the counter: "Two specials."

The shop was in the basement of a building near Sendai Station occupied by an insurance company, at the end of a subterranean row of bars and restaurants. It was near the electronics company where Akira was employed, and the two of them had often come here for soba in the days when Haruko had worked there as well. It seemed like the right spot for their reunion.

"Some things never change," Akira said again.

"You're right. The menu is exactly the same. But they've got wasabi in a tube now instead of the fresh-grated stuff they used to serve."

"I meant you. Do you really have a kid?"

"She's four years and nine months old."

"Well, I'm three years and three hundred and thirty-nine months old," said Akira, keeping a straight face.

"You can do that in your head? That's quite a talent."

"Comes in handy in the dating world," she laughed.

Dating! Haruko smiled at the memory of single life and studied Akira more closely. She was short and slender, her hair dyed brown and curled. Her eyelids were heavy, her lips full. She wore little makeup. Though it was chilly in Sendai in late November, she only had a black sweater on.

"You know," Akira said, "I always wanted to ask you what you thought of me when we worked together. We sat next to each other all that time. Did you think I was an idiot, never talking about anything but men? You must have hated me. But you were always so polite. Was that just to keep me at a distance?"

"I admired you."

"Don't be ridiculous."

Though they were the same age, Haruko had envied Akira's energy, her constant, animated commentary on life—the cute salesman visiting the office, the idiosyncrasies of her current boyfriend, some sexy underwear she had discovered. "There was no discouraging you."

"'No discouraging'? You make me sound like a cockroach," Akira said, lowering an eyebrow in mock offense.

"I always thought you were so cool. When your boyfriend called during work, you'd just tell the boss you wanted to take time off and leave—and the amazing thing was, no one held it against you."

"Not that I did that every day."

"Often enough!" Haruko laughed.

"You just have to pick your spots. Know when you can get away with it."

"Pick your spots. . . ."

"But I'm always ready to leave early if something special comes up."

"Okay, what if I call someday and tell you I'm getting divorced?"

"I'd be out the door in a flash."

Then maybe I'll do just that, Haruko Higuchi thought.

The restaurant, she noted, was not particularly crowded for noon on a weekday, and at first she wondered whether it might be struggling to keep afloat, but then she noticed a new flat-screen TV mounted high on one wall, the sort of thing you wouldn't buy if you were about to go out of business.

The TV was tuned to the noon news. It was a national broadcast, and yet the shot showed a local scene, the front of Sendai Station. Below the banner of the network, the sight of the familiar building was disconcerting, as though one's own home had suddenly shown up on the news. The caption on the picture announced that Prime Minister Kaneda's motorcade was about to leave the station.

"Sendai's caught Kaneda fever," Akira observed, glancing up at the screen, her chin propped on her palm. "Everybody at our office went out to watch instead of going to lunch."

"The security is amazing. They've closed a lot of roads," said Haruko, remembering the police lines she'd seen on her way there. The men had been wearing padded armor, like baseball catchers, with "Miyagi Prefectural Police" across the chest.

"I suppose the local bigwigs would be in trouble if anything happened to a popular new prime minister. A whole lot of trouble. . . ." Akira took one last look at the TV and turned her attention to the lunch that had just arrived.

They talked about Akira's boyfriend as they ate their soba. They had met at a party; he was three years younger than her, a serious sort with a baby face, who was anxious to please no matter what she asked of him. "It's like I found this lamp—I just rub it and he pops out ready to do my bidding."

"A genie."

"But the best part is his name: Masakado! Like the shogun. I'm going out with Taira no Masakado! Lord of all Japan!"

"And where does Lord Masakado work?"

"That's sort of interesting, too," she said, her voice rising slightly, as though she'd suddenly realized something else to his credit. "Have you ever heard of a 'Security Pod'?"

"Those things they've installed all over the city?"

"The ones that look like R2-D2 from *Star Wars*."

"Are they really collecting information?" Haruko asked. They had been touted as a way to "promote public safety." But it was unclear what they were recording and who had access to the information.

"According to Lord Masakado, it doesn't amount to much," Akira said. "He thinks satellites are more accurate and efficient. The pods basically take pictures in the area right around them and record cell phone transmissions. But we live in a surveillance society, that's for sure."

"So what's his role in all this?"

"You might say he's in maintenance."

"He maintains surveillance on society?"

"Not exactly. He cleans the lenses. They go around in a van and check each pod, make repairs, wipe the lens. Pretty exciting, no?"

"Any wedding plans?"

"Wedding? Plans? Next question. But speaking of marriage, how's yours going?"

"I'm not sure what to say."

"Well, what about the kid? Boy or girl? Cute, I'm sure."

"A girl. And cute—I suppose." Haruko paused for a moment, resisting the urge to launch into a description of Nanami. "But, back to you, are you thinking of marrying Masakado?"

Akira stopped, a noodle suspended in mid-slurp between her chopsticks, and stared at Haruko. Then, after a moment, moving only her lips, she sucked up the rest of the noodle. "You only get one card at a time," she said at last.

"I don't follow."

"Well, for example, when you're dealt the ten of spades, you have a problem—should you hold it or throw it in for another card? Tens are tricky that way. You might get a better card. In that sense, aces or fours are a lot easier to figure out."

"So, Masakado is the ten of spades?" Haruko tried to imagine how the man would feel about the comparison. "I'll bet he's really a face card."

"No, afraid not." She smiled and shook her head. "Though I would say he *looks* like a jack." Akira's affection for her boyfriend showed in the line of her smile. "But what about you?" she asked. "Did you settle for a face card on top of the deck? Stand pat when you were dealt your husband, game over?"

"Well, he wasn't exactly the first card." Haruko grimaced. "Though I guess he did turn up pretty early in the game."

Akira slurped her soba more enthusiastically, as if enjoying these confidences. When she had finished another mouthful, she stuck a finger in the air. "That's right, you used to talk about a guy you dated in college—good-looking but flaky."

Haruko nodded, summoning up Masaharu Aoyagi's face in her head. Akira's prying was like pulling the plug on a keg of wine, among a stack of them piled precariously against a wall. Her memories of her time with Aoyagi began flooding back. She fumbled for the cork, her fingers slippery, and barely managed to push it back in the hole. The torrent stopped, but bits of things, like scraps of photographs, tumbled into view—glimpses of their earliest days at college, Aoyagi's boyish face when they'd first met, and later his stunned look when she'd announced she was leaving him.

"Do you remember that delivery truck driver who was in the news for a while a couple of years ago?" Haruko said eventually.

Akira, finishing another bite of soba, looked puzzled for a moment but then stuck her finger in the air again. "I do. You mean the nice-looking guy who was all over the TV for catching a burglar? How could I forget that face? For a while there, Sendai had the hots for him like it has for Kaneda now. I suppose I got a pretty good case myself," she admitted. "Good-looking but a bit rough around the edges. In the end, though, I could never understand why people got so worked up about it all."

"Because the woman he rescued was a star," Haruko said.

"That's right. What was her name?"

"I don't remember anymore."

"Which is exactly my point," Akira said, adding a little hot water to her bowl.

Haruko shook her head. "I suppose everything fades away eventually. The star's name, the truck driver, old boyfriends."

"Though they must go on doing something somewhere, even after we've forgotten them. . . . But where is that little girl of yours today?" she added.

"At kindergarten."

Akira fixed her with a skeptical look. "Are you sure you didn't make her up?" She held Haruko's gaze for a moment before breaking into a smile.

The TV screen was still filled with familiar buildings, scenes of downtown Sendai along the main street heading south from the prefectural offices and city hall. The sidewalks were jammed, despite the November cold. Haruko wondered where so many people could have come from, while life elsewhere in the city went on as usual. She remembered that someone had once told her that thirty percent of worker ants in a colony aren't actually working at any given moment. So the crowds here were that thirty percent, she decided.

"They're that desperate to see the prime minister?" Akira said.

"Maybe because he comes from Miyagi, they feel like they know him."

"Though no one around here paid much attention when he ran in the primaries. The governor all but laughed at him, said he was too young to have a chance. But once he became prime minister, they were just begging him to come back for a hometown parade."

"It does seem like a lot of fuss," Haruko pointed out. "It's not as though he won Olympic gold."

"And he's already been in office six months. I suppose he was paying them back by delaying the parade until now." Her tone was cynical. "Serves them right for not backing him from the start."

"There he is," murmured one of the customers behind Haruko. A car passed slowly from left to right across the screen. For a moment she thought it was snowing, but then realized they were throwing tickertape from the buildings along the route. There was something old-fashioned about the scraps of paper fluttering down on the parade. The festive mood of the crowd was unmistakable, and you could almost feel the anticipation as a patrol car cut across the screen, and then a long convertible came into view.

"There he is, that's Kaneda," the man behind Haruko said. They couldn't hear much of the broadcast since the TV was mounted so high on the wall, but they could tell that an excited announcer was repeating the prime minister's name.

He was seated in the back of the convertible, waving to the crowd. The camera zoomed in for a close-up, revealing the face of a man who was still young—at fifty, the youngest prime minister in Japanese history. An unusually dignified face, with undeniable charisma. Full eyebrows, a well-formed nose, piercing eyes, relaxed manner—he might easily have been mistaken for a movie star. A face that showed traces of innocence and experience in equal measure. The members of his own Liberal Party joked that his carelessly styled hair was still jet-black because he hadn't suffered enough, but his expression was subtle, notoriously difficult to read: were those slightly pursed lips smiling or bracing for the next challenge? The slim woman seated next to him looked serene and well bred, and perhaps slightly cold.

Akira pointed at the screen, addressing the man in the limousine. "We're counting on you," she said.

Haruko remembered a debate she'd seen on TV between Kaneda and his opponent, the venerable Labor Party boss, Makoto Ayukawa. Though Kaneda was said to have played rugby in college, he had looked slender, almost delicate, next to the older man. His manner had been understated and respectful, but he had fixed Ayukawa with a sharp stare throughout the debate. When Ayukawa had accused him of being young and overly idealistic, Kaneda had responded without missing a beat: "I got into politics because I wanted to turn ideals into realities."

13

"My husband said it all along."

"What?" asked Akira. "That he's lucky to be married to such a good-looker?"

"No," Haruko laughed. "That too few politicians are ready to lay down their lives for the country."

"He can say that again. They either die of old age or off themselves after a scandal."

"He says Kaneda seems like one of the few who might," said Haruko.

"He can say that again, too."

At first, Haruko wasn't sure what she was seeing. As Kaneda's limousine crept across the screen, something white dropped into the picture—as though a curious bird had swooped down on the car . . . though the tail was too long for a bird. It was probably just a clump of tickertape, or so she thought.

She still couldn't hear the announcer. The white object descended on the limousine.

"Is that a toy plane?" someone murmured. Haruko wasn't sure whether it was Akira or someone behind her—or a voice in her own head.

The camera caught the propellers spinning over the small body of a remote-controlled helicopter as it hovered for a moment above the car. Then the sound of an explosion filled the room, white smoke billowed across the screen, and the picture seemed to warp.

For a moment, Haruko thought something had happened to the TV, but the picture quickly returned, showing the street through a veil of smoke and people fleeing in every direction. The pavement where the camera was focused seemed to be on fire.

The silence in the soba shop was broken only by the hushed voice of the announcer saying, "A bomb! A bomb!"

PART
TWO

THE AUDIENCE

Day One

Toru Tanaka dropped his head back on the pillow and gazed at his left leg on the bed below him. It had started to itch inside the cast, so he pulled himself up a bit and glanced around for the ear pick he used to scratch his leg.

"Hey, Tanaka," said his roommate. "Looking for the pick?" The curtain down the middle of the room had been left open. The white-haired, slack-mouthed man in the next bed had casts on both legs. His face was round, his eyes wide-set. Toru shook his head, annoyed at being so easy to read.

The man, Yasushi Hodogaya, had been in the room when Toru arrived. Toru had only recently turned thirty-five, and this sixty-something room-mate was old enough to be his father, but Hodogaya had decided they were going to be buddies, members of the "brotherhood of broken bones." Worse yet, he never missed an opportunity to play up his twofold injury, reminding Toru how much worse off he was having broken both legs.

Annoying, too, was his habit of muttering insults at the TV screen while a chess program was on, as if he played better than the experts on the show. But Toru knew nothing about chess, so he had no way of knowing whether Hodogaya's criticism was justified.

Fortunately, despite the casts, Hodogaya would often jump out of bed and leave the room on a pair of crutches, sometimes for long periods. He seemed so mobile that Toru had to stop himself from asking when his roommate planned to check out.

"Hey, Tanaka. You know who that was came to see me?" Hodogaya asked one day.

"How should I know?" said Toru.

"You'd never believe me if I told you."

"Then don't tell me."

Hodogaya would have been approaching retirement if he had worked for a respectable company, and work might have been the last thing he'd have wanted to discuss. But, perhaps because his job seemed a bit shady, he was always anxious to talk about it. He told stories of his adventures in the underworld that were probably mostly bluster, claiming to be friendly with various thugs and yakuza bosses. But Toru had to admit that the men who came to visit him were pretty tough-looking, something Hodogaya took pleasure in pointing out.

Now, as the pair of them lay in bed, someone appeared at the door of their room and knocked. It was the boy from the room next door, also on crutches.

"What's up?" said Hodogaya.

"Toru!" said the boy. "Did you see what happened? On TV?" It struck Toru as odd and a bit annoying to have a boy of middle school age calling him by his first name, but he had decided it was just his way of being friendly.

"TV?" he said, looking over at the set on the table against the wall. He reached for the remote and switched it on. The hospital charged for TV privileges, but he had bought a prepaid card and earphones. "Seen what?"

"What *happened*!" said the boy. "At least we won't be bored in here for a while," he added, before disappearing as quickly as he'd come. Toru wondered what all the fuss was about as a man with a solemn expression appeared on the screen. He was holding a microphone and had a bandage around his head. The background looked familiar, until Toru realized it was right here in Sendai—along the main street dividing the city from north to south.

"That's right," said Hodogaya from the next bed. "The parade's today. Kaneda's coming, the new prime minister." Almost simultaneously Toru noticed the headline streaming across the bottom of the screen: "Prime Minister Kaneda assassinated by remote-controlled bomb." He grabbed the earphones and put them on.

"Things are finally calming down, but traffic is still at a standstill and the city is in chaos." The announcer's voice was tense; he had obviously been injured in the explosion.

Toru watched the screen intently, vaguely aware that Hodogaya had turned toward his own TV and put on his earphones. The broadcast was jumpy and confusing, with a constant soundtrack of honking horns and barked orders from the police—clearly not the program the producers had planned—but as he watched, Toru began to grasp what had happened.

Kaneda, who had been elected six months earlier as the first opposition party candidate to become prime minister, had been riding through downtown Sendai when a remote-controlled model helicopter had appeared from the top of a textbook warehouse and descended toward his open limousine. As it neared the car, it had exploded.

The TV station replayed the event again and again, as though the footage spoke for itself: the blast, the nearly unrecognizable remains of the car, the big zelkova trees in the median snapped in half. Apparently no spectators had been killed since the avenue was wide, but a number of people had been injured in the ensuing panic, and some were still unconscious. The bodies of the prime minister and his wife had not been positively identified, the announcer said, but the fact that he already referred to them as "bodies" seemed to say it all.

"Shit," Toru muttered, and knew that he'd be watching TV for a while. It was lucky to be here in the hospital—what better place to watch the aftermath unfold? Still, until they had something concrete to report, the talking heads on the tube were like dogs worrying an old bone. Eyewitnesses were apparently easy to come by, since just about everyone who had been present was trapped in the congestion and roadblocks and had little to do for the time being but wander around. Most of them talked excitedly about the noise and smoke at the moment of the explosion, and about what they did afterwards. In most cases, this amounted to nothing more than running as fast as they could, but they all seemed eager to tell the story. A number of young people came on claiming to have caught the explosion on their cell-phone cameras, but when the images were put up on the screen, they were disappointingly grainy and indistinct.

The prime minister's number two man, Katsuo Ebisawa, ventured out just once. He was nearly seventy, but he was built like a rugby player and whenever he had appeared with the much younger Kaneda, he had looked like his bodyguard. All he would say now was that the government was gathering information and that the police would report soon, before he vanished from sight.

At 2:00 P.M., the police held a press conference. For the media, and for Toru sitting in front of his TV, it was the first substantive moment in the coverage. The official who appeared before the cameras was from the National Police Agency rather than from the Miyagi Prefectural Police. He was introduced as Ichitaro Sasaki, the assistant division chief for General Intelligence in the Security Bureau.

"Title sounds like a software upgrade," Toru heard his roommate say without removing his earphones. "And he looks like Paul McCartney." He was responding to Sasaki's baby face, big, droopy eyes, and mop of curly hair—Toru had to admit there was a resemblance. "Wonder if Paul's up to the job?" Hodogaya added.

Questions were fired at Sasaki one after the other, but he just glanced at his watch from time to time and said next to nothing. Eventually, this strategy seemed to subdue the reporters, and he answered a few questions briefly but authoritatively.

"Where did the helicopter come from?" asked one reporter.

"We think it came from somewhere in the textbook warehouse."

"Can you be more specific?"

"Possibly from a window, or from the roof. We're looking into that now."

"Roadblocks have been set up along all the highways," another reporter broke in, "and train service in and out of the city has been suspended. This isn't an investigation—it's a blockade. Won't this create havoc for businesses, not to mention for the citizens of Sendai?"

Sasaki didn't bat an eye. "At the present time, we don't know who did this or how many of them there are, but we have to prevent them from leaving the city if at all possible. For the next few hours, we are asking for understanding and cooperation from all the affected parties, including the transportation industry. Once the proper checkpoints and investigatory measures are in place, we believe we'll be able to resume train service and open the roads. Our prime minister has been murdered, and those responsible are still at large. I'm afraid some inconvenience is inevitable. Would you rather that we worried about the effect on private individuals and businesses and let the killers go free in the process?" He stared at the reporter who had asked the question. "If that's what you're proposing, I think we have a few questions of our own for you."

"Are you cooperating with the Miyagi Prefectural Police?" someone else asked. "Is it normal for the National Police to step in so soon?"

"Is there some reason we shouldn't be here?" Sasaki shot back. "The prefectural police are providing their full support," he added. "It may be an odd way of putting it, but the fact that the crime occurred in Sendai is the one bright spot in this tragedy. Thanks to the Security Pods that were installed here last year, we've been able to collect a great deal of information, and I'm convinced we'll soon have the culprit or culprits in custody." Then he basically gave the networks their marching orders: "In response to this crisis, we are asking the media to cooperate in gathering information from the citizens of Sendai and passing it along to the authorities. You can play a vital role in encouraging public vigilance."

The commentators on the news special immediately began to review the press conference, while the announcer recapped the situation. Toru got out of bed and hobbled off to the bathroom on his crutches. After emptying his bladder, he stopped for a cigarette on the way back. In the smoking area, too, the assassination was the sole topic of conversation.

"It's the title that really matters. When you give something a name, you create an image for it, and images influence people." The speaker, seated on a bench along the wall, was Toru's neighbor, the middle school student. It occurred to Toru that the boy shouldn't be here even if he wasn't actually smoking.

"What are you talking about?" he said, sitting down next to him.

"Kenji here's wondering when they came up with this 'General Intelligence Division,'" said the boy, pointing at a wrinkled older man. "He says they used to call it 'Public Safety' or 'Central Investigation' or something like that." Toru was mildly impressed that the boy called the old man by his first name, too.

"When did they change it to General Intelligence?"

"Three years ago," said the boy. "When they reorganized the Security Bureau."

"How do you know so much about it?"

"You have loads of time to read up on stuff like that in here," he said. "Seems there was too negative an image with 'Public Safety,' and 'Peace-Preservation,'

'National Security,' and the rest of them. They all sound a little scary—I guess some people in Japan are nervous about anything with 'national' in the title." Toru had never heard a kid talk like this, and he realized it made him uncomfortable. "So," the boy continued, "they needed something vaguer, a bit more abstract, and 'General Intelligence' was born. When you hear the name you're not exactly sure what they do, but everybody knows 'intelligence' is important. So the division that handles it must be okay. Anyway, it *sounds* a whole lot better than 'Public Safety,' that's for sure."

"Says who?" said Toru, lighting a cigarette.

"You've heard of 'appreciation payments'?" said the boy.

"No." The kid was beginning to get on his nerves.

"You must have, Toru," he said. "That's what they call the money the government supposedly pays for the upkeep of American soldiers stationed in Japan. When people hear 'appreciation payment,' they feel like it's some sort of charity they're giving to the troops themselves, but the truth is the money goes straight into the U.S. treasury. Another example of strategic naming. You get it all the time, tricky words like 'appreciation' or 'hometown' or 'youth' or 'white-collar.'"

"Is that so, professor?" Toru said, unable to take much more of this.

The boy frowned. "Well, all I know is that the politicians and the rest of the big shots never tell us much of anything; everything happens behind the scenes. But we'd better keep our eyes open—you, too, Toru." He looked at the old man as well, as if to say "Including you."

Perhaps because the boy had lumped them together this way, the old man seemed to decide that he and Toru were now friends. "You know," he said, "they put those Security Pods in everywhere, and they're keeping track of everything we do, but nobody seems to complain . . . to me, that's the really scary thing."

"I guess," said Toru, sounding only vaguely interested. He blew out a thin stream of smoke. "But they're probably better than a higher crime rate. That's why they put them there in the first place."

"But what about that serial killer? All that 'intelligence' and they still haven't caught him." A string of murders starting about two years earlier had been the excuse the authorities used to make Sendai the test city for the new surveillance system.

A number of people had been stabbed to death in the area around Sendai Station, always on Friday night. The victims were young and old, male and female—a middle-aged man whose face had been slashed, followed the next time by a young woman whose head had almost been cut off. Since all the bodies had been mutilated with knives or blades of some kind, people in the city began referring to the killer as "Cutter," and before long the facetious nickname had given its unseen owner a kind of creepy familiarity. There were also several victims who survived the attack, and they reported that after he had cut them, he put his face down next to theirs and yelled "Surprise!" This bizarre behavior added to the terror, but it fueled curiosity at the same time. Eventually, the whole country was talking about Cutter, the Sendai serial killer.

The police searched frantically, but Cutter left few clues, and the fact that he was an equal-opportunity killer made profiling difficult. More than a year and twenty victims later, they had little to go on. It was said that a special unit had been deployed for the investigation, and that the officers in the unit had been authorized to use means that went beyond the normal scope of the law. It was unclear what that involved, but to date it had not resulted in Cutter's capture.

At one point, some monthly rag ran a picture with the headline "Cop Confronts Cutter." The grainy image was straight out of a comic book: a gun-toting officer chasing a grim-faced, middle-aged man in a suit. The caption was corny enough: "Wounded Cutter, escaping by the skin of his teeth, vows revenge. Killer remains at large in Sendai." But the speech balloon above Cutter's head—"Surprise!"—was over the top, and no one paid much attention.

Then, a local network affiliate caused a fuss by trying to get an exclusive interview with the killer. Apparently, a man claiming to be Cutter had contacted the station and offered to give a tell-all interview. The station had been skeptical at first, but after a good deal of back and forth, they began to think they were dealing with the real thing. They invited him to come to the studio, promising not to inform the authorities; but in the end, someone on the staff apparently decided this was a bad idea and called the police. The man who claimed to be Cutter was arrested when he arrived for the interview, only to turn out to have no connection with the crimes. The TV station was criticized for compromising ethical standards in pursuit of ratings, and a number of senior people lost their jobs.

Still, media shenanigans aside, the citizens of Sendai were terrified of this phantom killer and stopped going out at night, with the result that business at bars and restaurants dropped off drastically. In due course, when the daughter of a local business owner was murdered, a bill was proposed in the national assembly to "restore peace and security by the introduction of mechanical means." The fact that the business owner's son-in-law was a veteran member of parliament for the ruling party probably had something to do with the hasty way the bill reached the floor of the Diet, but given the circumstances there was no public objection. After all, who was going to quibble when so many innocent people were being killed? Under normal circumstances, this kind of conspicuous invasion of privacy would have caused a violent outcry, but Cutter's yearlong reign of terror had apparently convinced Sendai, and perhaps the rest of Japan along with it, and the measure sailed through the assembly.

Soon after its passage, "data-gathering terminals"—the Security Pods—began appearing around the city. They were designed to increase the quality and quantity of information available for crime prevention and investigation. In practice, the pods recorded and stored a picture of almost everyone who passed near them, day or night. They also kept track of user information for transmissions from cell phones and other mobile devices.

"In America, they passed the Patriot Act right after 9/11. . . ." The boy was still holding forth.

"Has a nice ring to it," said Toru.

"But it's another example of strategic naming. It sounds good, it's 'patriotic,' but in reality it lets the government record telephone calls and emails and just about anything else, no questions asked."

"What do you mean?"

"In the past, when they suspected someone was up to no good, they got a search warrant and then they could gather information on that person. Now, no one knows who's a terrorist and who's not, so they gather information about everybody and then decide who's suspicious. The whole game has changed, in America and everywhere else."

"I thought Americans cared a lot about their freedom."

"But wouldn't most people agree to more government surveillance if they thought it could prevent terrorism? Look at us: nobody said a word when they installed the pods in Sendai."

"I don't think anybody thinks of it like that," said Toru. "They just want that murderer caught."

"I'm sure you're right. But you know what I think? I think they cooked up the whole Cutter thing."

"Cooked it up?"

"They needed an excuse to put in the pods. I'm sure of it. Japanese people will put up with almost anything if you frighten them enough. The whole thing just sounds fishy. What killer is going to yell 'Surprise!' as he chops your head off? It's right out of a manga."

Toru laughed. If only the world were as simple as this kid made it out to be. "People can't be fooled that easily," he said.

"Then how did all those pods get here?" said the boy.

As soon as he got back to his room, Toru put on his earphones and turned on the TV. A telephone number, fax number, and email address flashed across the screen along with a message asking anyone with information to contact the studio. There was something almost offensive about the email address beginning "kaneda_scoop@."

But tips—often contradicting one another—were beginning to come in and were immediately broadcast. A tall man with a face mask had been seen talking suspiciously on a cell phone in the crowd before the parade. Several men in suits had been studying a map on the observation deck of the building across from the station. Two men were arguing in a white car parked on a street near the site of the explosion. Two other men, one clearly wearing a disguise, had been heard talking about a sexual assault on a pedestrian bridge. A young woman in the crowd had suddenly started waving just before the explosion. . . .

One of the announcers on the news special wondered aloud whether passing along all these reports before they could be confirmed might add to the confusion. The moderator seemed caught off guard by this and had no response other than to frown angrily, but one of the news analysts jumped in almost immediately to rescue him.

"In the first few hours after an incident of this nature, it's important to lay out all the cards on the table and get the large view, without ignoring any possibilities. If you start out being overcautious, you can end up delaying the investigation." What he meant, of course, was "If it's good for ratings, who cares whether it's true or not."

About this same time, Makoto Ayukawa called a news conference. Though Kaneda had beaten him handily in the election for prime minister, his Labor Party, which had governed Japan for most of the postwar period, still held a substantial majority of seats in parliament. Ayukawa was utterly composed on camera, the very image of the head of the dominant party.

"The late prime minister is, I'm sure, in all our prayers." His voice was quiet and dignified. "I would like to emphasize," he continued, "that in this time of crisis, we put aside party differences and unite behind the effort to bring to justice those responsible for this atrocity."

"I bet Ayukawa did it!" laughed Hodogaya. They had turned off the TV and started dinner.

"You think it was payback for the election?" Toru said. It had clearly been humiliating for Ayukawa, who had been counting on a third term as prime minister, to lose to an opponent as young as Kaneda, but he doubted he would have gone as far as assassination.

They turned on the TVs again when they'd finished eating. Some experts on remote-controlled helicopters were now being interviewed, men who flew the models in and around Sendai. They were a strange assortment—an older fellow with a handsome shock of white hair, a businessman type in horn-rimmed glasses, a young guy in a grubby T-shirt who could have been a student.

"It's a 90," said the white-haired man as they watched the tape of the explosion. The rest of them nodded agreement. They were apparently discussing the size of the engine on the helicopter.

"Can you tell what model it is or the maker?" asked the interviewer.

"It's an Ooka Air Hover," said the young man, his voice going shrill from eagerness or nerves. The others seemed to concur. They watched the footage over and over, asking for different camera angles or a wider shot, and they added details about the helicopter, the kind of gyro it used, the type of muffler.

"They say it took off from somewhere on top of the textbook warehouse," said the moderator, bringing out a large photo that showed the helicopter in front of a brick building. "How far away could you stand and still control its flight?"

The men looked at one another for a moment, as if trying to decide who should answer.

"Well, it would depend on the transmitter and the antenna," said the older man, "but you could be at least two kilometers away without any problem. But you really can't do much unless you can follow the flight visually, so they were probably standing where they could see it. You control these things by keeping track of their position in the air, and that would be hard to do if you were too far away to see."

"There was no wind today," added the kid in the T-shirt, "so it was probably a pretty easy flight; but bad weather would have made it much trickier. They also had the extra weight of the bomb. You'd need somebody who knew what he was doing." The rest of the group nodded. Then they took a closer look at the photograph and pointed out where the silhouette differed slightly from that of a normal Ooka Air Hover—no doubt where they had attached the bomb. It was a shame, everyone agreed, that the machine had been vaporized in the explosion since it would have revealed additional information.

"So it's safe to say that this flight could not have been managed by a novice?" asked the moderator.

"It would depend how much practice they had at hovering."

"You could probably manage if you practiced every weekend for a few months."

"Perhaps," said the white-haired man, "but I think it would still be impossible for a beginner, especially with the destabilizing weight of the bomb and the problems involved in such a dangerous undertaking. I suspect this was done by a fairly experienced flyer."

"Are there many people with these skills?" asked the moderator.

"Oh sure, lots," they said, like a Greek chorus.

"But"—the white-haired man again had a reservation—"there aren't so many places you can fly, so right here in Sendai the number is actually fairly small. Nor are there lots of shops where you could get an Ooka Air Hover. It should be possible to find out who bought one recently."

"Could it have been secondhand? Or could someone have brought it from elsewhere?"

"That's certainly possible."

"In which case, it might be difficult to determine where this particular machine came from."

"I suppose so."

"And anyone who planned something like this would be careful to cover his tracks," said the moderator, obviously satisfied that he'd made a point.

Ichitaro Sasaki of General Intelligence showed up on the program late that evening. "We have a number of promising leads, and we're following up on every one of them," he said. "But we will still need to keep the city under tight security, and in particular the area around Higashi Nibancho Avenue will be closed off for several more days, so we ask for your continued cooperation." Somehow, as he spoke, Paul McCartney, who had looked so unimpressive, began to seem reassuring, someone to be depended on.

After the interview, the news special came to an end. Perhaps everyone was simply worn out from all the excitement, or maybe they had finally begun to feel guilty about replaying the same few seconds of the bomb exploding for the umpteenth time. But as soon as the show ended, the station began to run a hastily assembled video biography of Prime Minister Kaneda, covering his life from the early years, through his days in business, and on to his political career. There were shots of him looking almost heroic as he announced his first run for parliament, tapes of eloquent speeches, debates with crafty political opponents, coverage of the primaries, his dramatic win in Sendai, his debate with Ayukawa in the general election, and his inauguration, all leading up to the climax—today's parade through the city and the appearance of the model helicopter. Knowing the ending, Toru turned off the TV and closed his eyes.

Day Two

He checked the clock: 7:00 A.M. But when he pulled aside the curtain that divided the room, Hodogaya was already watching TV.

"Now it's really getting interesting," he said, twisting to look at Toru and pulling one earbud out. He seemed to feel sorry for this roommate who was late for the show. "The police held an emergency news conference a couple of hours ago, while we were asleep."

"To say what?"

"They seem to have a suspect."

Toru turned on his own TV: a face and the name Masaharu Aoyagi flashed across the screen. Toru's first reaction was that the man didn't look particularly dangerous, but then it occurred to him to wonder how they had this picture if he hadn't been arrested yet. The date running under the image was about two years ago—a still from a popular news show. Why would the suspect, Masaharu Aoyagi, have been interviewed on a TV program back then? In the picture, he was wearing the familiar blue and white uniform of a well-known delivery company. The man was tall and lean, and the photographer had apparently caught him off guard, because he was frowning slightly and scratching his head. Toru finally figured out where he had seen the picture.

A couple of years ago, a very popular young actress had got into a nasty situation in the city. She was originally from Sendai and was in the habit of sneaking back to an apartment she kept there when she had time off. She had been home alone when a man had forced his way into the apartment and attacked her. Fortunately, this Masaharu Aoyagi had been making a delivery at just the same time.

When no one answered the intercom, he'd decided to leave a printed message; but he thought he heard a crash and a woman screaming inside the apartment, so he pressed the buzzer again. Still no answer. Very cautiously, he turned the knob and pushed open the door—to find a man attacking a woman. He managed to pull him off and hold him down until the police arrived.

"Did you know the apartment belonged to Rinka?" asked a reporter.

"I had no idea." He sounded a bit shaky as he answered.

"But when did you realize it was her?"

"I'm afraid I don't know much about celebrities," Aoyagi muttered. "I don't even watch TV," he added, obviously embarrassed. The reporters burst out laughing.

"She's very well known. You really don't watch TV?"

"No, I'm busy with work." Aoyagi looked down and barely whispered his answer. The reporters surged closer. With long, tousled hair and a deadpan expression, he might have passed for a slightly eccentric movie star himself, but there was something fresh and unaffected about the way he dealt with the media. From soon after the incident, he attracted a great deal of attention, and in due course became a minor celebrity in his own right, if only for a short time.

The news shows sent film crews to cover him at work, and there were interviews with his coworkers and his boss. Once, when his delivery route became known in advance, a crowd gathered along the way in the hope of catching a glimpse of him—and that, too, was reported on the news. Worried that all of this disruption would affect business, his employer initially asked the media to keep their distance while he was at work, but when the furor continued they started thinking about using him in a commercial. He turned them down cold, however, and the idea was dropped; but the excuse he gave, that he didn't want anything to interfere with his job, only made his stock with the public go up.

"Weren't you frightened when you realized the attacker had a knife?" The reporters were still asking their questions on the old videotape.

"It all happened so fast," he said.

"They say you had no problem subduing Rinka's attacker. Have you done judo or something?"

"No," he told them, scratching the tip of his nose, "it was just a move a friend taught me when I was in school. . . ." His unease in the face of all this attention was enough to make anyone feel protective. "A leg sweep. You bring him down with a leg sweep and then kick the shit out of him—that's what my friend said."

Toru was surprised to realize that it had been more than two years ago that he'd seen the driver interviewed on TV. The media had been all over him for a while, but in less than six months he had faded again into obscurity. The "man of the hour" becomes just another man once enough time has passed.

But now, two years later, he was back in the spotlight, a suspect in an assassination. Or so it would seem.

"It's hard to believe he could have done it," said the announcer as the archival footage came to an end.

"It certainly is," agreed a woman who specialized in ferreting out celebrity scandals. "I covered the story, and he seemed to be a very sweet boy, though he was a bit jumpy sometimes."

The announcer nodded as a piece of video that had played earlier came on the screen again. A tense and embarrassed Masaharu Aoyagi stood talking into a microphone, but this time the technicians managed to zoom in on his right hand, showing his fingers twitching violently. Then they panned down his legs, which were shifting and fidgeting. The tape was in slow motion at the end of the interview, focusing on the way his mouth went slack as he finished talking. His lips seemed frozen in a smile, his eyes wary, as though he preferred his own company to these people here in front of him. The expression passed almost instantly, caught only by the slow-motion photography, but to Toru it felt as if he'd had a glimpse of something dark and cunning behind the driver's pleasant face.

Someone on the news show said that Aoyagi had quit his job at the delivery company three months ago—which was, no doubt, the lone piece of good news for a company in an otherwise embarrassing situation. There was some comfort that the suspect was at least a "former" employee.

"Toru!" The middle school boy said loudly as he spotted him in the smoking area and came to sit next to him. "Getting interesting, don't you think? The police must be pretty desperate if they've already named a suspect."

"Well, when somebody kills the prime minister right in front of them, I guess their asses are on the line. I'd say they're desperate. But," he added, bringing up something that had been bothering him, "we don't really know that this Aoyagi did it yet, so it seems a little soon to be shouting his name all over the place."

"I bet they have plenty of proof already; or maybe, since it's an emergency, they just want to arrest him as soon as they can and worry about his rights later."

"You think they really have proof?" Toru said.

"Well, they seem to be able to check phone records and stuff with the Security Pods. They should be able to come up with something if they use them right."

"Sounds like you actually like the idea of a 'surveillance society.'"

"Not me! It's like 'Big Brother Is Watching You.'"

"Pretty much," said Toru.

There was some new information in the morning at Sasaki's press conference. He reported that another, smaller explosion had occurred just after the one that killed Prime Minister Kaneda, this one on a side street nearby. A car had burned and a concrete wall had fallen over. At first, it was thought that the damage had been caused by the blast from the remote-controlled helicopter, but the investigation had revealed that the explosion came from inside the car. A man's body was discovered in the driver's seat.

"There was a bullet wound to the head of the body. We are trying to get a positive identification now, but the driver's license recovered from the car belonged to Shingo Morita of Aoba Ward in Sendai. Furthermore, we have learned that Mr. Morita was a college friend of the suspect, Masaharu Aoyagi."

"Can you tell us what evidence led you to Aoyagi?" asked a reporter.

"An officer encountered a man behaving suspiciously in the vicinity of the textbook warehouse immediately after the explosion. While he was running an identity check, the man managed to escape. Several officers in the vicinity pursued the suspect, but he eluded them and is still at large. The owner of a liquor store was attacked some time later," Sasaki added. His face was nearly expressionless, though the hangdog eyes looked a bit strained.

"Anything else?" prompted another reporter.

"Several hours ago, we received a tape from the surveillance camera at a shop selling remote-controlled models here in Sendai."

"The helicopter?" called another reporter. Sasaki nodded significantly.

"It shows a man purchasing a helicopter like the one used in the attack . . . a man who bears a strong resemblance to the person who fled from the scene of the second bomb."

"Was it Masaharu Aoyagi?"

"The shopkeeper has identified him," Sasaki said. "Furthermore, according to our investigation, Aoyagi had a part-time job at the Todoroki Pyrotechnics Factory in Sendai while he was in school."

"Todoroki Pyrotechnics?" echoed another reporter.

"They make fireworks," Sasaki explained. "In other words, he would have some familiarity with the use of explosives."

"Is that how he made the bomb?!"

"We're not prepared to say at this time, but we are seeking the cooperation of Aoyagi's former employer."

"Were there other factors that led you to Aoyagi?"

"Well," Sasaki said, as though throwing one last bone to the dogs, "there was the matter of a phone call we received from him." A clamor rose from the press pool. "I'm not at liberty to reveal the details, but he has been in contact with us by telephone and has confessed to the crime." He went on to announce that the police were relaxing the security measures around central Sendai to some extent and that transportation was beginning to function normally again. But the reporters had lost interest in highways and trains, their attention now focused on Aoyagi.

The program broke for a commercial. "Try our special béchamel sauce!" chirped a man clutching a frying pan and smiling from behind a thick beard. "From our kitchens to yours." He was a well-known chef from a fancy French restaurant that had a branch in Sendai. Toru was surprised to see him hawking sauce on TV, a sign, he thought, that the man was reaching the end of the line. Should have stuck to the restaurants, he thought indifferently.

The program picked up again after the commercial. Up to this point, the producers had little but the footage of the explosion to work with, but the addition of Aoyagi gave them new material. Old tapes from his days as a hero deliveryman were played one after another—with particular attention given to a brief scene showing Aoyagi gesturing angrily at a group of girls who had followed him on his rounds. He might have been chasing off a pack of dogs. The camera lingered on his face, and at normal speed it appeared unremarkable enough, but the slow motion replay caught a hint of wildness in it. Even Toru could see that Aoyagi was good-looking, but it occurred to him that there was something menacing about him as well.

At this point, the coverage switched to a news conference hastily called by the senior staff in the delivery company where Aoyagi had been working. Everybody's getting in on the act, Toru thought. Next they'll be holding one to announce there weren't enough reporters to cover all the news conferences.

The proceedings began with the company president reiterating that Aoyagi had quit three months earlier and was no longer their employee. "But it would be a terrible shame if he is indeed involved in this incident," he concluded noncommittally. The manager who had supervised Aoyagi was asked whether there had been anything in his record that might have aroused his employers' suspicion. With apparent reluctance, he admitted that there had been some trouble. "What sort of trouble?" a reporter wanted to know.

"A number of packages were sent to addresses on his route but it was never clear where they'd come from; it seems the delivery receipts showed Aoyagi himself as the sender." The camera came in for a close-up of the manager's face, his serious expression contrasting oddly with the cartoon cats on his tie.

"Aoyagi's name was on the receipts?"

"But we had no reason to think he had written them himself, so we assumed it was some form of harassment, that he was being targeted somehow."

"It never occurred to you that Aoyagi might have sent them?" asked a reporter. "You never had any suspicions?"

"We had no reason . . . ," the man mumbled, fidgeting nervously with his cat-tie. "It seemed too odd. . . ." The reporters began firing questions at him, their tone growing increasingly insistent.

The cameras also cut repeatedly to shots of the front of the building where Aoyagi had been living. The police were searching his apartment, so the media were kept at bay for the moment, but the building was surrounded by photographers.

One of them had found a perch in an office building across the way and was probing the apartment with a telephoto lens, though very little could be seen through the crowds of police and crime scene investigators. The one thing he did turn up was a small photograph hung on the back wall of the room, and a pulse of excitement went through the TV studio when an enlargement of this image revealed it to be a portrait of Prime Minister Kaneda with a crude "X" drawn over his face.

"What could he have had against Kaneda?" somebody wondered aloud.

One of the men on the panel of experts, identified as a retired detective from the Metropolitan Police, spoke up: "About a year ago, there was a campaign to relieve congestion in urban areas by prohibiting on-street parking, and Kaneda was a major supporter. Maybe Aoyagi saw him as an enemy of delivery drivers who park on the street in the course of doing their job." The other panelists seemed impressed by this analysis.

It was unclear whether it was the same footage the police were using, but the TV station also aired a tape from the security camera at the remote-control model shop. The picture was in black and white, but the face of the man coming up to the register was quite clear. He turned aside and kept his hand over his mouth—perhaps aware of the camera—as he paid for an Ooka Air Hover.

"There's no way to be absolutely sure, but there is a strong resemblance," said one of the commentators. He sounded absolutely sure. Toru, too, thought the man looked exactly like Masaharu Aoyagi.

There was also a report that Aoyagi had been eating a meal at a little *tonkatsu* restaurant one street off Higashi Nibancho Avenue not long before it happened.

"It was before noon, so the place was still empty. He sat right in that chair, eating lunch and watching TV." The owner, a man in a white jacket with thinning hair and glasses, glared at the chair as though it were somehow cursed. "They had a lot of stuff about Kaneda on the TV before the parade started, and it was a little creepy the way he kept griping about it. I had a bad feeling about him as soon as he walked in the door."

"And you're certain it was Masaharu Aoyagi?" pressed the woman holding the microphone in his face.

"You don't believe me? Of course it was. We give free seconds on rice, and twice he called me over to ask for more. Didn't leave a single grain in his bowl. Pretty weird, don't you think? Who has an appetite like that before he goes out and kills somebody?"

"But are you sure it was him?"

"What do you mean 'Am I sure?' I said it was, didn't I? Wait a minute," he added, disappearing into the kitchen. When he came out, he was holding a credit card. "Here, have a look at this. He forgot it when he left."

The woman took the card and held it up for the camera. The name at the bottom read "Masaharu Aoyagi."

"What did I tell you?" said the shopowner. "He was muttering all sorts of crazy stuff about Kaneda. Seemed pretty weird to me."

"You should probably turn this over to the police," said the woman.

There was also a tape from the security camera in the parking lot of an apartment building somewhere. It had caught some suspicious activity the night before.

"I thought I heard glass breaking in another apartment," said a man who was apparently a resident of the building with his face blurred to protect his identity, "but when I looked out the window, I saw a guy opening the door of a car in the lot." The footage from the security camera was fuzzy, but it was clear enough to make out a figure moving from car to car and trying the doors.

"Looking for a getaway car," said one of the panelists.

"While the police are conducting their investigation, where is Masaharu Aoyagi and what is he doing?" said a serious-sounding voice as the screen was filled with a close-up of Aoyagi. Then they broke for a commercial.

Toru let out his breath, realizing that his shoulders had gone rigid and he'd been staring a hole in the TV. His roommate seemed to be coming up for air as well.

"I don't get it," Hodogaya said. "Two years ago he was some minor celebrity, and now he's supposed to have done this?"

"Maybe he missed the spotlight. They made such a fuss over him for a while and then just dropped him. Maybe he wanted back in."

"Well, I feel sorry for Kaneda if Aoyagi killed him for a few more minutes on TV."

Toru nodded. He could see how a prime minister might prefer to be assassinated for political reasons or at least in some kind of conspiracy.

"But they'll wind this up in no time," Hodogaya said, as if watching the chess program on TV.

When the show returned after the commercial, there was an interview with a man who was filmed from the neck down to disguise his identity. His voice, however, had not been altered. "Right from the start, I thought there was something funny about that burglar story," he was saying. The caption explained that the man had lived next door to the starlet Rinka at the time of the break-in two years ago. "The insulation in the building is pretty good, pretty soundproof, so I always wondered how he could have heard her screaming through the door. Seemed pretty unlikely to me. I always thought he set the whole thing up, for some reason."

Back in the studio, the host apologized for allowing the account number to be seen when they had broadcast the picture of Aoyagi's credit card. "The account has been deactivated," he said.

"And this just came in," he added. "We have received an important piece of information from one of our viewers." He went on to explain that a housewife in Izumi Ward had sent in footage that she had shot several months earlier at a riverside ball field north of the city. She had been recording a little league game there—the backstop, the kids in uniform, the opposing pitcher—when a remote-controlled model helicopter had suddenly floated up in the background. "Is that a helicopter?" says a voice on the tape, apparently belonging to the woman shooting the film. At this point, the camera angle shifts, swinging down to focus on a man standing on the bank of the river, and zooming in on the controller he's using to fly the machine.

The man in the picture seemed somewhat nervous—and looked exactly like Masaharu Aoyagi.

"He was practicing," murmured one of the panelists as the tape ended. "That seems pretty clear."

Then they moved on to an interview with a woman who was identified as working at a well-known chain restaurant. "He came in last night, sat down right there, and ordered some pasta." She spun around and pointed frantically at a table behind her. "When I went over to take his order, he was real grumpy and mean. Then a police officer showed up and things got out of hand."

"In what way?" asked the interviewer at the restaurant.

"He started throwing around chairs and breaking windows." The camera moved to a shattered pane of glass, while the reporter pretended he'd just realized the extent of the damage. The TV theatrics seemed a bit overdone to Toru.

The studio had also received a tape of Aoyagi's call to the police, which had just been released. The voice of the officer he had spoken to had been edited out, so the recording was a bit jumpy.

"This is Masaharu Aoyagi," a voice said. And then, "I did it."

The TV station, ever prepared, had called in a voice-print expert, who claimed that the voice on the tape was identical to Aoyagi's from recordings made two years earlier at the time of his brief celebrity.

The special broadcast continued. Kaneda's deputy in the Liberal Party, Katsuo Ebisawa, held a news conference outside his official residence. He announced that he was assuming the position of acting prime minister, as the constitution required, and emphasized that the authorities were still in a fact-finding mode.

"My party is providing any information it can concerning Masaharu Aoyagi and cooperating fully with the police investigation," he added.

"How?" a reporter shot back. He seemed almost surprised when Ebisawa began to answer.

"Letters slandering Prime Minister Kaneda have been arriving at our party headquarters for the past two months. Similar letters have also been mailed to the prime minister's residence. Masaharu Aoyagi's fingerprints have been recovered from these letters."

The uproar in the press pool forced Toru to pull off his earphones. He stretched, reached for his crutches, and stood up. Hodogaya had turned off his TV and was flipping through a manga. "Taking a leak?" he asked.

Toru nodded. "Sick of the tube?"

"Completely," said Hodogaya.

"This is just the beginning," said Toru, feeling sure there would be much more to come.

"They'll catch him soon enough. He's making a good game of it, but he's an amateur all the same." Hodogaya's tone made it clear that *he* was no amateur himself, and Toru knew that he was likely to launch into another dubious story of some exploit in the past; and sure enough, the next words out of his mouth came in the form of advice to the fugitive. "If it were me, I'd go underground," he said.

"Literally? Underground?" Toru was barely able to contain his laughter.

Hodogaya bristled. "Every city in this country has an underground system," he said, as though addressing a classroom. "Two systems, to be more exact: the sewers and the storm drains."

"Is this a long story?" Toru interrupted, starting out of the room. "Afraid my bladder won't wait."

When he'd finished in the bathroom, Toru decided to go down to the first floor to look around. He found it easier now to navigate the halls on crutches. In the gift shop, he flipped through the weekly news magazines, but it was still too soon to have any coverage of the assassination. He read the sports papers instead.

Two young women stood next to him at the magazine rack. One of them was carrying a basket of fruit, a gift for somebody they'd come to visit.

"I can't believe it," one was saying. "They let out this stuff bit by bit, but it looks bad. And I liked him a *lot*. I was still in high school two years ago, but I had a major crush on that guy, the delivery man."

"I did, too," said the other girl. "Everybody did."

Toru was curious to hear what they had to say about Aoyagi.

"I don't know anything about bombs," the first girl said, "but that stuff he did on the train's disgusting. Completely gross!"

"I know! I was so disappointed. It's worse than killing the prime minister!"

Stuff on the train? This was new to Toru. They must have been watching a different channel, saw some new wrinkle. He swung around on his crutches and headed back to his room.

"It was about two months ago. I was on my way to work, on the Senseki Line. It was evening, but the train was pretty crowded. I remember this woman near the window saying 'Please stop!'" Toru had changed the channel to find a young man in sunglasses speaking into a mike. "We were all staring at him, pretty sure he was one of those train mashers, and then a few stops before Sendai Station, the woman grabbed the man's arm and pulled him off the train. They argued for a while on the platform. I had the feeling I'd seen him somewhere, and then I realized it was that delivery guy."

When the interview was over, the announcer read accounts from other witnesses who said they'd seen a man who looked just like Masaharu Aoyagi being pulled off a train in a groping incident two months earlier.

Then a small, pale woman who looked like a secretary came on with pictures she'd taken on her cell phone of a man and a woman arguing on a platform. There was no doubt that the man looked a lot like Aoyagi. "While I was shooting these," the woman said, "another man came along to help the girl, and the first man ran off."

An actress on the celebrity panel sniffed in disgust. "So, he's a coward, too. Assaulting that poor woman on the train is bad enough, but then to run away! It's awful!"

"It certainly is," said the moderator, sounding somewhat less indignant. Then he paused and pressed his fingers against the mike in his ear. "It seems we have a report just coming in," he said. Toru swallowed and adjusted his earphones. "A man resembling Masaharu Aoyagi was spotted just moments ago in the Kashiwahara neighborhood in Aoba Ward. The police pursued him, but he commandeered a car and fled, driving the wrong way down a one-way street. The car collided with an oncoming vehicle and struck a wall, but the man escaped in another car. An elderly woman was knocked down when he drove off, and was taken to the hospital with minor injuries."

"If he's still somewhere in Sendai, they're bound to get him soon with all those Security Pods," observed one of the commentators.

"There's a report of another crash in Sendai last night, and while there's no confirmation yet, we do know that one of the cars involved was a police vehicle. It seems likely that incident involved Aoyagi as well."

Toru punched his remote and changed the channel. A woman he didn't recognize was reading another bulletin: "This just in: a woman reports seeing a man resembling Masaharu Aoyagi driving south on Route 4." The broadcast was produced by the national network, but most of the live reports from Sendai used local talent. The network shows had all been forced to link up with the Sendai stations and were broadcasting anything they could get their hands on.

Next was a man who said he'd spoken to Aoyagi just before the incident. He was middle-aged and unshaven, and apparently had a small delivery business. "I used to run into Mr. Aoyagi all the time when I was out making deliveries," he said, adding the "Mister" despite the fact that he was twice Aoyagi's age. "Then he turned up again yesterday morning. It had been a while, so I was glad to see him. He was with another man."

"Another man?" prompted the interviewer.

"Yes, that's right," he said. "He's in a lot of trouble, isn't he?"

"You feel sorry for him, do you?" said the reporter, sounding shocked.

"I didn't say that," he protested. "My packages were wrecked, and I'm not sure what I'm going to do." It was unclear what this meant, but the man didn't seem particularly upset. In fact, he was almost grinning as he said it.

Another channel. This time it was a middle-aged woman with a surprisingly good figure. "He went that way," she said, pointing stage right. She seemed eager to tell her story. "A big man, with a big gun, going that way."

"And you're sure it was Aoyagi?" asked the reporter.

"I guess," said the woman. "But I was too scared to breathe!"

If the TV is this crazy, Toru thought, then the Internet must be a madhouse.

He was glad to be in the hospital where there were no computers, otherwise he would have been following the story around the clock.

"New eyewitness account!" trumpeted an announcer toward evening. To Toru, most of what they'd shown so far was junk, so he was amazed at their enthusiasm for each new dribble of information. But this time the clips were more impressive.

The video had apparently been shot a few hours earlier by a man who lived in the northern part of the city. It was looking down from a balcony and showed a group of men, some uniformed police and some apparently plain-clothes officers, standing with their guns trained on two other men. The arms of the man in front were pinned behind his back, with the second one holding a knife against his throat. A delivery truck was visible in the background.

"That's definitely Masaharu Aoyagi," said the announcer. "He's apparently taken a hostage!" Despite the shaky picture in the home video, he was quite recognizable. He could eventually be seen dragging his hostage out of sight down a narrow side street.

"The hostage was found later a short distance away, apparently unharmed," the audience was informed.

"*And where the hell is Aoyagi now?*" was Hodogaya's own sarcastic voiceover.

"Probably already offed himself somewhere," Toru muttered.

"I suppose they won't stop until he's dead."

"Game over," said Toru.

Hodogaya seemed finally to have lost interest in the television and was busy fiddling with his cell phone. When it rang a moment later, Toru wanted to remind him that they weren't supposed to use these things in the hospital, but Hodogaya hobbled out into the corridor.

Some time later, Chief Sasaki held yet another press conference, announcing that the investigation was moving toward a conclusion, but that the situation was nevertheless serious and potentially dangerous. "Masaharu Aoyagi is a desperate man," he said, staring into the camera. "Two people have died and five more have been injured during his attempt to escape." Someone broke in to ask whether the casualties were law officers. "No," said Sasaki. "They were innocent bystanders." At this, the reporters pushed forward, insisting on knowing who was to blame—blame being one of their specialties.

"Last night, Aoyagi commandeered a car, crashed it into a police vehicle, and then fled on foot. The body of a woman was found in the car."

"Was she killed in the crash?" asked a reporter.

"No," Sasaki answered. "She had been stabbed in the chest." More shouting from the press corps. "Therefore," Sasaki continued over the noise, "we have issued tranquilizer guns to the officers involved in the manhunt." The pressroom was suddenly quiet except for scattered gasps; Toru realized he had gasped himself.

There was something about the term "tranquilizer gun" that seemed brutish—Toru pictured a target painted on Aoyagi's back—perhaps because it equated a human being with a wild animal.

Toru knew from news reports that powerful narcotics had been developed for use in dart guns as a last resort, in response to the restrictions on the police using live ammunition. Though a culprit might be armed and dangerous, public sentiment still favored a nonlethal sedative over deadly force. So the research on these dart guns had been fast-tracked, and now that the tests had been completed and a quantity of them produced, the police apparently intended to use them on Aoyagi.

As if in support of this, the man Aoyagi had held hostage, who turned out to have worked at the same delivery company, said on television that "he's completely different from the guy I knew at work. I think he would have killed me. . . ."

At some point in the evening coverage, Toru glanced over at Hodogaya. His roommate had turned off his TV and sat there looking fed up.

"You give up watching?"

"It's getting pretty boring."

"You're right, the same stuff over and over."

Halfheartedly, Hodogaya mentioned something about a visitor—his usual ruse—then picked up his cell phone and headed outside. He was gone for some time, and while he was away Toru felt an odd compulsion to keep watching, as if it were his responsibility to keep track of developments for their room.

They were now showing footage of an interview with Aoyagi's father, apparently recorded earlier. The old man was speaking into a microphone in front of a house in a neighborhood identified as being in Saitama Prefecture. He was small but powerfully built and he seemed braced against the onslaught of reporters. He looked tanned and healthy, his short hair and bushy eyebrows reminding Toru somehow of a sailor. His answers were curt, to the point of being rude. Toru could understand a father's need to believe in his son's innocence, but at the same time it seemed a little ridiculous to insist he wasn't involved. But the little man went even further, urging his son on camera to keep running. The reporters seemed to disapprove.

Not surprising that Aoyagi would have a father like this, Toru thought in disgust. Between the two of them, they'd managed to piss off the whole country.

After the interview ended, they cut away for a while to coverage of various accidents and incidents around the city. A man who had kidnapped a baby was caught at one of the checkpoints; some characters who had been robbing people on the subway were arrested thanks to a tip from a witness; and the leader of a gang that had committed a murder in Tokyo several years back had suddenly turned up in a hotel in Sendai. None of these had anything to do with the Kaneda assassination, but it seemed that the arrests had been the direct result of information passed along by a tense and extra-vigilant public.

Later that evening in the smoking area, the middle school boy was holding forth again on his new pet theme: the tyranny of the surveillance society. "They know everything about everyone, thanks to those pods," he was saying. "They intercept every email and phone call, so they're solving all these other cases as a kind of side effect of the Kaneda thing." Toru wondered how a kid that young could get so worked up about it. It seemed the boy had also been following the news online. "And you wouldn't believe how many postings there are from people claiming to be Masaharu Aoyagi! But this isn't like looking for a needle in a haystack; they're hunting for this one guy and everyone knows exactly who he is and what he looks like. How tough can that be?"

Day Three

Toru awoke to someone tapping him hard on the shoulder—in fact, so vigorously that he found he was angry before he was fully awake. Floating just above him was Hodogaya's wrinkly face.

"What do you want?" he grunted. "And what time is it, anyway?" He was so groggy he could barely think.

"It's four," Hodogaya told him.

"In the morning?"

"Naturally."

Four o'clock was technically morning, but it was way too early to be awake. "It's still dark," he muttered.

Ignoring his protests, Hodogaya grabbed the remote from the bedside table. "Take a look," he said. "We're getting to the climax."

"What climax?" Toru said. He reached down to scratch under his cast, but stopped as he realized what he was seeing on the TV.

The screen was filled with a shot of the Central Park, a large open space used for concerts and other events just across the street from Sendai City Hall. With no playground equipment or fences to block the view, the camera caught the whole park at once. The sky in the background was dark, a mottling of black and deep gray, showing that this was live—before dawn.

Klieg lights had been focused on the park, illuminating one area like a spotlight on a stage. The camera panned slowly along the buildings at the perimeter, and uniformed men with rifles could be seen lining the roofs, their telescopic sights trained on the bright patch.

Then the angle shifted to a reporter standing in the street some way from the park, apparently kept back by the police lines. "The marksmen are waiting for orders," he said. The blades of a helicopter could be heard beating the air above him. This must have taken the shot of the rooftops. "Masaharu Aoyagi is reportedly coming here to surrender. And we've been kept at a distance since he has apparently taken another hostage."

Toru was surprised to see how quickly things had come to a head. "What happened?" he asked Hodogaya.

"About an hour ago, the police announced that Aoyagi had contacted them to say he was going to give himself up. He called the media as well."

"Why'd he decide to surrender all of a sudden? And why are they turning it into such a circus? I've never seen so many lights." Dozens of beams were trained on the park from the rooftops of the surrounding buildings. Our taxes at work, he thought irritably. "A whole lot of fuss, and all those guns, for one guy?"

"But they can't just shoot him, can they?" said Hodogaya. "Not on live TV. It's not a public execution."

"We're all watching if they do, that's for sure."

"They'd have a big stink on their hands."

"Which is why they've got dart guns. Not a public execution, a public sedation."

"Dart guns?" Hodogaya echoed, apparently hearing about this plan for the first time.

"They mentioned it yesterday; they're planning to use these new tranquilizer darts on him."

"Seems I missed something, too," said Hodogaya, sounding genuinely disappointed.

"Aoyagi's probably assuming they won't dare shoot him with all these cameras, but he never thought of darts."

"Poor bastard," Hodogaya sighed.

"You feel sorry for him?" Toru asked, but Hodogaya suddenly pointed at the screen.

"Look, is that a manhole cover?" A round shape was just visible on the ground near the center of the park.

"Could be," Toru said.

"I bet it leads to the sewers. There's a storm drain about six meters down."

"How do you know that?"

"I did a little research on the waterworks, for my old job."

"What job?" Toru asked, but without waiting for an answer he stuck the earphones back in—just in time to hear an announcer say that Aoyagi had appeared.

Then everything went suddenly quiet, as though the earphones had stopped working. A man had appeared out of nowhere in the park, his hands raised above his head. Thin and disheveled, he wore a black sweater over jeans. A disappointingly ordinary figure.

"So that's it," Hodogaya murmured.

Masaharu Aoyagi advanced slowly to the center of the park and stopped, then stared around the ring of buildings, as though staring down the barrels of the rifles trained on him. Perhaps it was tension, or exhaustion, but there was something of a wild-eyed dog in the way he looked.

As Toru reached under the edge of his cast to scratch, it struck him that the fun would soon be over—and that he would probably miss it. He had already forgotten where he'd felt the itch.

PART
THREE

TWENTY YEARS LATER

When Prime Minister Sadayoshi Kaneda was assassinated in Sendai twenty years ago, the media reaction was unusually frenzied. This was natural enough given the circumstances, but in hindsight we can see the consequences of the lack of balance in this response. Newspapers and the networks fanned the flames of public outrage by relaying undigested police reports and endless unsubstantiated accounts from ostensible witnesses. Despite the fact that the evidence against Masaharu Aoyagi was never more than circumstantial, from the very beginning of the incident the media identified him as the assassin with astonishing certainty—or, rather, it would be astonishing if this kind of error didn't continue to occur with dismaying regularity today.

Just how astonishing their errors were became apparent to me as I began to research the events of that period in preparation for this account. Under normal circumstances, almost anyone is capable of seeing reason, respecting civil liberties, and playing the game straight. But in times of crisis, clear heads seem to be in short supply, and everyone gets swept up in the excitement.

Even now, decades after the event, the facts of the Kaneda assassination remain unclear. Findings were published by the investigatory commission established less than a month after the assassination by Prime Minister Katsuo Ebisawa, Kaneda's successor, and headed by Supreme Court Justice Ukai, but the "Ukai Report" is a remarkably vague document that amounts to little more than a list of reasons why we don't know the full story.

Furthermore, since Ebisawa specified that all information gathered by the Ukai Commission, the police, and other agencies should be kept sealed well into the next century, further investigation is virtually impossible. There can be only one conclusion: the government that sealed the evidence was determined the incident should be forgotten altogether.

No doubt the majority of the population now subscribe to the theory that the assassination was the result of a conspiracy organized by Ebisawa, who was Kaneda's number two at the time of the incident. A memoir published by Ebisawa's legal counsel caused a considerable sensation a few years back by hinting at his client's participation in the affair.

In his lifetime, Sadayoshi Kaneda was compared to the youthful hero of legend, Yoshitsune, while Ebisawa was known as his faithful old retainer, Benkei. It would certainly be a shock if it turned out that Benkei had orchestrated his master's demise, but given the political path he was pursuing and his deeply jealous nature, it isn't difficult to imagine that this was in fact the case.

Ebisawa split from the Labor Party, which had enjoyed a virtual lock on power in the postwar period, and established the rival Liberal Party. He then worked for many years as the leader of the opposition, prodding recalcitrant MPs through their legislative paces. And time after time he stood as the Liberal Party candidate for prime minister, in each case losing to his Labor Party rival, sometimes by a narrow margin and sometimes in a landslide.

Twenty years ago, however, opportunity had come calling. The Labor Party was self-destructing in the wake of much-needed but ultimately unpopular tax hikes. The stage was set for a changing of the guard and with it, Ebisawa clearly believed, his chance to become prime minister. Just at this moment, however, a young politician, Sadayoshi Kaneda, emerged from Ebisawa's own party to hijack his ambitions. The elder politician suffered a crushing defeat in the primaries, and even at this historical remove it isn't hard to imagine the bitterness he must have felt.

In public, Ebisawa took the high road, praising Kaneda as the new voice of a more youthful party and promising to support his run for prime minister and even serve as his deputy. But according to the lawyer's memoir, he was simultaneously passing along campaign secrets from the Kaneda camp to the Labor Party leadership. Ebisawa was also said to be the source of a story that came out in one of the weeklies during the campaign, revealing that Kaneda's late mother had worked in a bar and had died from stab wounds during an argument with a customer. He seemed to have decided that if he was to be relegated to the role of kingmaker, it was better to annoint Makoto

Ayukawa, his old rival from Labor, than to allow the upstart Kaneda to prevail. But better for whom? For the country? The people? For his party? No, said his lawyer, Ebisawa wanted revenge, pure and simple.

So by the same logic, when Kaneda eventually won the general election despite the sabotage, Ebisawa decided to take matters into his own hands, to eliminate his rival and thus succeed him as prime minister—or so the memoir suggests.

It is not widely known that the route for the prime minister's parade in Sendai that day was changed at the last minute, nor that the new route was decided by then-mayor Sachio Sato, a college classmate of Ebisawa's. When this information is combined with the fact that the textbook warehouse, which happened to be along the new route, was owned by Sato's sister, the conspiracy theory begins to seem plausible. And while the victory parade in Sendai was managed by the prime minister's public relations office, it is said that the original idea for the visit came from Katsuo Ebisawa.

An equally persistent theory, however, contends that the assassination was the work of the Labor Party itself, manipulated by a greater and more sinister power. Whenever something mysterious occurs in Japan, something happening behind the scenes, the fingers always point to the same culprit, the mastermind, the puppeteer: the United States. Such, perhaps, is the fate of the powerful.

Twenty years ago, Japan was wrestling with the question of whether or not it should develop nuclear arms. A year before the election that brought Kaneda to power, the then prime minister Ayukawa came back from a meeting with the U.S. president and suddenly announced that he wanted to begin looking at the question of a domestic nuclear deterrent. Ayukawa was lambasted by the Liberal Party and the media, but he responded that he had never actually proposed developing an arsenal, merely that the issue be given due consideration. He wondered aloud whether a nation could govern itself or conduct diplomatic relations with others if it was unwilling to debate the difficult questions confronting it. And so a public debate was held.

But at the same time there were those who maintained that the idea of a nuclear Japan was simply part of a new U.S. defense scenario, that America wanted an armed Japan as one wing of its China strategy. Among the main proponents of this theory was Sadayoshi Kaneda. He gave voice to an uncomfortable feeling that was shared by most people at the time: namely, that American foreign policy in Asia had been muddled and inconsistent ever since the Pacific War, that the U.S. had no idea what to do with Asia, and that many of Japan's problems, including things as basic as the country's Occupation-imposed constitution, were the result of American ambivalence and misunderstanding. In the early days after WWII, the U.S. had sought to neutralize the Japanese threat through Article 9 of the constitution, in which the country renounced the right to military force. But when the Cold War began almost immediately afterwards, Japan was suddenly an important strategic asset; and while Article 9 remained in effect, the Americans urged the country to develop a military capability. Eventually, they began to campaign actively for the revision of the article itself.

Kaneda accused Ayukawa of being an American flunky, of encouraging a debate that was supposed to get the Japanese thinking for themselves but was actually just part of a larger U.S. design. He acknowledged that the idea of Japan rearming was a traditionally conservative one—and thus counter-intuitive for a liberal politician—but he felt that any government that simply followed the lead of the U.S. would be a laughingstock not only to the Americans but to the whole world. "The United States has never had a vision for Asia," he insisted, "so it is incumbent upon us to chart our own course in matters relating to defense. To take this further, it seems imperative that we develop a credible nuclear deterrent." He also proposed that Japan take steps to upgrade its technical know-how in the areas of strategic data collection and surveillance, especially if it proved difficult to acquire a nuclear arsenal in the short run. In other words, he argued, more than an offensive capability, the country needed a fast, accurate system for gathering data on the military strategy and preparedness of other nations. These were measures that could be taken within the framework of the constitution; and while he supported strengthening the missile defense system, he felt it was wise to put resources into acquiring such technological advantages rather than an arsenal of ABMs. Certainly, these kinds of innovations should be within the reach of Japan's technological prowess. "We may not possess the brute force," he said, "but we can make ourselves indispensable if we possess the most accurate information."

Another fact revealed in the lawyer's memoir is that Kaneda decided soon after becoming prime minister that he would visit China and the Korean peninsula and hold talks aimed at resolving longstanding territorial disputes and demands for Japanese acknowledgement of its actions during the war. But he was not intending to make unilateral concessions, just open discussions; and he was often quoted as wondering why China, in particular, reserved such special animosity for Japan when it had suffered at the hands of other adversaries, such as the British during the Opium Wars, who had never offered any apologies to the Chinese.

He was convinced, however, that Japanese politicians, who tended to be all bluster at home, lacked both the interest and the resolve to conduct a successful foreign policy. It never seemed to occur to them that they should be seeking common ground with their counterparts overseas. "There are no statesmen among us," he was known to say, and for that view he no doubt incurred the wrath of Uncle Sam, at least according to those who hold with the second conspiracy theory.

Then, too, there are those who tend to focus on the *site* of the assassination: the city of Sendai. In other words, they believe he was eliminated by a powerful local bloc.

Kaneda scored a victory in the primary elections despite being younger than the other candidates and virtually unknown. Several factors contributed to this upset, including the above-mentioned tax reforms pushed through by the Labor Party. But perhaps even more important was Kaneda's good fortune that the first primary in the election season was held in his home district of Sendai.

Like the U.S. system, the general election for a prime minister is divided into two stages: primary elections within the Labor and Liberal parties to determine their candidates, and then a general contest for prime minister. The primaries are held region by region, with the party candidate getting the most votes claiming that region. When the voting is finished, the candidate who has won the most regional elections becomes the party's nominee.

Since the primaries are held sequentially, it was particularly significant that the first one was in the city of Sendai, in Miyagi Prefecture. Sadayoshi Kaneda's early campaign was therefore conducted with the utmost care and planning. He made the rounds of all the businesses and organizations in his district, attending countless events in the six months leading up to the primaries, giving hundreds of speeches, and generally making himself known to his constituency. From the outset, he offered a fresh, fearless, new face, combined with a winning speaking style, and he quickly gained the allegiance of voters in his own party and eventually even some of those who had traditionally supported Labor.

Furthermore, Kaneda's charisma and self-confidence must have rattled Katsuo Ebisawa, who was running as a senior member of parliament and the heavyweight in the contest. Ebisawa's campaign became mildly hostile, asking voters whether they could really trust such a young, untested candidate, but this tactic backfired and ultimately strengthened Kaneda's position. Negative ads are a part of any campaign, but voters apparently took offense at a commercial that juxtaposed a particularly snooty-looking picture of Kaneda with one of an elderly, bedridden man. What the Ebisawa campaign did not foresee was that the negative reaction would be directed at Ebisawa as the source of the commercial rather than at Kaneda. Apparently, in the Sendai race, this was enough to tip the balance in Kaneda's favor.

Needless to say, a victory by a young unknown over the man who had been the face of the Liberal Party was big news, but in terms of the larger campaign, it was just a single, local win. Still, this local win proved decisive in Kaneda's victories in both the primary and general elections, victories that were driven in large part by almost accidental media attention.

Quite by chance, the victory in Sendai occurred just at a moment when there were no other newsworthy events. Thus, the morning talk shows and the noon news hours were happy to have Sadayoshi Kaneda to fill their slots. Of course, once TV latched onto the story, Kaneda's name recognition shot up and he won the next local election. As the wins piled up, the media dubbed him "a breath of fresh air," the coverage became still more intense, and ultimately it had a snowball effect. The best analogy is perhaps Jimmy Carter's overnight ascent in American politics. You could say, in effect, that it was the combination of the early win in Sendai and the power of the mass media that were behind Sadayoshi Kaneda's rise to the office of prime minister.

Kaneda's principal backers in the Sendai primary were the Physicians Association and a group of public casino owners. And though the point was never emphasized, it is common knowledge that the leadership of the doctors group consisted of a number of men who had known Kaneda in college, while the casino owners included several who had been at middle school with him. An interview in a weekly photo journal given just before Kaneda announced his candidacy by one of the casino owners attracted a lot of attention. The man had insisted that while his middle school teachers had given up on him early on in life, his classmate, Kaneda, had always been there for him. Ironically, the combination of the sober, mannerly Kaneda and the roughneck casino owner struck voters as refreshing rather than unsavory.

But a third and widely credited theory is that these two groups of supporters, the doctors and the casino owners, turned against him after the election and arranged his dispatch. The theory gained particular currency when it came out that shortly after becoming prime minister, Kaneda had begun studying health-care reform with his Liberal Party colleagues in parliament and that he had discussed budget reductions for public casinos with Katsuo Ebisawa in the same period.

This was certainly not a question of Kaneda betraying former allies. Well before the campaign, he had focused public attention on issues such as the deplorable working conditions in emergency medicine and the shortage of gynecologists; and he may genuinely have felt the need for more centralized control over issues ranging from the location of regional clinics to doctors' salaries. At the same time, business at public casinos had been on the increase and they had begun to show substantial profits. Thus, he seemed intent on cutting budget support to the casinos and using the savings to fund health-care reforms.

Still, it is possible to imagine that those special-interest groups who supported him in the primaries might—fairly or unfairly—have felt used and betrayed, and decided that Kaneda had bitten the hand that fed him. A writer who interviewed one of the casino owners some six months after the assassination quoted him as saying that the prime minister "just didn't get it."

There were a number of other theories as well. One holds that Kaneda's girlfriend, Hikaruko Kobayashi, went to the Labor Party and begged them to make an example of him for refusing to properly acknowledge her. Another maintains that he was eliminated by a group that saw him as hopelessly unsympathetic to gay causes. In the end, however, other than the fact that Kobayashi committed suicide after the assassination and that Kaneda did once fire a secretary who was known to be gay, there is no credible evidence to support either notion.

Ultimately, however, our inability to get to the truth of the case after all this time is due in large part to the fact that so many of those who were involved are now dead. As the years have gone by, a number have died of natural causes, but several—too many, some would say—died in other ways.

Most notable, of course, is the suicide of his lover, Hikaruko Kobayashi. Two months after the assassination, she was found hanged in a hotel room in Fukuoka. There was no note. Later it was revealed that her apartment in Tokyo had been ransacked, and her sister maintained that the diary she'd kept was missing.

Hideo Okura, who was covering the parade on the day of the assassination, was stabbed to death in broad daylight on a busy street less than a year later. A broadcast reporter for a local TV station, he was the one who first insisted he'd seen someone on top of the textbook warehouse. The Ukai Report concluded later that it was Masaharu Aoyagi on the roof of the building flying the remote-controlled helicopter, but Okura had told a local magazine that the man he'd seen bore no particular resemblance to Aoyagi.

Yuzo Ochiai, the owner of the model shop, has also died. A nondescript man in his late fifties, he owned a small store on the south side of town that sold various remote-controlled gadgets, including, it was said, the one Aoyagi had used. In the wake of the assassination, the networks broadcast the surveillance tape from his shop supposedly showing Aoyagi purchasing the helicopter. Six months after the incident, Ochiai struck a divider on the freeway and was killed instantly. The investigation revealed that his blood alcohol level was elevated, though his family insisted that he did not drink. In the course of my own research, I have learned that Okura's description of the man he saw on the roof closely resembles Yuzo Ochiai.

Junko Kusumi, a waitress at Nokkin, a chain restaurant in Sendai, is another witness who died soon after the incident. A man robbing a convenience store where she was shopping was accused of hitting her on the head with a hammer, though when he was arrested later he denied any knowledge of her murder. At the time of Kaneda's assassination, Junko Kusumi had appeared on TV saying that Aoyagi had broken a window and threatened the customers at her restaurant. But according to a friend who was interviewed after her death, Kusumi had regretted making her statement. She had apparently said it was the police who had used violence and made threats.

Tsuyoshi Kubota's name should certainly be included in any list of interesting players in the case. He was in his mid-thirties at the time, and busy committing a series of robberies in homes around Sendai. Two years before the assassination, he happened to have chosen a budding young celebrity named Rinka as his next victim but was caught in the act and apprehended by Masaharu Aoyagi, who had been making a delivery to Rinka. Given his extensive criminal record, Kubota was sentenced to seven years in prison but was paroled after five. It was barely a footnote in the weeklies, but Kubota was killed in a fight on the street less than two weeks after he got out of prison. It was said that he spent much of his sentence, however, boasting that he would kill Aoyagi when he got the chance.

Ai Kurata also died less than two years after the assassination. Around the time of the incident, reports surfaced that Aoyagi had molested a young woman by that name on a commuter train in Sendai. She died in a drunk-driving accident along a mountain road on the Oshika Peninsula, going over a cliff after failing to negotiate a curve. Another woman, Koume Inohara, was in the passenger seat and was also killed, but strangely there seemed to be no previous connection between the two. The only thing they had in common was the fact that they were both heavily in debt.

There have also been persistent and intriguing rumors regarding Tsuneo Okouchi, a college friend of Kaneda's who was said to have supported him behind the scenes during the election. Twenty years ago, Okouchi was director of the Sendai Hospital Center, and it was learned later from an internal complaint filed at the hospital that he'd had some sort of dealings with the police during the incident. The reason for this was never revealed, but there were rumors that the bodies of two people who had died under suspicious circumstances were processed in the hospital's morgue as though they had been patients. Okouchi had clearly taken measures to conceal these activities from public scrutiny. There was, in addition, a magazine report that two of the doctors who had assisted in the disposition of the bodies committed suicide soon afterwards. Okouchi later became head of the Physicians Association but died recently of liver cancer.

If we give any credence to the conspiracy theories, then there is no doubt that these deaths form an interesting pattern. Ichitaro Sasaki, the assistant division chief in the Security Bureau who coordinated the search for Aoyagi at the time, has also died by now. He retired shortly after the incident and effectively disappeared. It is said that he opened a flower shop in a small town north of Sendai, and that over time he came to look even more like an aging Paul McCartney. There has been, of course, considerable speculation as to why he dropped out of public life and refused to speak about the case.

The most common explanation has to do with a fact that was learned only after the commotion had died down: that his son was in a serious car accident in Tokyo during the hunt for Aoyagi. Though the son survived, it was said that the event forced Sasaki to weigh his career against his family and that he chose the latter.

There are those, however, who contend that Sasaki stumbled across some highly sensitive information in the course of the investigation. During those three days—or, strictly speaking, two, as the chase ended on the morning of the third—the Security Pods picked up information from every corner of the city. That data has never been divulged, but there is no doubt that an extraordinary number of phone and email messages were recorded and analyzed and nearly as many pictures were taken of the general public, implying that someone gave tacit approval for a massive invasion of privacy.

Normally, this kind of infringement of civil rights would cause a strong backlash, but given the circumstances it is probably understandable that few objections were raised. Most people would have felt insulated, since the data collected was ostensibly focused on Masaharu Aoyagi and those associated with him. But the rumors surrounding Sasaki's retirement point out that he had access to all the data, and there is speculation that somewhere in this sea of information he uncovered a national secret of some kind. This line of reasoning holds that it was considered unsafe for him to remain on the police force and that he was offered early retirement and a generous pension in exchange for his silence.

There are still others who say that the strain of those few days exhausted and broke him, forcing his retirement, or even that he had his face altered with plastic surgery and is still out there somewhere pursuing the truth about the assassination. According to the latter camp, the man running the flower shop was someone else again, who had undergone an operation of his own.

On the face of it, these theories seem utterly absurd, but my research revealed that they were fueled by rumors about a certain plastic surgeon who died ten years ago. He had originally done work for celebrities in Tokyo but had retreated to Sendai, supposedly due to suggestions that he was not properly licensed. The rumors stemmed from reports about something he said on his deathbed: apparently a photo of Ichitaro Sasaki had appeared on the TV—perhaps as part of a special on the tenth anniversary of Kaneda's death—and he is said to have murmured that he, too, had been involved in the incident. It was inferred from this that Sasaki had undergone plastic surgery, but a more likely explanation is that he was referring to work he had done on Rinka, the actress Aoyagi had rescued two years prior to the assassination.

Mamoru Kondo, a detective who worked on the investigation with Sasaki, also retired less than a year after the incident. According to an account in his diary, which was made public on the Web by his family after his death, Kondo had objected to a gag order and suppression of evidence concerning an illegal search that had been conducted on an associate of Aoyagi's, and he had clashed with his superiors in an attempt to ensure the safety of the man in question. For his trouble he had been forced out of his job. The authenticity of the diary has been questioned in many quarters, but one can't help wondering whether Kondo's intervention didn't save Aoyagi's friend from being permanently hushed up.

Finally, there was some discussion on the Internet about the fate of Detective Taro Matsumoto of the Miyagi Prefectural Police. It seems that he had been devoting his off-duty hours to a personal investigation of the Kaneda assassination, and that his interest in the affair had been sparked by a posting he had read on an Internet bulletin board during the incident that had been signed "Masaharu Aoyagi." Of course, any number of people claiming to be Aoyagi had popped up on the Net during those three days, but Matsumoto felt that a few of these messages could not be easily dismissed, and he pursued his investigation based on these online leads.

Whether due to his superior skills as an investigator or his superior imagination, Matsumoto had developed a pet theory that there had been another intended scapegoat for the crime, and that Aoyagi had only been pressed into service after the original candidate suddenly died of heart failure on the Sendai subway that morning. In other words, according to Matsumoto, the plot was so elaborate that it included several possible fall guys. Matsumoto died from his injuries in a taxicab accident ten years ago.

At present, when so many voices that might have spoken about the incident have been stilled, we can only speculate as to the true facts and wonder what we might learn if Masaharu Aoyagi could come back to tell us what happened to him. I must confess that I paid a visit to his grave in preparation for writing this report, but needless to say, the dead do not give up their secrets.

Only one thing is certain: that no one now believes what so many of us did twenty years ago when the media stirred up such a frenzy and hounded Masaharu Aoyagi as the murderer of Prime Minister Kaneda. But we will never know what Aoyagi thought and felt for those forty-eight hours of frantic flight.

PART
FOUR

THE INCIDENT

Masaharu Aoyagi

At 11:00 A.M., Masaharu Aoyagi found himself walking past a line of second-hand computer shops in the neighborhood to the east of Sendai Station. When he caught sight of a truck parked by the side of the road ahead, his expression relaxed into a smile.

"What are you grinning about?" His companion, Shingo Morita, was wearing an orange down jacket. He had been sensitive to the cold ever since their student days, and there was no doubt that the November wind had a bite to it. But if you brought out the down coat now, what would you wear in February when the cold really set in?

"I used to see that guy when I was driving." As they approached, the man stacking boxes in the back looked up. Aoyagi glanced at his watch. "Right on time, as usual, Maezono," he said. "Some things never change."

"Been making this stop forever," Maezono nodded. "Same time, same place." His face was wrinkled, and Aoyagi knew he must be well into his fifties, but he looked ten years younger in his dark blue uniform—perhaps because he stood ramrod straight as he lifted the boxes. "No rest for the weary."

"Can't complain about that, can you?"

"Back when you were on TV all the time, I thought you'd take away all my customers," Maezono said, running his hand through his short, graying hair. His eyes were deep-set, like knots in a gnarled log. The boxes under the tarp on the back of his truck were neatly stacked. "But now I've got so much work, I even do evening deliveries." He sighed. "Have to hurry to catch the show I watch at nine."

"As regular with the TV as you are with the boxes!" Aoyagi laughed.

"Guess you could say that," Maezono grinned. "My run is out in the suburbs. I'll drop it off early and I should still make it home in time."

"Must-see TV," Aoyagi chuckled. "See you later," he added, sensing that Morita was getting impatient.

"You should try to be less conspicuous," Morita said as they walked away.

"Why? What do you mean?"

"I mean, you should be less conspicuous."

"Is this the voice of the forest speaking?" Aoyagi laughed.

"It is indeed. A peaceful, lakeside forest."

When they had first met at college more than ten years earlier, Shingo Morita had explained that the character in his name—"mori" for "woods"—meant that he had a special affinity for this type of scenery, and that from time to time he could hear it "speaking" to him. He'd repeated the claim often, and when his friends teased him, asking what the forest was telling him, he told them with a straight face that it revealed the future. "I know what's going to happen," he used to boast.

"You're psychic?" some girl would ask him at a party—for it was always in a crowd that he made this claim.

"Well, I suppose you could say that," Morita would answer, puffing out his chest a bit.

"So what did you want to talk about today?" said Aoyagi, changing the subject. Morita had called a week earlier to ask if they could have lunch, saying he had something important to discuss. "It's important for *you*." It seemed an odd thing to say after all this time.

"Does it have to do with what happened on the train?" Aoyagi had asked. Two months earlier, while riding inbound on the Senseki Line, a woman had accused him of groping her, though he had never laid a hand on her. Coincidentally, it was then that he had also run into Morita for the first time since graduation.

"It does," Morita said.

Aoyagi had all the time in the world to meet an old friend, living as he was on his unemployment check. Nevertheless, he couldn't imagine what Morita might have to say.

"What's wrong with this?" he asked as Morita marched by another restaurant, part of a big chain. They hadn't agreed on a place to eat, but maybe Morita had something particular in mind.

"It's full," he said.

"How do you know without checking?"

"I know."

"The voice of the forest?"

"You guessed it."

"Same old Morita," he murmured.

"People don't change."

"I suppose you're right," Aoyagi conceded. "That guy we ran into, Maezono, is exhibit A."

"How so?"

"Well, he's self-employed and his whole business is regular customers—pick up something at the same time and place every day and deliver it somewhere else at the same time and place. But he's famous for his schedule between jobs—every driver in the business knows where to find him: from 12:30 to 1:30, he's having lunch and then taking a nap under a pedestrian bridge near where I live; at 4:00, he's reading magazines at a bookstore out on the highway; at 6:00, he's having dinner, always at the same place. He's always on time, never varies his routine. We used to set our watches by his truck."

"The joys of the regular life?"

"Maezono says that getting through his day on schedule gives him a sense of accomplishment, like putting together a model exactly according to the instructions."

They had come to a fast-food place and Morita paused. "This okay?" he said. Aoyagi had no objection—fast food was about right in their case. They went in and ordered at the counter, then climbed to the second floor carrying their trays. The room was empty but they sat at the very back.

"Still giving these places the professional once-over?" Aoyagi asked.

"Not really," Morita laughed. "Not anymore." There was a hint of nostalgia in his voice.

"I wonder if the Society for the Study of Adolescent Eating Habits is still in business?" Aoyagi said, giving the full name of the club they had founded during their undergraduate days here in the city.

"The Friends of Fast Food?" Morita corrected. "I doubt it. Even in our day, it was only you, me and Higuchi, and Kazu." Morita used their nickname for their friend, Kazuo Ono, who was a year behind the other three in school.

"I heard that Kazu went out recruiting after we graduated and rounded up a bunch of new members," Aoyagi said.

"But I don't think it lasted long after that. I guess there wasn't really anything very exciting about going around town keeping track of all the new menu items at fast-food places. I can see why no one kept it up."

"How can you say that? You were the driving force behind it."

"Youthful exuberance," Morita said, folding over a French fry and stuffing it in his mouth. Aoyagi recognized the old habit, and Morita seemed to realize what he'd just done. "I guess the way we eat never changes either," he said. "What do you think man's greatest strengths are?" he asked suddenly.

Aoyagi grunted noncommittally and bit into his hamburger.

"Trust and habit," Morita said.

"Rust an abbi?" Aoyagi repeated, his mouth full now.

"You haven't changed either," his friend said, pointing at Aoyagi's lunch. He had eaten around the edges of the bun, leaving the center for last—just the way he always had.

"This isn't much of place, though," said Aoyagi, as he folded the wrapper from his burger. "I suppose you can't take off points for having an old guy working behind the counter, but he didn't even look up when he took our order. And that's weird, too," he added, pointing at the security camera on the ceiling above them. "It's not even aimed at anything."

"The place gets a C or a D," Morita said, reviving their old rating system. "And the 'Special of the Day'—C at best. Don't think I'm hurrying back for that."

Aoyagi studied his friend as they talked. He'd let his hair grow since they'd graduated, which suited him, but there were dark circles under his eyes. "You know," he said, "I didn't think you were in Sendai."

"Sorry. I kind of fell out of touch."

"When my New Year's cards started coming back, I figured you'd moved. But I guess I never thought we'd lose track of each other so soon."

"There was just a lot of stuff going on." Morita stirred his drink with his straw.

"What kind of stuff?"

"You and Haruko breaking up, you saving that girl and getting famous, you . . ."

"That was all my stuff," Aoyagi interrupted. "Was it really my fault?"

"After that, I was busy working in Tokyo and it was hard to stay in touch. But you could have called me, especially when you and Haruko split up. You must have needed a shoulder to cry on."

"I did call," Aoyagi broke in, "but your phone had been disconnected."

"Oh. I guess I had a lot going on then, too."

"Well, I really did call," Aoyagi said.

"And you really don't give up easily."

"You just didn't answer." Aoyagi laughed, worried things were getting too heavy. "Are you still working in Tokyo?"

"I've been at the Sendai branch since last year."

"I guess I never figured you for the business type." And he certainly didn't look the part, with his hair that long. On the other hand, his friend had always had a way with words that would have been useful in the business world.

"Turns out I'm not," said Morita. He bent another fry in half.

"Why do you say that?"

"Because I always know how a deal's going to turn out."

"The voice of the forest?"

"Naturally. So I always know what the other guy is going to do, whether I can make a sale, whatever—I know everything ahead of time. It's a big advantage, but it kind of takes the fun out of it. You end up just going through the motions. Still, I always did everything exactly by the book. Know why?"

Aoyagi was about to say no, when the traditional answer to the familiar question popped into his head. "Because you're a pro," he laughed.

"That's right," nodded Morita. "A pro. I wonder how old Todoroki is, anyway. Still churning out fireworks, you think?" How many times when they'd worked at his factory had they heard Todoroki say he did this or that because he was "a pro"? "And do you suppose his son ever came back to work for him?"

"Who knows?" said Aoyagi, picturing Todoroki's bearlike face. "But tell me, Mr. Morita, does that voice from the forest really still speak to you?"

"It really does."

"Then why haven't you ever considered a career in gambling?"

He was quiet for a moment and Aoyagi thought he suddenly looked older, and a bit sad. "You don't believe in this power of mine," he said at last, "but it got you out of that scrape with the woman on the train."

Aoyagi groaned, remembering the incident two months earlier. "Now that you mention it, how did you end up there that day?"

"My powers," said Morita, sounding serious. "I just happened to be on that train, but in another car. Then, one stop before Sendai Station, it hit me—someone I knew was in trouble. So I got off and looked around, and there you were—sort of hard to miss, actually, facing off with that half-crazed banshee. And somehow I just knew that she was trying to frame you as a groper."

"You even knew I hadn't done it?"

Morita nodded. "The powers, my friend. But why were *you* on that train?"

"Because of a weird phone call," said Aoyagi. The police had called his house that day to say that his driver's license had been found on the beach at Matsushima. He'd gone to check his wallet and found that it was, in fact, missing.

"How did it get to Matsushima?" Morita asked with a laugh.

"How should I know?" He had been genuinely puzzled since he hadn't been anywhere near the place in years. "But I decided I should go get it." The whole chain of events still seemed improbable.

"And the groping thing happened on the way back?"

"You mean the frame-up."

"I'm afraid you were guilty the moment the 'victim' grabbed your arm for a citizen's arrest. Try going to the police with her hand on your arm to prove your innocence. They would never let up till you confessed."

"I see what you mean," said Aoyagi.

"It didn't matter that she was lying. An accusation is as good as a conviction these days. That's why I grabbed you and dragged you out of there."

Aoyagi remembered the sound of the woman's voice crying out on the train. He had no idea it had anything to do with him until he turned to look at her. A chill ran straight down his back when she grabbed his arm. "Keep your hands off me!" she had screamed. He didn't know what she was talking about, but he could feel himself blush and start shaking anyway.

"There's something a little too nice, too easygoing about you—makes people want to take advantage of you," said Morita.

"Was *she* trying to take advantage of me?" Aoyagi could still see the woman's thick makeup as she faced him on the platform. There was something of the hustler about her, but the anger in her eyes had seemed genuine. "Do you think maybe I did it?" he asked Morita.

"Well, did you?" his friend shot back, pointing a French fry at him.

"No. But in the years since we last met, I might have turned into a major creep. . . ."

"But that didn't happen," said Morita, without waiting for him to finish. "When we were in school, didn't you always say the one thing you couldn't stand were assholes who felt up women on trains? You were full of the milk of human kindness when it came to snotty teachers, sexist jerks, and those shitheads who forget to return adult movies to the video store—even that slasher who killed people behind the station didn't seem to bother you much. But you could never abide a regular old groper. Or did I get it wrong?"

"Well, I don't remember about the slasher." Aoyagi forced a smile. He also didn't quite buy the part about adult videos. "My dad couldn't stand guys who did that kind of thing. Maybe I got it from him." He frowned, remembering that his father had once attacked a man who had been caught groping a woman and nearly kicked him to death. "Or maybe I've changed in the last eight years."

"From a guy who can't stand gropers . . . into a groper yourself? I suppose anything's possible, especially with erratic types like you." Aoyagi couldn't tell whether he was serious or not. "Maybe the shock of breaking up with Haruko turned you against all women, and you started molesting them in your need for revenge."

"A bit too plausible for comfort," Aoyagi said.

"By the way," said Morita, changing the subject again, "when I was working in Tokyo I ran into Kazu on the subway. He's the one who told me you two had split up. Shocked the hell out of me."

"I was pretty shocked myself," said Aoyagi.

"She dumped you, I suppose."

"How did you know?"

"The forest. But I could have guessed anyway. And she's married now, with a kid," he added.

"The forest tell you that, too?" Aoyagi's eyes were open wide.

"No, I ran into her," Morita said. His tone was offhand. "Last year, just after I got back to Sendai, at a department store near the station. She was with her husband and their little girl. And the funny thing is, she's still Haruko Higuchi."

"What do you mean?"

"She married a guy named Higuchi."

"You're kidding."

"She saw me first," Morita continued. "She came up and introduced me to her husband. He said she talks about the old college days all the time. Seemed like a nice guy to me."

"I've never met him," said Aoyagi. "I didn't even know his name."

"Curious?" Morita asked.

"About what?"

"How you stack up against him."

"No, let's not go there," said Aoyagi.

"I'd call it a draw." His eyes narrowed. "He has qualities you don't, and you've got some he doesn't. He seemed a bit wide-eyed and clueless, maybe."

"The type who knows how to share a chocolate bar?"

"Chocolate bar? Yeah, maybe so. Actually, he reminded me a little of you. . . ."

"So, did you get me here today just to make fun of my love life?" Aoyagi stuck his lip out, pretending to pout. "It's been six years since Haruko and I broke up. It's ancient history."

"Well, then," Morita said, leaning forward, "how about that Rinka. Did you do it with her?" His tone was neutral but the intentness in his look made Aoyagi wince.

"Are you serious?"

"But you were her knight in shining armor, you came to her rescue. Didn't she owe you something? I'm sure you got friendly. So, did you do it?" This was the same old Morita, getting all worked up at the mention of a woman and wanting to know everything in detail. In reality, though, he had been something of a late bloomer himself; shy as anything when left alone with a girl, usually not even getting around to holding hands by the end of a date.

"Of course we did it. Lots," said Aoyagi, grinning and looking down at his lap. Morita let out a whoop.

"Seriously?! What's it like, with a showbiz type?"

"Can't you tell by looking at her? We went at it all night, and she kept screaming 'I'm dying, I'm dying!'"

Morita's eyes grew wide. "I never thought you had it in you!"

But then Aoyagi burst out laughing. "It was a computer game," he sputtered. "A martial arts game, and when her guy was on his last legs, she'd scream 'I'm dying!'"

Morita looked stricken. "You are so fucking boring," he muttered.

"Nothing happened. She was always busy with TV shows and interviews, but she finally asked me over for dinner to thank me. We played computer games a few times."

"You were always too serious," Morita said.

"Some things never change. I was a serious driver, too."

"But you quit?"

"I didn't want to make trouble for the company."

"Seems to me you were their best advertisement."

"There was some trouble," Aoyagi said, scratching the side of his head.

Masaharu Aoyagi

It had started about six months ago. He had been out in his truck making his rounds as usual when his cell phone rang. First it vibrated, then the light came on, and finally the tone—it always felt like having a small animal in his pocket. He thought it might be from one of the houses where he'd just left a "delivery attempted" notice.

Easing down a narrow, one-way street, he turned left at the intersection and pulled over. Then he took out the phone and answered it.

"Is this Aoyagi?" a man's voice said.

"Yes, who is it?" The sudden intrusion of an unfamiliar voice reminded him how it had felt when the whole world—or at least the TV audience—seemed to be watching him: the sick stomach, a tightness in his cheeks. He had truly hated all the attention, his role as "man of the hour." And to make matters worse, the whole thing had happened just as the company was putting all its management systems online, including information about the drivers' routes and work schedules, and even their cell phone numbers. Access had supposedly been limited to employees and the drivers who contracted with the company, but somehow the system had been hacked and Aoyagi's profile became public knowledge.

Occasionally someone would wait for him along his route or, more often, call his cell phone. They all had something to tell him—ranging from friendly messages of support to accusations that he was a "cocky bastard." Either way, he found dealing with them exhausting, so he was relieved when the TV shows had gradually begun to move on from his story, and the calls had slowed and stopped. It worried him to think that this might be another one after all this time.

"Who is it?" Aoyagi asked again.

The man asked a question instead of answering. "How long are you going to keep working?"

"Until nine or ten o'clock, if I've got something time-sensitive," Aoyagi said without thinking. There was a cold laugh at the other end of the line.

"No," the voice said. "I meant, when are you going to quit your job?"

"Quit?"

"If you don't quit soon, I'll be very unhappy. And when I get unhappy, I can make lots of trouble." Then the phone went dead. Stunned, Aoyagi had sat staring at the blank display.

"What the fuck? What kind of threat was that?" Morita stabbed yet another v-shaped fry at him as he spoke.

"At first I thought it was just a crank call," said Aoyagi.

"It wasn't?"

"They kept coming. He called to threaten me, then he called the company to tell them to fire me. Still, I managed to ignore it until things started happening with my deliveries."

"What things?"

"Well, for one, they suddenly increased, a lot."

"Doesn't sound like a problem—business booming."

Aoyagi flattened the little box that had held his French fries. "An unbelievable number of packages starting coming to addresses on my route, all with similar handwriting and all from somewhere in Tokyo. But the weird thing was that my name was written in as sender on every one of them."

"Could have been someone else with the same name," Morita suggested, but he was beginning to frown. "It's possible. But what was in them?"

"Nothing much—candy, saké—but the people getting them had no idea where they were coming from, and it seemed creepy having my name on them. The company didn't know what to do."

"I see what you mean. It's a bit too elaborate—and expensive—to write off as a prank."

"And a bit too scary."

Morita scratched his head. "Curiouser and curiouser. But it still wasn't worth quitting over."

"The guy on the phone said that worse things would happen if I didn't quit. Of course, the company reported everything to the police."

"So, again, you didn't have to quit."

"No, I suppose not," Aoyagi admitted. Despite the threats, no one had asked him to go, there had been no need to give in.

"So?"

"To be honest, I think I'd been looking for the chance to get out."

"Something of a pattern with you, it seems," said Morita.

Aoyagi realized how much he enjoyed sitting here after all these years, listening to his old friend's categorical, if slightly ill-informed, opinions.

"There was a guy on my route named Inai," he said.

"Sounds like the first line of a limerick."

"Maybe," said Aoyagi. "Anyway, this Inai was never ever at home. He was constantly ordering stuff by mail, but he was never there when I showed up to deliver it. The crack in his door was always stuffed with delivery notices."

"So?"

"So one day this Inai really did disappear. He left a note on the door saying that his packages should be left with the building manager and that he'd be back 'at some point.' It seemed pretty odd."

"'At some point'? What was that supposed to mean?"

"I realized that most of the stuff I'd delivered there was from sporting goods stores or travel agencies. One of the other drivers told me later that he was probably getting ready to go off on some kind of adventure."

Morita grinned. "Adventure? What was he, a cub scout?"

"The thing is, ever since Inai took off for parts unknown, I've been thinking I should do the same," said Aoyagi.

"You always were pretty suggestible," Morita laughed. "Maybe you just needed something more exciting than driving a delivery truck."

"Maybe. I've certainly felt as though I've been drifting, not qualified for anything."

"What, in particular?"

"I don't know. Something, anything." His tone grew more insistent as if to cover his embarrassment. "Anyway, I told the boss I didn't want them harassed on my account and I quit."

"The asshole who was calling you was probably one of Rinka's fans," said Morita.

"I'd have thought so, too, if it hadn't been so long since the whole thing happened." There had been some contact with people who were clearly obsessed with her soon afterwards, but most of them had just wanted to thank him for helping "their Rinka." He'd been almost favorably impressed by this brush with the world of fandom.

"Then maybe it had something to do with the groping thing," said Morita. "You're a good-looking guy, serious, responsible. Then you became a hero overnight. Who wouldn't be happy to see you arrested for groping some woman on the train? What's more fun than watching the golden boy screw up?"

For a moment, this scenario almost made sense. Maybe the mystery of the lost license in Matsushima was somehow just another piece of the puzzle. "And is this the forest talking again?"

"No, this is me." Morita took a deep breath and glanced at the clock on the wall. "Ready to go?" he said.

"Where to?" Aoyagi asked, hoping they might finally be getting to the reason Morita had wanted to see him.

"Not the west side of the station. There was a huge crowd, roads blocked off."

"For Kaneda's parade," said Aoyagi.

"Did you want to go have a look?"

"No, not really." He'd been impressed by what he'd seen of Kaneda on TV, but not enough to want to brave the crowd. He hadn't even remembered to vote on election day. "I'm just glad I don't drive anymore. It's a pain when they start blocking off streets, and the whole city goes to hell if you can't use Higashi Nibancho."

"Unfortunately, that's exactly where we're going."

"Why?"

"That's where my car's parked. We can talk when we get there." Mystified, Aoyagi followed him down the stairs and out into the street. From behind, he could see that his friend was beginning to go gray.

Masaharu Aoyagi

Several months earlier, Masaharu Aoyagi had stopped his truck and glanced over at the list on the passenger seat. He had all the deliveries memorized, but it was always worth double-checking. The guy who had shown him the ropes when he'd first started driving had always said that you were more likely to make a mistake when you were quite sure you wouldn't. His instructor, Iwasaki, wore his hair slicked straight back, and though he was only a year or so older than Aoyagi, he'd been married with a kid by the time he was twenty and was building a house now. Still, he had a teenager's passion for rock-and-roll, and he was always saying how he was going to "rock the world." He really meant it. He also liked to point out that the "iwa" in his name meant "rock" in English. "It's Destiny," he insisted.

Once the training period was over and Aoyagi got his own route, he didn't see much of Rock Iwasaki. But he did run into him from time to time when the drivers went out drinking together. Iwasaki would invariably bring his guitar along, even for karaoke, and start in on a Beatles riff without being asked. It had always made Aoyagi happy to see someone enjoy himself so much.

Iwasaki used the word "rock" in response to just about any situation he encountered, good or bad. When he was given a particularly dumb assignment or an unpopular route, he'd mutter "This does not rock"; but if something good happened—a raise for the drivers, for example—you'd hear him practically shout "That rocks!"

But Rock Iwasaki had also taught him a lot of things during the training period that had stuck with him. Some of them were technical aspects of the job—the right way to carry boxes or use a hand truck—but others had more to do with attitude. "You've always got to show up at the door with a smile on your face," he used to say. "And never let on that a box is too heavy or the weather's too hot. That's why they call it the *service* sector!" Still other lessons were more like warnings: "Driving your truck when you're dead tired is like playing with a loaded gun. Stay alert, stay alive!" And once Rock had shown him the butterfly knife he kept in his glove compartment—"You never know when one of these will come in handy." The blade didn't look as if it was meant for peeling apples.

Aoyagi had also seen him stop his truck out of the blue, hop out the door, and tell a guy in a suit walking along the street to watch what he did with his cigarette. "You flick that around," he said, leaning in on the man for emphasis, "and it's going to end up in some kid's eye." He'd said later that his daughter had nearly lost an eye from somebody's discarded cigarette.

On more than one occasion, Iwasaki had spoken of the dangers of hip-hop music. "It just doesn't rock," he insisted. Aoyagi had found this particular prejudice a bit odd, but he recalled that Morita had once said much the same thing. Aoyagi had just confessed that he had started to like hip-hop. "How can you listen to that crap!" Morita had said. At the time, it had struck him as strangely conservative, but today he felt nostalgia even for his old friend's idiosyncrasies.

Aoyagi got out of the truck and retrieved a small box from the back. He checked the shipping label—Hasama House, Apt. 302, 3-8-21 Higashi Kamisugi, Aoba Ward, Sendai—and tucked the box under his arm. "I bet Inai's not in again today," he murmured, as if humming to himself.

A man in a yellow uniform was just coming out the door. "How's it going?" he said as he spotted Aoyagi. He worked for another delivery company, but his route must have been similar to Aoyagi's since they kept bumping into each other. The guy was in his late forties, with a daughter about to take the high school entrance exams, Aoyagi remembered.

"Not bad," he said.

"Headed for Inai's?"

"Not in again, I suppose."

"For quite a while, according to the note."

"What note?"

"The one on his door. It says to leave his deliveries with the manager."

"So he's off on a trip?"

"Better yet, an 'adventure,' according to the note."

"So Inai's an adventurer?" said Aoyagi, as the other driver headed back to his truck. He went in and took the elevator to the third floor to check the note. It sounded ridiculous, and yet something about reading it made him feel good. When he went to drop off the package, the building manager scowled at him through his beard.

"I'll take it," he said, "but I don't know what the fuck to do with this stuff, or when this guy's coming back."

"He didn't say?" asked Aoyagi.

"He paid a year's rent in advance, so it may be a while."

With a murmur of surprise, Aoyagi put the box down in front of the man.

"You know the fire extinguisher outside Inai's door?" the manager asked abruptly. He still sounded grumpy.

"I think so," Aoyagi replied, remembering that he'd seen one just a moment ago.

"Well, he's got a spare key taped to the bottom of it. Go put this in his apartment." He picked up the box Aoyagi had just deposited on his desk.

"He won't mind?"

"Who gives a shit? And do me a favor, take this with you," he added, handing him the package the other driver had just left. It was unusually light. "It's darts," he said, pointing at the shipping label. "Says so right here."

"You mean, like the game?" Aoyagi asked.

"Do you know, like, some other kind?" Aoyagi didn't mind the sarcasm, but winced when the manager threw an imaginary dart somewhere near his head: "You'd think he could have waited until this shit had arrived."

"Maybe he decided to go in a hurry. By the way"—the question had been on his mind since the other driver had mentioned Inai's trip—"did you see him when he left?"

"On his way out the door? Yeah, I saw him. He was carrying this huge backpack."

"How did he look?" At this, the manager finally eased up a bit.

"You know, now that you mention it, he looked like a kid heading off on a field trip, all excited, shining eyes. Like a big kid."

Aoyagi took the boxes up to Inai's apartment. When he got back to his truck and was starting the engine, he found himself wondering whether things might have been different if he'd been more like Inai, if he'd let himself set out on some adventure. Maybe if he had, she might not have left him.

Masaharu Aoyagi

Six years earlier, Aoyagi had finished his route and gone to Haruko Higuchi's apartment instead of going home. He was planning to stay over, since the two of them had a date to see the first showing of a new movie the next day. When he opened the door, she stuck her head out of the kitchen to greet him. He had been coming here since their student days and felt almost as much at home in her apartment as he did in his own. He even had his own space in the shoe cupboard in the front hall.

"I ordered pizza," Haruko said as she came and sat down on the rug.

She'd had problems at work, she told him at some length. "Just because I came up with the idea, my boss refuses to support it," she explained.

"I'm sure it's not because it was your idea."

"The costs would be practically nothing, so why does he insist it show a profit immediately?"

"You're right, that doesn't seem fair," he agreed. The TV was on low; everyone seemed to be enjoying themselves as usual.

"I'll run the bath," Haruko said eventually, getting up. As she did so, Aoyagi noticed a bar of chocolate on the little table next to them.

"Mind if I have some?"

"Help yourself," Haruko called back from the bathroom. Aoyagi tore off the paper and carefully broke the foil-wrapped bar in half. "They were giving them out at the office," she said as she came back into the room.

Aoyagi looked down at the two pieces of chocolate. He had tried to make the halves even, but the break was jagged. He compared the pieces for a moment and then held out the one in his left hand to Haruko. Instead of taking it, however, she stopped and her face darkened as she stared down at it.

"What's wrong?" he asked.

She took a few short breaths. "I've been thinking," she said, her tone bright and a bit manic, "that maybe we should break up."

Aoyagi winced. "Here," he said, as if he hadn't heard, holding out the chocolate again.

"I've been thinking about it for a while."

"What are you talking about?"

"I saw you just now. After you broke the bar, you checked to see which half was bigger and you gave that one to me."

"I guess," he said, nodding. There was no reason to deny it.

"I've always liked that about you, how careful you are, and thoughtful." From her tone it was somehow clear she didn't think she shared these qualities herself. She took the piece of chocolate from him and quickly broke it again. The resulting halves were even more jagged and unequal, crumbs everywhere. "Take it," she said, holding out half to him. He looked up at her. "Meaning, this is more me. Meaning, I'm fine with a little less careful—a lot less, in fact. I'm not going to get mad if my half is a bit smaller. We've been together a long time, ever since graduation. You don't have to handle me with kid gloves. Don't you see?"

"Just because we're sleeping together doesn't mean we can't be nice to each other," Aoyagi protested.

"That's not what I mean!" Exasperation was creeping into her voice.

"All this over half a bar of chocolate?"

"Over your insisting on me *always* getting the bigger half, over your even noticing there *is* a bigger half."

"And that hurts your feelings how?"

"I know it doesn't make sense," she said, frowning now.

"This isn't about the chocolate, is it?"

"You know it isn't. Do you remember something you said not long ago about your job, now that you're used to the route? You said that one day is starting to blend into the next, that you can't tell the difference between yesterday and tomorrow anymore."

"I was tired, I might have felt that way at the time."

"But it's the same with us. We're too used to each other. We've been together too long, and we're too comfortable. We're too willing to settle for things the way they are."

"Now hold on," Aoyagi tried to interrupt.

"It's as though we're here in the same room but not really *together* anymore."

"Now wait," Aoyagi said, waving his piece of chocolate at her. "Where are you coming up with all this? You're talking, but you're not making any sense."

"We're like an old married couple—and we're not even married yet." Haruko let out a little laugh. "It's not fun anymore."

Aoyagi suddenly thought of the trip they had made to Yokohama just last month. They'd spent a lot of time searching for a restaurant the guidebook had recommended, but when they finally got there, they were so badly treated they were tempted to walk out. In the end, though, they decided to take their revenge by ordering every item on the menu, lingering endlessly over each course, and monopolizing the table as long as they possibly could. They knew it was a pointless protest, but they had laughed about it later. Had the fun already stopped by then? Exactly when had it stopped?

"You know I've been playing that game again," she said, glancing over at the aging computer in the corner of the room. She had hauled it out of the closet not long ago and taken to playing a game she had loved in college.

Aoyagi nodded. "Feeding that creepy fish." The peculiar game involved nothing more than looking after a thoroughly unlovable talking fish.

"Well, the fish said something that hit the mark."

"It doesn't even look like a fish."

"I know, but it said something after I fed it. It said 'Don't settle for too little.'" Aoyagi couldn't tell whether he was expected to laugh or cry. "And it hit me—it was talking about us, about you and me."

"I'm not sure I like having my future decided by a talking fish."

"Do you remember those stamps they used to put on our homework in elementary school? A gold star with 'Excellent!' underneath, or just 'Good effort!' if you hadn't really done so well."

"I remember."

"Well, if we go on like this, we're headed for a life of 'Good effort.' I'm sure of it."

"And I'm sure you're out of your mind," said Aoyagi.

They sat facing each other in silence, and he went home before the pizza arrived. At the time, he had felt more bewildered than sad; perhaps most of all he'd been angry that she had made up such a silly excuse for dumping him. And part of him was convinced that she would call before long to say she was sorry, to plead temporary insanity, perhaps.

There had been no call after a week, but he had managed to stay calm. When they'd quarreled in the past, he had always been the one to offer a truce, even if he wasn't to blame, so he took comfort in the knowledge that he could always call her when he felt ready to patch things up. Besides, he was swamped at work.

After ten days, he called her, but to his surprise her attitude hadn't changed. She insisted they give the breakup a chance to work. He couldn't see how they'd know whether it was working if they didn't ever get back together, but he realized he was grasping at straws.

When Haruko pulled out, she left a gaping hole. A huge, invisible hole in his head and heart. Aoyagi had pretended to ignore it, busying himself with checking, stacking, lifting, running, delivering. He knew that the best way to cope was to keep moving, but as he went on his rounds, he kept seeing things he wanted to tell her about. Funny things, like the woman who wrestled with her determined Saint Bernard until she finally gave up and let the leash drag her along like a water-skier. Or a window washer high up above the street exchanging an awkward bow with a woman working in an office on the other side of the pane. When he realized there was no Haruko to listen to these tales, he wanted to curl up in a ball. And finally when he couldn't stand being so miserable, he tried calling Shingo Morita—only to get a recorded message saying that his number was out of service.

One day as he sat daydreaming on a park bench, a child dropped a crumpled sheet of paper as he walked by. When Aoyagi picked it up and handed it back to him, the little boy smoothed out the sheet and held it out for him to see. It was a crayon drawing, and at the top was a gold star with "Excellent!" stamped underneath.

Aoyagi forced a smile. "You should be proud," he said. "I never got better than 'Good effort.'"

"You never got a gold star?" the boy said, unable to hide his scorn. Aoyagi had never known how much he wanted one until now.

Six months later, he went to a shop that dealt in secondhand computer games and on a whim bought the one with the creepy fish. Perhaps it was a form of rehabilitation, a way of testing how much of the hole he'd been able to fill.

At first, he was just going through the motions, tending the computer aquarium according to the instructions; but gradually he grew more intent on the game until, to his complete amazement, he was stopping people at work to tell them about the condition of his virtual fish. One evening at the end of the second week, the fish suddenly turned to look out at him.

"Don't settle for too little," it gurgled.

"You shit!" said Aoyagi, stabbing his finger at the screen. "That's what you told her. That's what fucked everything up." The fish ignored him and swam calmly away through glowing blue pixels. "But you know," Aoyagi muttered at its receding tail, "if I'd given her the smaller half that day, she'd have been mad about that instead."

The fish ignored him, but finally turned back with a withering look. "Did you say something?"

Masaharu Aoyagi

"Did you say something?" The voice woke Aoyagi from a light sleep.

"Sorry, did I doze off?" There was a slight ache in his head as he shook himself awake. He realized he was in Morita's car, with the back of his seat dropped down.

"You were talking in your sleep, must have been dreaming," Morita said. The engine was off, but his hands were gripping the wheel and he was staring intently through the windshield.

Perhaps he was just groggy from his nap, but Aoyagi thought he felt the car rocking. He checked the clock on the dashboard: just before noon. It had been no more than a few minutes since they'd walked from the east side of the station, threaded their way down an alley, glanced at the roadblocks set up for the parade, and found their way to Morita's car, parked on this side street.

They could see a little clot of motionless cars further down—drivers who had ignored the warnings about the street closures and now had nowhere to go—and a group of parade-goers who had stopped in the middle of a crosswalk, but otherwise the street was nearly deserted. Though it was noon on a weekday and this prime minister was news, the crowd seemed paltry compared to the crush for the Star Festival or a big fireworks display.

As they had passed through the tunnel coming out of the station, Aoyagi had spotted a man in a red Panthers sweat shirt selling a magazine outside a game center. He went over and bought one, and the man bowed politely. It was something produced twice monthly for the homeless to sell on the streets.

As they fell in step again, Morita glanced at the thin publication under his friend's arm. "Interesting?" he asked.

"At ¥300, it'd better be," Aoyagi answered. The cover showed a picture of a well-known guitarist who fronted for a foreign rock band. "But the point is, the guy who sells it gets to keep most of the profit."

"So the price is a donation?" There was more than a hint of disdain in his voice.

"The price is his salary. I buy the magazine, his job is to sell it."

"Sounds like charity to me." This was apparently a dirty word to Morita.

"I don't think I'd last three days hawking magazines like that. Looks like hard work to me."

"Except they don't have anything else to do," said Morita.

"And what 'they' would that be?"

"The homeless."

"Which would you rather be? A homeless guy who works his ass off or a stiff in a suit who hangs out at a coffee shop reading manga?"

"If it had to be one or the other, I guess I'd be the suit."

"Me, too," Aoyagi confessed.

"But did you notice?" Morita said, apparently still not ready to let the subject drop. "The guy selling the magazines was humming 'Help!' by the Beatles. The perfect soundtrack for begging."

"I didn't notice," Aoyagi muttered.

"Though I suppose he could get in trouble for using the tune without paying royalties."

"A scary thought," said Aoyagi, though he doubted whether the Beatles worried about copyright infringement in a Japanese subway station.

Outside the station they walked west along Minamimachi Avenue until they reached the side streets beyond Higashi Nibancho. There they found Morita's car next to a tiny park that occupied a corner lot. Aoyagi remembered that as soon as they'd climbed inside Morita had produced a plastic bottle of water from somewhere and offered him a drink. He had taken a sip, but after that there was a blank when he must have fallen asleep.

"There must've been something in it," Aoyagi said, laughing and holding up the bottle as his head finally began to clear.

"What would be in it?" Morita said without turning to look at him.

"No, it's just that I fell asleep out of nowhere, like I'd been drugged." It struck him as an odd thing to say but he couldn't help it.

"You were," said Morita. "I put a sedative in the water."

"That's not even funny. Not your usual kind of joke at least."

"Have any interesting dreams?" Morita turned to look at him at last.

"Now that you mention it," said Aoyagi, feeling embarrassed, "I dreamed about splitting up with Haruko."

"The chocolate?"

Aoyagi flinched visibly. "How do you know about that?"

"How do you think?" Though the day was clear and bright, it was dark in the car, which was parked in the shade. "There are several possibilities," he said. His face was expressionless, his voice low and flat as though reading from a legal document. "One," he said, holding up his index finger. "I heard about it from Haruko herself."

"When you ran into her? Why would she tell you that?"

"Two," said Morita, holding up another finger. "Kazu told me."

"And how would Kazu know?"

"Three. You mentioned it while you were talking in your sleep just now."

"I did?" Aoyagi stammered.

"Four," said Morita. "The forest told me." As he said this, he gave a deep sigh. For some reason, Aoyagi was reminded of the way Haruko had sighed as he handed her half the fateful chocolate bar—and then he realized what the two things had in common. Then, as now, he had the queasy feeling that he was about to hear something important and very unpleasant. "Actually, it wasn't the forest," Morita continued, looking as though he might start laughing at any moment. "You probably never believed that crap about seeing the future anyway."

"I wouldn't say that," said Aoyagi. "You got quite a few predictions right, didn't you?"

"I did?"

"Sure. You remember the data processing class, in our freshman year? You knew exactly what was going to be on the final exam."

"The guy who taught it reused his old exams in a three-year cycle. I just figured out the schedule and borrowed an old one."

Aoyagi wasn't sure where these confessions were leading, but something about the tone of them worried him. "And when I asked you if Haruko would go out with me, you were certain she would."

"That wasn't hard. When somebody asks you a question like that, you just say what you know he wants to hear. Maybe I should have told you not to bother, that it wasn't going to work out in the end."

"Then what about the Friends of Fast Food? You always knew ahead of time what they were going to introduce on the menu. You'd say mango desserts were coming up that summer, or sesame buns would be in favor that fall—and you were almost always right."

"A business like fast food is always two steps behind the rest of the world. The TV had been full of stories about how good sesame is for you. All I did was figure out that the burger joints would catch on eventually and stick it on their buns, and voilà, a prediction. If you make enough of them, some come true."

"But when we went to the beach and the parking lots were all full, you'd say 'Go that way,' and we'd always find a spot. I thought you could actually see where the empty spaces were." He remembered Morita murmuring that the information was coming to him "from the forest."

"I just pointed us up the narrowest, least likely streets. Inconvenient spots are always the last to fill up, so it was a matter of probabilities. When it was really crowded, it didn't work, as far as I remember."

Aoyagi looked over at his friend. "What are you telling me?" Why was he insisting now that it was bullshit?

"You remember when I mentioned Haruko's husband? You said something about a chocolate bar. You probably didn't even realize you said it out loud, but I knew it must have been important, something that happened between the two of you. And that's the key to my parlor trick."

"Trick?" Aoyagi echoed, feeling somehow drained all of a sudden. "But how did you show up on the train?" he said more quietly. "How did you know I would happen to get mixed up with that woman? Didn't you say that was the forest?"

Morita had been gripping the wheel as they talked. He let go now and turned toward him, looking troubled.

"Listen," he said, glancing at his watch. His eyes were wide and bloodshot. "There isn't much time, so I'll have to keep this short."

"I'm lost."

"You got mixed up with that woman, but it didn't just 'happen.' You were set up."

"Set up? By who? The guy who forced me out of my job?"

"I guess we could start there," said Morita. "It's all connected. They wanted to ruin your reputation, make it impossible for you to stay at your job. So the calls started, first to you, then to your boss. Then they set you up on the train to try to make it look like you were some kind of pervert."

"'They'? Who are you talking about?"

"The people who ordered me to help them, to fuck up your job and your life," Morita said, speaking with more urgency now.

"Ordered you? Who ordered you?" He could tell that there was no hint of humor left in Morita's voice, and he was suddenly frightened. His hand fumbled for his seatbelt. Seeing what he was doing, Morita reached down to stop him.

"Don't," he murmured.

"What?"

"Just listen. They've been drawing you in, and they're about to spring the trap."

"Morita? What are you talking about?"

"Let's see if I can make it simpler. I haven't told you that I've got a family, a wife and a son."

"Just like that? When did this happen?"

"Soon after graduation. My boy's already in elementary school. Hard to believe, isn't it."

"I'll go further than that. I *don't* believe you."

"But it's true. As soon as I got to Tokyo, the woman I was seeing got pregnant and we got married. But she had this hobby—more of an addiction really. She went out every day to play pachinko, even took the baby with her. Of course she lost, and she started borrowing to keep playing." Morita was speaking quickly, hurrying through his story. "Strange, isn't it? Pachinko's supposed to be fun, but you can get in trouble fast. She never said a word to me until it was too late, until she was up to her neck in debt. I didn't even believe her at first, when she came to tell me."

"Look," Aoyagi interrupted, "I'm sorry, but I'm still not following you."

"I was doing everything I could to pay back what she owed, and then not long ago I had a strange call. They said they'd cancel her debts if I helped them out on a little project." He glanced down at his watch again.

"What project?"

"They told me I had to help you get away from somebody who was going to accuse you of something, and then make sure you were in a certain place at a certain time."

"What kind of 'project' is that?" he said, looking around the car, then seeing the bottle of water.

"I didn't understand myself. First, they told me to find you on the Senseki Line and if you were in trouble, to tell you to run. It seemed weird, but if it was really going to help you, I didn't see any problem with it. At least that's what I told myself."

"But you really did help me."

"No, I didn't," Morita said, his voice beginning to crack. "They didn't want you arrested. They just wanted you to be seen with that woman accusing you of molesting her."

"But who are 'they'? Seen by who?"

"By the other people on the platform. So that later, when you were accused of another crime, it would seem more plausible because those people would speak up and say they'd seen you bothering that woman."

"Another crime?" Aoyagi croaked. "What other crime?"

"I didn't know myself," said Morita. "They just told me to get you in this car and keep you knocked out till twelve-thirty. And they gave me this bottle to do it."

Aoyagi looked from the bottle to the clock on the dashboard. Just noon. "And once they had me asleep, what were they going to do?"

"I didn't know. I knew it wasn't right, but I tried not to think about it. Those loans had made me crazy, and I thought if I just did what they told me, the problem would go away. That's all. But as we were walking here from the station, I began to see that something really bad was going to happen, something I could never make right. And seeing you after all this time, and realizing you were exactly the same guy . . ."

"I don't know what you're trying to tell me, but I think I'd better find out real soon," said Aoyagi.

"Then listen!" Morita nearly screamed, turning to fix his eyes on him.

"To what? What are you saying?"

"That I've just realized what's going to happen. You saw all those people on our way here? They've come for the parade, to see Kaneda. And d'you remember what we used to talk about sitting around after class?"

"Yeah—all kinds of stuff." The meetings of the Friends of Fast Food had involved staking out seats in some restaurant and shooting the bull for hours on end. It was usually just the four of them—Aoyagi, Morita, Haruko, and Kazu—but they had talked about anything and everything. From the totally banal—girls in other departments, new movies, what they'd buy if they won the lottery—to subjects worthy of a student debating society, "the right to collective self-defense and the peace article in the constitution" and the like. They always sat at the back of the restaurant and they always took their time, letting the conversation run its natural course. The very length of the sessions had seemed to give them weight. Aoyagi could still see them—Haruko, Kazu, and the two of them—huddled around the table.

"But, remember all the time we spent talking about the Beatles, and the Kennedy assassination? We all liked the Beatles, but Kazu was the one into the Kennedy thing, at least at first."

"Now that you mention it." Kazu had been unusually insistent. He was absolutely convinced that Oswald hadn't shot Kennedy, and thought it was scary that the truth had never come out. For a while, they had just listened to him hold forth, but eventually they all got interested and started reading up on the incident. It became something of a group obsession. Kazu had somehow decided that Oswald was a victim, that they had framed him, and they knew what would happen to him after he was arrested. It seemed to infuriate him. When the others asked him who "they" were, he had scowled. "The ones with all the power, the bosses," he'd said.

"After the Kennedy assassination," Morita continued now, "there were reports that Oswald had been a CIA informant."

"I remember reading that."

"And before the assassination he had been handing out flyers for the Communist Party in some little town. He did it because the CIA ordered him to, apparently because they wanted to give the impression that he was some sort of activist."

"That was the theory."

"Well, I think they had that woman accuse you of molesting her for similar reasons. I had a hunch what was going on, before, but I refused to let myself think about it."

"You're going to have to spell it out. I'm still not with you."

"I think the whole thing with the woman was just background, setting you up for the main event."

"Main event?"

"Has anything else strange happened to you recently? Other than losing your job?" Morita asked. His tone was now more frantic, and Aoyagi could feel panic growing in himself as well. His mind ran over the events of the past few months. His driver's license turning up in Matsushima was definitely odd. Then Koume Inohara's face popped into his head. "It wasn't exactly strange, but I did meet a girl at the unemployment office when I was picking up my check."

"What kind of girl?" In the old days, Morita would have whistled at this kind of admission and demanded details. Now he just stared hard at him.

"Just a girl. A few years younger than me."

"Did she come on to you?"

"Not exactly. We were sitting next to each other at the computers where you can search for job vacancies."

"Are you dating?"

"We're friends," Aoyagi said, shrugging. It was the truth.

"Sounds fishy to me."

"No, we're really just friends," Aoyagi insisted, though he realized that he probably hoped the relationship would develop into something more.

"I'm not talking about your relationship," said Morita. "I mean the girl herself."

"What's fishy about meeting a girl?"

"Then why did you mention her? Your enemies now may be the people who look least like the bad guys, me included."

"Well, you look a lot like a bad guy at this point."

Morita closed his eyes and rubbed his hand over his face, taking a moment to collect himself. "You're right," he said as he opened his eyes. "I'm probably overreacting. But you've got to be careful. Don't trust anyone. Otherwise, you'll end up like Oswald."

Aoyagi glanced down at his watch, not sure what to say to this. "Still ten minutes to go," he said, almost giggling. "Good thing I'm not still asleep."

"They'll probably kill him during the parade," Morita said.

"Is that supposed to be funny?"

"It's what I figured out. When I saw you drop off after drinking from that bottle, I finally realized what was going to happen. I actually got out and looked under the car."

"Under the car?"

"That's what they always do in the movies, stick a bomb under the car to blow up the star witness."

"Pretty corny plotline," said Aoyagi. "Your bad guys aren't very original."

"No, but they've been around a bit too long to worry about that." Aoyagi felt relieved to see a smile on his friend's face, but the relief faded almost instantly. "Even the bomb's not original—it was so obvious, an amateur like me found it right away." Morita was still grinning, but his face looked ghastly. "Not that it makes any difference whether I found it or not. They know I can't get rid of it."

"Are you serious?" Aoyagi blurted out, finally understanding the desperation in Morita's eyes. "We've got to get out of here!"

"*You've* got to," said Morita."

"Not without you."

"Where would I go?" He startled Aoyagi by now saying, "Do you remember *Abbey Road*? The medley?"

It was the Beatles' eleventh album, released before their last, *Let It Be*, but actually recorded later. Something that Paul McCartney stitched together for a band that had already dissolved. He took the eight songs in the second half of the album, which had been recorded separately, and mixed them into a long medley. Morita had often said how he liked the way Paul had closed it out with "The End."

"I was humming 'Golden Slumbers' from it while you were asleep," Morita said.

"A lullaby? For me?" The lyrics were, in fact, almost exactly like a lullaby, with something strangely moving about Paul's full, straining voice.

"Remember how it begins?" Morita asked, and then started to hum the opening line. *Once there was a way to get back homeward.* "It always makes me think about hanging out with you guys back in school."

"That was hardly home," Aoyagi muttered.

"It was for me, the way we were back then."

They fell silent for a moment, and this time Aoyagi didn't bother to try to think of anything to say.

Finally, Morita reached over and took something out of the glove compartment. It was several seconds before Aoyagi realized what it was. "A gun?" he murmured.

"Weird, isn't it?" Morita said, looking down with an odd little smile at the thing in his hand. "Who'd have thought I'd ever have one of these?"

"I don't know," said Aoyagi blankly. "Who?" He had never seen a real gun before. It looked as if it might go off at the slightest touch.

"They told me to bring you here today. And if I couldn't get you to drink out of the bottle, I was supposed to use what they'd left in the glove compartment. I wondered what they meant, so I checked earlier."

"What the hell's going on?" Aoyagi said, not hiding the panic in his voice.

Morita put the dull, black barrel up to his eye. "Looks like the real thing," he said quietly. "In other words, these guys have no trouble getting their hands on something like this, or getting it into my car."

As he spoke, there was a violent shudder and the sound of an explosion. The air seemed to crack open and shock waves swept over the car.

Aoyagi sat stunned with fear, but Morita seemed suddenly more relaxed. He looked around to see where the noise had come from, but he didn't appear overly concerned. "That's the bomb," he murmured.

"Bomb?"

"Time's up, my friend," he said. "You've got to run. It's not healthy to stay here."

"Then let's go."

"Not me. If I go with you, they'll take it out on my wife and my kid. There's only one penalty for not following orders. I know what kind of people I'm working for." He made no effort to keep his despair to himself. Yet, at the same time, he seemed calmer than before, and Aoyagi felt he finally had a glimpse of his old friend. It was as if the Morita of long ago had come back, and it seemed all the more important not to let him go.

People were rushing around in the street outside. They could hear muffled voices in the distance and feel a rumbling under the wheels.

"I thought you were going to sleep at least an hour," Morita was saying. "So I would have had to leave you here. But when you woke up early—well, that was just luck. At least, that's what I decided."

"Luck? Who for?"

"I shook the car a little," he continued, "to see if you'd wake up. I just sat here and waited, but I hadn't decided what I'd do if you really did come to." Aoyagi remembered now that the car had seemed to be rocking gently, like a boat at anchor, when he woke up from his nap. Morita reached out and adjusted the angle of the rearview mirror. "At any rate," he said, waving the gun, "you've got to get moving. I'll be staying here. I'm not sure what these guys will do, but I don't think I want to cross them anymore. I'll just sit here. It's my way of apologizing for having failed them. I think it's better that way."

"You're not making any sense!" Aoyagi groaned.

Morita's eyes narrowed as he stared at the mirror. "There are two cops coming up behind us," he said. "If you're going, now's the time. Go on. If you don't, I'll have to use this. You know me, I overact." He was laughing now. "Remember that job we had cleaning the city pool?"

"I remember," said Aoyagi.

"The whole time we were scrubbing that sucker, there was a security camera on us."

"I don't remember that." His voice was almost a whisper.

"You don't remember the little drama we acted out for the camera?"

"Morita, please!" Aoyagi pleaded.

"I would tell you to run. 'Run! Aoyagi!' I'd yell at you. 'Get out any way you can! Get out and live your life!' It was our little joke." Aoyagi was near tears. He opened his mouth but no words came out. "When you rescued that girl," Morita hurried on, his mind apparently wandering now, "they interviewed you on TV and you said you used a judo move to bring down the bad guy."

"You taught it to us," Aoyagi managed to murmur.

"I was watching the tube with my boy. I told him I knew you. He was real impressed."

"Morita?" He stared into his friend's eyes.

"Don't worry about me. All good children go to heaven. . . . At least that's what they say." The hint of a smile played around his mouth.

Aoyagi said nothing, and Morita began to sing "Golden Slumbers." "*Once there was a way to get back homeward*," he sang, and then, softly, "*Golden slumbers fill your eyes. Smiles awake you when you rise.*" Aoyagi had trouble following the English, but the last line stuck in his head—a smiling face at the break of day.

He turned to Morita to make one final plea, but his friend had lowered the back of his seat and closed his eyes. "*Sleep pretty darling, do not cry,*" he sang quietly, this time in Japanese. It was as if he were singing himself a lullaby.

Masaharu Aoyagi

Aoyagi jumped out of the car and closed the door. When he turned to look back, he saw two uniformed policemen close behind him. They had evidently come down this side street from Higashi Nibancho. He couldn't see what was happening out on the main street, but it was clear that crowds of people were milling about, and he could hear shouts and general confusion in the distance. Sirens were coming this way fast. He looked up at the sky and realized that smoke was drifting between the buildings.

He looked back inside the car. Morita was still slumped behind the steering wheel, eyes closed. Aoyagi reached for the handle on the passenger side, but as he did so he heard someone yell "Don't move!" One of the policemen had crouched down a few steps away and his hand was fumbling for something at his belt. Without thinking, Aoyagi straightened up and put his hands above his head.

"That's right," the cop said. "Don't move." He had drawn his gun. To Aoyagi, who had never seen a real one before today, guns seemed to be multiplying before his eyes. Obviously, something big had happened. He could hear Morita's words echoing in his head: "You'll end up like Oswald."

Oswald had been shot dead by a man named Jack Ruby while he was being transferred to jail. The report on the assassination concluded that both Oswald and Ruby had acted on their own, without the support of any larger organization or political group. But Aoyagi remembered how that conclusion had infuriated Kazu as they had argued over the Kennedy affair long ago at their fast-food debates.

But before he could remember anything else, there was an explosion near his head and the rear window of Morita's car shattered. One of the policemen must have fired his revolver. "Get down!" he yelled, moving slowly toward Aoyagi. "Face down on the ground!"

Aoyagi glanced at Morita through the window. Who should he listen to? A trigger-happy cop or his old friend? It was an easy choice. He ran.

He dodged across the street. It took some nerve to turn his back on a man pointing a gun at him, but this was no time for caution. If they intended to shoot him, he would at least give them a moving target. But was it better to duck into a building or get away down another street? He decided a building could become a trap.

Behind him, the cops were yelling for him to stop. Their voices were sharp, as though in the same breath their hands were reaching out over the distance he'd covered to slip under his arms and pin them back. He caught sight of a liquor store on the corner. This had not been his district when he was driving the delivery truck, but he'd been down this street any number of times. A map of the area unfolded in his head. If he turned left, he'd come immediately to an alley on the right. . . .

A white-haired man emerged from the shop, wiping his hands slowly on his apron. He called something to someone inside. He looked back around just as they were about to collide, and Aoyagi had to swerve to avoid knocking him over.

Another shot. Glancing back, he saw that one of the cops was crouching down and aiming his gun. He thought for a moment that he'd been hit, but there was no pain, no shock of impact. Then he realized that the shopkeeper was falling backward onto the sidewalk. The collapse seemed endless, as though he were seeing it in slow motion, and as he fell he looked up at Aoyagi with a puzzled expression. When at last he came to rest in a heap, there was blood spurting from his shoulder. A woman came running out of the shop. Aoyagi stopped and started to bend over the man, but then caught sight of the cops out of the corner of his eye and took off again. He was fairly sure the shopkeeper was still conscious when he left him.

The police were still after him. As he ran, Aoyagi began to realize that something wasn't right. This wasn't the Wild West. Japanese police didn't draw their guns for every little offense. And they didn't ignore an injured bystander to go on with a chase.

As soon as he dodged into the narrow side street, there was an alley to his right. Then, if he turned left at the next intersection, he would come out on a bigger street running east and west. He had managed to open up a bit of distance on the police, so he fumbled in his bag and pulled out his cell phone. But who to call?

He realized with amazement that he was completely out of breath. Was he already so out of shape just three months after quitting his job?

People were beginning to drift out of the buildings on either side, and when he looked up, he saw that many more had opened windows to peer out. For a moment, he had the scary feeling that everyone was staring at him, that they were there to keep an eye on him and point him out to his pursuers. He felt outnumbered and trapped, and he was tempted to lie down on the ground and surrender. But then he realized that no one was looking at him at all, that their attention was focused further off to the east, to the parade on Higashi Nibancho, where Morita had said the killing would take place.

Aoyagi emerged into a narrow, one-way street to find a scene of utter chaos. Smoke was billowing into the air, and people were running in every direction as if they'd lost their minds, hurtling down sidewalks, threading their way through stopped cars, scattering in wild flight. He reached out to stop a man in a suit who came running past.

"What?" the man shouted.

"What happened?" Aoyagi asked.

"There was an explosion."

"But where's everybody going?"

"Running to see? Running away? Who knows?"

"Was there much damage?" he pressed him.

"Enough," said the man, turning to hurry off with the nosy bystander's sense of purpose. "I don't think Kaneda could have made it."

Kaneda dead? The news stopped him in his tracks. It seemed unreal. But one word kept coming back to him from Morita's ramblings: Oswald.

Just then, the air seemed to billow out from behind him—from the area he'd just left. There was a loud crack, a gust of wind, someone screamed. The people running near him stopped and all eyes turned in the direction Aoyagi had come from.

"Another bomb?" someone wondered.

Unsure where to go now, he ran to his left, then turned and ran back the other way. Suddenly, through the crowd, he caught sight of a taxi stopped in traffic. The "For Hire" light was lit, and without a second thought he made his way over and jumped in the back seat.

"Looks like another one," the driver said. His hair was long, but the strip of forehead in the rearview mirror was wrinkled. Their eyes met in the reflection.

"Was that really an explosion?" Aoyagi said.

"Sounded like one."

"Can you get us out of here?"

"Where to?" the driver asked.

"The east exit," he blurted out. His first impulse had been to say "any-where," but thinking better of it, he had fixed on a destination that would put some distance—and Sendai Station—between him and the two cops. He realized where he really wanted to go was back, back to the hamburger joint, back to Morita and their conversation before all this had started. If he could just go back, this chaos might go away, and he would find himself sitting across from his friend again, calmly watching him bend a French fry in two.

"East exit?" echoed the driver. "Don't know if that's going to work. I forgot about all the streets they closed off for the parade or I would never have come in here. I was just trying to figure out a way around this mess."

"Can you see how far we can get?"

"You got it, buddy."

Just then the car ahead of them began to move. The cab driver pressed the lever to close the rear door, put the car in gear, and immediately made a hard right turn. "If I do a U-turn here, we might be able to get around the station. Sound okay to you?" He seemed to have suddenly come to life. Aoyagi wondered why he'd bothered to ask, since they were already on their way, but he grunted his approval and sat back.

As the driver made his way aggressively through traffic, Aoyagi found his mind going over something Morita had said . . . how the bad guys always put a bomb under the car in the movies. . . . And, to his horror, he finally realized that the second explosion must have been under Morita's car. He pressed his face against the window, but the world outside was a blur.

"I caught a glimpse of a cop in the mirror just now," said the driver. "First time I've ever seen one with his gun out like that."

"A cop?" Aoyagi murmured.

"Yeah, just now. He was right behind you on the street. They must be on high alert. Doesn't look like the Sendai I know."

Masaharu Aoyagi

"Doesn't look like the Sendai I know," said Kazu, glancing over at Aoyagi in the passenger seat.

"It's a bigger town than you think," Aoyagi said. He was in his second year of college, student backpack on his lap. He reached inside now and fished out a paperback he had just bought.

"What's that?" Kazu asked.

"It's called a 'book,'" Aoyagi laughed. "I feel like my brain's turning to mush from all the hamburgers and bullshit with you and Morita. Thought I might try reading once in a while."

"Wouldn't be Dostoevsky by any chance?" Kazu asked. Aoyagi jumped and turned toward him with a startled look. "Did I guess right?"

"How did you know?"

"I was talking to Morita the other night, and he said you'd be reading Dostoevsky soon."

"But how did he know?"

"A few days ago we were out drinking with Haruko and she asked if we'd ever read Dostoevsky, said everybody should try him at some point. Morita told me later that he was sure you'd decided on the spot to read him." Kazu seemed unimpressed by the prediction. "I guess you're more of a softy than I thought," he added.

"Softy?" said Aoyagi, feeling a bit offended.

"But it was really Morita who put Haruko up to the whole thing. He wanted to see how susceptible you were."

"Susceptible?" Aoyagi said, not quite following.

"You see," Kazu giggled, "she's never read Dostoevsky herself."

"Shit," muttered Aoyagi.

"Except for a manga version of *Crime and Punishment.*"

"Shit," he repeated.

"And I thought 'Dostoevsky' was some kind of Eskimo," Kazu confessed.

Aoyagi suddenly wanted to toss the paperback out the window.

"You made a wrong turn somewhere," Aoyagi said.

"I guess so," Kazu laughed quietly. He didn't seem very upset; in fact, he almost seemed to enjoy being lost. "Morita's maps aren't too helpful."

"Let me have a look."

Kazu fished a sheet of paper out of his jacket pocket and passed it over. Helpful it wasn't. The map had a cross, indicating north and south, and arrows snaking west on Route 48 to a place marked "Here!" in big letters. Along the way was a complicated intersection where several roads came together. It had been circled, and a note had been scribbled underneath: "Gets pretty messy here!" That was it.

"He sure is out in the boondocks," Kazu observed noncommittally.

"When we started school, he was living in this fancy place downtown."

"I know. He let me crash there once after we'd been drinking. Why would he have moved out of a place that was that convenient?"

"He probably decided that 'convenience is not the mother of invention' or some crap like that," said Aoyagi.

"The voice of the forest?" Kazu chuckled. "How long has he been talking about that?"

"As long as I've known him." Aoyagi remembered their first meeting at a party soon after classes had started in their freshman year. For some reason, Morita's head had been shaved at the time. He recalled how the guy had introduced himself—Shingo Morita—explaining that because his name had the character for "woods" he was specially attuned to them, "to hear and be guided" by them. Aoyagi had thought at the time that he was seeing the first evidence of the dangers of binge drinking.

"Do you buy it?" Kazu asked. "About the voices, I mean."

"It's a load of shit, if you ask me."

"I suppose so," said Kazu. "Anyway, at the moment I wish we had the 'voice of the GPS' to guide us to his new apartment."

Aoyagi tried calling on his cell phone to ask for better directions, but for some reason there was no answer.

"Why would he be out without his phone?"

"I guess he's relying on the voices."

Though they were sure they were lost, they had continued on their way until they came to a dead end. There had been a wrong turn to the right back there somewhere, made inadvertently. The road had grown increasingly narrow and headed uphill until, at some point, they were positive they were on the wrong track. But Aoyagi, at least, had lacked the honesty to admit their mistake and head back the way they'd come. At the top of the slope they came to a parking lot that looked like a trailhead. Here they stopped and got out of the car.

"Where are we?" Kazu asked.

"Don't ask me," said Aoyagi. They looked back, down on the roofs of the shabby houses scattered along the road. Cinderblock walls fronted the yards.

There was nothing else to do but turn around, but as they took one last look down the hill, Aoyagi let out a low whistle. He had suddenly recognized a yellow car parked in front of one of the houses close by. Even the license number was familiar. Kazu realized at nearly the same moment. "That's Haruko's, isn't it?" he said.

"Looks like it," said Aoyagi. He walked down to the car and examined the dent in the bumper.

"Well, if it isn't Masaharu and Kazu," said a voice. He looked up to see Haruko waving at them from a short way down the hill. Exchanging looks, they went to meet her.

Haruko was wearing jeans and a black, hooded coat. Standing next to her was a short man with a thick beard. He had a large nose, droopy eyes, thick lips. Aoyagi was just thinking that he looked more bear than human, when he growled, "The whole point of moving the factory out here was to get away from people. So how come they keep wandering in?" He must have been close to fifty, but his hair was jet black. The white scarf around his neck reminded Aoyagi of the markings on an Asian black bear.

"That's right," Haruko said, nodding solemnly. "They don't want just anybody showing up here."

"Anybody at all," the man said, frowning at her now.

"I'm sorry," Kazu stammered. "I didn't catch your name. Are you Haruko's father by any chance?" The mere mention of this possibility made Aoyagi stand up a little straighter and fix his collar.

"No," the man said, grimacing as if he didn't care much for the idea. "I run the factory here."

"This is Mr. Todoroki," Haruko said. "Of Todoroki Pyrotechnics? You've never heard of it? Either of you?"

"Pyrotactics?" Aoyagi murmured. "Sorry, no."

"*Pyrotechnics*! Fireworks!" Haruko corrected him, her eyes shining. "Mr. Todoroki's factory makes the *big* ones, the ones they use in the shows downtown."

Every summer, for three days in early August, Sendai held the country's most famous celebration of Tanabata, the Star Festival. But the night before the festival began, there was always a huge fireworks display on the banks of the Hirose River. For nearly two hours, the sky would be filled with spectacular bursts of light and sound. Aoyagi and Morita had watched for the last couple of years from the roof of a building on campus.

"You make all those . . . here?" Aoyagi said, looking more closely now at the buildings stretching up and down the street.

"That's right." Todoroki scratched his forehead, his eyes narrowing. "And we've got a shitload of gunpowder around, so we get a little jumpy when a car we don't know comes nosing up a dead-end street like this."

"That's right," Haruko echoed. "You guys should be more careful, poking around like that. Guess you got lost?"

"And not just them, either," Todoroki frowned, again turning to Haruko.

"It's *pyrotechnics*," Haruko said, apparently oblivious. "'Pyro' as in 'fire,' and 'technics' meaning 'art.' Fire-art. And do you know what they call the gunpowder inside?"

"No," said Aoyagi, "and I'm sure you didn't either until Mr. Todoroki told you just now."

"They call it 'stars.' Cool, isn't it? Putting 'stars' in rockets and shooting them up in the sky. Sounds like fun."

"Have there always been fireworks?" Aoyagi turned to ask Todoroki. "You hear about the great shows they used to have even in the Edo period."

"They weren't as spectacular as they are now, but they did love their fireworks back then. They used to have competitions where they'd get firework-makers from all over the country to show their stuff."

"Mr. Todoroki," said Haruko in a sweeter tone of voice. "Do you think we could help out here?"

"As in, a 'job'?"

"That would be cool," Kazu chimed in.

Todoroki frowned and shook his head. "No, I don't think so. Gunpowder's nothing to fool around with, and there's lots of other dangerous stuff. No, it wouldn't work."

"Then can we come watch sometime when you shoot them off?" Kazu said. At the thought of fireworks, he was almost an excited little boy again. "I've always wanted to see from close up, how you light the fuse and everything!"

"No," said Todoroki, shaking his head again. "I'm afraid that's not possible." But then he seemed to have another thought. "Can the three of you shovel snow?" he asked.

"Absolutely," Haruko said without a moment's hesitation.

"It gets pretty deep around here in January. My crew has to waste time shoveling before they can get down to work. Think you could handle snow removal and general cleanup?"

"Would it mean we could get a peek at the fireworks from time to time?" Haruko said, beginning to wheedle.

"Could be," Todoroki grinned.

"Actually, we're professional shovelers," Aoyagi said, smiling now, too.

"Born to shovel," Haruko chimed in.

"Shovels 'R Us," Kazu offered.

"All right," Todoroki laughed. "Just keep your shovels away from my fireworks."

At this point, Aoyagi's phone rang. "Where are you?" Morita's voice barked. "Lost?"

"I think we got where we wanted to go," said Aoyagi.

"No you didn't," Morita protested. "I'm here and you're not."

"No, I mean you should come right over and meet us."

"No, you come here."

"But if you don't come here, you won't see the fireworks," he muttered into the phone.

"Where are you?"

"Just come. And bring your shovel."

"What?"

"I'll explain when you get here."

Masaharu Aoyagi

Aoyagi heard the driver say that things didn't look good and he opened his eyes. He must have closed them at some point without realizing it.

"Trouble?"

"Like a parking lot," the driver said, pointing at the street ahead of them. He had apparently been planning to use the tunnel under the Bullet Train tracks to get to the east side of the station, but they had stopped well short of the entrance. The traffic light ahead was green, but no one was going anywhere. Clearly, they had been lucky to make it this far.

"They've got everything blocked off, even the highways," the driver said as he fiddled with the volume on the radio. And I just got a call from my dispatcher saying we're all supposed to head back to the garage. Anyway, we're not going anywhere soon, so you're probably better off walking. They said things are clearer on the other side."

When the door opened after he'd paid the fare, the noise and confusion of the city swept over him, sirens and anxious shouts and all the other sounds of disaster. He stood for a moment next to the cab, but he felt as though the noise was urging him along. The people on the sidewalk were all hurrying by with serious faces. Aoyagi fell in step with them.

He decided he should go home. When he got back to his apartment, he could sort things out. The TV and Internet would have details, and he could try to find out what had happened to Morita.

He cut through Sendai Station and came out of the east exit. The driver's information had been wrong: traffic was at a standstill here, too. Stoplights had lost all meaning, and pedestrians wandered among the motionless cars.

Aoyagi ducked into a side street next to a discount electronics shop and headed north. It would take him about twenty minutes to get home. Pulling out his cell phone again, he dialed Morita's number. He needed to know if he was all right.

Morita had always hated gadgets and had resisted cell phones, but just two hours earlier, Aoyagi had teased him about having acquired one. "Once I started working, I couldn't really tell clients I was morally opposed to talking to them," Morita had explained as Aoyagi had punched the number into his own phone. He could hear the system trying Morita's number, but then a recording came on to tell him that it was turned off, or possibly out of signal range. He couldn't help feeling that his friend had gone where no phone would ever reach him again.

The streets grew less crowded and chaotic as he approached his apartment. Some young mothers with strollers stood talking in the little park across the street while their toddlers played in the sandbox. A line of fir trees had been added along one edge, perhaps in anticipation of Christmas.

As he reached the familiar entrance of his building, the conversation with Morita in the car and the flight from the police had begun to seem unreal. If that had been real, how could life here still be so peaceful and normal? He looked up at the laundry drying on the balconies above him as if marshaling more evidence.

He pulled open the heavy door and went inside. After checking his mailbox, he walked over and pushed the button on the elevator. It took him a moment to notice the men standing on either side of him. Or, rather, he had noticed but had paid them no attention, assuming they lived in the building. He was startled when one of them spoke up.

"Mr. Aoyagi?" It was the man to his right. His face was flat and featureless; narrow eyes under thick eyebrows. As Aoyagi nodded, the other man took a step toward him.

"Masaharu Aoyagi?" he said. This one was tall and wore glasses. Both were in dark suits with the same lapel pin—Aoyagi couldn't make out the company.

"Yes," he said, feeling tense. "But do I know you?"

The man to the right suddenly reached out and grabbed his arm, twisting it back to secure a hold on him. Aoyagi bent over in pain, his legs giving way. "What do you want?" he grunted.

"Shut up," said the man. "And don't move."

Against the white shirt inside his open jacket, he'd seen a strap and, cradled under his arm, what looked like a gun.

He had no particular plan in mind, but he could still see Morita's desperate expression in the car and hear his voice: "Run!" he'd said. So, planting his legs, he pulled back sharply and twisted at the same time. Then he pushed as hard as he could against the chest of the man on his right, who tottered for a few steps before falling on his back.

In the meantime, the taller one had grabbed at him from behind, so Aoyagi spun to face him, swinging the bag on his arm to his shoulder. He shoved the second man, and felt him immediately start to push back. He reached out with both hands for his arm. "The moment your opponent steps in with his right leg, plant your left leg next to his." Aoyagi could hear Morita's voice in his head, just the way he explained the move to them back in the cafeteria. "Use your whole upper body as well as the leg." He moved now almost involuntarily, as he had two years earlier when he'd run into the person in Rinka's apartment. He stepped in and swung his leg as hard as he could while pulling on the man's lapel. The man's legs went out from under him. "Pull his upper body toward you," he could hear Morita saying. A second later, the man's back hit the floor with a thud and Aoyagi fell hard on top of him.

He recovered almost instantly, scrambled to his feet, and started to run. It worked, he heard himself telling Morita. For all the good it would do him.

He flew out the door and ran to the right—directly into the path of an old man pushing a bicycle. He lived in the building and, though Aoyagi didn't know his name, they had always exchanged a friendly hello.

"Hi," said the old man.

"Hello," Aoyagi shot back, dodging the bike without slowing.

He ran straight down the street as fast as he could, starting to pant almost immediately. After a few seconds, he heard a crash in the distance behind him. Without stopping, he craned his neck to see the two suits tangled up with the old man and his bicycle.

He followed the street out to the four-lane highway that ran through the neighborhood. Traffic was heavy, but perhaps because nothing at all was moving on Higashi Nibancho, it was hardly unusual. As he pelted down the sidewalk, his lungs gasped painfully for air and his legs started to cramp as if to keep them company.

He caught sight of a pedestrian bridge over the road and headed toward it. At the very least, the other side of the road was that much further away from those men. But as he started up the steps, he lost his balance and his legs crumpled under him. A young woman in his path jumped out of the way—probably assuming he was drunk—and scrambled down the rest of the stairs.

Aoyagi grabbed the railing, pulled himself to his feet, and started up again. Glancing back, he couldn't see anyone following him. From the top of the bridge, he looked down on the cars passing beneath.

He wanted to sit down, to rest his weary legs and aching lungs, but he told himself he had to keep going. Then a wave of dizziness hit him, his eyes blurred and he felt light-headed. He stopped and leaned against the wire mesh that lined the bridge, staring down at the traffic. The road looked like a silver stream reflecting the sunlight, teeming with Honda fish, Mazda fish.

Bent almost double, he had made his way to the middle of the bridge when he saw three cops in uniform coming up the stairs on the other side. He considered trying to slip past them with his head down, but he could see that one of them had already noticed him; he had to turn back. The cop yelled something—the words were loud and sharp, like warning shots. He turned and ran back the way he'd come, but halfway down the stairs he stopped again. The two men from his apartment building were at the bottom.

A little noise slipped from his lips and tumbled down the stairs, swelling until it reached the men. They looked at him, and as they did, Aoyagi began backing up the stairs. But at the top, he saw the policemen starting toward him from the other side.

He thought of the judo move; this was stupid, he knew, but it was the only thing he could think of using. Would it work again? With real cops? Three of them? It didn't seem likely. Out of ideas, he looked down at the road.

The cops coming from the far side were in uniform. The two guys from the building were not, but judging from the gun he'd seen, they probably were police as well. Since he hadn't done anything wrong, he could just let them arrest him and then explain what had happened. Once they checked his story, he would be out in no time. That was what he wanted to believe, but Morita's voice was still ringing in his ears: "You'll end up like Oswald," he'd said, before his sad little lullaby. And then there was the bullet in the liquor-store owner. A shudder went through him as he remembered the blood pouring from the man's shoulder. The bullet had been meant for him.

Something wasn't right. He had to keep running. Get away—and stay alive.

He could feel Morita's voice urging him on, not just in his head but in his whole being. Get out of here! No time to stand around thinking—yet he stood frozen. It was easy enough to say, but where was he going to go?

The men in suits were running up the stairs, guns drawn. The cops were almost on top of him. Aoyagi put his hands in the air.

As he did so, he caught a glimpse of his wristwatch. Ten after one already? Then something else flashed into his head. He looked right and then left, as if checking to see where he was. He could feel Morita inside him: not the weary, defeated Morita he'd just left but the self-confident one he'd known in school, the one reminding him now of "trust and habit."

Exactly! He turned and in one motion leaped up onto the railing. "Don't move!" someone yelled, and he could feel somebody lunge toward him. He looked down for one second and the height sent a chill through him, but the next instant he jumped.

The bridge vanished and he was falling through space. It was like evaporating, his body temperature dropping with the rest of him. As his speed increased, he had a quick flash of himself as a puddle of flesh on the pavement. He wanted to close his eyes but couldn't.

He was aiming for the bed of a truck parked on the shoulder of the road— a truck with a cloth canopy. A truck that belonged to his methodical friend Maezono whose schedule never varied. Today was no different.

He tucked into a tight ball just before he hit the cover. He could feel the stacks of boxes underneath as he sank into the cloth. Pain shot through his arm and his heart raced with fear, but the canopy held. He bounced up, scrambled to his knees, and crawled down to the pavement.

Haruko Higuchi

Haruko Higuchi and Akira Hirano were staring at the television in the soba shop. At first it had been hard to grasp that there had been an explosion, but as the details slowly emerged, anxiety ran through the customers around them. The owner came out from behind the counter to watch. "Like a bad movie," he muttered. No one complained or tried to get him back to the kitchen.

"I bet it's a madhouse out there," Akira said at last. Since the restaurant was below street level, they couldn't see what was going on outside. "Must be nothing but fire trucks and ambulances."

To Haruko it seemed that the place had darkened, the air grown thick. It felt as if they were in the one safe refuge, and the outside world had become uninhabitable. They couldn't get out even if they wanted to.

"You'd better go get your daughter," Akira said. "The traffic will be impossible."

"You're probably right," Haruko nodded, impressed at how calm her friend appeared. She stood up, but all the other customers seemed to have come to the same conclusion, and there was a long line at the cash register.

"Who would do something like that?" Akira said as she fished some change out of her purse.

"Maybe a rival who wanted him out of the way?" said Haruko.

"Or a crazy who was planning to commit suicide and decided to go out with a bang?"

"It could be. You'd have to be crazy to do it that way."

They finally reached the head of the line, paid for their lunch, and left the restaurant. Climbing the stairs to the street, they were surprised to see that it was a sunny day.

"Is that smoke?" Akira said, pointing in the direction of Higashi Nibancho. Something white seemed to be rising to meet the fluffy clouds that dotted the pale blue sky, as though the clouds had grown a tail.

"I can't believe this happened here," Haruko said. If they started walking along this very street, in fifteen minutes they'd be at the spot where a prime minister had been killed. It seemed inconceivable.

Hearing a beep from her pocket, Akira took out her cell phone and checked her email. Haruko checked hers as well. A moment later, Akira let out a little cry.

"What?" Haruko asked.

"It was from Masakado. He wants to know whether I'll go snorkeling with him this Saturday!"

Haruko burst out laughing. "Pretty relaxed, isn't he? Do you think he doesn't know what's happening?"

"Maybe not. He's off today, and he's probably just hanging out at a coffee shop reading manga. But he's on to something whether he knows it or not: it seems like the whole world could be going to hell, but we just go along as usual, show up at the office, go to the beach. World War Three could start, but I doubt they'd cancel a good party for it."

"I see your point," Haruko said. A major disaster happens right here in Sendai, and all I really care about is whether my little girl is okay, how long my husband is going to be away on business, what to make for dinner, or the price of some lipstick I found on the Internet.

It was after seven when Haruko had a call from her husband, Nobuyuki, who was in Osaka on a business trip.

"I was in a meeting all day so I didn't know. I couldn't believe it when I got back to the hotel and turned on the TV. It must be crazy there. Are you and Nanami okay?"

"Calm down," Haruko laughed. It was out of character for him to put more than two sentences together.

"But I've been worried about you, really," he said.

"Then I guess you should drop everything and come home." She was trying to sound insistent. "If you're really worried, that's what I would do."

"Hello?" he said, his voice muffled. It was a trick he often used when he wanted to avoid a subject. "I didn't catch that. Must be a bad connection. What did you say?"

Familiar with the routine, Haruko didn't bother trying to continue the conversation but instead held the phone out to her daughter who was playing at her feet.

"Daddy? Are you coming home?" Nanami asked.

"How are you, sweetie? I'm afraid I've got some more work to do here."

Haruko reclaimed the phone. "That's better, static-free again. Now can you hear this? Why don't you come back?"

"I can't. I've got another meeting tomorrow."

"But can it really be all that important? What would you do if something happened to us?"

"I'd come straight home, of course."

"Then pretend it has," Haruko said, not wanting to let him off the hook.

"I'm really sorry, but I can't now. And anyway, you're both all right."

"We are," she admitted. "Things are crazy and Nanami's kindergarten is closed tomorrow, but that's about it."

"I'm glad to hear it," he said. They talked only a minute more.

"What did Daddy say?" Nanami asked when her mother was free again. She trailed after her, tugging at the hem of her skirt.

"He said he'd come home when you start eating your cucumber," said Haruko.

"Then we should just let him stay there," said Nanami. She didn't like cucumber.

"Poor Daddy," Haruko laughed.

The footage of the prime minister's parade and the flight of the model helicopter played nonstop on the television in the background, like news-worthy events from some distant country.

But these events were much closer to home. The next morning, she was sitting at the kitchen table spreading jam on a piece of toast, after switching on the TV. Her hand froze in midair. The image on the screen was that of the prime suspect in the case—a man she knew very well. "What have you done?" she murmured in spite of herself. "What can you have done?"

"Who's that?" Nanami said, pointing. "Is he a bad man? What did he do?"

Haruko tried to focus on what the announcer was saying. The pictures were from two years ago, background clips from a news show when Masa-haru Aoyagi had rescued that young celebrity while making a delivery. "It's shocking to think it could be him," the announcer was saying, with a tremor in his voice. Haruko nodded unconsciously. That's him, she told herself, but what kind of joke is this? What are they saying about him? The announcer added that he had quit his job three months earlier. She continued watching the program, but she couldn't make out why he was a suspect.

Realizing she was still spreading jam distractedly on the toast, she stopped and took a bite. It was impossible to swallow at first, but a sip of milk helped to wash it down. She got up and found her cell phone, deciding that she should simply call him, but then realized she didn't know his number.

"Are you calling Daddy?" Nanami asked. "Mommy, is something wrong?"

Haruko Higuchi

"Is something wrong?" a voice had asked Haruko eleven years earlier, and then, too, it had made her realize that she had been staring blankly into space. The voice was that of Kyoji Takeda, a teacher at the cram school where Haruko worked. Haruko's position was temporary, only for the winter break from college, but Takeda was five years older and a full-time employee. One of the other part-timers had said that he'd been head-hunted away from another well-known school the year before. Haruko didn't know whether this was true, but it was clear that he was liked and trusted by the students.

"Sorry," Haruko said looking quickly back at the tests she'd been grading. "I was daydreaming."

"The little ones are still pretty cute, aren't they?" he said, dropping into the chair next to her. Haruko was in charge of an elementary school class.

"They are," she agreed. "A bit naughty sometimes, but basically sweet."

"Then they hit middle school and suddenly they're all grown up."

"I know what you mean," she said, remembering her own middle school days.

"There's only a year between sixth and seventh graders, but somehow there's all the difference in the world. You know why?"

"Puberty?" Haruko said, holding her index finger up like a child giving a clever answer.

Takeda burst out laughing. "I suppose that's part of it. But basically we all take our cues from the people around us. Sixth graders are the oldest kids in the elementary school, so they set the tone for all the younger ones. But once they're in middle school, for better or worse, they come under the influence of the ninth graders—who are in the full throes of puberty. So, even though they're only a year older, the seventh graders act like they've suddenly aged three years."

"Which is why sixth graders happily run around in shorts at school, but seventh graders suddenly wouldn't be caught dead in them." Haruko liked seeing her boys in shorts, but by middle school it was mostly long pants and uniforms.

"Plus puberty." Takeda smiled again. His horn-rimmed glasses gave him a serious look, but he had a pleasant, easygoing way about him.

"Why did you decide to become a teacher?" Haruko asked, beginning to pack her books away in her briefcase. The topic didn't particularly interest her, but it seemed like a reasonable question to ask. Instead of giving a glib answer, though, he looked unexpectedly thoughtful.

"I don't know," he murmured. "I suppose I like working with kids."

"Makes sense," she said. She realized that she didn't dislike him, but there was something about his self-confidence that made her uncomfortable. "Though it hasn't been so long since you were a kid yourself," she said.

"Flattery will get you everywhere," he laughed, then abruptly changed the subject. "Do you ever think about what you want to do with your life? When to get married, that kind of thing?"

"Marriage?" she said. "I always thought around thirty." She'd never given the matter much thought but tried to sound as though she had. "But I can also see myself staying single a lot longer."

"Then there's not some guy out there you've got your eye on?"

"Definitely not," she said, frowning with mock distaste.

"You're kidding. You don't have a boyfriend?"

Haruko could feel the conversation heading somewhere she didn't want to go, but she could hardly ignore the question. "No," she said. She could also feel the pressure to ask the next question in turn, as much as she didn't want to: "And how about you? Is there anyone special?"

"No, no one."

"No?" she said, as flatly as she could. And with that, the conversation died as though sucked into a hole that had opened up in the air. How awkward, Haruko told herself, getting to her feet.

"Can I drop you at the station?" he said, getting up, too. His tone was utterly natural. "I was just leaving myself." He glanced at the clock on the wall and her eyes followed his. Nearly nine.

Kyoji Takeda was a good driver. He drove fast, changing lanes frequently and passing slower cars one after another. "Haruko," he said, as he stopped at a red light, "do you have any plans for this evening?"

Maybe because it was warm in the car, she had started to feel sleepy almost as soon as they'd left the school. "No," she answered without thinking. "Nothing in particular."

"Why don't we go and see how Saihoji Temple looks at night?" he said, as though the idea had just occurred to him. Haruko wondered why she would want to go somewhere she'd been to dozens of times before, but in her sleepy state she was about to grunt her assent, when the light turned green. Something about the color her half-open eyes had seen made her think of Aoyagi—perhaps because the first character in his name meant "green"—but as his face popped into her head, she sat bolt upright and let out a yelp. "What?!" Takeda almost shouted, his head snapping back in surprise, making the car jerk.

"I nearly forgot!"

"Forgot what?"

"I have a date! Could you drop me on Hirose Avenue? Please?" she said, putting her hands together in mock supplication and closing her eyes to avoid seeing his reaction.

"No problem," he said, and she felt the car accelerate.

"I'm sorry, and thanks," she said, thinking he was hurrying for her sake.

Takeda grunted and started punching numbers on his cell phone. "It's me," he said when the call went through. "You want to go out for a drink?" He seemed to have forgotten about Haruko already.

"I was afraid you weren't coming," Aoyagi said as she got out of the car and ran over to him. He was wearing a black jacket, standing in front of the Fashion Building where they had agreed to meet. There was something appealing about the way he stood there, back hunched against the cold, hands deep in his pockets.

The lights of the city seemed brighter than usual as the crowds made their way through the arcades. Traffic was heavy on Hirose Avenue. Aoyagi had joined the knot of young people waiting at a popular meeting spot.

Haruko smiled and shook her head. "No, I was the one who wanted to go. Why would you think that?" She had spotted an ad for a one-night, late-show revival of an old horror film and told Aoyagi that they shouldn't miss it. How could she tell him now that she'd forgotten all about it until a few minutes ago?

"Well, I suppose because you weren't here when the movie started," Aoyagi said.

"Am I that late?" She checked her watch and gave a startled shrug as though just realizing the time. "I wish they could have waited for us."

"I don't know what kind of movie theaters you go to, but I don't think they usually do that."

A group of people about their age were talking in a tight circle nearby, their hands as deep in their pockets as Aoyagi's.

"I'm sorry I made you stand out here all this time," she said.

"I've been calling your cell and texting you for the last hour. Didn't you notice?"

"Oh!" she blurted out, groping in her pocket for her phone. "I did. I just got them."

"Just got them?" Aoyagi snorted.

"I was at work, and the phone was turned off."

"You could have checked your messages."

"I was going to, at 9:30," she said.

"The whole point of a cell phone is that you have it with you, so people can get in touch."

"But it wasn't an emergency," she pointed out.

"But if it had been, what good would it have done to check at 9:30? I could have been dead for all you'd know."

"Okay, okay. I get it. I'm sorry."

"And who was the guy in the car?" He pointed at the line of traffic along Hirose Avenue.

"Oh," Haruko said, understanding at last what was bothering him. "That was Kyoji, Kyoji Takeda. He teaches at the school."

Aoyagi snorted again and stuck out a lip. Then he pointed his finger at her. "And that suit, that's what you wear to work?"

"School rules. Teachers have to wear suits."

"Do you know how much time I spent trying to decide what to wear tonight—just to go to the movies with you?"

"And you look very nice," she said.

"That's not what I mean!" he bleated. He seemed on the verge of a tantrum, but apparently thought better of it. "Oh well," he said more quietly. "You want to get something to eat?"

"Sure. There must be a burger place open late."

"We don't have to be Friends of Fast Food tonight."

"I suppose not."

"You know," he said, sounding more serious, "this is the first time we've been out together, just the two of us." Haruko nodded, just realizing this fact herself.

Aoyagi took a deep breath and then gave an odd little laugh. "Oh well," he said again, and set off down the street. Haruko fell in step next to him. "Would you really have checked your phone at 9:30?" he asked.

"Of course," she said.

"Well, after this, just be on time."

"Without fail!" she laughed.

Masaharu Aoyagi

Aoyagi checked the clock. Four already. He looked over at the thick curtains covering the windows and wondered whether the lights were visible from outside. Leaning against a wall, he looked around the room. It felt strange to be waiting here in an apartment where he had made so many deliveries, as though the doorbell was about to ring and he would see himself come through the door with a package.

A map had been thumbtacked to the wall. It showed a large country somewhere, but Aoyagi couldn't tell which one. Changes in elevation were marked with fine gradations of color, and he imagined Mr. Inai trudging through this variegated landscape.

Three hours ago, Aoyagi had jumped from the bridge onto the canopy of Maezono's truck, and then down to the pavement. A quick peek had confirmed that his friend was napping peacefully in the driver's seat. It was hard to believe anyone could sleep so soundly that he wouldn't notice a body falling on his truck, and Aoyagi was tempted to tap on the window and wake him up. But there was no time.

He must have shocked the men on the bridge by jumping, but it was only a matter of time—seconds at most—before they realized what had happened and came after him. He jumped the guardrail, bolted down the sidewalk, and turned in at the first corner. What the fuck? he muttered over and over to himself as he ran.

He needed a place to rest, and think. The idea of another taxi occurred to him, but the danger of being trapped in traffic was too great. A coffee shop or a movie theater? No, if they did manage to find him in a place like that, there'd be no room for him to slip away.

So that left a house or an apartment. He needed someone to hide him until he could explain what had happened, until everyone had calmed down. "Hide him?" The words made him wince. Why did he need a place to hide when he hadn't done anything wrong?

He wanted to call someone to ask what was happening to him. But who? He wasn't sure he knew anyone in Sendai who would want to hear from him now, who would believe what he had to say. The first person who came to mind was Morita—and his absence amazed and frightened him. Then he thought of Kazu. When he'd turned a few more corners and put a little more distance between himself and the bridge, he took out his phone. It had been more than two years since they'd talked. Not since Aoyagi's fifteen minutes of fame. Kazu had called, all excited. "You bastard! Getting to meet Rinka. I've been telling everybody, I knew you back in the day!" Aoyagi managed to retrieve the number he'd stored after that call, and he dialed it now.

As he listened to the phone ring, he slowed to a walk; he was out of breath and his hand was shaking. Finally, the recording came on, asking him to leave a message. He hesitated, tempted to hang up, but just then a cat jumped out of a hedge on the side of the road. The tone sounded. "It's me, Aoyagi," he said, almost involuntarily. Then he didn't know what else to say. After a few moments of silence, the tone sounded again and his time was up.

He closed the phone. Where to go? What to do? He was out of ideas, and he felt sure he was still being followed. As he glanced around, he realized these streets were on his old delivery route.

He had let himself into Inai's apartment with the spare key hidden under the fire extinguisher. Now, with the curtains still closed tight, he was watching the TV. At first he had kept the volume off, but the solemn look on the face of the announcer made him want to know what he was saying.

The apartment was a mess. The table was buried under piles of papers and packages, and the boxes stacked by the closet suggested he had been preparing to move. But Aoyagi wasn't convinced that he'd be away for a whole year, despite what the building manager had said about his paying the rent in advance. Maybe he didn't know how long he'd be gone; or, even if he had planned on a year, what was to prevent him from losing interest along the way and coming home early? Still, whatever his long-term travel plans were, Aoyagi was fairly sure that Inai wouldn't be coming back this afternoon. In all the time he'd made deliveries here, he had never once found him home at this hour. It was a place he could shelter in for a while.

Noticing a Walkman sitting on the desk, he began opening drawers. In the bottom one, he found a tangle of cords, from which he extracted a pair of earphones. They turned out to be the kind he'd seen used with cell phones, with a tiny microphone attached, and he wasn't sure how to use them. With a bit more tugging at the mass of wires, though, he managed to unravel a pair of black earbuds.

Every channel was replaying the same scenes. The limousine gliding down Higashi Nibancho, the camera moving in for a close-up of the dignified, determined profile. Then the little helicopter fluttering down from the text-book warehouse . . . and the explosion.

Aoyagi gripped the remote. A remote-controlled helicopter? As the images scrolled past in an endless loop, he stared hard at the whirling toy. Was it just a coincidence? He took out his phone and began slowly punching a number. Koume Inohara's name came up on the display.

"Oh dear, I just can't make this work. It must be me. Am I doing it right?" From the beginning, Koume Inohara had an odd way of speaking rather for-mally while sounding quite familiar. Her short frame, clipped speech, and slightly aggressive style somehow worked together. She had been busy for a while with the touch-screen on the job-placement terminal at the employ-ment office and then suddenly turned to Aoyagi for help.

"Let's have a look," he'd said, moving over to try her screen. It was frozen and he had no luck with it either.

"Good," Koume laughed. "I'm glad it's not me." Her hair was shoulder length, dyed a light brown. "But how will I ever find a job if I can't even get the computer to work?" There was something appealing about her even when she was grumbling.

"Maybe it thinks you need a little more time off," Aoyagi said, trying to cheer her up.

"Maybe I do," she laughed. And so they had struck up a friendship two months ago. He had run into her again when he went to check the job postings, and they had started having lunch together from time to time. One day she'd asked if he had any hobbies. He told her he didn't, and when he'd asked about hers she said it was a little unusual: "Remote-controlled model helicopters."

He pressed the send button on his phone. "Be careful. Don't trust anyone," Morita had said. Aoyagi felt himself tense up when the phone rang. Trust and verify, he told himself. There was no answer and again he was told to leave a message. The voice was the same as the one on Kazu's recording. You again, he smiled to himself. She seemed to be the only one willing to take his calls.

"It's me, Aoyagi," he said. "Sorry I've been out of touch. I saw the whole thing about the helicopter on the news. I couldn't believe it." He paused, not sure what else to say. "I guess that's it," he added before hanging up.

He remembered how innocent and happy she had looked when she invited him to come with her to fly the helicopter. "You won't believe how much fun it is!"

On the TV, Kaneda's limousine was once again being engulfed by the explosion. The screen filled with smoke. There were glimpses of dark figures staggering around in the aftermath. He had been sitting with Morita nearby when all this had happened. Then there was the other explosion. Could it really have been Morita's car? He tried to chase the scene from his head, with little success.

Viewers were told there were roadblocks on all the highways in and out of Sendai, and that service on the Bullet Train and all the local trains and buses had been suspended. "It is unclear whether this crime was the work of an individual or a group, but someone was controlling that helicopter and we have every reason to believe that person is still at large in the city of Sendai." The serious-faced speaker was identified as a "writer" by the caption at the bottom of the screen. Aoyagi had the eerie feeling the man could see him through the TV screen, see him sitting here in Inai's apartment.

They also replayed a news conference given by the police. The assistant division chief from General Intelligence in the Security Bureau was doing the talking, a baby-faced man named Ichitaro Sasaki, who seemed unusually calm and collected given the circumstances.

From his experience with the media two years earlier, Aoyagi knew how uncomfortable it was to have a microphone shoved in your face. When they kept pushing it closer and closer and repeating their questions, you felt as though you had to say something, even if it made no sense.

So he was impressed by Sasaki's ability to remain calm in the face of a roomful of shouting reporters. His attitude seemed to suggest that the more the reporters indulged in wild speculation, the more determined he was to conduct a thorough and careful investigation. When they had run out of steam, he made a short statement.

"The fact that the crime occurred in Sendai may be the one bright spot in this tragedy. Thanks to the Security Pods that were installed here last year, we've been able to collect a great deal of information, and I'm convinced we'll soon have the culprit or culprits in custody."

Aoyagi had seen the Security Pods around town but he didn't know much about them. They had appeared quite suddenly, perhaps because the police had failed to make an arrest in the case of a serial killer who was terrorizing the city. You could spot them in the bushes around a hotel, in the corner of a pedestrian underpass, in public parking lots, and they lined all the major streets at intervals as regular as the city's famous zelkova trees.

"They've got the suckers everywhere," one of his fellow drivers had told him when they first began popping up around town. "Now they'll know everything we're up to."

"Everything?" Aoyagi had wondered.

"They're like those cameras that catch you speeding and take a picture of your license plate, but these catch you at everything else."

"Like what?" Aoyagi said, not convinced that the cute little pods could be so insidious.

"Well, for one thing, they'll know when we park illegally to make a drop-off. And I heard they can eavesdrop on your cell phone."

"What about privacy laws?" said Aoyagi. "They can't listen in when you haven't done anything wrong."

"Which is why they're not telling anybody." There was something plausible about his friend's paranoia, and yet the pods looked innocent enough, sitting right out in the open for everyone to see.

Aoyagi stared at his phone. He wasn't sure why they'd want to know who called who or how they'd use the information, but it was unsettling to think that the device in his hand was always sending out a signal. He was about to turn it off when it suddenly began to vibrate and the display lit up with the name of the incoming caller.

"Kazu," he said, as he pushed the talk button.

"Aoyagi, my long lost-friend," Kazu's voice said.

"'Long-lost friend'?" said Aoyagi. "What are you talking about?" Kazu had never used such fancy language.

"Well, you are," he said. "A long-lost friend."

Aoyagi didn't have time to argue. "Sorry to call out of the blue, but I was wondering if you could put me up at your place tonight."

"My place?" His tone made it clear he didn't think much of the idea.

"I'm not sure," Aoyagi hurried on, "but it looks like I'm about to be homeless."

"What happened? Did they kick you out?"

"I lost my key." It was the first lie that came into his head, but it would have to do. "I can't get in touch with the manager, so I was hoping I could crash with you. Are you still in the same apartment?"

"Yeah, the same place. But do you think you can get a key tomorrow?"

The gears turned in Aoyagi's head. He could come back here to Inai's if he had to, so maybe there'd be no need to impose on Kazu. "I think so," he said.

"But other than being homeless, what have you been up to, my old friend?" Kazu said.

"I quit my job," Aoyagi told him, noting that he was now an *old* friend. "I'm collecting unemployment at the moment."

"Is that so?"

"How about you? What's up with you?"

"Can you talk?"

"Sure." The question seemed strange, as though Kazu was worried about using up Aoyagi's cell phone minutes. "It's been a while; I thought we could catch up a bit."

"So what are you doing?" Kazu said.

"I just told you. I'm unemployed."

"I meant, what are you doing right now?"

"Talking on the phone with you," he said.

"I know, but where are you calling from?"

"I'm at a hotel," Aoyagi lied. He could hardly say that he was being chased by the police and had broken into a stranger's apartment.

"Well," Kazu said abruptly, "call me again if you need anything." And with that he hung up. Aoyagi stared at the phone in his hand. The parade was still making its endless way across the TV screen, but he couldn't bring himself to put the earbuds back in. The only thing he could figure out in all of this was that no one seemed to be able to figure anything out. That's why the TV showed the same pictures ad nauseam, and the talking heads yammered on about nothing. He held out the remote and switched it off.

The light faded behind the curtains and shadows spread along the walls. Aoyagi rose and made another circuit of Inai's room. The pile of boxes brought a thin smile to his lips. Many of them still had packing slips attached to them, including some he must have delivered himself. He felt as though he was meeting an old traveling companion in an unexpected spot.

Somewhere in the middle of the stack, he noticed a box with markings from a well-known brand of health foods. Moving some other boxes, as though playing a giant game of Zenga, he managed to extract this one and put it on the floor. It was full of a kind of energy bar that he had often eaten when he was too busy to get a real meal. He wasn't sure why Inai would have bought a whole case of them—some sort of closeout deal or promotion—but that didn't stop him from stuffing handfuls of the bars into his bag. It was out of character for him to take something like this, but he noticed that the expiration date on the bars was already past and comforted himself with the thought that he could replace the ones he was taking with a fresh supply later.

He moved a few more boxes to reach the closet door. On a shelf inside was a small library of guidebooks and other materials relating to outdoor survival, as well as field guides to plants and insects. Maybe Inai really was off on an adventure. On the bottom shelf was a futon and, next to it, a length of white rope. Squatting down and pulling these out, he found a tightly rolled sleeping bag right at the back.

The other shelves in the closet held Inai's clothes, shirts and sweaters folded and arranged as neatly as in a shop window. And behind them, a knitted cap. The colors were a bit too bright for his taste, but he put it on and went to have a look in the bathroom mirror. Not a bad start on a disguise.

Back in the living room, he opened his bag again and tried to make room for the rope and the cap. But now the zipper wouldn't close. Another trip around the apartment. He was amazed how quickly he was overcoming his scruples—but he had little choice. He found a backpack, navy blue and nondescript but bigger than his bag. Unzipping it, he began repacking.

Another peculiarity of Inai's housekeeping: his refrigerator was full of CDs rather than food. It was turned off, so the disks weren't cold, but it still struck Aoyagi as a strange place for music. Unlike the neatly folded clothes, the CDs had been stuffed in at random—and if the disks were here, where was the food, anyway? He decided Inai must eat out all the time and had therefore pressed his refrigerator into service as a media cabinet. He noticed a little sticky note on the door: "Today, you are a CD rack." It was even dated. He wasn't sure whether the note was a suggestion to the refrigerator or a reminder to himself, but there was no doubt that Inai was one strange character.

As he was trying to close the refrigerator door, a stack of disks fell over and several of them slid out onto the floor—and there they were, amid the scattered cases: the Fab Four, walking across Abbey Road.

He went back into the living room. Pulling the connection out of the TV, he plugged the earphones into the stereo, put the CD in the tray, and pressed the button to skip to "You Never Give Me Your Money" at the beginning of the medley.

As the quiet piano music started, he could feel himself relax. Before he knew it, he was curled up on the floor, clutching his knees to his chest. The familiar voice murmured softly in his ears, and the shifting rhythms began to make him sleepy. It was still early, but he was exhausted. Maybe he hoped everything would go back to the way it had been if he could only sleep. He had the feeling Paul was whispering to him over and over—"All good children go to heaven."

At some point, the music had ended and the disk had stopped. Aoyagi was almost asleep, but the sound from the intercom made him sit bolt upright. Pulling off the earbuds, he looked around for his backpack. He got up and peered down the hall toward the door.

The intercom rang again and his eyes searched the room. The monitor, complete with a video screen, was next to the light switch. He could see the manager and hear him telling the two men in the center of the picture that this was the only empty apartment in the building. Two men in suits, though they didn't look like the two from his own building.

"Open it," one of them told the manager.

The camera must have been mounted above the door, since it looked down on the men, making them seem almost like children waiting for a friend to come out to play. But the charm of the scene was lost on Aoyagi, whose heart was racing. How could they have found him here?

What could have led them to Inai's building? There was some chance they were going door to door in Sendai, in which case it was just a matter of time before they got to this apartment, but to arrive so quickly at the one place he'd chosen to hide—it seemed a little too easy. The monitor clicked off, perhaps on an automatic timer.

He padded down the corridor as quietly as he could. For some reason the front door seemed a long way off. Dizzy from the fear they'd come bursting through it, he almost stopped short. But his feet kept moving under him, and he stepped down into the cement-floored entrance hall. He could hear them just outside. After checking that the chain was latched, he grabbed his shoes and retreated down the passage.

A sliver of evening sky was visible through the gap in the curtains as he shouldered his new backpack. It held the contents of his old one, plus the energy bars and the rope. He turned back to the boxes for a moment, wondering whether there was anything else he should take.

The intercom sounded again, and he looked at the monitor. The men were still staring at the door, the manager behind them holding the fire extinguisher. His hand fumbled under the canister. "The spare ought to be here," he said.

"Could somebody be in there?" said one of them.

Aoyagi could see the manager reach into his pocket and hand over his own keys. The lock clicked as he got up, pulled the rope from his pack, and headed for the balcony.

He could hear the door opening behind him and the chain going taut. Someone called out. Shouldering his pack, he turned long enough to push over the mountain of boxes. They were heavier than he'd thought, but he was able to bring them down in a hip-deep pile in front of the door. It wouldn't slow them down for long. Several of the boxes had broken open as they hit the floor and their contents scattered. He felt bad about the damage, but he also noticed something useful in the mess and without thinking shoved it in his pocket.

At this point, the chain must have given way and he heard the door swing open. Someone called his name and footsteps came down the hall. He pulled aside the curtains, opened the sliding door, and stepped out onto the balcony. As he wrapped the rope around the rail, the rows of houses stretching away in the evening light seemed unusually peaceful, in contrast to the shouting in the room behind him; apparently the boxes had worked better than he'd hoped. After one more loop around the rail, he let the rest of the rope fall—not quite to the ground but close enough.

Then something exploded. The window next to him shattered, and Aoyagi covered his face in his hands. Shards of glass rained down around him. As if in a dream, he threw his leg up over the railing, then hesitated, wondering whether the rope was properly secured.

"Aoyagi! Stop!" yelled one of the men. He swung the other leg over the railing and hung from the rope. There was a creaking noise and his body rocked to one side, pulled by the heavy backpack. The railing groaned.

He grasped the rope in both hands, wrapped his ankles around it below, and began sliding down. At the second floor, he checked the distance to the ground: just a little more and he could jump.

The creaking grew louder and he glanced up, wondering whether the knot would hold. They were above him now, looking down. "Stop or I'll shoot!" yelled one of the men. Aoyagi nearly lost his grip on the rope. They were leaning over the railing, and he was staring down—or up—the barrel of a gun, aimed carefully at him.

Aoyagi was shaking, but he managed to let go of the rope with his right hand and fumble in the pocket of his jacket. He found the object he'd borrowed from Inai's broken box: a dart. Gripping it in his free hand, he leaned back. There was no time to aim. His left arm clutched the rope tighter and his right arm let fly in the direction of the balcony above.

He heard the sound of scraping metal: the extra weight from his throw must have broken the fittings on the flimsy railing. The rope went limp in his hand. As he fell back, he thought he saw the dart stuck in the face above him.

Legs drawn up to his chest, he landed in a row of azaleas under Inai's balcony. His knees struck his chin and the shock left him dazed. But a moment later he was up and running again. Glancing over his shoulder, he could see the two men watching him go. One of them was holding his cheek, but the other was aiming a gun—though the shot never came.

He ran down a row of cars in the parking lot to the south, checking for unlocked doors. Though he knew it might be useless with roadblocks ringing the city, he wanted a car. He needed to escape the fear and exhaustion, if only for a few hours or a few miles.

One of the energy bars fell from his pack, but he didn't stop to pick it up: he had spotted a lock button protruding above a door. Opening the driver's side, he reached in by the steering wheel—no key. He checked the sun visor and the glove compartment. Still no luck.

Slamming the door, he took off again.

He ran out to the road and followed a narrow sidewalk. There was a guardrail to his left, the street side, and a line of telephone poles to his right. At one point, as he hustled along, his shoulder struck one of the poles and he nearly doubled over from the pain; but he rubbed the shoulder, gritted his teeth, and ran on.

How had they found him? There was only one possibility. He remembered what the police chief had said on TV—about Sendai and the "one bright spot in the tragedy." The Security Pods.

As he ran, he pulled his phone from his pocket—the likely culprit. But it wasn't clear whether they could find him just because the phone was turned on or because they'd intercepted the calls he made. Maybe they could trace a call to a general area but not an exact location. They might have known he was in Inai's building, but not which apartment—so they had relied on the manager.

He remembered Kazu and thought he should call him back. But would they get a fix on him as soon as he hit "send"? With the power down, he slipped his phone back in his pocket.

Coming out on a major road, four lanes with wide sidewalks on either side, he slowed to a walk, took the cap out of his pack, and pulled it down over his eyes. He had come some distance from the site of the explosion, and the people he passed seemed less agitated.

Ahead to his right was a bus stop. He pulled the cap further down on his face as he approached. A woman in high heels was studying the timetable.

"Is there one coming soon?" he asked her.

"I was just checking," she said, frowning slightly. She straightened and turned toward Aoyagi. "Seems like I've been here forever."

"With all the roadblocks, the bus company probably can't keep up."

"Roadblocks?" she said, frowning again.

"The explosion today?" Aoyagi said. "They've got all the highways blocked off, and they set up checkpoints."

"What explosion?" Her voice was high-pitched, her eyes hooded over. "What are you talking about?"

Cars were passing by. No bus, but traffic was moving. You might not be able to get out of the city, but you could still get around in it, though there were probably traffic jams here and there.

"You mean you haven't heard? Prime Minister Kaneda was killed by a bomb." He realized his voice was too loud and might have frightened her. But he had merely aroused her curiosity.

"Kaneda? Who's he?" she said, taking a step toward him. "And why'd they kill him?"

Aoyagi looked around. He had run here all the way from Inai's place, but there was still a chance those men could have followed him.

"Look, I'm sorry—I'm in a bit of a hurry."

"Oh, don't be," she said. "Didn't somebody famous say 'Haste makes waste' or something?"

"Who was that?" said Aoyagi.

"I don't know. I heard it on TV. Some guy trying to set a record for knocking over the most dominos. . . . But tell me about this bomb," she said, her lips pursing and puckering. "Who did it?"

The back of his neck prickled and he turned slightly. Standing in the distance was the man with the gun who'd been at Inai's building. Apparently he hadn't spotted Aoyagi yet.

"Hi there," a voice called. Aoyagi turned to find a big foreign car pulling to a stop in front of them and a man leaning out the window. "Looking for a date?" the man said. His hair was frizzed in a perm, and the arm hanging out the window was fleshy. His face was flat, his eyes hidden behind dark glasses.

"I'm waiting for the bus," said the woman, sidling up to the car, "but I don't think they're running. How about a ride? I'm already late for a party."

"Hop in," he told her. "But who needs a party? I'm already here. . . . And who's this?" he said, turning toward Aoyagi.

"I just met him," said the woman, on her way around to get in the car. "But did you know that somebody named Kaneda got killed? Big politician?"

"Never heard of him," said the man. Aoyagi was stunned, but also a bit envious, that anyone could be so ignorant. She's off to her party, he's out cruising, and I'm here in the Twilight Zone—except it's real. What a joke. "But that's probably why the town's crawling with cops," the man added.

"You get in, too," she said, coming back around to grab Aoyagi's arm. "You can tell us all about it on the way." He didn't resist when she pulled him toward the car.

As he slid into the back seat, he nearly gagged on a cloud of sickly sweet air freshener, and he had to shove aside a slew of CD cases. Slouching down, he peered out the window. The man was still there on the sidewalk.

"Where're you headed?" the woman asked from the front seat.

"Just hope it's not far," said the man driving, craning around. "Takes forever to get anywhere with all these cops. What is this anyway? Safe Driving Week?"

"It's the bombing," Aoyagi said levelly.

"Right! You said that, and somebody died?"

As he listened to them babble away, Aoyagi felt a slight sense of relief. The police knew where he lived and where he might be going; they knew his name and what he looked like. But no one else—including these two—seemed to have any idea who he was or how he might be connected with the assassination. He had begun to believe that everyone in the city was after him, and he found it a bit reassuring now to realize he was wrong. Maybe there was somewhere he could hide. He'd try Kazu first.

Masaharu Aoyagi

"To what do I owe the honor?" Ten years earlier, Kazu had looked annoyed as he opened the door to find Aoyagi and Morita standing outside. "Do you know what time it is?"

"Sure," Aoyagi laughed, looking down at his watch. "It's eleven." Kazu was living in an old, ramshackle apartment building thirty minutes from downtown on foot.

"Have you two been out drinking?" he asked. His hair was wet and he looked as though he had just pulled on the dark blue sweat suit.

"Sorry," said Morita, leaning on Aoyagi's shoulder. "Were you already in bed?"

Kazu sighed. "I was, and not planning on entertaining two boozy upperclassmen."

"The best-laid plans . . . ," Morita muttered. His face was bright red. "Don't make us stand out here. When your elders and betters come calling on a cold December night, you don't usually ask them in?"

"I don't," said Kazu calmly. He rarely got really angry—which they saw as both a strength and a weakness in his personality. "Anyway, you'll have to wait a minute while I clean up a little."

With that he disappeared, and they were left in the open air, leaning against the railing and staring up at the night sky.

"Whadda we do if he never comes back?" Aoyagi said.

"We'll talk about it in years to come, 'the night Kazu never came back,'" said Morita.

"Then I hope it snows," said Aoyagi. "It makes a better story with snow."

"If it starts to snow, I'm sure he'll let us in."

"I wouldn't, if I were him."

"Why's that?"

"Because I'd want to see what we'd look like buried in snow."

"You're right, that does sound interesting, present company excepted," Morita murmured. At this point the door opened again.

"Do come in," said Kazu.

"Generally speaking," said Kazu, launching into a sermon as soon as Aoyagi and Morita were seated, "you wait until December when girls get all moonie over Christmas, and then you throw a party and you find a date. It's pretty simple, really. Except you haven't done it." Kazu's apartment was modest—just two small tatami rooms—but neat by student standards. Yet there was something depressing about the holes that dotted the paper closet door.

"True," Aoyagi nodded solemnly.

"But, but," Morita stammered mournfully, "if Aoyagi spends Christmas with Haruko, can I come see you, Kazu?"

"You can if you don't mind watching me make out with my girl," he said. At this, Morita's mouth fell open, his lower lip trembled, and he began to rock as though in pain.

"You, too? Since when?" he moaned, like a man who had been betrayed.

"Since a while ago. I met her at work."

"How'd *you* get a girl?" he said, pointing at Kazu's grubby sweat suit. "Just look at you!"

"They're pajamas," Kazu said.

"I wouldn't wear that even to sleep in."

Kazu turned toward Aoyagi, as if to say that he couldn't talk to Morita in this condition. "So, to what do I owe the pleasure of your visit?" he said again, with mock formality. "I thought the plan was to introduce our friend here to a girl this evening."

"That's right. He said he absolutely had to find a girlfriend before Christmas," said Aoyagi. "So I arranged a date with a girl from the place Haruko used to work."

"But you struck out?" Kazu asked, turning back to Morita.

"Not exactly. We had fun," he said, waving his finger like a maestro's baton. "Well, *I* had fun."

"And what about the girl?"

"She seemed to be enjoying herself," Aoyagi said. "And Morita was a little quieter than usual—he even managed to avoid mentioning the 'voice of the forest.'"

"I'm sure all the little wood sprites and fairies were weeping."

"We had dinner, and a few drinks. Then we went to a karaoke place."

Kazu passed them each a mug of tea and leaned back against the closet door to sip his own. "He's a good singer, so that should have been okay."

"And sing he did, like a regular rock star. Some song by that group everybody's listening to. . . ." Aoyagi's voice trailed off as he failed to remember the name of the band.

"You mean Fiber Optic?" said Kazu, his eyes growing wide. Aoyagi nodded. "But you *hate* them," Kazu said to Morita.

"You cud say dat," Morita nodded, his voice beginning to slur badly.

"But he found out the girl was a big fan," said Aoyagi.

"And you knew one of their songs?"

"Well," said Morita, slumping forward, "I practiced a little."

"He was fantastic," Aoyagi put in.

"But how could you sing that trash? It's like selling your soul to the devil."

"You know," Morita said with a thin smile, "a liddle Fiberopic woulda been a small price to pay to not spend Christmas alone."

"But it didn't work out?"

"It was looking good when we left the karaoke place," said Aoyagi. "Haruko and I were walking a little ahead, but I could hear them talking. I thought everything was going great. But I guess in the end she just wasn't interested."

"I sent her an email after we said goodnight," Morita told him.

"But you don't have a cell phone, do you?" Kazu asked.

Morita groaned. "I borrowed Aoyagi's, but she never answered. Our little romance was DOA."

"You don't know that," said Kazu. "What did you say in the mail?"

"I said 'I had a lot of fun. Can I see you again?'" Morita recited.

"Doesn't sound like you at all," said Kazu. "Which is good."

"That's what I thought. But she never answered."

"Maybe she's the type who likes to keep you waiting awhile. Or maybe you weren't receiving mail right then. Did you check with the call center to see whether the system was working?"

"So many times I think I pissed them off. 'You *haven't* got mail' is my new call name. But I can't say I was surprised." Morita fell silent, staring at his lap. The refrigerator thrummed in the kitchen and there was a low creaking in the walls somewhere. The closet door rattled as Kazu shifted position.

"But you know, Morita," said Kazu, speaking up at last, "who needs a girl who doesn't recognize your true value? I hate to see you all messed up over this."

Morita looked up and sighed. "Shit," he muttered. "It was close, though."

Kazu looked puzzled.

"Shit," Morita said again, running his hand through his hair.

"Guess I win," said Aoyagi.

"Win what?" said Kazu.

Morita sounded glum. "The truth is, the girls put off our little party till tomorrow."

"What does he mean?" said Kazu, turning to Aoyagi.

"You see, Morita was nervous about meeting this girl tomorrow, so we went out drinking tonight to help him relax. But he kept saying he didn't know what he'd do if things didn't work out, so to shut him up I told him you'd take care of him. Then he started saying you weren't really that nice a guy."

"What the fuck are you talking about?"

"So, we decided to try a little experiment, just in case—to see how you'd react if we showed up here with a sob story."

"And we made a bet," said Morita. "Aoyagi bet you'd be nice to me, and I bet you wouldn't."

"You see, he really is a good guy," said Aoyagi, smiling.

"What the fuck?" Kazu muttered again, looking more than a little annoyed at being made the butt of their joke.

Aoyagi took a sip of tea. "Anyway, Morita, now you've got a backup plan for tomorrow," he said.

"And when you crash and burn, you really think you can come here?" Kazu said.

"This was just a rehearsal," said Morita. "I'm counting on you."

Masaharu Aoyagi

"To what do I owe the honor?" said Kazu, as he opened the door of his apartment and found Aoyagi standing outside. Surprise and then suspicion showed on his face in quick succession.

"I know it's sudden, but I need a place to crash tonight," Aoyagi said. Kazu's hair had grown since they'd last met, and he seemed somehow more substantial. Maybe he'd just gained weight. "Sorry to call out of the blue," he added.

"I tried calling you back."

"Oh? I had my phone off."

"Well, come in," Kazu said, stepping aside to let him pass. Aoyagi bent to remove his shoes and then followed him into the living room, where he slipped off his backpack.

The room was sparsely furnished, just a low table, a TV, and a jumble of cables that seemed to belong to one of the newer game systems. Aoyagi murmured his thanks again as he sat down and leaned back against the wall next to the closet. When Kazu disappeared into the kitchen, he took a few deep breaths to calm himself and checked the blue-black bruise that was forming where he had hit his arm against the telephone pole.

"How long has it been?" Kazu said when he came back from the kitchen carrying two mugs. He handed one to Aoyagi, who let the steam warm his face for a moment.

"I'm not sure," he said. "I think the last time was when you helped me move out of that apartment."

"That's probably right," said Kazu, lowering himself to the floor. He picked up a cushion and offered it to him.

"Office closed today?" Aoyagi asked, waving off the cushion. Kazu had gone to work for the local government soon after graduation. "I didn't think I'd find you here this early."

"I quit that job a couple of years back."

"No kidding? Why?"

"Got sick of the place. I was just too serious, I guess. I got everything done during regular business hours."

"A model employee," said Aoyagi.

"I thought so. But it didn't sit well with the guys I worked for. They fooled around all day and then stayed late to collect overtime. Since I was going home at five, they pretended I didn't have enough to do and really piled it on. They even took work away from guys who did next to nothing to give it to me. This pissed me off. Especially since I knew their overtime was coming out of my taxes."

"Can't say I blame you," Aoyagi siad. Kazu was as idealistic as he'd been back in school.

"So I quit. I wanted them to see how much they needed me, how hard it would be if I wasn't there to pick up the slack."

"And did they see the error of their ways?"

"Not exactly," Kazu laughed. "I don't think they even noticed I was gone."

"So, you could say your decision was a bit hasty?"

"A bit. I kick myself every day."

"So what are you doing now?" Aoyagi asked.

"Working at a shop," he said, mentioning a clothes store in the Fashion Building downtown. When Aoyagi admitted he had never heard of the brand, Kazu laughed. "A good-looking guy like you should pay more attention to his appearance. You'd clean up real nice," he said. "For example, where'd you get that lump of a backpack?"

Aoyagi looked down at his bag and gave it a pat. "I'm over thirty," he said. "Too old to worry about how I look."

"You've got it backwards. This is when you have to start worrying. If you don't, you'll slide right on into middle age before you know it. . . . And while we're on the subject, how's your love life since you and Haruko split up?"

For a moment, Aoyagi almost forgot he was a wanted man as he was drawn back into the mindless leisure of their student days.

"Well, there is someone I've been seeing," he said, thinking of Koume Inohara.

"If it feels right, go for it," Kazu said, without much enthusiasm.

Not knowing how to respond, Aoyagi changed the subject. "Have you seen Morita?" he asked. The bloodshot eyes and desperate voice came back to him. Was he still alive? Feeling his face begin to twitch, he pressed his mug to his lips.

"Morita?" Kazu said. "We went out for a drink when I was in Tokyo on business with my old job."

"Did he seem different?"

"Well, he's married."

"With a kid, I hear," said Aoyagi.

"I have to admit, I was shocked when I found out."

"I know. He didn't seem like the type."

"When I saw him, he hadn't heard you and Haruko had broken up." They said nothing more for a moment and sipped their tea. Aoyagi wondered how much he should tell Kazu about what had happened. And he wanted him to turn on the TV, to see what they were saying about Kaneda. But first, he thought, he would ask if he remembered their old talks about things like the Kennedy assassination. Before he could open his mouth, though, Kazu spoke up.

"There's something I wanted to ask you."

"What's that?"

Kazu peered down into his mug. "Did you do it?"

Aoyagi almost choked. Was he asking whether he'd killed Kaneda? But how could he think that? Were they already talking about him on television?

"Well? Did you?" Kazu said, looking him in the face now. His eyes widened. "You *did*! Unbelievable!"

"No!" he blurted out. "I didn't! How could I?!"

"You sure?" Kazu said. Confused, Aoyagi studied his friend for a moment.

"Would you rather I had?" he asked.

"Well, not everybody gets to do it with a girl like Rinka. I guess they get standoffish when they're that famous."

Aoyagi could feel the tension draining out of him. "Maybe," he murmured, taking a long, slow breath.

"'Maybe,' nothing. You were hot shit when all that was happening. The hero of the hour. And Rinka seemed *so* grateful. I thought for sure you were getting it."

"Morita said the same thing," Aoyagi said, realizing how different the words sounded to him now. "Can I turn on the TV?" he added.

"Sure." Kazu put down his mug and handed over the remote. At that moment, the phone rang and he picked it up. "Sorry," he said on his way out of the room. "Go ahead and turn it on."

A shot of the parade came on the screen. Then, as it faded, the announcer began reading a rather commonplace list of things observed by witnesses to the assassination: a large man wearing a face mask poking at his cell phone; a group of men studying a map on an observation deck across from the station; a woman who had been gesturing wildly in the crowd just before the explosion. But one of them made Aoyagi's heart skip a beat: "Two men were seen arguing in a white sedan on a side street just a short distance from the parade route." That was us. Morita and me.

He tried to stand, suddenly appalled at the idea that they thought he was implicated in it, but then sank back to the floor. At least he hadn't been identified by the media yet. Glancing at the door, he could see a somber-faced

Kazu out in the corridor, nodding over and over with the phone pressed to his ear. There was something ominous in his expression.

The TV switched to a commercial. He stared at the screen until Kazu came back.

"Everything okay?" Aoyagi asked.

"Yes, fine."

"Your girlfriend?" he teased, hoping to find a cheerier subject.

"Uh, yeah," said Kazu, sounding surprised.

"Having a fight?"

"Yeah, sort of."

"It's always something."

Looking down at his feet, Kazu told him, "Actually, she's coming over now."

"I see," he said, getting up and shouldering his pack. "In that case, I'd better be going. You two try to patch things up."

Kazu muttered something inaudible. "Will you be okay?" he managed to say finally.

"I'll be fine," Aoyagi lied.

"If you go left out the front door, there's an all-night restaurant straight up the street. A place with a big red sign."

"Sounds great," Aoyagi laughed.

"Could you wait there?"

"The big red sign?"

"I'll talk to her and tell her what's going on, then I'll call and you can come back here."

"You really don't have to bother," said Aoyagi.

"But we've got a lot to catch up on," said Kazu, looking serious.

Aoyagi saw no reason to refuse. On the contrary, he was grateful for the offer of shelter and someone to talk to. "Okay," he said. "I'll hang out there for a while, but if you need some space with her, just let me know."

"I'm sorry," Kazu added as he followed him to the door.

"Just sort things out with her."

"I will."

"You know, there was something I've been wanting to ask you, too," said Aoyagi.

"What's that?"

132

"Do you remember that night Morita and I showed up at your place unannounced?"

Kazu chuckled, his expression softening. "You mean the night he was 'rehearsing' for rejection?"

"It didn't hit me at the time, but later I got to wondering . . ."

"Wondering what?"

"Was your girlfriend there, in the closet?"

"What makes you ask that, after all this time?"

"It was just a feeling I had. I guess it's too long ago to remember."

"No, how could I forget? We were just—you know—'getting friendly' when you showed up."

"But you had that gross sweat suit on."

"It was all I could find," Kazu laughed. "I threw it on while she got in the closet."

"Well, sorry for the interruption!"

"Anyway, after you left, we had a good laugh. She said I had the weirdest friends."

There was one other thing. "Is the girl who's coming over now the same one?"

"No, of course not," said Kazu, as if he thought it odd to still be seeing the same girl. "But I sometimes wonder what happened to her. The last time I saw her we had a huge fight. Then she used the fire extinguisher to do a number on my apartment. A real bomb scene."

"A fond farewell to remember her by."

"Yeah, guess you could say she 'extinguished' the fire in my heart."

"Oh, please!" Aoyagi groaned.

"Do you think about Haruko much?"

Aoyagi felt blindsided by the question. "Not much," he said.

"Girlfriends are funny that way. When you're with them you feel like you know everything about them. But once you split up, you lose track of them completely."

"I know what you mean," Aoyagi murmured. Slipping into his shoes, he stood in the open door. "I won't mind if you two fool around a while before you call," he told him. Kazu gave a halfhearted smile.

"Aoyagi," he said.

"What?"

"I'm sorry, really."

"Don't worry about it. I'm the one who dropped in out of the blue."

"I just didn't know what else to do." He looked crushed.

Aoyagi caught sight of the fire extinguisher in the hall. "If it turns out she came to finish the fight, make sure you hide that," he said.

"Will do." There was a hint of relief in his smile. Aoyagi had turned to go when Kazu spoke up one more time: "You really didn't do it?"

Aoyagi stopped. It didn't seem worth the trouble. "Of course I did," he said. To his surprise, Kazu looked shocked.

"Really?" he murmured.

Aoyagi smiled and headed for the elevator.

It was hard to miss the big red sign. The dinner hour was over, so the place wasn't crowded—a couple of women at one table, a few people eating alone. A sour-faced manager tried to take him to a table by the window, but he asked for one at the back. It made him nervous to be too visible.

He wasn't really hungry, but he ordered pasta and something to drink. Then he just sat, staring into space. His exhaustion was becoming a line of tense muscle down the back of his neck, and he thought he might feel better if he could close his eyes for a few minutes, with his head down on the table. But almost immediately the images from the news and the announcer's droning voice began replaying in his brain. And then there was Morita. As drowsy as he was, he knew he would never get to sleep.

When the food arrived, he took out his cell phone and put it on the table. Only then did it occur to him that he would need to turn it on to get Kazu's call. He held the phone in his left hand while he twirled some spaghetti with his right. An image of a Security Pod flashed into his head: a little rocket-shaped capsule—or just a glorified mailbox, maybe? Was there one nearby intercepting every radio wave in the vicinity? But even without the pods, couldn't they locate a cell phone just by its signal? The phone in his hand seemed insignificant yet dangerous as well.

He pressed the power button. There was a faint musical tone and the display came to life. A second later, the phone rang, as if someone had been waiting for that very moment to find him. It was unnerving.

At first he thought they'd found him, and then that it might be Kazu, but it was Koume Inohara's name that appeared on the screen. He put the phone to his ear.

"Masaharu?" she said. "I've been trying to get you all day." She was a couple of years younger than him but she talked to him like an older sister.

He lowered his voice and glanced around the restaurant. "I'm sorry. I've been kind of busy."

"I kept getting your message box."

"You heard about the helicopter?" he said.

"That's what you were calling about?"

"It just seemed pretty incredible."

"Where are you now?" she asked. He could feel his hand tense at the question. Morita had told him to be suspicious of her—to be suspicious of everyone—unless he wanted to end up like Oswald.

He started to say that he was waiting for a friend, but suddenly questions began forcing their way into his head. Was it just a coincidence that she should call him now and want to know where he was? Was it a coincidence that they'd met in the first place? That she'd been sitting next to him at the employment agency and had complained about the unusable terminal? Or had the whole thing been arranged?

"I'm going to see a friend," he said. Better to keep it vague. Her murmur was equally noncommittal. He realized she had never revealed much about herself yet always seemed to be sounding him out, trying to find out more about him. Once the suspicions started, though, there was no end to it. Everyone looked like the enemy.

"But it is pretty weird," she said. "It's not every day they kill a prime minister with a model helicopter!"

He was startled by her choice of words. And somewhat relieved. How could someone so straightforward be involved in any of this? "Do they know what kind it was?" he asked.

"I haven't been watching, but I heard Ochiai is going to be on TV tonight as some sort of expert."

"Ochiai?"

"The man who owns the shop where I bought your helicopter."

Aoyagi looked across the room to the parking lot, dyed red by the sign over

135

the restaurant. He realized Kazu might be trying to call. "I've got a lot going on right now, so I'm going to hang up," he said. "I'll call you back later."

"Later? I was hoping we could go out somewhere."

Why not? It didn't make much difference whether he stayed at Kazu's or got together with her. He didn't have anywhere else to go. And since Kazu's girlfriend was coming over, it probably made sense not to bother them.

A waitress passed his table, glancing in his direction and then moving on. Perhaps she didn't like him talking on the phone, or maybe she just had other things on her mind, but there was something oddly inquisitive about her. She disappeared into the kitchen and didn't come back. He suddenly felt anxious.

"I'll call back," he said again.

"You know, I can always tell when something's bothering you," Koume said. "Are you all right? Has something happened?"

"I'm fine," he replied. Haruko had once told him that the one thing she didn't want to become was a person who could lie with a straight face. They had been watching a politician on TV trying to wriggle his way out of some scandal.

After hanging up on Koume, he sat staring at the display on the phone. He knew he should turn it off, but instead he dialed Kazu's number and listened to it ring. The waitress brought his order, seeming flustered as she put it in front of him.

"What's up?" Kazu said.

"I just wanted—" Aoyagi began, but Kazu cut him off.

"What's up?" he repeated.

"Sorry, are you in the middle of something?"

"No, not really."

"It's just that I don't think I'll be able to use my phone much longer."

"Low battery?"

"Yeah," said Aoyagi, realizing he had actually become one of those people who could lie with a straight face. "I know it's a lot to ask, but would you mind coming to get me here if it turns out I can stay at your place? Or calling the restaurant?"

"Come get you there?" Kazu muttered and was silent for a moment.

"Kazu?" he said at last.

"Look, I'm sorry."

"About what?"

"I'm really sorry."

"What do you mean?" Aoyagi said. He wanted to tell his friend to forget about him and look after the girl. "Kazu," he started to say, but the line went dead. For a moment he considered calling back but then let the phone fade out. When he looked up, the waitress was standing over him. Startled, he sat back abruptly, banging his knees against the bottom of the table. The coffee cup rattled.

"Excuse me," she said, blinking nervously. Aoyagi was tempted to stand up and leave the place without another word. He was reaching for his backpack when she managed to get out the rest of her question. "Aren't you the deliveryman?"

He looked at her again. She was smiling now and blinking even harder. "I used to see you on TV. I was a big fan."

"Thanks."

She opened the little notebook she was holding. "Could I get your autograph?"

"I'm not a celebrity," he stammered, shaking his head. "I'm not even a deliveryman anymore." He had asked hundreds of people for their signatures on his rounds, but it felt very strange to have someone ask for his, and even stranger to be refusing. He had never known what to do when people were reluctant to sign his delivery slips, but the girl gave up easily enough, turning to go with a disappointed look. Feeling guilty, he got up and headed for the bathroom at the back of the restaurant, taking his backpack with him just in case.

He looked at himself in the mirror. There was a scratch on the side of his face, and he could feel the bruises on various parts of his body. His eyelids were puffy; his jaw hurt where his knees had hit. He rinsed his hands, ran them under the air-drier, and left the bathroom. As he was making his way down the narrow passage toward his table, he noticed that the automatic door at the front of the restaurant had just swung open. He stopped and instinctively retreated a step.

Five men came in the door. No one he recognized. Some in suits and some not, but all five were well built—like an amateur rugby team going out for dinner after practice. They had a hard look, clearly not the office crowd stoking up for a long night.

The short, middle-aged man in the lead flashed an ID of some kind at the manager, while the other four looked around the room. These guys obviously played on the same team as the ones who had shown up at Inai's apartment.

The one at the back was especially impressive: almost 190 centimeters tall, crew cut, broad shoulders, muscular chest—like a black belt in some martial art. He had earphones on and was carrying a firearm so casually it could have been an umbrella. It seemed incredible that anyone could walk into a restaurant with a gun in this city, in this country. Which may have been why the other customers paid no attention to the new arrivals or this man's shocking accessory. Maybe they thought it *was* an umbrella?

Aoyagi stepped back, then turned and ran back to the bathroom. Opening a window in one of the stalls, he dropped his pack to the ground outside. Then he climbed onto the toilet seat and used the window frame to haul himself up. His heart was pounding. He knew they could come bursting through the door at any moment, but the thought somehow made him waver. He managed to pull the upper half of his body through the window, then found he couldn't twist around. Finally, spurred on by the fear that someone might grab his legs, he slithered out. His jeans caught on something and he felt a pain in his leg, but he stretched his hands above his head and let himself fall to the ground.

The shock disoriented him for a moment. Groaning, he sat up and brushed the dirt from his hands. Then the wall next to him shook, and there were shouts and loud banging. A gun went off inside. He needed to get away, to put a safe distance between himself and these men. But what was safe now?

Masaharu Aoyagi

"Legally speaking, the safe distance isn't clearly specified." Aoyagi, Morita, Haruko, and Kazu were sitting on the ground like well-behaved schoolchildren, listening to Todoroki. He wore a pair of light blue pants and a white T-shirt, and they could see his belly wobble every time he gestured at them.

Morita had kidded him that he should wear something a little less revealing, but the boss had brushed this off. "I should show up in my birthday suit. Give you kids a real thrill!" They had groaned at the thought.

The sun had set and the sky was fading to a deep indigo. Todoroki's staff had been talking about the weather all afternoon. It was the first clear day in some time, perfect for fireworks. Last year, they remembered, it had rained. Aoyagi and his friends sat a short way off, on the banks of the Hirose River, watching the professionals set up for the Star Festival fireworks display—their "VIP seats" a reward for having shoveled snow at the factory all winter.

"Hey Rocky! We may be VIPs, but this isn't exactly a 'seat,'" Morita had pointed out. Everyone at the factory called the boss "Rocky"—short for Todo-*roki*. They had found it hard to use the nickname at first, but as winter changed to spring and they became regulars, they had taken to calling him "Rocky," too.

"So there's no law that says how far away you have to keep people from the fireworks?" Haruko said.

"No, some places have ordinances that fix the distance, but they're inconsistent and pretty confusing. The truth is, if you're a hundred meters away and someone gets hurt, that's not a safe distance—no matter what the law says. But we're pros," he added. "We don't have accidents. That's why they let us work right here in the middle of Sendai." Aoyagi thought it would be nice to be able to say you're a pro at something and mean it.

The launch mortars had been set up on the riverbank, wired in separate groups for each element in the show. Todoroki's men had just finished attaching all the fuses and doing the final tests.

"I thought you just tossed a match into the tube and ran like hell," said Morita.

It had surprised them to learn that everything was controlled by computer, that a laptop could manage all the timing and the ignitions, but it was even harder to believe that middle-aged, do-it-yourself Rocky would rely on a keyboard and processors for his big show.

"You really know what you're doing?" Morita had asked him, pointing at the tent where the fuse wires converged on his laptop.

"Of course—we're pros," Todoroki said again. "In the old days, when fireworks were fancy toys for warlords, no one worried much about efficiency,

139

but it's a business now—digital-age rocketry—and we know exactly what we're doing." He tapped clumsily at an imaginary keyboard.

"You could blow up the whole city typing like that," Kazu laughed.

"No worse than Aoyagi pressing the button on the elevator. Have you noticed?" Haruko said, as though the subject had reminded her of a joke she'd been meaning to tell. When she had their attention, she held her thumb straight up. They stared at her for a moment.

"You're right!" Morita said. "He does. Like he's giving you the thumbs up. It's sort of weird."

"There's nothing weird about it," said Aoyagi. "My mom and dad do it."

"Sorry, definitely weird."

"No, not normal!" Todoroki nodded emphatically.

"You sure?" Aoyagi said, sticking out his thumb. "Okay. I'll try it your way."

"But you can't teach an old dog new tricks."

"You can. People can change," Aoyagi insisted.

"Not you," Haruko laughed. "What about the way you leave rice in your bowl?"

"Rice?" he murmured, growing flustered.

"He does! He does!" Morita said, his head bobbing again. "I've never met a grown man who couldn't clean his rice bowl." It was true. Aoyagi wasn't particularly conscious of it, but now that they mentioned it he realized he did have a habit of leaving bits of rice clinging to his bowl. This, too, had never struck him as strange—though he knew most people ate more neatly—it was just the way he was raised. Morita pressed home the point. "You must have grown up rich to leave that much rice."

"It's cruel, like genocide, to finish up every last grain," Aoyagi murmured. His father had once said something like this to him when he was young, and it had impressed him. But as he said it now, it sounded like nonsense. "At least, that's what my dad used to say."

"Your old man's weird, too."

"Maybe so," he allowed.

"But it seems a bit boring to shoot them off with a computer," said Haruko.

"Not at all," Todoroki explained. "The fireworks themselves are completely handmade, down to the last detail. We're artists. So who cares who lights the fuse? You can use a computer—you could even rig a cell phone to set off the whole show." He wriggled his fingers again, this time as if dialing a phone.

"Hope you don't get a wrong number," said Morita, dialing, too.

To Aoyagi, a cell phone was going too far—cheapening something so spectacular. But he took some comfort in the fact that these signs of change didn't seem to faze Rocky, the consummate pro, for whom the magic of fireworks never changed.

The last light faded from the sky, and the noise from the crowd gathering on the bridge above them grew louder. They were no doubt as anxious as Aoyagi for the show to begin. Next to him, Haruko sat with her head thrown back, supporting herself with her arms stretched out behind. "I'm going to get a stiff neck if they go straight up," she said. Aoyagi grunted. "But it's incredible to see them from so close."

"Oh, I forgot to mention," said Todoroki. "Don't leave as soon as it's over. You've got to help clean up."

"'You' meaning who?" said Morita.

"All of you, of course."

"You might have said something a bit sooner," he grumbled. He didn't sound too upset. "By the way, Rocky. Does your son plan to take over the business at some point?" They had heard that his only son, who looked exactly like him, had graduated from college a few years back and was working for a company in Aomori.

Todoroki frowned. "The prodigal son," he said. "It's possible."

"Did he really get the police after him for shooting off fireworks in school?" Aoyagi asked. They had heard the story from several people at the factory. Rocky nodded and frowned again.

"I let him hang around when he was a little kid. He had a real knack for the business." It wasn't clear whether he was proud of the fact or not. "But he's a rebel, and reckless. So he's not cut out for a delicate job like this."

"If you can do it, he can do it," Morita teased.

"Then I imagine he'll show up one of these days to take over." His tone suggested the subject was closed. "But you know," he added in passing, "a fireworks display isn't about size." They looked at him, ready for the next pronouncement from their pyrotechnic guru. "Different towns have different budgets, different ideas about what they want. But what really matters in the end isn't how grand a show is—it's about the hometown girls who got married and moved away coming home in the summer to visit, to show off their children to the grandparents, and the whole family coming out to watch. That's the same everywhere. All sorts of people getting together outside on a warm evening and looking up at the sky. Everybody sighs and says how pretty they are, how exciting. And then they get up the next morning and go back to work, promising themselves they'll be sure to go again next year. That's what I love about this job." They stared wide-eyed at so much sentimental stuff. But he soldiered on. "And I'll tell you something else I like about it. Thousands of people watch the same fireworks at the same time; and who knows, maybe an old friend you haven't seen in years could be among them. You might even start thinking about the same thing at the same time, maybe something that reminds you of this friend."

"That reminds me," Morita giggled, "never to ask a pyrotechnologist for his thoughts on life!" His hand shot up and he made a swishing noise, like a rocket. As the others joined in, Todoroki turned with a smile and headed off to make his final preparations.

The fireworks were even better than they had imagined—and a very different experience from watching them on a roof miles away. From a distance, the Star Festival show had been visually spectacular, but up close you experienced it with your whole body. The boom shook you to the core. A streak straight up into the sky. An explosion. Brilliant light. Sparkling flashes floating to earth. Fading in the night. Darkness. And again. There was nothing to do but look up, mouth open.

Aoyagi felt each explosion in his belly. Then, an instant later, an enormous flower bloomed in the sky, only to dissolve in a shower of sparks that made the most delicious crackling before they fizzled out. One after the other, the rockets streaked up, forming layers of blossoms as their screams rained down on the four of them below. They knew it was just a fireworks show, but somehow the power and immediacy made it seem like the explosion of countless man-made stars.

Then they stopped, at least for a moment: a brief pause to allow the breeze to carry off some of the smoke that filled the air. Aoyagi used the time to look down at the technicians from Rocky's factory who were hard at work right in front of him. Their faces were lit up like schoolboys on a field trip. In the primitive thrill of fire, any weariness, any troubles they felt had been swept away. And there was Todoroki in his T-shirt. He glanced over at them and grinned, holding up two fingers, the sign of victory.

"Unbelievable!" Morita hissed.

Aoyagi looked at Haruko sitting next to him. Her eyes were still fixed on the sky, as if staring at an afterimage. "Haruko," he said, lowering his voice so that no one else could hear. She turned to look at him, and he wanted to go on, but no words came. He'd spent the last few days picturing this moment and rehearsing what he planned to say—to no avail.

"What?" she said.

"There's something I've been wanting to ask you for a while now." He could feel the tension in his face, his jaw start to tremble. "Do you want to go with me?"

Her expression clouded over for a moment, and Aoyagi felt as though he was flaming out like a defective rocket. He wished he could take back what he'd just said.

"Go with you where?" she said, looking doubtful. "To the bathroom?"

"Not that kind of 'go,'" he said, his frown growing deeper. An explosion shook him then. The show had started again. A giant star was born overhead, dissolving just as quickly in a chorus of crackles. Haruko looked back at the sky, and he decided he should give it one more try. He was about to say her name again when she suddenly laughed out loud.

"It took you long enough to ask," she giggled.

Haruko Higuchi

A pale streak of light lingered in the sky even after it had started to drizzle, so Haruko had thought it would stop soon if they could just put up with it for a bit. But it hadn't stopped and the day had gradually darkened until it was hard to tell whether night had fallen—at which point the skies opened up and the drizzle became a downpour. Caught without an umbrella, she let out a little groan and looked around for shelter.

There was nothing. The buildings along the street didn't even have eaves. She wanted to speak to Aoyagi, but the pelting raindrops washed away her voice. He scratched his head and looked at his watch. "Still got an hour till our reservation," he said.

"What are we supposed to do? Swim there?" She put her hand to her head and felt that it was already soaked.

"This is what we get for picking such a fancy place. It was way out of our league to begin with."

"But it's our anniversary," she said.

Aoyagi had been less than enthusiastic from the moment she proposed they celebrate their three-month anniversary. "I can see the point after a year together, or even six months, but isn't this a bit soon? Besides, I've never done anything like this before."

"Neither have I," Haruko had admitted. "But you take a car in for its first checkup after a month; so we can think of this as a three-month inspection rather than an anniversary." In fact, she was just looking for an excuse to go to a famous French restaurant that had opened a branch in Sendai.

"Of course!" she heard him say now through the rain.

"What?"

"I just remembered," he said, smiling as he grabbed her wrist and pulled her along. He turned a corner into a larger street that ran toward the campus. It was raining even harder now, as though a waterfall had descended over the city. The street was filling and the wipers of the cars driving past worked so frantically they seemed about to fly off.

Aoyagi turned off the street into an overgrown vacant lot. A road had run through it at some point, but it had long since been abandoned to the thick undergrowth. He pushed his way into the weeds, and Haruko followed, unable to stop him to ask where they were going. Mud kicked up behind them as they ran.

At last he pointed into a clump of grass that was nearly as tall as Haruko. They plunged in, but it wasn't until they were almost on top of it that she realized he had been heading for a car—a yellow sedan hidden in the weeds. The rain clattered on the hood.

"Get in," he said, circling around to the driver's side.

"How?"

"I'll unlock it." He bent down and reached under the car, then straightened up. Hearing the locks pop open, she pulled at the door and climbed in. "Nice weather we're having," he said, gazing out at the rain through the windshield.

"Whose car is this?" she said.

"Beats me." He rubbed his head, sending drops flying everywhere. Then he reached into the back seat and produced a towel. "For you."

"And whose is this?"

"Beats me," he laughed, then sniffed at it carefully. "Seems clean enough."

"Yuck!" she snorted.

"You'll catch a cold," he said. It was warm for November, but not warm enough to sit around soaking wet. "Anyway, I think it's Kazu's, so I doubt you'll catch anything fatal."

"Is this his car?"

"No, not his," Aoyagi said as he inserted the key and turned the ignition. Nothing happened. "Must be the battery," he muttered.

Ever so carefully, Haruko began drying her hair with the towel. She was reluctant to use it, given the questionable provenance, but she was even more reluctant to catch a cold. When it was almost dry, she leaned back, feeling the cold of the seat through her jacket. "How did you know this was here?" she asked him.

He looked a bit sheepish. "Rumors, probably. Everybody knows about it. Some guy must have abandoned it here rather than pay to get rid of it."

"And the key?"

"In the wheel well."

Haruko studied him for a moment with raised eyebrows and then turned to look out the window. The rain was pounding so hard she wondered if it would dent the roof.

"Anyway, it seems like a good place to wait," she conceded.

"I'm glad you think so. An umbrella wouldn't do much good in this, even if we had one. I just wish we could get it running, for the heater."

"It would run if you got a new battery."

"You think so?" Still staring out at the rain, he began humming cheerfully to himself.

"What's that?" she asked.

"The theme song for our little yellow car," he said, repeating the tune a few times. Haruko almost wanted to join in.

What had seemed like a passing shower had long since exceeded the label, and it was pelting down.

"It won't be easy to get to the restaurant. Do you want to cancel?" she asked.

"Me? No, why do you ask?" He tried to sound shocked.

"Well, *haute cuisine* isn't exactly your style."

"Since I can't even clean my bowl, you mean?"

"You said it."

"But I'm a reformed man," he said. "I even read a book on etiquette, just for tonight." He mimed using a series of knives and forks, beginning at the outside. "On the other hand," he said, glancing out the window and checking his watch, "it's pretty bad out there. Let's give it a few more minutes. If it looks like we can't make the reservation, we'll call them."

"They'll understand if we're late, with the weather like this."

"But will they even let us in if we're soaked to the skin?" he said, looking down at his jacket. Then he looked at her. "I hate to mention it," he said, "but your unmentionables are worthy of mention."

Flustered, she looked down at her shirt. Her bra was visible where the material was dampest, but it was hardly indecent. "You think so?" she said. "Perhaps that's because you've got your eyes in the gutter."

"Touché," he said.

"Oh!" she crowed suddenly. "I just remembered."

"What?"

"Something Kazu said when we were sitting around in the cafeteria. About how he never had to worry if he didn't have the money to get a room. He had a 'free love hotel.'"

"He said that?"

"He was talking about this car! He meant you could bring someone here— this is the hotel!"

Aoyagi turned beet red. "You could be right. I think Kazu may have brought girls here. But I'm not, I never . . . I haven't."

Haruko had settled back triumphantly but then sat up again. "Do you think that towel . . . ?" She was almost gagging.

"No, no. I'm sure it's new, probably just for wiping the seat. Kazu said he would leave a clean one for the next guy."

"Next guy?!" she nearly screamed. "God, you're all vile!" She pushed her hand against the window. "Open this, I can't breathe."

"You'll get soaked," he said.

"I don't care! I'm sitting on the bed in a low-rent love hotel!"

"At least it's dry," he murmured.

"Now I remember," she said, punching futilely at the window button. "Kazu told you to be sure to use it, too. 'You should try it out, Mr. Aoyagi,' he said."

"He did? But I never did!"

"No? But Kazu always adds that 'Mr.' for you and Morita when he wants to get your attention. It's his way of showing respect for you as upperclassmen. But he only uses it when the situation calls for it. Do you remember that time we were in the cafeteria and Morita was bad-mouthing that professor?"

"Isn't he always bad-mouthing a professor?"

"This time, though, the guy was sitting almost next to us, but Morita didn't know it and he kept going on about how terrible he was. So Kazu started saying 'Mr. Morita . . . uh, Mr. Morita.'" Morita had frowned at him, but then started in about the guy's taste in ties, how he'd actually worn one with an octopus pattern on it. So then, of course, the rest of them couldn't help looking over at their neighbor; and there they were, hanging down in front of him—a line of bright pink octopi. Everybody burst out laughing.

"I wonder if the professor noticed?" Aoyagi said.

"I don't see how he couldn't have. But he played it pretty cool. He just sat there. But when Morita found out what had happened, he was furious with Kazu for not telling him." Kazu had insisted that there was no way he could have said anything with the man sitting right there; and besides, he'd given him a signal: "You should watch out when I add that 'Mr.'" he had said.

Aoyagi's cell phone rang at that point. It occurred to Haruko that it might be the restaurant, but it was unlikely they'd be calling customers to confirm reservations, even in this rain. Aoyagi checked the display. "My mother," he said.

"Your mother? It's not like her to call, is it?"

"No." He answered, but his greeting was cool, followed by a few unenthusiastic grunts. "No, same as always," he said, smiling for the first time.

Then, "No, what can you do? It won't do any good to say anything." And he hung up.

"What was that all about?" Haruko asked.

"My dad. In most ways, he's a pretty average guy, but he has this obsession with those lechers who feel up women on crowded trains. He can't stand them, has a fit every time you even mention them."

"Nothing wrong with that," Haruko murmured, a bit put out by the new topic.

"I agree, but there are limits. Once, when I was in high school, my mother got a call from a lady who lived in the neighborhood saying he was at the train station making a scene. When we got there, he had this guy pinned down on the platform and he was beating the shit out of him. Apparently he'd caught him groping a girl on the train and pulled him off—which was okay, I guess, but then he couldn't control himself and started punching him."

"What did you do?"

"My mother was crying and tugging at him, and finally some station cops managed to separate them. It was pretty bad." Aoyagi looked as though the scene was playing out in front of him. "She was calling just now to say the same thing happened again. He caught another one and beat him up."

"I'm not sure I blame him."

"But he's driving my mother crazy, and then she calls me—though I don't know what she thinks I can do."

"Still, in a way it's a good deed."

"But he doesn't think about the consequences. He just reacts on the spot, goes berserk. That's not right. He needs to take a step back, do things deliberately."

"All of a sudden, you're for deliberation?" she laughed.

Aoyagi called the restaurant about the reservation. "They were pretty nasty," he said after hanging up. "I guess you don't cancel on a place like that at the last minute."

"It's a famous restaurant, but that's still no reason to be rude," she agreed.

Haruko Higuchi

"Mommy?" said Nanami. "Are you dreaming?" Haruko had been sitting at the kitchen table staring at the television. Every channel was showing footage of Masaharu Aoyagi. Nanami was playing on the floor, stopping from time to time to ask to be taken outside. What good was having the day off from kindergarten if she didn't get to go to the playground?

"But the people on the TV said it's dangerous to go out today," Haruko lied. "There was that bad trouble downtown yesterday."

"You mean the bomb? I think Daddy's worried. Somebody really important died."

"That's right," said Haruko, thinking how odd it was that children learned so young about the concept—and the reality—of death. Maybe it was the TV, or manga, or video games. She remembered how dismayed she and her husband had been one day when Nanami, barely a toddler, had brought them a grasshopper she'd caught and announced that it had died. She had wanted to know where it had gone now that it was dead.

Nobuyuki had answered without any hesitation, "It's not there anymore," pointing at the stiff little creature in her hand. "It's here." He pointed at her chest.

"Here?"

"In Nanami's heart," he said.

This had seemed a bit too sentimental to Haruko, but then again she supposed it was true that people lived on after death in the memories of the ones who loved them. They had laughed, though, when Nanami made a face and said it was "yucky" to have a bug inside her. She threw the thing across the room. Nobuyuki had been forced to reassure her that it was good and dead, and would never get inside her. He had tossed the bug out the window.

"Is he a bad man?" Nanami whispered now. Haruko looked up at the screen to see a picture of Aoyagi from his days as a delivery driver. Unsure how to answer, she reached for her mug on the table.

"I don't think so," she murmured.

"He's not?"

"No, he's just a regular man. I bet you'd like him." She stopped herself from adding "as much as your mother did."

They showed a close-up of Aoyagi, with a somber voiceover. "At the time, he was a fresh-faced hero, but looking at this picture now, it seems clear that something darker was lurking beneath the surface." The shot showed him looking back over his shoulder, and there was, in fact, something a bit sinister about his expression seen at such close range.

"Bad man!" Nanami shouted, accustomed as she was to reacting to TV cues.

In spite of herself, Haruko was impressed at how effectively they had made Aoyagi into a villain, though their image had nothing to do with the character of the man she'd known. If an insistent photographer had yelled his name from behind until he turned around, the shot might well have looked like this. But it took a certain devious skill to extract the expression from its context and emphasize the negative side of it.

As she stared at the picture, it seemed to blur, and that horrid fish from the game long ago swam across the screen. "Don't settle for too little," it said, giving her a nasty look. Was it possible that Aoyagi had taken the advice to heart and decided he had to do something big? A moment later, she was watching the owner of a *tonkatsu* restaurant being interviewed, and—perhaps it was just her imagination—something about his face reminded her of the fish as well.

The man reported that Masaharu Aoyagi had been in his restaurant when the prime minister's parade was getting started. "It was before noon, so the place was still empty. He sat right in that chair, eating lunch and watching TV." He bristled when one of the reporters asked whether he was absolutely sure it was Aoyagi. "You don't believe me? Of course it was. We give free seconds on rice, and twice he called me over to ask for more. Didn't leave a single grain in his bowl. Pretty weird, don't you think? Who has an appetite like that before he goes out and kills somebody?"

Haruko was so absorbed in the TV that she didn't hear Nanami at first.

"Mommy? Mommy, what's the matter?"

"Nothing's the matter, honey." Didn't leave a single grain in his bowl? Aoyagi?

She wanted to scream at the TV that he didn't eat like that, not even after she'd teased him endlessly. Or maybe he'd changed after they split up. After all, when they were together, she would never have imagined he could turn into someone who managed to rescue that actress. So maybe he'd also turned into someone who didn't eat like a slob. It wasn't out of the question.

For some reason, Nanami was no longer in the room. She called her name and ran out into the corridor. When she reached the front door, she was crouching there putting on her shoes.

"Mommy won't take me out, so I'm going myself."

"Okay, okay," Haruko said, slipping into her own shoes. "Wait a minute and we'll go together."

Three other mothers had brought their children to the park near their building. While the kids swarmed over the swings and slides, the women talked about the assassination. Haruko knew the names of the children but not the mothers. She doubted they knew hers, either.

One of them said how frightened she was. "But it doesn't even seem real," said another. "And the man who did it is probably right here in Sendai. We were living in Niigata until last year, but we knew all about the deliveryman. He was on TV a lot."

"Well, you can imagine what it was like here, in his hometown," said another woman. "Everybody was talking about him, at least for a while. I actually saw him once," she added. Her child was clinging to her leg like a koala in a eucalyptus tree.

"Mrs. Higuchi, you've been here in Sendai all along, haven't you?" said another woman with two koalas of her own.

"Yes," she admitted. "But, you know, that man seems pretty normal to me, pretty much like anybody else, except that he rescued that woman." The words slipped out before she knew she'd said them. But to her relief, the other mothers seemed to agree—reminding each other that he was just a deliveryman, and a particularly good-looking one at that.

Nanami, who had been hanging about following the conversation, suddenly spoke up. "I like him, too," she said. "He's pretty." The women burst out laughing.

"Still," one of them said, now frowning, "you can't tell a book by its cover."

"You're right. And it's bad enough if he did this thing at the parade, but they're saying on TV that he was also caught groping a woman on the train. I draw the line there," she said. Startled, Haruko turned to stare at the woman.

"It was apparently a while back, but someone saw him running away after it," said another woman.

"Why would a handsome guy like that go after women on the train?"

"They say it's a sickness, that they can't stop themselves. It doesn't matter what they look like, or how they do with women otherwise. I guess they need the danger to get their kicks."

"I guess," Haruko mumurmed.

"I hope they catch him soon," someone else put in. "But you know, there's a weird guy who's been hanging around here, too," she added.

"I heard he tried to talk to Ken on the playground."

"I wonder if that could be this Aoyagi? . . ."

They seemed to have decided that Aoyagi was responsible for every crime that had been committed recently in the whole country, and that his capture and imprisonment would usher in a new era of peace and security. It might have been funny if it weren't so frightening. What if she told them now that she had once dated this Aoyagi? She was sure they would turn on her instantly, and that she and her family would be driven out of the neighborhood. Hiding her feelings as best she could, she lingered a few minutes while Nanami pulled up the grass at her feet.

Unexpectedly, one of the mothers turned to Haruko and commented that she must be about the same age as the suspect. It may have been nothing more than an idle observation, but it struck her as odd. Unsure how to answer, she hesitated, and then muttered something vaguely, as if she hadn't quite understood. Anyway, at that moment Nanami tugged at her sleeve.

"Mommy, I have to go potty," she said.

Haruko said a hurried goodbye and left the park as quickly as she could.

"Can you make it home?" she asked as they came to an intersection.

"Don't worry, Mommy," her daughter said. "I don't have to go."

"But you just said—"

"I knew you didn't like talking to those ladies," Nanami said, twirling a branch she had picked up somewhere.

"You mean you were rescuing me?" Haruko laughed. Nanami had a habit of using this ploy to escape uncomfortable situations herself, but her mother now had a new appreciation for her little trick. "You clever girl," she said.

"Did I help?" she asked.

"You certainly did."

"Good!" Nanami shouted. "Then I'll help next time, too."

"Okay," said Haruko. "We'll have a signal. When I scratch my nose, you say you need to go potty."

As they were walking home, Haruko found herself thinking again about the charge that Aoyagi had been caught molesting a woman on a train. Could he really be such a monster? She said the last word aloud without quite realizing what she was doing.

"Monster? Where?" said Nanami, looking around frantically and sticking her arms out in the pose of the hero from one of her TV shows.

Haruko remembered how much Aoyagi's father had hated these people, how he had caught a few of them on the train and then beaten them up. She had been rather curious about him, but when they actually met—the one and only time—he proved to be a short, well-built man, the judo teacher type, who impressed her as serious and stable rather than some sort of lunatic.

They had been on their way to Disney Resort and had stopped in at Aoyagi's parents' house. He had said he just wanted to introduce her and they'd be on their way, but they had insisted on making them dinner. To their credit, they didn't seem to assume they were engaged, but his father had stopped at one point to say how glad he was to see them together. "My son may seem a bit thick at times," he said, "but his heart's in the right place."

"You really think so?" Aoyagi's mother laughed, smiling at her husband.

"Well, at least he's not the type to ever bother a woman on the train," said his father. "He might be capable of killing someone, but never of molesting them."

Haruko looked startled. "Really? That doesn't sound too reassuring somehow."

"Don't get me wrong," he added quickly. "I'm not condoning murder. But there are times when killing somebody is unavoidable—self-defense, for instance, or if you were protecting your family. It's a 'never say never' kind of thing."

"Is it?" Haruko murmured, suppressing a giggle.

"Which is why I say that there's a remote possibility that Masaharu might kill someone—there's no way of knowing until he's confronted with the situation. But no extenuating circumstances, nothing would ever make it okay to attack a woman like that. No one could ever tell you he felt up a woman on a train to protect his children. That's what I'm trying to say."

"Well, thanks for that, Dad," Aoyagi said. Sometimes he found it hard to believe that he was related to this man. "But you're right about one thing," he added. "I'd never be able to bother a woman on the train—not after seeing how you beat the crap out of those guys."

"You don't mean 'not able to,' dear," his mother started to correct him.

"Yes he does," his father broke in. "He'd never be able. He's not strong enough."

Haruko and her daughter walked along holding hands. "Could he really have?" Haruko murmured, lost in her thoughts.

"Could he really have?" Nanami echoed. As she smiled at the girl, Haruko wondered how Aoyagi's father was taking the news that was all over the TV. Not only were they blaming the assassination on their son, they were accusing him of having molested women in the months leading up to it. She found herself worrying about his parents, realizing their house must already be surrounded by reporters and cameras. "Are you all right, Mommy?" Nanami said, pulling on her sleeve.

Haruko took her cell phone from her bag and scrolled through the address book to Morita's number. She pressed "send." After a few rings, a young woman answered. Haruko explained that she'd been trying to call Morita.

"Nobody here by that name," the woman said and hung up.

It was the number he'd given her last year when they'd run into each other at a department store by the station. She had never called him, nor he her, and she realized the number might have been wrong from the start. Next she tried calling Kazuo Ono, their old friend Kazu. They, too, had exchanged numbers the last time they met. Now she dialed without allowing herself time to reconsider.

The phone rang over and over, and she had the sinking feeling that both Morita and Kazu had gone somewhere beyond her reach. Though they'd been out of touch, she had always felt she could contact them if she wanted, but now that she was trying, they were nowhere to be found.

"Hello," said a voice at last, but instead of relief, Haruko felt a flash of disappointment. It was a woman's voice.

"Excuse me," she muttered, unsure what to say. She thought she should apologize and hang up.

"Hello?" said the voice again. "Is that Ms. Higuchi?"

"Yes?" Haruko blurted out, startled to be called by her name. Nanami looked up.

"This is Kazuo Ono's phone. Your name came up on the incoming-call screen. He's mentioned you—you were friends in college, weren't you?"

"Yes, that's right!" Haruko said. She felt as though this woman was her last hope of a connection with the outside world.

"I'm Kazuo's girlfriend. He can't talk right now." The woman's voice had grown quieter.

"I see," said Haruko. "Can I ask why?"

"He's in the hospital, and he's unconscious."

"The hospital? Is he sick?"

"He got hurt last night."

"Hurt?"

"Hurt?" said a little echo. Nanami was squatting at her feet, playing with a pile of twigs.

"I found him at his apartment. It looked like somebody had beaten him up. He was covered with cuts and bruises."

"I don't understand," Haruko said, her voice rising. "Who beat him up? Was he robbed?" Somehow, she was sure he hadn't been, even as she asked the question.

"You know Mr. Aoyagi, don't you?" the voice on the other end of the line asked.

"Aoyagi? Yes, why?"

"Well, I think he rescued Kazuo. At least, that's what Kazuo told me when we were riding here in the ambulance."

"He saved Kazu? But he's in a lot of trouble himself," Haruko said.

"That's what I thought. I don't know what's going on."

As she stood with the phone to her ear, Haruko recalled more of her visit to Aoyagi's parents, as though suddenly drawn back to that day long ago.

"One year in elementary school they told us to write an essay about our winter vacation," Aoyagi said. He sat frowning next to his father. "Everybody else wrote about what they did on New Year's Day, but I wrote a little masterpiece called 'Perverts Must Die,' a title and topic supplied to me by my dear old dad." Haruko bent double with laughter, but Aoyagi's father seemed unfazed.

"You were pretty proud of it at the time," he said.

"I was a kid. I didn't know any better. At any rate, thanks to my careful education, I've got a phobia about train mashers—though not for the same reason women have."

"You do, don't you?" said his mother in her mild way. She had apparently not been following the conversation. "You always had trouble remembering how to write 'pervert.'"

Masaharu Aoyagi

Once he had cleared the window above the toilet and picked up his backpack, Aoyagi made his way around the building and out to the sidewalk. It was dark now and the restaurant through the window looked like a scene on a well-lit stage. He could see the men moving among the tables. The short man who seemed to be the leader stood talking with a waitress and the manager. Then he showed them something—a notebook or a photograph perhaps—and the waitress was gesticulating.

Aoyagi slung his pack over his shoulder and pulled out his cell phone to check that the power was off. Was that how they'd found him? He started walking, but just as he did so there was a deafening crash behind him. Spinning around, he could see that the plate glass window at the front of the restaurant had shattered and the customers stood wide-eyed at their tables, as though frozen in the act of getting up to leave.

The man with earphones was crouching in the pool of glass, brandishing the gun—and for some reason Aoyagi found the scene almost funny, it was so incongruous: an all-night restaurant, broken glass, a gun . . . all in Japan?

It was as though reality itself had shattered with the glass. Someone started screaming in the restaurant.

He took a step, but his knees buckled under him and he crumpled to the pavement. Almost at once, he was scrambling to his feet again, urging himself along. But only his head seemed to be racing; his feet refused to obey and he stumbled awkwardly down the sidewalk. Trucks were whizzing past him. On the side of one of them, in a flash of headlights, he recognized a whale, the trademark of one of the rival delivery companies. The prime minister had been killed, but the trucks were still running. He felt a pang of sympathy for the drivers who'd be coping with traffic jams and roadblocks all over the city.

He remembered how the drivers used to say that the country couldn't function without them. Everyone was talking about the Internet, but the Internet moved information, not real things. For that, you needed trucks and drivers. And if that was the case, shouldn't they be treated a little better? They certainly thought so themselves, if almost no one else did. Two years earlier, though, when the TV had been making such a fuss over his encounter with the burglar, some guy on one of the shows had reminded the viewers, who tended to see truck drivers as road-hogging bastards, that they were, in fact, the backbone of the country's commerce. There'd been a lot of jokes among his fellow drivers about how he had single-handedly raised their social status, but in actual fact they were genuinely pleased and grateful. Would those same drivers be furious with him now for sending their social capital plunging?

He turned into a bigger street and slowed his pace. The sidewalk was nearly deserted and the streetlights seemed to glare down at him; it would be too conspicuous to keep running.

He thought of Kazu—someone else to worry about. Would he show up at that restaurant once he'd patched things up with his girlfriend? And if he did, would he run into those men? Their conversation on the phone a bit earlier ran through his head. There had been something strange about his voice, something troubled. Aoyagi stopped short. He pulled out his phone and stared at it again. Could it be? Could Kazu have tipped them off and not the signal itself? He looked up and glanced around. A young couple passed by, and from the opposite direction he saw three rowdy kids in school

uniforms with their hair lacquered in strange shapes. As Aoyagi stood looking at them, the boy nearest him turned and met his gaze. He felt exposed, as
if the lights in Sendai had gone out, leaving him alone illuminated, like the
star of some horror movie.

What had Morita said?—"Your enemies now may be the people who look
least like the bad guys"—just a few hours ago, sitting in his car, with the sad-
dest look on his face Aoyagi had ever seen. "If I go with you, they'll take it
out on my wife and my kid."

The signal at the crosswalk turned green, and Aoyagi hurried to the other
side.

He had been there just once before, several years earlier when his TV was on
the blink and he'd wanted to see Japan play in a World Cup match. It had
seemed like a long shot, but he'd headed off in the direction of Sendai Station one evening. He had heard about something called an "Internet café,"
and he remembered the other drivers saying they sometimes watched TV online, but he had no idea how to do it and had gone in with low expectations.
In the end, though, he'd liked it a lot better than he imagined.

The place was down a flight of steps from the street. A door slid open, and
there was a line of booths, each equipped with a computer screen. He remembered his friends had said the place had few rules, that there was no need to
become a member or even show any ID. Nor had they installed security cameras the way so many other places had. He sat down in a booth, logged on,
and began scanning news sites. He was afraid that his name would be everywhere, with a hi-tech "Wanted" poster of his face prominently displayed. But
there was no mention of him at all. Nothing. To his surprise, he felt a twinge
of disappointment, but mainly a huge sense of relief.

Morita had said they would turn him into Oswald, but at least as far as the
news was concerned, it hadn't happened yet. Maybe he'd blown the whole
thing out of proportion. Someone had killed the prime minister, but no one
was saying that it was Masaharu Aoyagi. Still, the minute he allowed himself
to relax, he was confronted with all the things he's seen and heard in the last
few hours: Morita's shattered look, Kazu's guilty-sounding voice, the faces
of the men chasing him, the dart in his hand, the shopkeeper's blood, the
policeman's gun, the window exploding.

He felt the side of his face; the bleeding from the cut had just about stopped. But nothing had been blown out of proportion—he knew that now. There was no denying that they were after him. The accusations weren't being made public yet, that was all. But they would be at some point, and when they were, the shit would hit the fan, and he wouldn't be the only one to get dirty. It would affect everyone he knew. He was sure of it—and the knowledge made him feel sick.

He wasn't very good with a computer. In college, he had written papers on one and searched for cheap drinking spots, but after graduation he didn't have much need for it. Then, when he'd become a media darling for a brief period, the Internet had been flooded with anonymous and largely inaccurate information about him, and in the end he'd decided that the whole trumped-up thing was annoying and more than a little scary.

Opening a search engine, he tried typing in the name of his old company. The homepage that popped up was a good deal more elaborate than the one he remembered, and even the cartoon beagle on the logo seemed somehow cuter. He felt the tension in his face relax a bit. He remembered there was a rumor that the dog was based on a drawing by the owner's son.

Moving the cursor to the address line, he added a few characters and hit "return." If he remembered correctly, that should take him to the employees' system page. A log-in box appeared, asking for his employee ID and password. His should have been erased as soon as he quit, but he tried typing them anyway, on the off chance that someone had neglected to update the system. No such luck: the log-in failed. Searching his memory, he came up with another ID and entered it in the box. Then he typed "ILOVECATS" for the password. Praying that these hadn't been changed, he gingerly clicked the mouse.

One of the managers at the company had been a notorious cat-lover. His neckties invariably featured cats, and his desk was strewn with photographs and figurines of cats. This feline affair had apparently been caused by a bitter divorce that convinced him that only his cat truly understood him and could be trusted. He took great pride in announcing that his password for the site was "ILOVECATS," though they had tried to explain that there was no point in having a password if you told everyone.

As Aoyagi stared at the screen, the log-in box vanished and the employees' page began to load. "I'm in!" he blurted out, then glanced around nervously. The guy in the next booth was busy with his own virtual life.

He knew where he wanted to go: the drivers' log. When the page came up, he moved the cursor down the list to a name, clicked again, and then checked the route and schedule.

Logging out of the employees' portion of the site, he returned to the homepage and clicked on a button labeled "Package Pickup." When the form appeared, he filled in the blanks. After so many years of making pickups, it was the first time he had ever requested one. He made up a name for the "requester's" box, and then chose the address of a building on the route of the driver he had just checked, a building northeast of the station that he'd visited many times himself when he was still working for the company—and one that wasn't too far from the Internet café.

There was another café—this one devoted to coffee—on the third floor of the building. Aoyagi managed to remember its name and typed it into the form. The owner must have run the business as a hobby, since he was only there a few days a week; the rest of the time, the café was shuttered.

More blanks to fill in. What did he need picked up? Three large boxes. But then his hand paused. Next to the "Date and Time" box was a warning that pickups had to be scheduled at least a day in advance, and that no same-day service was available. In point of fact, Aoyagi wanted the pickup in an hour, but that was probably out of the question. He remembered that customers had sometimes phoned to ask for express service, but he couldn't risk calling attention to himself. He glanced at the time on the control bar of the computer. It was past six o'clock now; he would have to settle for the next morning. Fifteen hours to go, he thought, sitting back in his chair. Where would he be and what would he be doing fifteen hours from now? He found it hard to imagine. Still, this was better than doing nothing. He hit the button to schedule the pickup.

When the request finished uploading, he pressed the power button and turned off the computer. The coffee he'd brought to the booth was cold. He downed it and then went to the counter to pay. A moment later he was back on the street.

He walked north, choosing a direction at random. It seemed best to head away from the station. He tensed up whenever he passed people on the sidewalk, and soon realized he might have been better off staying in the dark computer booth.

After wandering aimlessly for some time, he was stopped at a crosswalk waiting for the signal to change when he caught sight of a pay phone. It looked oddly out of place at the end of a line of vending machines by the door of an optician's shop, orphaned in only a few years by the cell phone craze. As he was waiting there, it occurred to him that he might have messages on his answering service. He knew now that it was too dangerous to use his phone, but it should be safe enough to check his messages from a public landline.

Taking some coins out of his pocket, he fed them into the phone. Then he found his address book, checked the number of the message service, and dialed. When the call connected, he punched in his password and a friendly, robotic voice told him he had one new message. He pressed the receiver tighter to his ear to shut out the noise of the traffic behind him and punched the number to retrieve the message.

"It's me, Kazu. Are you okay? I know you said the battery was dying on your phone, but I'm worried." He sounded hesitant, like a kid unable to make himself clear. "If you get this message, *when* you get this, please get out of that restaurant. I'm going myself now. . . . You know, I don't believe you did it. You could never have done something like that. But the police showed up here and I was scared." Aoyagi's hand closed tighter around the receiver. "They called me before you got in touch the first time. I'm really spooked, so if you get this, get out of there right away." Scowling at the phone, Aoyagi took a few long breaths. The warning had come late. He had taken this advice long ago.

The voice trailed off and Aoyagi thought the message had ended, but then Kazu spoke up again, sounding even more tense. "*What? What are you doing here?*" Aoyagi could hear anger in his voice, and fear. "*How did you get in? What do you want?*"

The message ended abruptly, and the bright, metallic voice came on to announce the date and time it had been recorded. Just fifteen minutes ago. How could he find out what had happened? Someone had forced his way into the apartment. He thought he could guess who.

Cars rushed by, and the noise seemed so threatening that he crouched down as if to protect himself. Something rattled in his backpack—the energy bars were probably broken in pieces by now, but he had a feeling something much more important might be broken soon.

Masaharu Aoyagi

He decided to call Kazu's cell phone. There was some danger they could find him, even calling from a pay phone, but the fear in the voice on the message reverberated in his head like the echo of a *taiko* drum.

To retrieve the number, he had to turn on his own phone, and as he pressed the button he had the feeling that the invisible radio waves were broadcasting his location throughout the city, that everyone in Sendai now knew where he was and was coming to get him. His heart pounding in his chest, he checked the call record, found the number, and punched it into the pay phone.

"Hello," said Kazu's voice.

"Kazu?" he blurted out, almost yelling into the phone.

"Aoyagi?"

"Are you okay?" There was a rustling noise and then another voice came on.

"Masaharu Aoyagi?" The tone was harsh.

"Who is this?"

"Security Bureau, General Intelligence, Central Police Force," the voice said, quick and low. It occurred to Aoyagi that this was a job, not a name, but the man on the phone apparently had no intention of identifying himself further. "We know you did this. You can't get away, so you'd better think about your options. It'll go easier if you give yourself up."

"But I didn't do it. I'm innocent." In his wildest imagination, he had never thought he'd be saying these words.

"That's what they all say," said the voice. His line, too, was like something out of a bad movie.

Aoyagi shook the receiver in his hand, wanting to yell at it: "I didn't do it! Why can't you understand that?" Then he saw it out of the corner of his eye. At the edge of the sidewalk, in a clump of azaleas: a Security Pod. Tiny red and white lights were flashing on the dome. Was it watching him? He turned his back.

"Aoyagi! Get out of there!" He could hear Kazu suddenly yelling in the background. Then a groan.

"Hey! What's going on?" he shouted into the phone.

"What do you think?" The voice was calm and even.

"You can't hurt him!" They were police. They were supposed to serve and protect.

"And why would we do that?" said the voice. Then Kazu screamed, and the pain in his voice was like nothing Aoyagi had ever heard.

"Kazu!" he called into the phone.

"You've done a terrible thing," said the voice. "You've assassinated the prime minister and created a national crisis. Thanks to you, we're in a state of emergency, and in a state of emergency bad things can happen to people. It's unavoidable. Do you know why?"

"No, I don't know anything anymore," he stammered.

"Because we have to keep a bad situation from getting worse."

"You're out of your mind."

"I can assure you I'm not," said the man, bristling for the first time. "Just look at what America did after 9/11. How many innocent people do you think got hurt when they went after the men who planned the attack?"

"We're not America," he barked at him.

"You're right. I'm glad to say we're not. But that doesn't change the fact that you've committed a crime."

"But what does this have to do with Kazu? If you want me, come and get me. But leave him alone."

"If you're worried about your friend, there's a simple way to assure his safety. All you have to do is turn yourself in at the nearest police station—or come find us here at this apartment. As soon as we have you in custody, Mr. Ono can resume his normal activities."

"You won't get anything by hurting him."

"On the contrary, I'm counting on getting you."

A low tone sounded and Aoyagi realized he was almost out of time on the call. He was about to feed another coin into the phone, when it occurred to him they might have already traced the call. "I didn't do it!" he said once more into the phone, louder than before.

"Would you say so if you had? Only the guilty deny their crimes." The voice was as calm as ever, the tone categorical, almost patronizing. Aoyagi could feel himself getting furious.

"Okay, then I did do it," he said, switching tactics. There was a pause at the other end. "If I confess, does that mean I didn't do it?"

"I don't think you've fully grasped the situation."

"What happened to Morita?" he wanted to know, trying to find a way past the icy tone.

"Morita?" said the voice, hesitating for a moment. "Oh, you mean your other friend? The one you killed?"

"Killed? What are you talking about?"

"You planted a bomb in his car, didn't you?"

For a moment, Aoyagi was too shocked to speak. He could still hear the blast that had gone off just as he'd jumped into the taxi that afternoon. His mind went blank. His friend's name floated slowly up to fill the void.

"So what happens now? . . . ," the voice started to say, and the call ended. Aoyagi stood holding the receiver.

Masaharu Aoyagi

It would be asking for trouble to go back to Kazu's place. That much was obvious. Even a child could figure it out. Like a deer wearing a bull's-eye on its back wandering into a lodge full of hunters. Or maybe a pigeon. He remembered Morita when they were in college telling him about a bird called the passenger pigeon, which once roamed over North America in flocks of two billion or more, but was now extinct due to overhunting. Hunters in those days would catch one of these birds, blind it, then release it and let it flap around. The rest of the flock would see the frantic creature, assume it was feeding, and come to join it—at which point they became a flock of sitting ducks. Morita had seemed to enjoy the grimmer details.

And now, years later, he felt he had become one of these pigeons himself. With Kazu the bait. If he went to see what had happened to his injured friend, they would have him in their sights. He had one dubious advantage over the passenger pigeon: he knew it was a trap, but was still dumb enough to be walking into it.

"So this is really stupid," he muttered to himself. Yet his feet set off in the direction of Kazu's apartment, and the further he went the quicker he walked. I'm going to get my friend back, he told himself.

As he got close to Kazu's place, however, he thought of his parents: his father, laying into the molester on the station platform, his mother standing over them looking horrified. He stopped. "You can't just react. You need to take a step back, do things deliberately." He'd heard someone say something like that once. Who? Then he realized he'd said it himself—though he no longer knew when or where or to whom. Probably to Haruko, he guessed. At any rate, the thought of his impetuous father brought him up short now.

What were his chances of doing any good at all if he simply barged into the place? He didn't know how many men were there, but if they'd come to arrest him, they probably had brought reinforcements. He spun on his heels, heading back the way he'd come, and took out his cell phone as he went.

The area around the station was quieter than usual, and the discount electronics store was nearly empty. The recorded sales pitches and music playing inside seemed louder than ever with no one to hear them. But he found the empty, brightly lit space somehow reassuring, as if the strange and disturbing things that had happened since he'd met Morita that afternoon were all illusions, and these air conditioners and tumbling dryers and vacuum cleaners—and the normal life they promised—were the true reality. He wanted to think so.

But his eyes wandered to the line of wide-screen TVs in the entertainment section, and a dozen pictures of Kaneda's parade pulled him back to his own reality. It was the same footage he'd seen at Inai's apartment, the same car, the same crowds, the same unthinkable explosion over and over.

One TV at the end of the line was tuned to a different channel, and the volume had been turned up. "It's a 90," a white-haired man was saying, while a row of heads nodded in the background. At times like this, the networks assembled a panel of experts. This particular group was all men, though their ages and outfits were unusually varied. Aoyagi wondered what they could have in common, but as he watched, it soon became clear. The "90" in question was the size of an engine, and the men were all hobbyists who flew remote-controlled helicopters. He had a feeling he'd seen the white-haired man somewhere.

"It's an Ooka Air Hover," he could hear one of the others saying, and his fists clenched as he realized it was the same model he had at home. It was no coincidence that his helicopter was the same as the one used in the assassination; everything had been carefully planned. Including Koume Inohara? He froze there in front of the televisions. It was Koume who had urged him to buy the model, to get involved with the hobby in the first place. Could he trust her?

A shop assistant approached, perhaps finding it odd that anybody should linger so long in front of the TVs, or maybe just hoping for a sale. "Can I help you?" he said. But, realizing he couldn't very well ask him about Koume, Aoyagi mumbled an awkward answer and moved on.

He picked up a digital voice recorder and headed for the register. Pulling out his wallet, he was about to hand the clerk a credit card when it occurred to him that they might be tracking his purchases. This kind of paranoia would have seemed ridiculous to him yesterday, but the gunshot at the restaurant and the fear in Kazu's voice forced him to admit that nothing was impossible—that he should expect anything. Just before he handed over some cash, though, he had one more change of heart and used the card. It might be useful to reveal his location at this point.

Pocketing the recorder, he made his way to the video-game section at the back of the store, where he bought a hand-held "Fudebako-dai" game unit. When they first came out, these had been so popular it had been almost impossible to find one; but now that the fad had passed, they seemed to have them in stock.

"You don't need the software?" asked the clerk when he had asked for just the tiny player.

"No. I heard it's like a normal TV without the software."

"That's right!" beamed the clerk. "Works like a charm." He seemed so proud of the little gadget you would have thought he had invented it himself. "Wonderful reception. Crystal clear picture indoors, on the road, anywhere at all."

Leaving the store, Aoyagi went into the station and stopped in front of a trash bin, where he extracted the recorder and the game unit from their packaging. He installed the batteries, stowed the instruction manuals in his pack, and got rid of the wrappers.

He made a quick test message on the recorder, erased everything and, after checking to be sure no one was near, spoke into the microphone. It was a little embarrassing talking to a machine with so much emotion in his voice, but he willed himself into the part. "I'm getting out of Sendai now," he said as emphatically as he could. As he pressed the stop button, he glanced over at the clock in a game arcade. Please still be there, he thought, and humming the tune to the Beatles' "Help!" he set off again.

Masaharu Aoyagi

When Kazu's building came in sight, Aoyagi hesitated. He gritted his teeth, as if winding up gears in his belly, and forced himself to go on—then noticed that the tune had changed at some point: he was humming "Golden Slumbers" now. *"Golden slumbers fill your eyes. Smiles awake you when you rise. . . . Once there was a way to get back home."* Paul had been trying to reunite a band that had come apart, trying to imagine a road that led back home. But in the end, there was no way to get back, to be together again, and he had been left to stitch together a medley from the random songs on the second side of the album.

Aoyagi had first heard that story sitting in a hamburger joint, so it was almost certainly Kazu or Morita who had told it. He had pictured Paul, hunched over a tape recorder in a tiny room, desperately mixing the eight songs to make a whole. He felt now that he could understand the feelings behind it. And even if the attempt was futile, he too was going to try to find a way back to that time and those friends, or at least to help one of them who was in trouble now.

The short walkway that led from the street to the door of Kazu's building was lined with hedges. Beyond them, in the half-light, he could see a small area set aside as a playground. Avoiding the path, he hid just inside the concrete wall that surrounded the grounds of the building. He leaned against the wall, checked his watch, and then went over the conversation he'd had just a few minutes earlier with the man in the Panthers sweat shirt outside the game arcade—the same one who had sold him the magazine earlier in the day.

"You want me to use this to call your friend?" he'd said, holding the phone and confirming Aoyagi's instructions.

"All you have to do is hit 'redial.'" That would be the number for Kazu's cell phone.

"And I don't have to say anything?"

"You just play this message and make sure they hear it." Aoyagi held the recorder up to the phone and demonstrated how to work it. The man scratched his beard.

"I'm pretty old for all these gadgets," he said. "I'm an analog man." He muttered to himself as he tested the buttons, but Aoyagi found his bashful smile reassuring—like a curious child with a new toy. It was impossible to tell how old he was.

"Just play back the message," he said. "And I'm sorry to ask you to do this while you're working." The man smiled for a moment, revealing a row of yellowed teeth.

"Happy . . . to . . . help," he said slowly—in English. His pronunciation was perfect.

The plan was simple. If they were tracking his whereabouts through his cell phone and the Security Pods, he would turn their snooping to his advantage. When the magazine man played his voice from the recorder, the people in the apartment should turn their attention to Sendai Station—giving him a chance to get in to help Kazu. He had asked the guy to call Kazu's number at seven o'clock. He could only hope he'd remember—and figure out how to work the recorder and phone.

Pushing himself up on the wall, he tried to figure out which window was Kazu's—far right on the second floor, he decided, furthest from the elevator but right next to the fire escape. Then he heard footsteps and a voice and crouched down again with his back against the wall.

"The east entrance," a man was saying. He had just come out of the building and was talking to someone on his cell phone. "He called. That's right, definitely Aoyagi's number, and his voice. I'm on my way and I want you to meet me there. He said he was leaving town on the bus, I think, but I don't know if we can trust him."

Feeling like a latter-day ninja, Aoyagi crouched in the bushes and considered his options. The man with the phone, still absorbed in his conversation, passed by and crossed the street. Aoyagi could see he was headed for his car, a large sedan with odd stripes down the side. As he opened the door on the driver's side, he was visible under the streetlight for a moment: frizzy hair, lanky frame, age hard to tell. The car rumbled to life like a waking animal.

Then another figure appeared out of the dark, almost next to him, and Aoyagi's back pressed hard into the wall. It was him. The powerfully built man from the restaurant with the earphones and the gun. There couldn't be two like him in Sendai, maybe in all of Japan. He, too, passed by and headed across the street. A second door slammed and the car pulled away.

His plan was working. The recording of his voice must have gone out from the station on schedule. "Kazu, I'm not coming back there," he had said into the microphone. "I'm taking the bus, so don't wait for me." They must have traced the call and were headed for the east entrance.

He didn't know how many men had been at Kazu's apartment, but there were at least two fewer now—and one of them had taken his gun with him. If he was lucky, they might all be gone.

"Get going," a voice inside him said—his own but perhaps Morita's as well. "Get going!" Leaving the cover of the wall, he crept through the bushes toward the fire escape.

Masaharu Aoyagi

The fire escape took him to the passage on the second floor; Kazu's door was the first on the left. A fire extinguisher caught his eye and he pulled it off the wall. Kazu had told him about an old girlfriend trashing his apartment with one of these—so it seemed an appropriate item to bring to this party.

He tightened the straps on his pack and shifted the fire extinguisher to his left hand, leaving his right free to grip the nozzle on the hose. Then he pulled the pin that released the mechanism and closed his hand over the lever. As he stood outside the door, about to press the button on the intercom with his thumb, he remembered how they had teased him, saying most people used their index fingers for pressing buttons. His hand stopped, and he reached down to try the doorknob instead. There was a chance the two men who had gone out to the car had left it unlocked.

The knob turned, and the door opened with a gentle tug. Easy enough. But should he sneak in or come in with foam blazing, so to speak? After pausing for a moment, he decided on the latter. If you were outflanking your enemy and attacking from the rear—especially when you didn't have much to attack with—then you should at least make a good show of it. Besides, as keyed up as he was, he didn't trust himself to manage the stealth option.

Yanking open the door, he ran through the hall banging the fire extinguisher against the walls and burst into the living room. Kazu was to his left, face up on the couch. He was pale and his eyes were closed. As he called his friend's name, Aoyagi sensed someone coming at him from the right. Without thinking, he swung the fire extinguisher and let go—catching the man in the face and knocking him flat on his back. He lay on the carpet like a stunned frog, arms and legs in the air.

Aoyagi went first to check on Kazu. "Hey!" he shouted, bringing his face close and patting his cheek. He held his hand close to his nose to make sure he was breathing, and then yelled at him again. "Kazu! Wake up! This is no time for a nap!"

Kazu's eyes fluttered opened and he murmured Aoyagi's name, but then drifted off again. Aoyagi could feel his face growing warm and his eyes welling. There was anger and sadness in his tears, but most of all he was crying because he couldn't understand how all this had happened. How had Morita and Kazu got caught up with him in something so terrifying?

The man on the floor began to stir. Aoyagi turned and watched him for a moment. If he tried to get up, he would be forced to deal with him . . . but the only thing he knew how to do was Morita's judo trick. So he fished the rope out of his backpack and bound his hands as tightly as he could. As he worked, the man opened his eyes and gave him a dazed look. Aoyagi was glad he hadn't been the one on the receiving end of that fire extinguisher.

He moved back to the couch to check on Kazu again. Then, thinking it would be better to have someone else call the hospital, he went to look for a neighbor. He pressed the buzzer on the intercom next door, but as he stood waiting, he began to worry that someone could be watching him on the monitor. Moving out of range of the camera, he waited a moment more. No answer. He could hear music coming from inside, but whoever it was refused to come to the door. How could people be so callous?

He knocked, lightly at first, then harder and louder. "Open up!" he yelled. "Please open the door!" As his voice died away, he sensed someone behind him.

"Hey, Aoyagi," said a voice. "The deliveryman shouldn't make such a fuss." There was a click, like a round dropping into the chamber, and when he turned he was staring into the muzzle of a gun.

Masaharu Aoyagi

The car they put him in had stripes down the side—almost certainly the same one he had watched pull away earlier. It was roomy inside, with thick carpeting on the floor. The man with the earphones was driving; Aoyagi had been thrown in the back. They had not handcuffed or tied him, but another officer had climbed in next to him. This one identified himself as Ichitaro Sasaki. With his soft face and stylish haircut, he might have been taken for the spoiled son of a rich family; but his manner was tough and down-to-earth. Sasaki had taken the knit cap off Aoyagi's head and stuffed it in his backpack, which he put on the seat beside him.

"Where are you taking me?" Aoyagi asked.

Sasaki ignored the question. "You almost had us," he said. "We thought you were at the station. We traced the call and knew right away that it was coming from the rotary at the east entrance. That's where we were headed," he said, waving his hand to include the man in the driver's seat. "But we got a call from headquarters on the way. Apparently there's a Security Pod right where you were supposed to be calling from, but you weren't in the picture—just some man with a cell phone and some other gadget who didn't seem to know what he was doing with either of them."

"A digital voice recorder," Aoyagi murmured, feeling the energy drain out of him.

"Of course," said Sasaki.

"Are you watching all of us, all the time?" he asked.

"Like I said on the phone, we're in a state of emergency."

"Those pods were there long before the emergency."

"Do you expect us to wait around for the bombs to fall before we take the necessary precautions?"

Aoyagi realized they might start roughing him up—the way they must have beaten Kazu—but he was almost resigned to it now. After all, this Sasaki seemed to think his "state of emergency" gave him the right to do anything he wanted. Still, he appeared to be calm enough at the moment.

It occurred to him to wonder whether Sasaki was absolutely convinced of his guilt. How could he be so certain that he had killed the prime minister? But his look was cold and objective rather than vindictive, so on the off chance that he was dealing with a rational person, Aoyagi tried again. "I'm being framed," he said. "Can't you see that?" Sasaki looked at him with more intensity. "Can't you see I didn't do this?"

"We went through all this on the phone," Sasaki said. "That's what any guilty man would say. Tomorrow we'll release your name as the prime suspect, along with your picture and all the rest. The press will make a lot of noise—you're not unknown, after all."

"What makes you think that?"

"You were a hero. Rinka's savior."

"I never asked for any of that."

"Whatever you say," Sasaki chuckled.

"What proof do you have that I did this?" Aoyagi demanded.

"Actually, the evidence is pouring in."

"What evidence? From where?"

"Unfortunately for you, from everywhere," Sasaki said, closing his eyes for a moment. He opened them slowly again and looked at him. "The owner of a *tonkatsu* place says you had lunch there before you went to do it; the tape from the security camera at the model shop shows you buying the helicopter; and someone caught you on video flying the thing by the river." He sounded as though he was reading from a list.

"That's strange," said Aoyagi, his voice ragged now. "I didn't have *tonkatsu* today." He tried to remember the name of the place where he'd eaten with Morita. "And it wasn't me who bought the helicopter." It was true he owned one, but Koume Inohara had gone alone to the store to buy it for him; he had merely paid the bill.

"The camera doesn't lie," Sasaki said. His tone was even, almost pleasant. The car made a left turn and Aoyagi felt his weight shift, but Sasaki's back remained straight. "It's definitely you on the tape; no one's going to question that."

"It can't be me. It's a look-alike," he said, though he could hear how silly this sounded as soon as he said it.

"I'm going to give you a chance," Sasaki said. "Or to be more exact, I was told to give you a chance."

"A chance?"

"The chance to confess. I haven't cuffed you yet—you're not officially in custody. We can drop you off at the nearest police box. Things will go much easier for you if you turn yourself in and admit what you've done before we process you and formally charge you."

"Easier? Even though I haven't done anything?"

"When we go public with all this, everyone you know will be pulled in—your family and friends, even your coworkers. The press will hound them. You know something about that. But you can prevent things from getting out of hand by confessing now."

"How would confessing change anything? The reporters will come just the same." Sasaki said nothing. "I'm not going to confess," he continued, "because I didn't do anything." He would repeat this until they believed him.

"Then we'll take you in now." The tone was still flat, but he spoke a little louder. "But if you confess, we'll try to see that things go a little easier for you. This is a terrible thing you've done, but even so there might be extenuating circumstances, something in your background we can emphasize to get a little sympathy out of the media."

"There's nothing in my background and nothing in the foreground—I had nothing to do with this!" Aoyagi's frustration was mounting.

"I mean, we could create the impression that something in your childhood led you to do it."

"Create the impression. . . ." The conversation was getting so weird that Aoyagi was unsure what he was trying to say.

"We can still stir up a little sympathy for you—it's a matter of creating the right image."

"You mean you'll manipulate the facts," said Aoyagi.

"The image," Sasaki corrected. "That's the nature of these things. Images may not be based on much of anything, but they stick to you like nothing else."

As Sasaki talked on, Aoyagi realized that there was something very odd in all this. Why were they driving around talking? Why hadn't they simply taken him to the police station? Why all this effort to get him to confess beforehand? If they were really in a "state of emergency," why didn't they just lock him up and worry about proving their case later? Why did they sound as though they wanted to make a deal?

Slowly it began to dawn on him: Sasaki, or whoever he represented, was anxious to get this whole thing settled as smoothly and quickly as possible. They didn't care one way or the other about the truth. Who did it, or why, or how—none of that interested them. Their only concern was explaining the assassination in a way the man in the street would find believable—maybe even a little entertaining.

If they simply arrested him and dragged him off to jail, they must know he would plead innocent. And even if they had a tape of him at the model shop and a witness who could testify that he ate *tonkatsu*, he knew he hadn't committed the crime. He would deny his guilt in court, and even if they convicted him, there would be some people out there with lingering doubts. They knew they wouldn't be able to convince everybody, especially with trumped-up evidence.

So they would keep pushing until they could say they had a confession to add to all their evidence. They needed to keep distractions and digressions to a minimum, to find a neat plotline to sell—or get the media to sell for them.

As he began to see the larger picture, he felt less indignant than simply overwhelmed and exhausted. If they weren't interested in the truth, was there any way for him to prove his innocence? Even if he could somehow find the real culprit and bring him in, would that change anything? He felt dizzy, and more powerless than ever before in his life.

"Not buying it?" Sasaki asked, apparently realizing Aoyagi had stopped listening.

"Just not sure what you're selling."

"A lifeline for Japan's most notorious criminal."

"If I meet him, I'll pass along the message."

"You, my friend, have wandered into a swamp. The more you struggle, the faster you'll sink, and the more likely you'll be to drag others down with you. But if you stay nice and calm and do exactly what we say, then you just might keep your head above water." There was still no expression whatsoever in his voice.

"Sorry," he told him. "From down here in the swamp, it still feels like drowning to me."

Sasaki was quiet for a moment, but he held Aoyagi's gaze. He was studying him, like a zookeeper observing an animal to better understand its habits and characteristics.

The car came to a stop, and Aoyagi thought they might have arrived at the police station, but when he looked out he realized it was just a red light.

"Shouldn't you have the sirens blaring since you've got Japan's most notorious criminal in the car?" he asked.

"We would if we were in a hurry to get him somewhere."

"You're not?"

"We've got our man," murmured Sasaki. "Now we just have to get him to Tokyo."

"Tokyo?"

"Funny thing about this country—everything important seems to happen in Tokyo."

"Then I guess I'm getting the VIP treatment."

Lights flashed in his head, his vision went cloudy, and his neck snapped back. It took him a moment to realize he'd been punched, but when he could sit up again, Sasaki looked almost as calm as ever. There was no doubt he had hit him, but no evidence he had moved at all. Outside the window, everything else looked normal as well. He forced himself to put up a brave front—let them see any weakness, he thought, and that was it. Trembling inside, he said something about the lousy traffic.

"Just temporary. It'll all be over soon. Once we announce we have the culprit in custody, things will get back to normal."

"Maybe," said Aoyagi. "But that's exactly your problem. The culprit's still on the run, and you're giving him a chance to escape."

"You planning to escape?"

"Not me," he said. "The real killer." Sasaki punched him again. This time he saw it coming and knew what was happening when the pain spread through his cheek and his head spun around. He turned to look out the window, determined to hide his pain and fear, but as he did so, he realized several things at once. They were stopped at a red light. A truck was parked on the shoulder on the opposite side of the road. They were on a side street near Route 4, running east–west through Sendai. The truck, with its cloth canopy, was familiar.

So Maezono's truck had survived their last meeting. He could still feel the jolt in his bones as he had dropped onto the stiff material from the bridge, and the sensation of the boxes crumpling as they broke his fall. He felt a pang of guilt, realizing the driver would be held responsible for the damage. He remembered that Maezono had said he had evening deliveries when they'd talked earlier in the day, and that he had to hurry home for a TV program. It must be starting soon, Aoyagi reflected. Hope he makes it in time.

But maybe Maezono could help him. The thought flashed through his mind as his eyes dropped to the handle on the door next to him. His hands were still free and it was within reach—stranger still, it didn't seem to be locked.

He began frantically working out a plan. Open the door, jump out, dodge traffic, make a dash for the other side, hop in Maezono's truck. He'd be surprised, of course, but Aoyagi was sure he'd help him. Or nearly sure.

But he had to do it now, while they were still stopped at the light. He could see Maezono just climbing back into the driver's seat—there would never be another chance. Voices inside—his own, Morita's, and now Kazu's—were urging him to run again. Keeping his eyes straight ahead, he reached slowly toward the handle with his left hand, then suddenly yanked at it as he pushed the door with his right. At that point he should have been leaping out; instead, the handle just scissored back and forth.

"A shame," Sasaki murmured. Aoyagi could feel his face flush, and then go pale. "It's a dummy—standard issue on police cars. The door on your side opens only from the outside."

Masaharu Aoyagi

"I knew that," Aoyagi muttered, staring out the window and struggling for composure. Maezono's truck pulled into traffic and passed them going the other way.

"Sorry to spoil your fun," said Sasaki.

"Does he always wear those earphones?" Aoyagi said, jerking his chin toward the man in the driver's seat. He needed to change the subject, to keep Sasaki from seeing how frightened he was.

"Kobatozawa?" Sasaki said with a shrug.

What could he say or do to keep himself from breaking down? He took a deep breath and held it for a moment. As he breathed out, he felt the strength draining from his body and he began to shake. His mind went blank.

The car was moving again. Kobatozawa gripped the wheel and maneuvered through the traffic. He turned right and headed south on a street that was nearly empty. The car finally picked up speed.

"What's going . . . to happen to me?" he said at last, his voice cracking.

Sasaki looked at him. Kobatozawa muttered something he couldn't catch—or he might just have started humming.

"You're going to Tokyo with us. You'll be charged with the murder of the prime minister. Fortunately for you, this is a democracy and we don't condone torture or capital punishment, not often anyway. Your picture will be in every newspaper and on every television station, and I'm afraid to say there may be consequences for your family."

Aoyagi knew from experience that attention from the media could be a form of torture. "What should I do?" he whispered.

"There's only one thing you can do," Sasaki told him. "Confess immediately. Acknowledge guilt for everything you've done."

"Everything?"

"We already know the whole story. If you confess to everything, there'll be less pain for yourself and your family."

"The whole story?" But it wasn't his story. The words came through a haze. Whether from exhaustion or a need to escape his situation, he suddenly felt like going to sleep.

"You have nothing to worry about," Sasaki was saying. "Just leave everything to us."

Leave what to you? Aoyagi wondered, but he couldn't bring himself to respond. Maybe it was better to stop struggling and do as he was told. He had done everything he could, tried his best. Gazing at the streetlights flashing by outside, he comforted himself with the thought that he hadn't given up without a fight. Well done, Aoyagi, he told himself.

So this Sasaki said he had "nothing to worry about." He thought it over. Nothing to worry about. He felt better. To a man in the desert dying of thirst, this "nothing to worry about" was the sight of fresh water. He would follow orders now and drink his fill.

The car jerked to a stop. We're there, he thought, before seeing that it was just another red light. Now that he'd entrusted himself to Sasaki and resigned himself to being taken to Tokyo, every delay was an added irritation. But when he looked outside again to see if the light had changed, out of the corner of his eye he saw a car coming fast and straight toward them. His brain registered an older white sedan to their right rear—and then the impact.

At first it felt like another punch. The world lurched before his eyes and his head swam. But this time the whole car started to spin. Aoyagi managed to grab hold of the seat in front of him while Sasaki clawed at the air. They fell against the door on the far side as the car skidded, finally coming to rest against the guardrail pinned by the white sedan.

Aoyagi sat dazed for a moment. The only clear sensation was the pain in his neck where it had banged against the seat behind him. But Sasaki sat up almost immediately, and as soon as the car had settled, he leapt out. Kobatozawa had thrown open his door as if trying to rip it off its hinges.

Aoyagi watched in amazement as a man in a black parka climbed from the driver's seat of the other car. He was beginning to realize it had deliberately run them off the road. A head of disheveled hair was pressed up against the window on the passenger's side.

"Friends of yours?" Sasaki said, sticking his head back in the open door. "A rescue attempt?" By the time Aoyagi understood the question, it was too late. He could only feel amazed at his own stupidity for having missed the chance to slip away in the excitement.

There was another jolt. He clutched his knees and rolled himself into a ball, wondering how much more of this to expect. The car rocked again, and someone's back slammed against the door next to him. It was the man from the other car, thrown by Kobatozawa. Things weren't going well. He was short and slim, more like one of the students who hung out in this neighborhood than a grown man, and Kobatozawa shoved him into the side of the car again and again.

Sasaki was still standing outside the other door. Finally he told his driver, "Okay, enough!" Then he made a call on his cell phone.

A moment later, he slipped back into the car. "Put your hands together," he said, grabbing Aoyagi's wrists. "We're changing cars." Before he knew what was happening, he had handcuffs on and was being dragged out onto the street.

The night sky was clear and dotted with stars beyond the bright lights of the city. He could see now how efficiently the white car had trapped them against the guardrail. A number of cars passed, but none slowed or stopped, the drivers probably unwilling to get involved in the aftermath of an accident. A small knot of pedestrians had gathered, but Sasaki waved some ID at them and told them to keep back. They retreated several steps but most stayed to watch.

Kobatozawa gave one last shove with both arms and sent the smaller man flying against the car. There was a yell from the crowd on the sidewalk as he staggered up. "Someone call the police!"

"We are the police," Sasaki shouted almost instantly. "And we've got everything under control here." Aoyagi felt helpless with his wrists bound together. The man was in serious trouble.

Kobatozawa dived into the car, reached over to the passenger's side, and reappeared with a gun. There were horrified looks on the faces in the crowd as he turned on the man in the parka and pumped a round into the chamber.

Aoyagi could feel himself drifting away from the peculiar scene playing out in front of him. But he willed himself back. Kobatozawa thought the man had come to rescue him, so it was his fault if he was injured or killed.

"That's enough," Sasaki said again, more sharply this time, and his driver lowered his weapon. The man in the parka seemed to go limp. "We're done here," Sasaki barked, yanking at Aoyagi's arms. As he was pulled around, he caught a glimpse of the woman in the passenger seat. Under the streetlight, he could see that she still hadn't moved, and on the front of her white shirt he thought he saw a dark stain. They heard a grunt from behind.

He craned around. Sasaki, too, had turned to look. The man in the parka moved with surprising speed. His arm lunged forward, and Kobatozawa barely managed to dodge a knife thrust.

Close up, the little man looked less threatening than ever. His hair was receding and there was a shocked expression in his eyes, like a prairie dog that has just popped out of its hole. Aoyagi thought he might be one of those people who shut themselves away in their rooms, living on junk food and never coming out into the sunlight. But looks can be deceiving, for the man clearly knew what he was doing with the knife.

He spun around, tossed the blade to his other hand, and lunged again. There was nothing frantic about his movements; they seemed smooth and practiced. For several passes, Kobatozawa only just avoided the blade; but eventually he put some distance between them, dropped to a shooting stance, and fired.

The blast ripped the air, missing the black parka but shattering the windshield of their car. Someone screamed. Aoyagi's hands jerked to cover his ears, but the cuffs stopped him. He shut his eyes.

When he opened them again, Kobatozawa was clutching his arm, which still held the gun, and the knife was planted in his shoulder. Fully a head taller, he stood facing the other man. How had the parka managed to get close enough to do such damage? Kobatozawa tried to level the gun again, but in one swift move, his opponent retrieved his knife and caught him through the sleeve of his jacket. He frowned with pain.

"Don't move!" Sasaki yelled. He was still standing next to Aoyagi, but he had his own gun out now. He'd been holding Aoyagi's backpack, but put it down to grip the pistol with both hands. His stance looked professional and his aim steady—an easy shot at ten meters. The man's knife hand froze.

Aoyagi glanced at Sasaki and then down at his own handcuffed wrists. Confess everything, he'd said, and if he did, they would help.

Then Morita's voice again in the back of his mind: "Like Oswald."

Aoyagi had once seen a photo of Oswald at the moment Jack Ruby shot him. Ruby must have just stepped out of the crowd; the camera caught Oswald's face as the bullet hit him in the chest.

Was that it? Did they want him to give up and come quietly so they could send someone to finish him off? Dead men don't talk, and when he was gone they could make up any story they wanted to, turn him into any sort of monster that suited their purposes.

His body had begun to move. His handcuffed hands swung like a hammer, catching Sasaki in the back of the head. As he crumpled, Aoyagi grabbed his backpack, and then ran. Awkwardly, pack dangling from his cuffed hands, he ran. "Stop!" Sasaki yelled from behind, and there was the sound of a shot, but no shock, no pain. Somewhere far off someone screamed, horns honked.

Masaharu Aoyagi

He was gasping for breath and still trying to figure out how to run with his hands bound. The people he passed stared at the handcuffs and shrank away from him. It was easy to see why. Everyone in Sendai must be on edge after the assassination, so the sight of a handcuffed man running by was bound to turn heads.

He ducked into a narrow alley, hoping to find a place to rest for a moment. He tripped over a trashcan but stumbled on. More screams in the distance: maybe Kobatozawa was still playing cowboy.

Coming to the entrance of a small, rundown building, he ran downstairs to a landing halfway to the basement, dropped his backpack, and collapsed against the wall. After a few deep breaths, he studied the handcuffs, yanking his arms apart as hard as he could—though he knew it was futile.

"I can get those off you," said a voice from the top of the stairs. Aoyagi turned, and as he did so, he slipped and fell to the bottom of the stairs. "Sorry, did I scare you?" When the man moved slowly toward him, Aoyagi realized who he was. The slight build and startled look in the eyes—it was the young man who had tangled with Kobatozawa back at the car. Now that he could inspect him more closely, it was clear that he was older than a student, but his manner was hesitant. "Here, let me help you," he said, holding out his hand to pull him up. Aoyagi ignored the offer and scrambled to his feet, though it took quite an effort with his hands bound. "Then let me try this," the man continued, still holding out his hand. Aoyagi thought he was about to be stabbed, but suddenly noticed there was a small key resting in his palm. He held out his hands, and almost miraculously the cuffs fell away from his wrists.

"Where'd you get that?" he murmured, half stunned.

"This?" said the man, almost sheepishly. "I borrowed it from that guy back there. When he grabbed me, I had a chance to do a little research in his pockets." He seemed quite relaxed, with none of the reserve that would have been usual, given the difference in their ages. His hand moved slowly to the pouch on his belt; he took out a pair of glasses and put them on.

Aoyagi looked down at his own hands, which could move freely again. "Why are you helping me?" he said.

"Is that what I'm doing?" the man asked. "I don't even know who you are." Aoyagi looked up, startled. "I was following that thug in the car, and you just happened to be along for the ride."

"But you crashed into us. What about your car?"

"That old thing? I just borrowed it, too." As he listened to him, Aoyagi had the feeling he'd heard the lines before, as though he were watching a scene in some old movie—a story remote from everyday reality. Apparently, the young man had caught sight of the three of them leaving Kazu's apartment. "I knew it was him right away," he said. "No mistaking a guy wearing earphones and carrying a gun. I followed you, but when you got in the car, I stopped that white car and drove after you. I can't remember how long it's been since I drove a car." Aoyagi wondered how he had managed to "borrow" the thing, but he resisted the temptation to ask. The woman in the passenger seat had been unconscious, her head smashed against the window. Was it her car? And had his knife made the dark stain on her shirt? "They say your enemy's enemy is your friend. I could tell they were taking you off somewhere, so I guess you could say I was helping you."

"Did Kobatozawa follow you?" Aoyagi realized the knife was nowhere to be seen and wondered whether he had left it planted in one of the police officers.

"Kobatozawa?"

"The guy with the gun, did he follow you?"

"That's his name? Sounds like a bad joke." When he smiled, he looked quite harmless. "But I guess the joke was on him. Big guy like that, toting a gun, thought I'd be no match for him. But I won again today. Bet he's not talking so big now."

"But why did you take the key?"

"No particular reason. It just seemed like the neighborly thing to do—seeing as how we're kind of in the same boat."

"And what boat is that?"

"I think it's always best to complicate the storyline, so to speak. Stealing the key gives the impression that there's some sort of connection between us. The police will think so, and so will the media. And they'll all be wrong. It's the first rule of the fox—throw them off the scent, mix things up, distract them. The key didn't matter to me, but I thought I'd get you out of those handcuffs just for the heck of it. Pretty nice of me, if I say so myself. . . . But it's what I'm always asking myself: how come a nice guy like me doesn't have any friends?" Standing there facing him, Aoyagi suddenly felt like a kid cornered by a bully in an alley—though anyone seeing them would assume the roles were reversed, that he was threatening this little guy. "Strange name—Kobatozawa," he continued. "Can't say it suits him—too many syllables. Surprised he can pronounce it himself."

"Not any stranger than your name." Aoyagi blurted out what had been going through his head, though he instantly regretted it. He might be writing his own epitaph, but somehow he couldn't stop himself. "They call you Cutter, don't they? You're the guy who's been attacking people all over the city."

The man's eyes narrowed for a moment, but then his face seemed to relax. "Surprise!" he said.

"There was a picture with an article about you in a magazine a while back, after you'd already bumped off a lot of people. It was like a manga, you with your knife in a showdown with a big man with a gun." One of the other drivers had shown it to him. "We thought it was dumb, way over the top, more like an American comic book." They had all laughed at the picture at the time, but he now realized that it had been based on real events—on an earlier encounter between Cutter and Kobatozawa.

"I saw it," Cutter said in a flat voice. Then he gave him an impatient look, as if to say they couldn't stand there talking all day. "Coming?" And with a jerk of his finger he headed up the stairs and into the alley.

Aoyagi shouldered his pack. He couldn't have said why, but he didn't feel afraid of him really—a man whose crimes had terrified the whole city—and barely hesitated before following him. At one point, as if reading his mind, Cutter turned around. "Don't I scare you?" he asked.

"I guess you should," Aoyagi said, "but nothing makes any sense today, so this fits right in." It was a bit like putting fruit in a juicer: once it was all mixed up, it didn't matter whether you threw in any new stuff.

"So what did you do?" Cutter asked.

"I didn't do anything. They're trying to frame me for something, so I ran. Those two caught me, but thanks to you I seem to be running again—though I have to admit I'm pretty tired." Which is why I don't have the energy to get away from you, he decided not to add.

Cutter suddenly stopped and turned to look at him, his eyes scanning down his body. Then he reached toward him. Aoyagi would have jumped away, but Cutter's hand darted behind his back. "Look," he said, holding out something he'd apparently removed from him. "They're tracking you. They don't miss a trick."

"They must have put it on when we were in the car," Aoyagi said, taking the transponder and slipping it into a mailbox on the nearest building. "Let's go," he said.

Cutter seemed to know his way through the maze of narrow streets. They moved quickly, ending up at a rundown love hotel. They ducked into an old apartment building next door. It was dark, lit only by the neon sign of the hotel, but they made their way to the stairs at the back. Cutter opened the door of the first apartment on the second floor and switched on the light. The single bulb was covered with an orange shade, dyeing the room a somber shade of saffron. The apartment was just one six-tatami-mat room.

"What do they call you?" Cutter asked.

"Aoyagi." There seemed little reason to hide his identity. "How about you?"

"Miura."

"Is this where you live?"

"This dump? Are you kidding?" he said, sitting down at a low table in the middle of the room. Aoyagi sat across from him. "They've got the whole city wired with those pods. I needed someplace I could hide when things are hot."

"Are we safe here?"

"For the time being."

"But it's not yours?"

Miura's eyes moved to a photograph on top of a small bookcase against the wall: a man in a leather jacket standing next to a boy. "It's theirs," he said, nodding at the picture. "I'm just using it for a while."

"And where are they?"

He sat quietly for a moment, his mouth drawn into a tight line. "I gave them some money," he said at last. "They had this dream of driving all over the country, so I gave them enough to go and do it. They let me use this place in return—not a bad deal for them, I think. They're out there somewhere right now in a red convertible." Aoyagi made himself look away from the picture, certain somehow that none of this was true. "I bet you don't believe me," Miura said. "I bet you think I killed them."

"No, I don't," Aoyagi said, though he was far from sure he meant it.

"They say the Security Pods were put in to catch me, but it's a lie. I'm just a pretext. They talk about protecting the citizens of Sendai, but what they really want to do is watch them, everywhere, all the time."

"But you gave them the opportunity," Aoyagi said.

"They'd have found some other excuse if I hadn't come along. Politicians are brilliant at finding excuses—if not at much else. They create a panic—war, terrorism, whatever—in order to say that they need more power to deal with it. Did they really need all those pods for one kid with a knife?"

"Do they really work?"

"Sort of. As far as I know, each one picks up transmissions within a radius of a few dozen meters, but they've got hundreds of them around the city now, and more being installed all the time. They can get phones and data from Wifi, and they do voice recordings; and there's a fisheye camera in the dome that can film everything in a 350-degree radius around the pod. And apparently they can control it like a remote security camera to see what's going on in real time."

"And where does all that information go?"

"A computer system links the pods. So rather than sending the data to a central server, I think they access each one from the computer."

"It sounds like science fiction."

"It's like that movie! The one by Tony Scott, or was it Wim Wenders? Or maybe they both did one." Miura leaned forward, eyes shining.

But Aoyagi had never heard these names. "Like *Nineteen Eighty-Four*," he said, remembering the title of a book he'd read long ago.

"Like the eighties?" Miura muttered, looking confused. "Anyway, they can't see everything—not absolutely everything. Not the inside of this crummy apartment, for example. They don't have their bugs or their cameras in a place like this. I guess there's no point in watching you at home unless you're some big shot." Aoyagi told him that they had located him as soon as he used his cell phone. "They can usually tell now where a phone is if it's turned on," Miura explained, as if this were common knowledge. "When a call goes out from a phone, they verify the number from the base station before they make the connection." He sounded like a teacher keeping it simple for a slow student. "The site is stored in something called the 'home memory,' which is updated on an automatic basis. Apparently the pods can share data on your phone with the home memory, which means they can practically pinpoint a location. If you really want to stay out of their way, you should probably lose that phone."

"I already did," said Aoyagi. He had left it with the man selling magazines, which amounted to the same thing.

"Smart move. They're listening in on most calls anyway," he added.

"Listening in?" Aoyagi said, alarmed at this new possibility.

"I don't mean someone's actually listening, but they're being recorded. They store the data, and then they can access it when they need to. So, for example, they're probably looking at the records from all the calls you've made or received from that number. But if you look at it the other way around, the only thing they have to connect you to a call is the number, so it's fairly safe to use another phone."

"Why's that?"

"It's just common sense. It'd be almost impossible to find your voiceprint out there among all the calls being made. The data set is too big—it would take forever."

"So I could use someone else's phone?"

"Theoretically, except they might also be tracking the people you were calling, anyone connected to you in some way."

Aoyagi thought of Kazu. They had probably been watching his incoming calls. What about Koume Inohara? Did they know about his connection to her? Or had she herself been a trap they'd laid for him from the beginning? He still didn't know.

"But if they're recording everything, don't they end up with more data than they can handle?" Miura's explanation had raised some questions. "Even if they're only doing it in Sendai at the moment, there must be some limits to the storage capacity."

"I imagine they store the data for a given period and then dump it and start over. If they're covering the whole city, the cycle has to be pretty short—a day, two at most. Which means they can't go back and look at what happened a while ago—the data gets overwritten on a rolling basis."

"So they have no memory."

"It's a system designed for real-time pursuit in a high-profile case—like the bombing today at the parade. It'd be ideal for hunting down the guy who did that." He poked at the bridge of his glasses and stared at Aoyagi. "Oh . . . ," he murmured. ". . . And would you by any chance be that guy? Our local assassin?" An odd little pout turned down the corners of his mouth. Aoyagi hesitated for a moment, unsure what to say. "No! You're kidding! Really?!" He was almost shouting. "Let me shake your hand!" he said, grinning and holding out his own.

"But I didn't do it," said Aoyagi. "They're just trying to make it look like I did."

Miura let his hand fall back and was quiet for a moment. He blinked, pushed at his glasses, and studied him. "Interesting," he said at last, a smile revealing a row of crooked teeth. "So they're framing you. Funny, you don't seem like the type."

"Or not funny at all."

"So our Mr. Kobatozawa must be part of some special forces unit called up for the manhunt. They don't let regular cops walk around with a gun like that. Not in this country at least."

"I thought it seemed a bit weird," Aoyagi agreed. There was a sound somewhere outside and he stiffened and glanced at the window.

"Don't worry," Miura told him. "It's just check-in time at the love hotel. Folks still have to get laid, even if the prime minister's been blown to bits." He got up and disappeared into the kitchen, coming back with two cans of beer. Then he poured boiling water from an electric kettle into some cups of instant ramen. Aoyagi could feel his tension dissolving in the cloud of steam that rose from the Styrofoam tubs.

"While we're waiting for this to cook, why not fill me in," Miura said. "It doesn't seem like an easy thing to do—frame someone for the murder of a top politico. How'd they manage it?" He pulled the tab on his beer, tapped it against Aoyagi's, and took a sip. "I'm all ears."

Aoyagi was surprised that he felt no reluctance to talk about what had happened to him—on the contrary, he wanted to tell someone. "Where do I start?" he said.

"At the beginning. Your father, So-and-so Aoyagi, married your mother, Miss So-and-so, who gave birth to you, their eldest, in such-and-such city. A happy childhood, top marks at school, captain of the baseball team. . . ." It was a fair impression of the master of ceremonies at a wedding reception, and Aoyagi realized he had begun to smile in spite of himself. He wasn't sure why, but he felt at ease for the first time since he had jumped out of Morita's car.

So he started his story with meeting Morita that morning. There was a hint of irony in Miura's occasional interjections—"You don't mean it!" "Oh my God!"—but his face was rapt attention, like a jeweler appraising a stone. When Aoyagi had finished, he agreed that he was being framed. "You should be pissed off," he said.

"Thank you," said Aoyagi. "I am."

"Sounds like they've been planning this for months, laying traps for you. But why you? There must have been people who made more sense, who had some connection to Kaneda."

"I've been asking myself the same question." He put the beer can to his lips but then lowered it again. When he looked up, his eyes met Miura's.

"Think I put something in it?" he asked. "Wouldn't be the first time today. I guess you have to be careful, but you don't have to worry about me. I'm harmless." Aoyagi glanced at the window without answering. A sliver of light was visible through the crack in the curtains. Streetlights, he decided. "Well, at least have some ramen," Miura said, sliding one of the cups across the table. "Or do you think that's poisoned, too?"

Aoyagi picked up his chopsticks, feeling it would be childish to refuse. Steam rose from the broth as he pulled back the lid. It was the first warm food he'd had in hours, and his eyes watered as he slurped it up.

They had been eating for a few minutes, when Miura suddenly broke the silence. "No way!" He put down his cup and leaned forward. "I just realized why you look so familiar. You're the one who rescued that girl a while back. The delivery driver. I saw you on TV, lots of times."

Aoyagi smiled uncomfortably. He wasn't sure which was more disturbing—having his brief brush with fame come up in a place like this or having a serial killer as a fan.

"But don't you see?" Miura went on. "That's why they picked you. People love to see a hero fall from grace. Plus, you're handsome, so people envy you. We'd all be happy to see you go down for something like this. I have to give them credit, they found the perfect scapegoat."

"But that whole hero thing was just something the media cooked up to begin with," Aoyagi protested.

"No, they're right—it makes it more exciting if the least likely person turns out to be guilty." They went back to eating their ramen, drinking the soup to the bottom and setting the cups on the table at almost the same time. "So you're in a fix," Miura said. "What are you going to do?"

"I have absolutely no idea," said Aoyagi. "I was trying to figure that out back there in the car." He had decided he'd done everything he could, done his best but lost to a stronger opponent. He told himself he was living to fight another day, but at that point he had been resigned to being arrested.

Miura took off his glasses and wiped them with his handkerchief. "Being on the lam is hard work," he said. "They're looking everywhere for you, and they've sealed off just about every way out. But if it were me . . ."

"If it were you? . . ."

"I'd say your best bet was to hole up somewhere safe in town and wait. They'd have to go door to door, search every last house in Sendai to find you. But the trick is to hide someplace totally random." He had put his glasses back on. "Can you think of a place you've had absolutely no connection with before?"

Aoyagi knew the answer to this without thinking about it. "No," he said.

"Well, once the police name you as the suspect, just about anybody who spots you will turn you in. I suppose they'll be going public with your name any time now."

"Why do you say that?"

"You've shown them you can keep a step ahead of them, so they've figured out you won't go quietly." As he said this, Miura picked up the remote and switched on the TV. "They might have already made the announcement."

Aoyagi's eyes drifted to the screen as it came on in the orange half-light of the room. The footage of the parade and the explosion was still playing, though by now the commentators looked weary and the format had gone stale.

"You're causing quite a stir," said Miura. "I'm impressed."

"Don't be. I didn't do it."

"But congratulations, it looks like they haven't fingered you yet," he concluded after checking several channels. "But I'm sure they will by morning. It's just a matter of time now, and then you'll have to keep off the streets. If you so much as stick your nose out the door, someone will recognize you."

"What if I get a room in the hotel next door?"

"No good," said Miura. "You can't go in a place like that alone without attracting attention. You need someone to check in with you. Have you got a girl in town? One you can trust?" Though he looked like a kid who would die of fright in the presence of a real woman, he sounded like an old hand offering young Aoyagi advice. "And the police aren't stupid, you know. They'll start searching the love hotels, anyplace you can get a cheap room. So that rules out a capsule hotel, too. They'll show your picture around every flophouse in the city."

"How about an Internet café? I was in one earlier tonight."

"Same problem. Once they go public with the charge."

"Then what if I get in touch with a TV station or a newspaper and tell them I'm innocent, that I'm being framed. They'd want the story even if they didn't believe me. At least I might get them to listen to me, to look into it."

"It might work. The press doesn't really care about true or false, good or bad; they just want interesting. If they decide you're news, they'll be all over you. Though that could be dangerous as well." Miura seemed calmer now. "But what would you tell them? 'I'm being framed for the assassination of the prime minister. The cops are after me. But I'm innocent. Could you put that on the air, please?' What station is going to offer you airtime and shield you from the police?"

"I don't know," said Aoyagi. But it was the only plan he could think of. Then he suddenly remembered that something similar had happened not long ago. "But if they did, it wouldn't be the first time," he said, smiling at Miura.

"Yeah," Miura said, nodding slightly. "That guy who contacted a TV station saying he was me. He had their mouths watering, thinking they had a live exclusive with a serial killer."

"But then somebody got cold feet and spilled the beans to the police."

"They caught him, and the TV people got their hand slapped good and hard."

"All thanks to you," said Aoyagi.

"It had nothing to do with me. I can't help it if some Cutter wannabe goes and pimps himself to the press." "Cutter wannabe" sounded like a boast, but Miura's expression was all business. "And that just means they'll be even less willing to keep you undercover. If you call them I suspect you'll hear a lot of hemming and hawing."

"Even for something this big?"

"That's why they won't have the balls to cross the police." Aoyagi wanted to disagree. Weren't TV stations known for bending the rules? But Miura continued as though reading his thoughts. "They don't ever really do anything reckless; they've got lawyers checking everything beforehand. In this country, they know there's always someone watching them, waiting to slap them down if they get out of line. Call them if you want to, just be aware that there's a good chance you'll find the police waiting for you if you show up at a TV station. You might even end up getting shot in all the excitement. Live and in color!"

"You think they're planning to shoot me?"

"You think they aren't? It would be pretty convenient to have you out of the way." Aoyagi felt like laughing, but somehow nothing came out. He reached for his ramen cup again, but when he realized it was empty he put it back on the table. His head felt heavy. "You got any ideas?" Miura was saying. "A plan?"

Aoyagi heard him and knew he was supposed to say something, but he was suddenly terribly weary. "Ideas," he repeated. Like a man with tired arms working a pulley, he tried to drag the thought from his head. He had an idea. He knew he did. He could picture himself at the Internet café, entering information on the screen. "Just one," he muttered.

He explained his plan to Miura as best he could, though his tongue was thick in his mouth.

"Not bad!" Miura said when he'd finished. "Using your connections. A package pickup. Not bad at all."

"But zero chance of success," Aoyagi mumbled, feeling defeated.

"No, not zero. Will he believe you?"

"Who knows? But the only thing I can do now is trust my friends."

"Hey!" Miura spluttered. "The fall guy for the greatest setup in history and he's still pinning his hopes on people! You're a dreamer, no doubt about it. But fine, if that's what you've got planned, you can stay here until morning. The main thing now is to get some sleep."

"I can't stay here," Aoyagi said, looking around the room. The ceiling felt lower than before, the walls so flimsy they might collapse at the slightest touch. But even in this seedy place, he felt sleep coming on.

"You're right," said Miura. "You can't stay long. That's not your answer. Let's imagine you did stay here. What would you do? Spend the time eating? Eating and eating. You could get fat, turn that handsome face of yours to blubber so you didn't look the same anymore, and then you could go outside. You just might manage it in six months. But we can't have that, can we? You can sleep here tonight, then go."

Aoyagi's eyes popped open again, though he hadn't realized they were closed. He had never felt sleep come on this suddenly. He noticed a cell phone lying on the table in front of him, and looked up at Miura.

"You can have it," he said.

"Where did it come from?"

"They haven't found the body yet, so no one's canceled the service. I tried it earlier." Aoyagi stared at him. "You're going to need one. The police can't connect you with this number, so it's safe to use it for the time being."

Aoyagi picked up the phone. He wanted to turn it on, but his eyes closed and his mind went blank. Why was he so sleepy?

"I'd better come clean," Miura said.

"What about?"

"I put something in the ramen. I knew you needed a good night's sleep. I'm thoughtful that way. And you've still got some time to kill before the pickup."

"The ramen?" Aoyagi managed to whisper, but his head was full of stones.

"Well, then," he heard Miura say. "If I think of anything useful, I'll let you know."

Aoyagi wanted to call out to him, to tell him to wait, but the words died in his throat and a moment later everything went black.

Haruko Higuchi

She was waiting for her when Haruko got to the hospital. She had answered Kazu's phone and identified herself as "Kazuo's girlfriend," and now she stood near the reception desk holding hands with a little boy. Her son, Tatsumi, was four years old, the same age as Nanami, and her own name was Ami Tsuruta. Haruko wondered whether Kazu could be the little boy's father, but decided he probably wasn't. The boy told her "Mr. Ono" was pretty sick, when they introduced themselves.

"Did you have trouble getting here?" Ami asked. "The traffic must be bad."

"We took a cab, but it was so slow we got out and walked the rest of the way."

Nanami, who had been standing patiently holding her hand, spoke up at last. "Mommy, who's Mr. Ono?"

"Mommy's friend," Haruko said. At this, Tatsumi, not to be outdone, announced in a loud voice that Mr. Ono was his mommy's boyfriend. Ami smiled a bit sheepishly. Haruko guessed she was in her mid-twenties—a good deal younger than she was at any rate.

"He hasn't regained consciousness yet," Ami said as they were riding up in the elevator.

"But he was awake when you found him?" Haruko said, thinking back to what she had told her on the phone.

"Just for a moment. He mumbled something about Mr. Aoyagi."

Apparently she had arrived at Kazu's apartment the night before without any advance notice. "I wasn't worried exactly. But he'd been acting a little weird." She had been staying at her parents' house in town for a few days; after her son went to sleep, she had called Kazu. He sounded so odd on the phone that she was sure something was wrong, and she decided to go and check on him.

"To be honest, I thought he was cheating on me," she said, obviously a bit embarrassed. "I know something about that from my ex-husband. Anyway, I never thought I'd find him like that, lying on the floor barely able to move." She was on the verge of tears. Tatsumi squeezed her hand.

A bell sounded and the elevator door slid open at the fifth floor. Ami and Tatsumi led the way down the corridor.

"What did he say before he lost consciousness?" Haruko asked.

"It was mostly just muttering and groaning, but I did make out the words 'police' and 'beat me.' Then he said that Aoyagi had saved him. He used to talk about his college friends, so I knew the name. But then this morning, on the news . . ." Ami had seemed calm when they met, but as she described the events of the past few hours she grew agitated.

"I saw it, too," said Haruko. "I can't believe they're saying Aoyagi did it."

"He doesn't seem like that kind of person. Not if he helped that actress . . . and Kazu."

"The Aoyagi I knew could never have done something like that. Of course, he didn't seem like the hero type either," she added.

"Kazu talked a lot about his famous friend from college."

"He told me, too," Tatsumi said, looking very serious.

"Have you been out of touch with him since graduating?" Ami asked. From her tone, it seemed she didn't know that Aoyagi and Haruko had been involved.

"I haven't seen him for some time," Haruko told her. "But how did Kazu get drawn into this?"

"I don't know," said Ami. "And they said their friend Morita was killed."

"What?" Haruko's body went rigid as she tried to take this in.

"Did you know him, too?"

"We were friends in college. . . ."

"They mentioned him on the news," Ami said. "But I suppose it could have been another Morita."

Haruko started to answer but then stopped. Noticing that her mother was strangely quiet, Nanami tugged at her sleeve. Haruko shook her head slowly. "No," she said. "I don't think so." Morita dead? Normally she would not have believed it, but given what had happened, anything seemed possible now.

"They said he was in a car near the parade. There was a second bomb and he was killed."

Haruko was stunned, and for a moment she felt light-headed. "Are they saying Aoyagi did that, too?"

"They made it seem that way."

"But why would he? . . . Morita?" It all seemed unreal to her. Ami watched her with a concerned look.

Aoyagi kill Morita? She ran this idea through her head repeatedly. That was what they were saying. But what could it mean?

They reached the end of the hall and stopped in front of a room. "Ono" was written on a card on the door. "They didn't let me in until just a little while ago," Ami said, opening the door.

Kazu lay on his back, eyes closed. Haruko felt a rush of nostalgia at the sight of him, but the bandages brought her up short.

"What happened to him?" Nanami asked, looking up at her. "What's he doing?"

"He's sleeping. He got hurt." It was all Haruko could do to get the words out. As she stared at Kazu, the time since their first meeting seemed to shrink to nothing, and she could hear him telling her he'd thought the Friends of Fast Food would all be horribly fat from eating hamburgers all day. "I never expected someone thin and healthy like you," he'd said. "Have you got a tapeworm?" It had been one of the strangest greetings she had ever heard, though he'd meant well. Then Aoyagi had spoken up. "If it keeps you from gaining weight, I could do with one myself." He had smiled at the new addition to the Friends. "We expect our members to stay in shape, look out for their health," she remembered him saying.

But Kazu was covered with tubes and patches and bandages. Who was looking out for his health now?

Had the world gone crazy? Kazu here—Morita dead. It would have seemed ridiculous, if there weren't the evidence in front of her.

"When will he wake up?" Tatsumi asked.

"I'm not sure," Ami told him.

"Have they contacted his parents?" Haruko asked, looking around the room for signs of other visitors. "I think they live in Niigata." She felt as though someone had been testing her memories of college all morning.

"I called them last night. I'm sure they're on their way, but it's not easy getting into Sendai right now." Haruko nodded. Less than a day had gone by since the assassination and the roadblocks were still in place.

Their conversation was interrupted. "Are you friends of Mr. Ono?" a voice suddenly said behind them. They turned to find an unfamiliar figure standing in the door. He had broad shoulders and a square face. His suit was badly wrinkled, and he didn't look friendly. "My name is Mamoru Kondo, from the General Intelligence Division in the Security Bureau. I'm investigating the incident," he told them.

Kondo sat across from Haruko and Ami in a coffee shop at the other end of the hospital. "The prime minister was killed by Masaharu Aoyagi, using a remote-controlled helicopter," he said.

"Do you have some kind of proof?" Ami asked, leaning forward over the table.

"Haven't you been watching TV? Aoyagi was caught on tape buying the helicopter. And several witnesses have seen him on the run since the assassination. The owner of a liquor store was injured during his escape, and shots were fired at a restaurant where he was spotted. He was even taken into custody briefly last night—though that's not public information at this point."

Haruko listened while keeping one eye on Nanami next to her in a booster chair. Kondo told them that Aoyagi had been apprehended outside Kazu's apartment, but he had managed to escape while he was being taken by car to a station.

"Why did he come to Kazu's apartment last night?" Ami asked, but Haruko interrupted her.

"Escaped? How?" she said. Kondo's face was as impassive as a Noh mask.

"Actually, Mr. Ono contacted us to say that Aoyagi had phoned him. We think that when Aoyagi learned Ono had reported him, he forced his way into the apartment and attacked him. Our agents arrived soon afterwards and arrested him. We're sorry your friend was hurt for cooperating with us."

Haruko wanted to tell Kondo he was wrong, that Aoyagi couldn't have killed anyone or attacked his friend, but she realized she had little chance of convincing him and would probably just draw suspicion on herself. But then, almost miraculously, little Tatsumi asked a question that had been bothering her as well.

"How did Mr. Ono know he was a bad man?" Yes, how could he have known? It made no sense. Aoyagi hadn't been identified as the suspect until this morning.

"I don't know the details," Kondo said, "but Ono said that Aoyagi gave himself away when he called. Aoyagi apparently asked for help with his escape, relying on their college friendship. That's when Ono called the police—and we were already investigating Aoyagi."

Tatsumi nodded.

"But how did Aoyagi get away?" Haruko asked.

"A man—we assume it was an associate—rammed the car and Aoyagi escaped in the confusion."

"An associate?"

"The car used in the attack was stolen. The woman who owned it . . ." Kondo paused for a moment, glancing at the children before continuing more quietly. "The woman who owned it was found stabbed to death." Ami's eyes grew wide. The story got wilder every minute, and Haruko felt as though a fog was settling over her brain. But she was sure of one thing: she could not make the image of Aoyagi in her head match the villain Kondo was describing. "We're using every resource at our disposal to find him. The Security Pods are providing good information, and we've distributed his photo to every hotel, hospital, and station. We assume there is a chance he'll try to contact Mr. Ono again, which is why I've been sent here."

"He's coming here?" Ami blurted out.

"Not necessarily, but the possibility exists. Could I get your telephone numbers?" he asked abruptly.

"Our numbers?" Haruko echoed.

"You were his friend in college, and Miss Tsuruta's a friend of Mr. Ono. Aoyagi may try to contact you for some reason. We've learned he communicated with at least one associate just a short time ago." From Kondo's tone, it was clear he had no intention of telling them who the "associate" might be or what sort of "communication" it was. "We feel there is a chance he could try to contact one or both of you. If he calls you, we can use the information in our investigation, provided we have your numbers."

"You're going to tap our phones?" Haruko said. Kondo's proposal had been more decorous, but it came down to that.

"The Security Pods can collect various kinds of information. In general, we use it only with prior permission, but in a national emergency like this, we're asking for your cooperation to make the best use of these resources. Think of it as a more sophisticated version of checking a license plate number."

Haruko remembered that Akira Hirano had said her boyfriend did maintenance work on the pods. "Welcome to the surveillance society," she murmured, the words slipping out almost before she realized it.

Though he must have heard, Kondo's expression remained unchanged. "As a precaution, we'll be checking the numbers of your incoming calls. We won't be eavesdropping, just trying to identify the callers. If Aoyagi calls, we can react immediately."

"I'm not comfortable with someone listening to my phone calls," Haruko said.

"We would appreciate your cooperation." The words were still polite but the tone was chillier.

"I don't mind," Ami said. "I'll cooperate." Haruko could understand how she felt. Seeing what had happened to Kazu, she must want the whole thing to be over as quickly as possible.

"I guess I will, too," she said. They could get her number easily enough, so there was little point in resisting.

"If you receive a suspicious call, we'd like you to try to keep the connection for at least thirty seconds."

"Thirty seconds?"

"We need that much time to trace a call. So please try to prolong the conversation as much as possible. The data may help us with our investigation."

"What should I do if Aoyagi calls Kazu's phone?" Ami asked.

"We'd like you to answer and talk to him. If at all possible, arrange to meet him somewhere." When he had finished writing down their addresses and telephone numbers, he seemed satisfied. He hadn't touched the iced tea he'd ordered. As he was about to get up, Haruko stopped him.

"Why would he do something like this?" she asked.

"That's what we intend to ask him, once we've caught him."

Haruko went back to Kazu's room. He was still unconscious, so she decided to go home for the time being. Ami offered to walk her to the hospital entrance; on the way she asked Haruko where she lived.

"Oh, I know the neighborhood. I've been there once," she said when she heard the address, sounding almost cheerful for the first time. Just by the front entrance, she stopped. "I'll call you if he wakes up," she told Haruko. Then she looked up at the sky outside. The clouds had lifted and a film of pale blue covered the city. The sun was warm. "When it's like this, it's hard to believe there are wars going on somewhere or that people are suffering and dying, isn't it?" She was smiling, but Haruko thought she might easily start crying. "Kazu says that good weather makes him happy, but it also reminds him that not everyone can enjoy it, that somewhere people are miserable."

"He said that?" Haruko murmured, surprised to hear that Kazu, their resident philistine, had become so sensitive.

"Actually, he said it was something Aoyagi had told him," Ami said.

"Aoyagi?"

"Kazu said Aoyagi used to say that clear days made him think about people elsewhere having a hard time—and that he'd always remembered it."

"Oddly enough, that sounds just like something he would say."

The children said their goodbyes and Haruko led Nanami down the path toward the street.

"Mommy," Nanami said when they'd reached the sidewalk. "Is your friend the bad man on TV? Was he your friend?"

"A long time ago," Haruko said. Did that mean they were no longer friends? She remembered that Akira Hirano had insisted at one point that there was a big difference between an old friend and an old lover.

"When you break up with a lover, you don't go back to being friends."

"Some people do, don't they?" Haruko had wanted to hold on to the hope.

"No, never. Or maybe in rare cases. But the principle holds: an ex-boy-friend should be out of your life for good. Still, it does seem strange," she'd mused. "For the time you're together, you see each other every day, but once you split up, you never see him again."

"He didn't look like a bad man," Nanami said, pulling Haruko back to the present. "He's handsome."

"He certainly is," she agreed before she was quite sure what to say.

It was noon, and the sun was directly overhead. A light breeze tugged at her hair as they walked along. It seemed impossible that Aoyagi was some-where nearby, under this same perfect sky, a fugitive, his life on the line.

Nanami was complaining that she was hungry, so Haruko took her to a res-taurant near Kita Yonban Street. As they sat down at a table by the window, she remembered that Kondo had said Aoyagi fired a gun in a restaurant . . . probably much like this one. Aoyagi with a gun? The whole thing seemed more and more absurd, as though she were watching a bad student play in which he had been forced to act.

The TV on the wall would normally have been showing a baseball game, but today, naturally enough, it was tuned to a special about the assassina-tion. Nanami suddenly pointed at the screen.

"Mommy, look! It's him!" She had released the straw she was sucking to make this announcement. It was footage of an interview during his previous brush with fame, and his quiet, almost hesitant manner was that of the man she had known.

There were several calls to her phone while they were eating. First from her husband, Nobuyuki. Haruko had left the phone on the table, and Nanami noticed his name on the display when it began to vibrate.

"Daddy!" she chirped.

Nobuyuki was not the most forthcoming man in the world, but his instincts were good, and when he got an idea in his head, he tended to act on it right away. This could be annoying, but at least he was consistent. So she was hardly surprised at the first words she heard: "I just saw it on the news. Isn't he an old friend of yours?"

"I'm amazed you remembered."

"I make it my business to know about my wife's deep dark past," he said. "You told me about him when he was on TV a few years back. So you can imagine my surprise when the deliveryman who rescued the starlet turned out to be the guy who killed the prime minister."

"I was just as surprised."

"Are you okay?" he asked, and though he no doubt meant it in a general sense, Haruko felt as though he had thrown her a lifeline.

"If I said 'No,' would you come home?"

He laughed. "I'm on my way."

"No, I'm kidding. Everything's fine. But the police did interview me."

"The police?"

"They thought he might get in touch, since we were friends. They want me to let them know if he calls. But it looks like they're snooping on every phone in Sendai already; if he calls me, I'm sure they'll know."

"Do you think they're listening to us now?" he asked. "Not a very pleasant thought."

"They're very busy people," Haruko laughed. "Once they find out it's just you, I'm sure they'll hang up." But she, too, found it disturbing that someone could be listening. Outside the window, the domed head of a Security Pod was peeking from the bushes, its tiny lights flashing on and off. "The officer who came to talk to me said it didn't work on calls that lasted less than thirty seconds," she added.

"That's probably right. It takes a certain amount of time to get things up and running, longer than you'd think."

"Good, then we'll keep the next one under thirty," Haruko said, laughing again.

"Got it. Anyway, I'll be home as soon as I can," he promised, and abruptly hung up.

"What did Daddy say?" Nanami drained her juice, then poked her fingers into the mound of pilaf on her plate.

"He's worried about us," she told her.

"That's easy for him to say," she said, her tone very solemn. Haruko tried hard to keep a straight face.

The display on the phone lit up: Nobuyuki again. She hit the talk button. "Hi. What's up?"

"In thirty seconds or less, did he really do it? Did you really go out with a guy who could do something like that?"

Haruko felt as though someone had punched her in the gut. She searched her memory, but she was sure she had never told him that she and Aoyagi were involved. "How did you get the idea we 'went out'?" she said.

"Oh, a little bird told me. See you." And the line went dead again.

"Went out with who?" Nanami wanted to know. Haruko smiled as the phone began to vibrate again. She checked the screen, expecting yet another call from Nobuyuki, but this time it read "Akira Hirano." With a quick, exasperated glance at Nanami, she punched the talk button.

"Haruko?" Akira said, her voice as bright as it had been the day before when they'd met for lunch. "How'd you make out getting home? The whole city was a mess!"

"It wasn't easy. How about you?"

"I was stuck forever. The prime minister of the whole damn country gets killed, but there's still a ton of boring work to do. The world could be coming to an end, but they wouldn't let us call in sick." Haruko relaxed as she listened to her reassuringly familiar complaints. She was apparently on her lunch break, which had gone into "extra innings," as she put it. "But they're keeping that boyfriend of mine busy," she added.

"Pod maintenance?"

"None other. Apparently the peace and prosperity of our fair city depends on those little robots. And the robots depend on my Masakado to keep them bright and shiny—so you could say he has our fate in his hot little hands."

"Even though he's not a face card?" Haruko said, remembering her description.

"Maybe a jack," Akira laughed. "But who'd have thought it would turn out to be that deliveryman? Weird we were just talking about him."

"Scary," she agreed.

"Actually," her friend said, giggling softly, "I feel like going out for a drink tonight. Want to come?"

"Sounds like fun. . . ," she said hesitantly, but she knew there was no way she could leave Nanami for the evening. Feeling the gulf between her own world and Akira's, she said goodbye and pushed "end."

Nanami was quietly eating her lunch. Haruko busied herself picking grains of rice off her daughter's lips and popping them into the little open mouth. Then she worked on her own plate of pasta for a while. As she was finishing, she looked up at the TV again. The scene was vaguely familiar. But where had she seen this place, and when? A crowd of men with cameras and microphones had gathered. Their faces looked serious, yet they seemed relaxed, as though they were putting on a show they'd done any number of times before.

A moment later it came to her: it was Rocky's place—the fireworks factory north of the city where she and her friends had hung out during their student days. And then she understood what was happening: the media had heard that Aoyagi had worked at the factory and had jumped to the conclusion that he had learned to make a bomb there—further proof that he was guilty. It was ridiculously oversimple—and just the sort of logic the press seemed to prefer. As if on cue, a reporter appeared on camera. "We now know that Masaharu Aoyagi became acquainted with the use of gunpowder during his time here at this factory," he said. Haruko sat staring at the screen, blinking with amazement.

"Idiots!" she whispered.

She and Aoyagi and the others had spent a good deal of time at Todoroki Pyrotechnics during their college years, but for the most part they had done little more than shovel snow in the parking lot, sweep up the factory, and move boxes. Todoroki, the boss, was a straightforward, generous type not too concerned about extraneous details, but he was a complete professional when it came to gunpowder and the fireworks themselves. So it would never have occurred to him to teach a bunch of college kids how to make a bomb. If Aoyagi had learned something at Todoroki's factory, he had absorbed the knowledge directly from the air and not the owner.

Haruko couldn't stop herself shaking as she stared at the TV. The more she heard—the reporter's pompous pronouncements, the idiotic nodding of the experts in the studio—the more convinced she was that their version of events was just another made-for-television fantasy.

"Lies," she whispered.

"Mommy? Are you okay?"

"I'm fine. It's just that I always thought that what they told us on TV was the truth, but now I see it isn't."

"I already knew that," the little girl announced, clearly pleased with herself. "I know they're telling lies, because they're always saying they're sorry on the TV." Even at four, she had apparently seen too many press conferences by disgraced officials or company presidents.

Haruko picked up the phone and checked the list of contacts. She had changed phones since her student days, but most of the old numbers had migrated over. "I'm going to make a quick call," she told Nanami as she put the phone to her ear. Staring at the shot of Todoroki's factory on the screen, she imagined the connection making its way into the building.

The busy signal buzzed dismally in her ear. Everyone in Japan must be trying to get through to Todoroki Pyrotechnics.

Next, she thought of calling Morita, but she remembered that the number she had didn't work. She realized she wanted to ask him directly if he was really dead. Knowing him, he would probably tell her quite cheerfully that he'd heard the "voice of the forest" calling to him.

Aoyagi on the run, accused of killing the prime minister; Morita dead in an explosion; and Kazu unconscious in the hospital. She reviewed the list again, wanting to find someone to question, to grab by the throat and shake until they told her why. Putting the phone back on the table, she looked up at the TV.

The shot showed a burst of flames, but just as she'd started to wonder what was burning in Sendai now, the camera pulled back and she realized the fire was on top of a stove. A bearded man with an affected voice was asking her to try his "special béchamel sauce." She recognized him—a famous chef who had opened a restaurant in Sendai, the place she and Aoyagi had once planned to go to. The place that had been rude about their cancellation when they were caught in a downpour. In the end, they had actually made it there a month later, just to prove to themselves they could, but the staff had been snooty and the food somehow unexciting. They had left feeling disappointed and a little self-righteous. Perhaps it was her imagination, but it had seemed that she and Aoyagi often ended up in places that weren't much fun—as though the two of them weren't being made welcome. Surrendering herself to the flow of memories, she stared out the window. The sky was still cloudless.

She remembered something that Todoroki had said to them long ago at one of the fireworks displays. "Thousands of people watch the same fireworks at the same time; and who knows, maybe an old friend you haven't seen in years could be among them." Could Aoyagi be watching this same commercial somewhere in Sendai? Could he be remembering that same night, feeling the same emotions? The thought was disconcerting, and sad.

Did he really do it? Her husband's question echoed in her head. Everything they had said on TV was preposterous. The man at the *tonkatsu* shop, the charge of molesting, the attempt to connect the bomb to Rocky's factory— and the idea that he had killed Morita . . . that was most absurd of all. But if he didn't do it, why were they chasing an innocent man all over Sendai?

Did you really go out with a guy who could do something like that?

She had never thought of herself as a particularly good judge of men—or of people in general—but she thought she knew what Aoyagi was capable of . . . and what he would never do as well. At the very least, she knew a hell of a lot more about him than those fools on the TV. She grabbed the check off the table and stood up to go.

Masaharu Aoyagi

He had hardly needed the drug Miura had slipped him; he would have collapsed under the weight of his exhaustion with or without its help. It was already eight the next morning when he opened his eyes. He had slept in his clothes, rolled up like a chrysalis fallen from its branch. The curtains were pulled back, but the room was deep in shadow, as though the whole building were hidden from sunlight. Miura had vanished, leaving behind nothing but the key on the low table. Apparently to lock up when he left.

He turned on the TV—and at the sight of his own face, he felt the floor give way and his body freefall. A shiver raced up his spine, his neck froze . . . as though he was jumping off the bridge onto Maezono's truck all over again.

"Did you know the apartment belonged to Rinka?" a reporter was asking him.

"I had no idea," his former self answered.

When the tape had finished, the announcer came on. "We believe this man is the suspect in the current incident."

He told himself to stay calm. It had happened now: they had named him. But he had known it was inevitable. No reason to panic—or so he tried to convince himself. He *had* to convince himself or he would go crazy with fear. He hit a button on the remote and the TV went dark.

Jumping up, he lurched toward the door and began to push his feet into his shoes. But then he remembered his bag and stumbled back into the room. He shouldered the pack and was about to open the door when he was suddenly overwhelmed by the feeling that a row of men with guns was waiting for him just outside. He went back into the room and peered through the window. The narrow alley below was empty. Above, a single crow spread its wings and left its perch on the telephone wires.

He switched on the TV again.

An innocent-looking, slightly younger Aoyagi was facing a microphone, though apparently with considerable reluctance. Unable to stand more than a moment of this, he was just going to turn the thing off when a line of text at the bottom of the screen caught his eye. "Do you have any information for us?" it read, followed by phone and fax numbers and an email address.

Miura had warned him not to count on the TV stations, but he was unwilling to give up on them just yet. He had always believed he could trust the police, or, barring them, the media if he was in trouble—and his current situation certainly qualified as trouble.

He pulled out the phone Miura had given him and dialed the number on the screen, using the block on caller-ID as a precaution. The line was busy, but after hitting "redial" for ten minutes or so, he finally got through.

Aoyagi managed a weak "hello," but the woman on the other end was apparently used to hesitant callers. "Do you have any information about the Kaneda assassination?" she said, her tone businesslike but friendly.

"Actually," he muttered, "I'm Masaharu Aoyagi." He'd imagined the woman giving a gasp of shock, her voice rising to a shriek of excitement at the prospect of an enormous scoop. . . . But the reality was somewhat different—completely different, in fact.

"Is that right?" said the woman, sounding almost bored.

"*The* Masaharu Aoyagi, live . . . right now."

"Could I get your address and contact information?"

As he sat with the phone pressed to his ear, mouth open, it slowly dawned on him: Masaharu Aoyagis must be a dime a dozen by now. Men calling the station and insisting—as a joke or under some delusion—that they were him. And this woman, whose job it was to field these tip-offs, had no way of knowing whether one of them was the real thing or not.

He wanted to hang up at this point, but he knew he had to try again. He repeated that he was *the* Masaharu Aoyagi, that he didn't have any "contact information" since he was on the run from the police, that he was not guilty of murdering the prime minister or anyone else, and that he wanted the TV station to help him communicate that fact to its viewers. By the time he had finished explaining all this, he realized the call had gone on too long, but he thought he could hear the woman he'd been talking to speaking to someone else. The conversation was too muffled to catch, but it was clear that she was reporting the situation to a manager of some sort who must have been near her position in the phone bank. A moment later a man's voice came on the line.

"Yajima here. I'm a producer. You say you're Masaharu Aoyagi?"

"That's right."

"I have to tell you, sir, that we've had a large number of calls from people claiming to be Masaharu Aoyagi, almost all of them wanting to take credit for the crime. But you're saying that you're being *framed* for it?"

"Yes, I'm innocent."

"But can you prove you are who you say you are?"

Aoyagi said nothing for a moment. How did you prove you were you? "If I can," he said at last, "can you protect me?"

"Protect you?"

"The police are after me."

"Then why don't you just tell them you're innocent?"

Aoyagi could feel his exasperation returning. He wanted to tell the man it wasn't as simple as that, that it was too late to "just tell" the police anything. Images of men in suits running after him and of Kobatozawa with his gun flashed through his head. "I want to stay at your studio until I can make them understand," he said.

There was no response, and Aoyagi felt a pang of disappointment, realizing he had been hoping for this concession above all else. Finally, Yajima spoke up again. "That would be difficult," he said. "First, we would have to verify your story. It would be irresponsible to simply pass it along to our viewers without doing this."

"And you think you're being responsible passing along the lies they're telling about me without verifying those?" He knew sarcasm would do him no good, but he couldn't stop himself.

There was another silence. "I'm afraid we're required to report any information you give us to the police," Yajima said eventually. "We received orders to that effect last night. So if you did come to the studio, we would try to protect you as far as we legally could, but we would have to let the police know that you're here." At least he had the decency to tell the truth.

So the story might go like this: he makes his way to the studio; he finds himself in front of a bank of cameras; but the cameramen turn out to be police officers who draw their guns and shoot him down. The employees of the TV station are horrified, but Ichitaro Sasaki appears from somewhere and calmly informs them that Aoyagi was armed and dangerous so they'd had no choice. The explanation seems suspicious and conspiracy theories are tossed around, but it's impossible to determine the truth. At any rate, Masaharu Oswald is dead, and the story ends inconclusively.

"Did you hear me?" Yajima said.

"I'll think it over and call again," Aoyagi said. What else could he say?

Yajima seemed to hesitate for a moment and then gave him a cell phone number—presumably his own—and asked him to call if something happened. Aoyagi grabbed a pen from the desk in Miura's hideout and wrote the number on his wrist.

Then he pressed a button to end the call and another to turn off the TV. "Run," Morita had said. And Miura had convinced him he wouldn't solve anything by hiding here. The call to Yajima had made that even clearer.

He fished in his pack for the knit cap, but then remembered that he'd been wearing it when Sasaki had caught him. They were probably looking for someone in a cap by now. They might even have a picture of him wearing it from one of the pods and would be showing it on TV. He threw it into the corner. Hat or no hat, plan or no plan, it was only a matter of time before they caught him.

He was headed north, keeping his head down as he walked. His destination was a building to the northeast of Sendai Station—a long way on foot, but he could think of no other safe way to travel. He would feel too exposed on a bus, and it was almost certain they had shown his picture to the taxi drivers. Yesterday, he had been relatively relaxed, but now just being outdoors made him nervous. He imagined someone grabbing his arm or running off to call the police.

As he waited for the crossing signal at a wide avenue, he thought the couple next to him glanced once too often in his direction. He headed toward the pedestrian bridge down the block instead, but then felt he might have attracted attention by suddenly changing course . . . which made him attract even more attention by dashing up the steps to the top of the bridge. From there, he caught sight of a Security Pod standing guard in the bushes below. He wanted to crouch down and scurry off the bridge but forced himself to cross as calmly as he could. An ambulance passed on the street and his eyes followed the flashing light until it vanished in the distance. He felt like giving up.

The traffic seemed to be moving more smoothly than it had yesterday. They were probably still searching cars leaving the city, but perhaps less thoroughly. A large delivery truck was parked on the side of the road; the driver was retrieving a package from the back.

When he reached the building, he ignored the elevator, opting instead for the dark staircase. The café on the third floor was closed and shuttered—apparently it still opened only when the owner was in the mood.

Aoyagi hid in the tiny bathroom. Since no one used it except the customers of the phantom café, it was unlikely anyone would find him here. Still, the narrow space in the stall made him feel trapped, so he decided to wait by the sink. A hard turn of the knob failed to stop the plinking drops which echoed in his head.

Shortly after nine, the elevator in the building groaned to life, and a moment later he could hear someone in the passage outside. "Shit. Who orders a pickup from a shop that's always closed?" A fist pounded on a door.

Very slowly, Aoyagi stepped out of the bathroom into the passage. "Iwasaki?" he said.

Eijiro "Rock" Iwasaki, hair slicked back as usual, turned to look and his mouth fell open. "Aoyagi?" he murmured, and then froze, propping himself against his hand truck. "What are you doing here? I came to make a pickup."

"I know, I'm sorry—I'm the one who ordered it."

His eyes narrowed. "You? Why?"

"I went online yesterday and filled out the form. I could tell from the route charts that this was your territory."

"I don't follow. What are you talking about?" He had a habit of smiling when he was upset or confused, and he was smiling now. To his relief, Aoyagi could see that he was neither scared nor angry. "But what am *I* talking about? You, my friend, are in deep shit."

"You've been watching TV."

"This morning. I was about to leave when my wife told me to come see. And there you were, the national bad guy. Things were crazy at the company, too. Phones ringing, people running around."

"I'm sorry," Aoyagi said again, bowing his head. Of course they would be swarming around his old workplace. "Must make it hard to get anything done."

"Not to worry." He seemed to be gradually regaining his composure. "So, I assume you didn't do it?"

"What do you mean?"

"I mean, I can't imagine you'd ever be involved in anything like that." Aoyagi studied the lined face for a moment, reminded of the times he'd seen it in profile during the days when Iwasaki had trained him on the job. Listening to music on the truck stereo, he used to comment on each song— "What's up with this? It doesn't rock *or* roll." But his face now looked tired. Aoyagi clenched his teeth and looked down, but Iwasaki must have noticed. "Now don't get all weepy on me," he said. "You heard me? I'm not even asking."

"I'm sorry," Aoyagi stammered, pressing his palms into his eyes. "It's just that I didn't expect you to believe me right away." As he wiped his cheeks, he realized how long it had been since he'd washed his face.

"You know what I think of those bands on TV that haven't got a clue? Same with the books that get popular these days—it's all a load of crap."

"I think I've heard you say something to that effect," he said, managing a smile.

"And that's pretty much what I think about everything I see on TV." Aoyagi felt a real sense of relief and gratitude—someone understood him, his situation, and more than that, his friend was still his friend, was still the same Iwasaki. "So," Iwasaki said again, "what do you need delivered?" He glanced down at the hand truck, draped with a pale, company-blue cloth cover.

"Actually," Aoyagi said, "it's me. I want you to ship me out of Sendai."

He blinked. Not wanting to give him time to think, Aoyagi launched into his idea. He'd been sure that Iwasaki would come with the covered hand truck in response to a request for a big pickup. He would hide under the cover while Iwasaki took him to his truck, and then they could drive out of the city.

"Still, beats me how you knew I'd be the one to show up here," he said. Aoyagi explained that he had accessed the homepage and the drivers' schedules.

"And I knew you would at least hear me out," he told him. Iwasaki rubbed his nose and cracked his neck. "I'm sorry to ask you to do this," Aoyagi added, not daring to meet his eyes, "but there was no one else. I know it doesn't *rock* at all—any of it."

"You're wrong," he chuckled. "It totally rocks. Let's get you packed. Is this going to be COD?"

Masaharu Aoyagi

He had never been on a hand truck before. After he climbed on, Iwasaki put a box over him like a lid. Underneath, he clutched his head to his knees and kept quiet. The cart swayed unsteadily and he could feel every bump in his back. "I parked a few blocks away," Iwasaki murmured.

He could tell when they rolled into the elevator. There was the sound of a bell and they sank slowly toward the ground level. But they stopped almost immediately and the door rattled open again. He heard a man's voice speak just above him.

"Ah, Iwasaki!" It was the owner of the building, the same man who ran the café. "Did you have a delivery?"

Iwasaki laughed, ignoring the question. "Do you usually take the elevator when you're only going down one floor? You'll get too fat to open that café of yours, which you practically never do anyway as far as I can see." The elevator stopped again and the door opened. The other man apparently got off before the cart began moving forward, though too slowly to avoid the closing door, which struck the side of it, sending a jolt through Aoyagi's body.

"Must be crazy at your place," the man observed. "Can't believe it's Aoyagi. I bet your boss is shitting bricks."

"Did you know Aoyagi?" Iwasaki asked.

"Sure. He was through here a good bit. Seemed like a smart guy, reliable. Hard to miss him after all that stuff on TV about him and that girl Rinka."

"He didn't impress me that much," Iwasaki said, perhaps a bit louder than was strictly necessary.

"Just goes to show you can never tell about people. Who'd have thought he'd do something like that. Anyway, must be murder for you guys."

"Not really, at least not for the drivers. I don't know if he did it or not, and he quit the company a while back anyway."

"But killing the prime minister. It's not like it's a parking ticket."

"You're right there," he said. Aoyagi held his breath and tried not to move. The café owner's loud voice had always bothered him when he'd made deliveries here, but now it provided welcome cover. "Why are you so sure he did it?" Iwasaki asked.

"They've got all those pictures of him, and they say there's lots of other evidence. It's him all right. What we don't know is what made him do it." Iwasaki didn't answer right away, and the cart started to roll. Then Aoyagi could hear the other man's voice behind them. "But you never told me what you were doing here. A delivery?"

The cart stopped. "A pickup," Iwasaki said. "They told me to come and I came."

"But there's no one else in the building right now. All my tenants moved out."

Again Iwasaki hesitated. "But *someone* ordered a pickup," he said at last, adding a spooky note to "someone." "Maybe your building's haunted." The cart began to move again. Aoyagi admired the attempt to dodge the question, but he was afraid it might have made the man suspicious anyway.

"Not my building!" he laughed from somewhere in the distance now. "No tenants, and no ghosts!"

The cart shook even more violently once they were out on the street. Every bump rattled the wheels and knocked Aoyagi's back against the frame. At least it drove any other thoughts away. They stopped again and a heavy door opened somewhere nearby. He raised his head a bit.

"When I get this off, you jump in as quick as you can." Iwasaki's voice drifted from above, and then light flooded the cart as the box covering him was pulled away. He felt like a convict hit by a searchlight in the prison yard. He scrambled up into the back of the truck, banging his pack on the door as he went. "Further back," Iwasaki said as he climbed up himself. "I don't have a big load today, so there should be plenty of room. But not much to hide under, I'm afraid. Pile some stuff around you in the corner." Aoyagi looked at the stack of boxes. Iwasaki was right: the truck was on the empty side. Still, he should be able to cover up.

"Thanks to all the ruckus yesterday, hardly anything came in today, so there's not much to do. Lucky, I guess."

"How so?" Aoyagi asked.

"My schedule's open—I can take you wherever you want to go." He rubbed his hands over his face and back through his neatly combed hair. "At least till noon—I've got a pickup here in town," he added, looking down at his manifest.

As they talked, Aoyagi became increasingly nervous about the open door of the truck. He edged toward the wall where the boxes were piled higher. "Okay," he said, "then could you drop me somewhere out of town before you head back here?"

"Take your pick," Iwasaki said, folding his arms in front of his chest. "North or south?"

"Any suggestions?"

"Well, I heard from a guy who came in from another prefecture that the security isn't so tight going north on Route 4 from Izumi to Fujitani."

"Then north it is."

Iwasaki chuckled again. "You're going to have to learn to be a little less trusting," he said. "You don't have to agree with everything I say. What if I was lying—or that driver was? But okay, let's head north for the time being. And you get in one of those empty boxes. Even if they stop us and ask me to open the back, they're not going to search every box in a delivery truck."

"Sorry to put you through all this," Aoyagi said.

"Not much we can do about it now," he replied, scratching the tip of his nose.

"I guess not."

"But you know, I did a fair bit of bragging about you the last few years, after you got famous. Told people I'd trained you, made a big deal about it."

"To your wife?" Aoyagi had met her once.

"And the girls at the club," he said, looking for a moment like a high school kid. "They were impressed when I talked about you, paid more attention to me. *Lots* more, if you know what I mean."

"I think I do."

"What I mean is—I owe you one. So, sit back and relax." But instead of closing the door, he started a typical driver's discussion about the best route for the run. He was against using the bigger roads, proposing instead to skirt the university hospital and take the tunnel under Rinnoji Temple to connect to the beltway, and eventually to Route 4.

"Whatever you decide is okay with me," Aoyagi told him. Since when did a package in the back have a say about the delivery route?

"Fine, then, just leave it to me." But as he was closing the door, he stopped again. "Aoyagi," he said.

"What?" He swallowed, imagining any number of questions that might be coming. Iwasaki seemed uncharacteristically hesitant. "What?" he repeated.

"I've been wanting to ask you. . . ." He stopped again for a moment, then seemed to force himself to go on. "Did you do it with that Rinka?"

Aoyagi burst out laughing. "That seems to be what everybody wants to know."

The door closed and the back of the truck went dark around him. When doors closed now, he had the helpless feeling they might never open again.

Masaharu Aoyagi

The engine turned over and the truck began to move. Aoyagi stumbled to the front of the cargo bay, right behind the driver's seat, and sat down. The engine thrummed in his ears like the heartbeat of a large animal; a beast now awake, breathing evenly—with him like a tasty morsel awaiting digestion in its bowels.

He climbed into a box as Iwasaki had suggested but left the top open. As his eyes adjusted to the dark, he opened his pack. He wasn't particularly hungry, but then again he wasn't sure when he'd next have time to eat. Unwrapping one of the energy bars, he began to chew it. He knew it was supposed to be sweet, but the wad in his mouth was flavorless, like damp cardboard—though still an improvement over Miura's spiked ramen. But there was no escaping the fact that he was sitting in a box in the back of a truck eating pseudofood.

As he poked around in his pack, his hand closed on the portable game unit he had bought the day before—which seemed already like the distant past. He inserted the batteries, punched a few buttons, and a TV picture appeared on the screen. The clerk had not exaggerated about the reception: even in the back of a moving truck, the picture was exceptionally clear. He fiddled with a knob to adjust the volume.

There, on the tiny screen, as he knew it would be, was his own face. Unable to watch, he flipped through the channels, but he seemed to be on all of them. He finally settled on some footage that appeared to be from a security camera in a store. Shot from behind the register, the scene showed the back of the clerk's head. "This is clearly Masaharu Aoyagi purchasing the helicopter," an announcer intoned.

The man across the counter from the clerk looked up, and for an instant his eyes stared straight into the camera as though he knew it was there. Then he looked away, but that instant was enough to be sure: it was Aoyagi's face. "What the fuck?" he muttered.

He had never been to the model shop. Koume Inohara had bought the helicopter and even put it together for him, so the scene on the tape had never happened. Still, there he was—in a still extracted from the footage now filling the screen—or someone who looked exactly like him. It was mind-boggling.

But come to think of it, he had seen the owner of a *tonkatsu* shop swear that he'd finished off a big lunch just before the parade. He had even shown the reporter Aoyagi's credit card. "What the fuck?"

Yesterday, before the parade, he had had lunch with Morita: burgers, not *tonkatsu*. He hadn't so much as walked past a *tonkatsu* shop. But someone—him, yet not him—had been there. He hugged his knees hard to reassure himself that the person balled up here in this box was Masaharu Aoyagi. But who was the man on the TV?

The truck stopped periodically, apparently at traffic lights; then it moved on again. Aoyagi's eyes were glued to the miniature screen. They were now showing a video, identified as something a viewer had sent in, of a little league game at a ball field near the river. By the time he realized they were focusing on a lone figure in the background flying a remote-controlled helicopter—and that the face was his own—he was past the point of being surprised. The face was his, but it wasn't him. He had practiced flying the thing once near the river, but only with a group of fliers, including Koume, who was helping him get started. He had never been there alone. What's more, he had never seen the clothes the Aoyagi in the video was wearing.

A double. The implications began to churn in his head. Someone built like me, surgically altered to look like me. At first it seemed like a ridiculous idea; but how else to explain these pictures? And then there was something Rinka had told him a couple of years ago.

"Everybody seems so sure I've had work done." They had been sitting in a hotel room playing a video game when Rinka had suddenly brought up the topic. "And that my boobs are fake," she added, giving them a friendly squeeze. Embarrassed, Aoyagi looked away.

In the wake of the incident at her apartment, Aoyagi had been mobbed by the media and by new fans; Rinka, too, had received extra attention, and the encounter had left her shaken. So they had not seen each other again until six months later, when Aoyagi had received a call from her saying she wanted to thank him in person. Her manager showed up soon afterwards and took him to the hotel.

Since she had included the manager in the arrangement, Aoyagi had no expectations—no, no hope, he told himself, that they would end up in bed—but he certainly wasn't expecting the first words out of her mouth when the door to the room opened. "Do you play?" She nodded at a video game console. "Will you play with me?"

Her manager had urged him to, saying how much fun it was for her.

Rinka laughed. "Don't get him wrong. I'm not sure he even knows what 'it' means." Then, for the next hour, as they played a martial arts game, she told him how grateful she was for what he'd done—while repeatedly beating the crap out of him on the screen.

"You're killing me!" she screamed at the rare moment she was doing badly.

While they played, Rinka had grumbled about the hardships of a celebrity's life, and it was then that she mentioned plastic surgery.

"I haven't had any work done on my face, nothing at all. But they said something looked different in a photo, and then there were all these rumors that I'd had my eyes done, or my nose. They can be *so* cruel."

Unsure what to say to this or even where to let his eyes come to rest on such a famous face and body, Aoyagi glanced around the room. As he did so, Rinka's avatar scored another knockdown, and the real woman pumped her fist in the air and let out a whoop.

"Can they really change you that much with surgery?" he'd asked. He wasn't particularly interested in the topic but it was something to talk about.

"They can," she said. "Completely . . . or at least that's what I've heard. But they say even a little work can make a huge difference. Of course, you have to have the right doctor. Did you know that one of the most famous ones is right here in Sendai?" She glanced at her manager. The conversation apparently made him uneasy, but he nodded. "You remember that super-famous singer who showed up in Japan recently?" she said, pronouncing the foreign name with a flourish. "Well, they say he came to get this doctor to make him some body doubles." Her hand played with the game controller.

"Body doubles?" he echoed, feeling as if he'd wandered into a spy movie.

"Apparently the paparazzi had been giving him such a hard time, he decided he needed some look-alikes as a diversion."

"Would they really fool anyone?"

"If the bone structure is close, it's almost impossible to tell the differ-ence. . . . I mean, I've heard it is," she added, glancing again at her manager.

"So we've heard," he said, bringing the topic to an end.

Aoyagi studied the image on the tiny screen more closely. An assassination like this was the result of a plan too big and sinister for one little person down here on the ground to comprehend. So it was possible that a double had been created—anything was possible. But this much was certain: when a giant moves, someone below is bound to get crushed.

But what could he do? How could you fight back? How could he get out of this mess and get back to his life? No matter how hard he thought about it, no plan presented itself.

What did they do in the movies? There were lots of cases of people being framed for crimes they didn't commit, sympathetic heroes running from the police while trying to prove their innocence. He tried to remember how these other poor dupes had managed to make it to the Happy Ending. Catch the real culprit—that was it. Keep one step ahead of the police, discover the truth, expose the plot, prove his innocence. Then everybody could go home more or less satisfied.

The real culprit? The giant had planned carefully, planted witnesses, faked credit cards, created a body double and perhaps even false friends . . . all to prove he was the guilty party. How was he going to find the real villain, much less bring him to justice, as the formula required? For that matter, was there a "real" villain in a plot this big and intricate? Had there been a "real" assassin in the Kennedy case? If it wasn't Oswald, then who was it? Someone had pulled the trigger, but was he the real killer? Or was there a figure behind him, pulling the strings?

What if, by some wild chance, Oswald had managed to survive long enough to stand in front of the cameras and shout that it was someone else, somebody lurking in the shadows? Would anyone have believed him? It seemed unlikely. It wasn't until decades later that other explanations began to seem credible—but even these were only speculation. Even now we don't know the full truth.

So what could Oswald have done? What could he himself do now? He tapped his feet on the floor, unable to keep still. Iwasaki would help him get out of Sendai, but then what? Closing his eyes, he hugged his knees and hummed. *"Sleep pretty darling, do not cry."* Morita's tune, the last time he'd seen him.

Masaharu Aoyagi

The truck veered left and stopped. At first he assumed it was just a traffic light, but this time they sat there until he realized something was different.

He switched off the game unit and slipped it back in his pack. Something was about to happen, but he didn't know whether that meant he should crouch down deeper in his box or get out and get ready to run.

Had they been pulled over for a search? Was Iwasaki still in front? Worst-case scenarios ran through his head as he shifted around to listen for sounds from the cab. If the police were questioning Iwasaki, he might be able to catch a bit of it. It suddenly occurred to him that the truck might already be parked at a police station somewhere and surrounded by men with guns. But he reminded himself of Morita's motto: trust and habit.

A moment later, when the door at the back began to rattle, he instinctively put his hands together and bowed his head, like a boy praying in church—though he had no idea whom to pray to. He prayed the only prayer he had ever prayed—the one that came to mind as his father was beating up the man on the platform—for it all to end soon.

But maybe this stop meant no more than the earlier ones. Maybe Iwasaki would appear any second now and apologize for the delay. Maybe he had one package he absolutely had to deliver. The door rattled again and then flew open. Aoyagi's stomach lurched.

Light poured in from outside, and he strained to keep his eyes from squinting shut. He was prepared for a phalanx of policemen silhouetted in the door, but it was just Iwasaki who jumped in with him. The worried look on his face made it clear that something had happened.

"You know how much I like rock?" he said. "One guitar chord and everything wrong in the world seems to come right. No complicated message—it is what it is." Aoyagi stared up at him. "So I'll give this to you straight, like rock, without beating around the bush." He stopped for a moment and smoothed back his hair. "There's been a change of plans. We're headed for the subway station at Yaotome. The police are coming and I'm going to hand you over there."

He didn't even feel as though he'd been betrayed; Iwasaki must have his reasons.

"I had a call just now," he said. "Who do you think it was?"

Glancing down at his pack, Aoyagi muttered "The police?" though it wasn't really a question.

Iwasaki shrugged. "That guy back at the café must have called the company, told them there was something funny about the pickup. Not hard to figure out—it's his building, no other tenants."

"Clever guy," said Aoyagi.

"Despite appearances."

"So then the company would have called the police."

"And the police called me. Asked if I knew the penalty for 'harboring a criminal.'"

"I'm not a criminal."

"I believe you, but somehow they'd found out about a little secret I've been keeping, and they are basically blackmailing me. You see, I've been doing some business on the side, moonlighting. On days off, I make deliveries for especially good customers on my own, charge them a lower rate, and everyone makes out—except the company. The guy on the phone said they knew all about it, and they would tell the company if I didn't cooperate. Feels like a fucking grade school tattletale, except they'll get me fired right when my daughter's starting all those expensive girlie lessons. I hate to put it this way, but it looks like I'm selling you out—I had no choice."

"I don't blame you," Aoyagi said. "Just make sure you get a decent price."

"I'm sorry," said Iwasaki.

"It's okay. I don't think I could stand making things any worse for you than I already have."

"I told them I'd turn you over in front of the subway station up ahead."

"And you stopped here to ask how I felt about it?"

"Something like that. To see how the lamb looks going to the slaughter, I guess." He paused for a moment. "Or not," he added.

"What do you mean?"

"Why should I do what those assholes tell me?" he snorted.

Aoyagi reminded him how dangerous it would be to do otherwise.

"Save it," said Iwasaki, smiling and scratching his ear. "I know I don't look like the type, but I cried my eyes out when I saw *Schindler's List*. I figure there are two kinds of people in the world: the ones who play it safe and the ones who'll take a risk to help a friend. I guess I decided which kind I want to be."

"But what can you do now?" Aoyagi asked.

"Well, for starters I'll do just what they told me to do. I'll take you to the subway station. I hope you don't mind, but I'll tell them this was all your fault, that you forced me into it. That should let me cover my ass." Then he went on to explain his plan. It was very simple—true to form for Rock Iwasaki, but Aoyagi realized it was his only chance of getting away without implicating his friend. When he finished, Iwasaki clapped twice. "Let's do it," he said, heading toward the back door of the truck. "Showtime!"

"How do I thank you?" said Aoyagi.

"Just get your part right." As he was closing the door, he called back one more time. "You know, a few rounds with the cops isn't half as scary as tangling with my wife."

Masaharu Aoyagi

Even inside the box locked away in the back, Aoyagi could follow their route in his head as though he were driving the truck. So he knew when they arrived at Yaotome Station. There was no time to think about what was going to happen, but he realized he wasn't particularly nervous. As he looked back at the cargo door, the boxes seemed to be holding their breath in the dim light, waiting with him for whatever the world outside had in store. It occurred to him that a man who thought of cardboard boxes as his friends was losing his grip, but at that moment the door began to rattle. Someone pulled on the lever and released the lock; he could hear voices outside, shouting. "Stop! Stay there!"

Sunlight flooded the back of the truck, and Iwasaki's voice rose above the others. "Relax," he called. "I can handle this." With a grunt, he leapt into the back of the truck.

"Get down!" somebody yelled from behind. "Get away from there!"

"Don't get all excited. I know him, I trained him. He'll listen to me," Iwasaki called over his shoulder as he came toward Aoyagi. He had foreseen exactly this moment when he explained his plan: "As soon as I get the door open, I'll come in to bring you out. They'll try to stop me, but I'll get the jump on them. Even the most badass cop isn't going to shoot me in the back when I'm trying to help them catch you." He marched through the boxes with his arms out wide—to block their line of sight, Aoyagi realized. Still crouching in his box, he slowly shifted his pack to his shoulder. Then he slid a butterfly knife from his hip pocket—the one that Iwasaki had given him just a moment ago. "I keep it in the dashboard. Comes in handy sometimes. When I get close, you jump up and hold it to my neck. Then slide around behind me and take me hostage." The choreography had been exact. "No, scratch that. It'll look staged if you just grab me without a fight. You'd better hit me or knock me down or something first."

"Hit you?"

"Or something. It'll be more convincing that way."

So Aoyagi followed instructions. When Iwasaki approached, he jumped up and grabbed him. Then he lashed out with his leg in a sweeping circle— the judo move again. As Iwasaki pitched forward, Aoyagi could see Kazu, all those years ago, falling in identical fashion with Morita poised above him.

More angry shouts outside the truck. "Aoyagi!" someone called. He glanced at Iwasaki lying at his feet, and then looked up to find he was staring down the barrels of a lot of guns. "If you knock me over, you've got to pull me up right away and use me as a shield. Wait around and they'll shoot you right there." He remembered Iwasaki's instructions.

Bending over, he grabbed Iwasaki, pulled him to his feet, and pressed the blade of the knife to his neck. Iwasaki slowly raised his hands, assuming the pose of a proper hostage. "Aoyagi! No!" he shouted.

Iwasaki had originally proposed that they stop short of the station; Aoyagi could then tie him up and get away. But they both knew the police were unlikely to buy this. So they had decided that Aoyagi would have to take him hostage right in front of their eyes.

Hiding behind his friend as best he could, he moved slowly toward the door of the truck. When he could see outside, he realized there were at least a dozen men—with more on the way, no doubt. Sirens wailed in the distance. A line of police cars had pulled up at the bus stop to the right. The sight of all those guns made his heart pound, his head swim. For a second he thought he might fall back into the boxes.

"Don't shoot!" Iwasaki screamed. "He's got a knife!" As they hopped down from the truck, the men drew back.

"Aoyagi, there's no point in running," said a plainclothes officer in front of them. "You can't get away."

"Don't come any closer or I'll cut his throat," Aoyagi shouted. Iwasaki had assured him that the police would behave reasonably, that they were trained to be cautious—and so far it seemed he was right. "Move back!" he called.

The ones in uniform glanced at the man in the suit who had spoken earlier, a detective probably. "A cop is just like any other working stiff," Iwasaki had told him. "He can't go shooting people anytime he feels like it; he basically waits around for someone to tell him what to do."

With obvious reluctance, the detective held up his hand and signaled for the others to retreat a few steps. Still holding on to Iwasaki, Aoyagi edged sideways toward the fence along the road. Then he began slowly backing away. The police followed at a distance. "So far so good," Iwasaki said under his breath.

"Sorry," Aoyagi muttered.

"We'll get to those apartments in just a second. You know what to do. The street doesn't go through the complex, so they'll have to follow on foot. You can run through to the river or head for the park. You're a driver, you know the layout."

"I'm sorry," he said again.

"No need to apologize," Iwasaki whispered. "Consider us even for my luck with the girls at the club."

"I'll remember to let your wife know how grateful you were."

"When this is over, we'll have you over and you can tell her in person!" Resisting the urge to smile—and ruin their whole show—Aoyagi looked up at the row of stony faces. He began to lose heart. Something told him they were about to shoot.

Iwasaki had assured him they would never endanger an innocent bystander, particularly someone who had agreed to cooperate but was now being held hostage. But his assumption was based on the normal code of conduct, and these were anything but normal times. This was a state of emergency. Remember Kobatozawa shooting out the restaurant window, Kazu lying half dead on the floor of his apartment? The rules had changed, or else the police weren't playing by them anymore. They had Masaharu Aoyagi standing in front of them, lined up in their sights, and they weren't about to let him get away. From the giant's point of view, it made no difference whether they shot him alone or with someone else. Absolutely no difference. But it made a difference to him. How could he let Iwasaki get hurt?

The detective had a cell phone to his ear, and Aoyagi thought he could imagine the exchange. "He's got a hostage. Do I have permission to take the shot?" All he needed was confirmation from someone up the chain of command, perhaps even their old friend Sasaki.

"Damn rubbernecks," Iwasaki muttered close to his ear, and Aoyagi followed his line of sight up to the apartment block across the way. Here and there, curious faces looked down from the balconies.

"Don't shoot!" Aoyagi suddenly blurted out. "And smile for the camera!" His hand moved away from Iwasaki's throat to point at the building. Iwasaki, of course, made no move to get away, though the police seemed to be too busy to notice. They turned to look in the direction Aoyagi had indicated: nearly everyone in sight had a video or digital camera trained on them.

The detective turned back to Aoyagi with a look of open hatred. Too many witnesses. There was resignation in his eyes.

Keeping the fence at his back and Iwasaki in front of him, Aoyagi retreated the last little stretch down the street. When he reached the corner, he pushed Iwasaki away and fled into the apartment complex.

Masaharu Aoyagi

He ran along the bank of the Nanakita River until he found himself under a large bridge. From the moment he released Iwasaki, he had run flat out, and he was gasping for air. Resting in the shadow of a piling, he noticed a plaque that should have told him the name of the bridge, but it was worn and illegible. Iwasaki had been right about running through the apartment buildings: not only did they have to follow him on foot, but they couldn't open fire with so many bystanders around. Still, he had stumbled along feeling certain that a hand would reach out and grab him at any moment.

He leaned against the piling, sinking down and putting his palms flat on the concrete behind him. If he curled up, made himself small, it might be harder to see him from the bridge. The blind of tall weeds on either side would help. As he sat and waited, the cool of the earth seeped through his jeans. His brain was frozen, overwhelmed by the task of recovering the oxygen it had lost as he ran. His gaze drifted out to the barely rippling surface of the river, lapping along in a gentle, rhythmic motion.

He struggled to keep his eyes open. The world around him blurred, and a huge weight seemed to have come to rest on his shoulders. He was suddenly afraid that he could no longer stand—but even that seemed to come to him through a dense cloud.

A siren wailing in the distance startled him awake. Hungry for news, he extracted the game unit from his backpack, pulled out the antenna, and hit the power button. As the screen lit up, he thought for an instant that he would see himself crouching here by the river, complete with appropriate voiceover: "And here we have the suspect, Aoyagi, busy with his computer game." In fact, what appeared was an elaborately produced commercial. Flames flickered up, filling the screen, then died away to reveal what appeared to be the kitchen in a fancy Chinese restaurant. As he watched, though, it became clear that the cuisine was French—a commercial for a packaged sauce marketed by a famous chef.

I've been there, Aoyagi thought, with Haruko. She had insisted they go to celebrate the anniversary of the start of their relationship—three months before? Something of the sort. Or rather, they'd intended to go on their anniversary but they'd been caught in a sudden downpour and had to cancel the reservation and postpone the visit to another day. In the end, after all the buildup, the food had not lived up to its reputation and the staff had been rude to them—a pretty miserable evening. Still, it seemed like a happy memory compared to the current state of affairs.

When the commercial ended, the screen showed a shot of an announcer with a microphone, and in the background a place he knew well. "Rocky," he whispered as he recognized Todoroki Pyrotechnics.

Rocky had told them that he had picked the location for the factory to avoid problems with neighbors—since there weren't any when they'd moved in. But as time went by, houses crept closer and closer and they started hearing complaints about the dangers of living near a fireworks factory. They were even asked to move out. "I was here first," Rocky liked to mutter—and, in fact, from the shot on the TV it seemed he had managed to stay put.

"We haven't been able to reach Mr. Todoroki for comment." The reporter seemed to be talking to the announcer back in the studio. "It's too early to say whether Aoyagi used the knowledge of explosives he gained here in the current incident, but it has to be considered a possibility."

Aoyagi no longer had the energy to feel indignant. His only concern was the trouble he must be causing Rocky. He stood up, closing his hand over the miniature TV. "Who made you judge and jury? You don't know shit about me." He felt more determined than ever not to give in.

As he swung his pack onto his shoulder, an image came into his head: the little yellow car in a clump of bushes where he and Haruko had taken refuge from the storm.

Haruko Higuchi

Haruko strapped Nanami into her car seat. "Where are we going, Mommy?" she asked. They had walked back from the restaurant and gone straight to the parking lot next to their building.

"I just remembered something we have to do," Haruko told her, closing the rear door. Climbing in the front, she adjusted the mirror and the seat.

"Mommy," Nanami called from the back, "are we going to get a cake?"

Haruko laughed. "Is that the only reason we get in the car?"

"To get a toy?" she tried.

"Not today." As she turned the ignition, she realized how rarely she had driven lately. She backed out of the space and left the parking lot. Her cell phone in the well next to the handbrake caught her eye; it made her uncomfortable to know they might be listening.

It had been so long since she'd been this way she wondered whether she could remember the route. "I wish we'd got that GPS," she murmured. Her husband had wanted one when they bought the car, but she had insisted they would never use it.

Nanami had heard her. "Don't you know where we're going?"

"I do," she said, "but the GPS makes it easier."

"To go where?"

"Memory Lane," Haruko laughed.

"Does it know how to get there?" Nanami asked. Haruko wasn't sure she knew herself; she would simply have to see how it went. She took Route 4 heading west, then turned right onto a narrower street that meandered through blocks of modest houses. The traffic wasn't heavy, but there was a steady stream of cars in both directions. Out of practice and distracted as she was, she found it hard to keep her mind on the road.

Fortunately, all the turns came back to her as she drove, and she was managing to find her way without going astray. Just then, Nanami began to complain that she needed to stop for the bathroom. "I think I drank too much juice," she said.

"Looks like they caught him."

Haruko started. While she was waiting in a convenience store for Nanami to come out of the bathroom, she heard a voice behind her and turned to find two girls reading at the magazine rack. She wanted to push in between them to see what they were looking at.

"You mean that Aoyagi guy? The one who killed the prime minister?" the other girl asked. The phrase rang in Haruko's ears.

"Somebody in class saw the police around a truck near the subway station at Yaotome," said the first girl. "She said he came out of the truck."

Haruko pretended to browse in a shelf of cosmetics as she tried to catch what they were saying. If they already had him, it was too late—and maybe he really was guilty. For a second she imagined that getting caught might be proof of guilt.

"I'm done, Mommy," Nanami said, smiling up at her now and wiping her wet hands on her mother's jeans. "I did it all by myself!"

The girls from the newsstand were in front of them in line when they went to pay for the candy Nanami had selected. They looked almost like twins, identical hair and makeup and baskets filled with magazines and junk food. A cell phone rang and one of them answered.

"Right now? Waiting to pay," she drawled, sounding slightly exasperated. "What? Really? He got away again? Really? Cameras? Think they got you? Really?" Haruko felt grateful for the girl's otherwise annoying habit of repeating everything her friend said on the other end. Then Nanami looked up at her for a moment, smiled, and turned to the girls.

"He got away?" she asked, tugging on a sleeve. "The bad man?" The girls seemed startled, but when they saw Nanami, they relaxed.

"That's right," one of them said. "He got away."

"The bomb man?" Nanami persisted. Her mother took a step closer.

"That's right. My friend said he had a knife."

"A knife?" Haruko echoed, but just then a clerk appeared at the next register and she moved over with Nanami to pay.

As soon as they were back in the car, she picked up the phone. She wanted to know where Aoyagi was, whether he had been arrested or not; but who could she call? She dialed a number and hit "send," though she was almost sure the line would be busy.

"Who is it?" Todoroki's familiar voice barked.

"It's me," she said, hurrying to add, "Haruko Higuchi. I used to work for you when I was in school . . . with Morita. . . ."

Silence. Maybe he didn't remember her, or didn't want to get more involved than he already was. She was beginning to think he'd hung up when he finally answered.

"Haruko?"

"You remember me?"

"How could I forget? Especially with your friend causing such a fuss."

"I'm sorry," she said, noting that he'd said "your friend."

"I assume you had nothing to do with it."

"No, of course not, but I saw the factory on TV and all the reporters. It must be a pain."

"I'm a pretty popular guy right now," he chuckled.

"I imagine they're making it hard to get anything done."

"Fortunately, this is our slow season. We've been able to keep the cameras outside, but the guys in the factory are a little unhappy. Only a few of them actually knew Aoyagi, but the reporters seem to want me, and they don't give up easy. Someone's constantly at the door or on the phone."

"And you always said pyrotechnics was a lonely business."

"Not anymore. I guess this is my fifteen minutes."

"But what do they want?"

"To know whether I taught Aoyagi anything about explosives."

"Did you?"

"Of course not, absolutely nothing at all. If that kid knows how to make a bomb, then I know how to make a rocket to the moon." Todoroki was laughing now, too. "When the first reporter showed up, I heard him out. I told him I didn't think he did it."

"But they cut that out of the interview. It was never on," Haruko said. The media seemed to do little more than reflect public opinion back on itself. Not that they lied exactly, but their truth was highly selective. "I don't think he did it either."

"And the part about Morita . . . more lies."

"I know."

"It's not easy to get rid of a nuisance like that," he said, forcing a laugh.

"I hope not," said Haruko, wanting to believe it. Her fist tightened around the phone when she remembered the police might be listening. She knew they were keeping track of her calls, and they would no doubt be curious when they saw she was getting in touch with the owner of the fireworks factory. But maybe if they heard the two of them say that they didn't believe Aoyagi was guilty, they might consider the possibility. She liked the idea of planting a seed of doubt in their minds.

"So to what do I owe the pleasure?" Todoroki said.

Haruko wasn't sure herself why she had called. "I just wanted to tell you how sorry I am for all the trouble."

"Very thoughtful of you. But I suppose we should both be more worried about Aoyagi. He's still out there somewhere. They said he took a truck driver hostage and then got away. I wonder where he's headed."

"Maybe your way," she joked, before realizing it wasn't out of the question.

She suspected Aoyagi might not have a lot of close friends he could count on in a pinch. But did anyone? How many people in a lifetime do we really come to trust? "So have you come up with any great new fireworks?" she asked, feeling the need to change the subject.

"One or two. But we still have all the old standbys. That's what brings them out on a summer night." Haruko remembered the displays she'd watched from Todoroki's staging area.

"Let's talk again soon," she said, and then started to give him her number.

"It's right here on my phone," he interrupted. "Even I know that."

"Very up to date," she said.

"Like my fireworks."

"But there was one thing I wanted to ask you," she said before he could hang up.

"How to make a bomb?"

Haruko frowned, wondering again who might be listening. "No, I want to know where I can get a car battery."

"A battery? Is yours dead?"

"Almost," she said, rubbing her hands along the steering wheel. "My husband told me to get a new one when I had time."

"So you're married, too?" Todoroki said.

"Life goes on."

"Well, you could get a battery at an auto parts store, and most gas stations carry them, though they're more expensive. I've got some guys around here with nothing to do. Should I send one over to give you a hand?"

"Nothing to do?" she said.

"With all this ruckus, I can't get them to settle down to work. My son went off to play pachinko and hasn't come back."

"But he came back from Aomori to work with you?" Haruko said. They had known how upset he was that his only son had gone off to live in another city without making it clear whether he intended to take over the factory.

"For the time being anyway. Ichiro has the skills for this business, but his personality's all wrong. He's too impetuous, a bit of a rebel. This morning he got so worked up we had to stop him from throwing a firecracker at the reporters outside."

"They would have loved that."

"That's why I made him go and play pachinko. But I think I can get in touch with him. Should I send him to help you with the battery?"

"No, I can manage." She thanked him and pressed "end." "Sorry that took so long," she said over her shoulder to Nanami. She pulled out of the parking lot and stepped on the accelerator.

A few minutes later, she turned onto the Sendai Kita Loop Road. It sloped gently downhill; traffic was sluggish. Perhaps people had decided to escape the confusion in the aftermath of the assassination, or maybe it was just a reaction to the lockdown yesterday. Soon she was sitting in bumper-to-bumper traffic. A sign for an auto parts store caught her eye on the left and she turned into the parking lot. "Is this Memory Lane?" Nanami asked. Haruko laughed and shook her head.

Helping Nanami out of her car seat, she locked the doors and headed into the store. On the way, she studied the traffic on the Loop: with so little space between cars, she should be able to tell immediately if someone was following her.

When she told the girl behind the counter that she wanted a car battery, her reply was curt: "What kind?" Haruko supposed she meant what kind of car.

"The normal kind," she said, matching the girl's tone.

"Compact? Mid-size?"

"I don't think it was a compact," she murmured. She had a vague recollection that it was yellow. "Can you buy a battery without knowing what kind of car it's for?"

A look of disdain showed in the girl's eyes. "There's all kinds of batteries. Even the same maker uses different ones depending on the model and the year. If you don't have the part number, there's no way to tell."

Haruko knew next to nothing about the vehicle. All she could think of was the tune Aoyagi had sung when they took shelter from the rain in it. Nanami pulled on her sleeve and asked what she was humming.

"It's the jingle from the ad for the car," she said, and did it more loudly so the girl behind the counter could hear. To Haruko's surprise a light seemed to go on in her eyes.

"Why didn't you say so?" she laughed, reeling off the make and model as though this were the way other customers placed their orders.

"I'm afraid I don't know the year," Haruko said.

"Well, let's see what we can do," said the girl, wandering off down a row of shelves. Haruko hurried after her. Stopping in front of the batteries, the clerk turned to look at her. "It's probably that one, or that," she said, pointing at two different boxes. "But I guess you could make either one work if you had to."

"Would you mind explaining how you hook it up?" Haruko asked. The girl gave her another mildly disapproving look but then apparently thought better of it.

"Yes, ma'am, of course. Let's go try it on your car." She didn't particularly like the "ma'am," but Haruko followed her out to the parking lot. When they got the hood open, Haruko was given a lecture on battery installation.

"Remove the negative cable first, then the positive one."

"You have to do it in that order?"

"If you don't, you could short out the engine."

"'Short out'?"

"Just do it in that order," said the girl. "Then you remove the old battery and clean the terminals. Finally, you connect the new battery, this time starting with the positive cable." Haruko nodded solemnly at each step, and Nanami, standing on tiptoe to see the engine, nodded along with her. "If you're planning to do it yourself, make sure you've got a wrench: but any gas station will do it for almost nothing"—the implication being that some assistance was clearly indicated in her case.

"Thanks," said Haruko. "Could you get rid of the box for me?"

Haruko Higuchi

"What's it for?" Nanami asked, looking at the large bag next to her seat.

"You'll just have to wait and see," Haruko said. To avoid traffic, she got off the Loop and headed north on back streets, but as soon as she thought she'd found a good route, the brake lights of the car ahead came on and she was stuck again. For a while, they inched along, until she suddenly realized they were coming to a checkpoint.

A number of police cars were parked on the shoulder, and an officer with a flashlight was signaling for cars to pull over. Several more of them were questioning drivers. Before she had time to think about what she would say—or even to get nervous—she was pulling up.

When she rolled down her window, a face was staring at her. Human—she could tell by the hat—but almost completely devoid of any character.

"Sorry for the inconvenience, ma'am," the man said. "But we believe the fugitive may be in Izumi Ward, and we're searching all vehicles in the area."

"Is that so?" Haruko said. For some reason, the words sounded unnatural even to her own ears.

"Would you mind opening the trunk, please?" Haruko bent forward and pulled the little lever under the seat. When she sat back up and looked in the rearview mirror, she saw that several policemen were lined up behind the car. One of them lifted the trunk. She knew she had nothing to hide, but somehow she still felt uneasy. "Is this your daughter?" the one at the window continued, peering in at the back seat.

"Yes," Haruko said, glancing at his face and then looking quickly away. Without thinking, she jiggled the keys hanging from the ignition, but then, worried that this would be taken for impatience, she dropped her hand to her lap. "It's just one man?" she asked, hoping to draw his attention away from the sound.

The policeman looked at her and waited a beat. "Yes, that's right."

"Does he have a car?"

"We aren't certain." She wanted to know more, but she realized she couldn't continue to question him.

"Where are you headed?" he asked.

"I'm not really sure myself."

"Well, the area is dangerous, so we'd prefer it if you could avoid unnecessary trips."

"I understand, and I'll be careful," Haruko said. The car shook as they slammed the trunk shut, harder than was strictly necessary. When she looked in the mirror again, one of the cops was giving the thumbs-up sign.

"Sorry to have inconvenienced you, ma'am. You're free to go," she was told.

As she was turning the key in the ignition, Nanami called out from the back seat. "Mister! That bad man is Mommy's friend." Haruko shuddered, and glanced involuntarily at the man still standing next to the car. His eyebrows rose, but she closed the window and pulled back onto the road, watching him in the mirror. The last thing she saw was a second man in a suit coming to join him.

Haruko Higuchi

"Did I say something wrong?" Nanami asked as they drove away.

"No, everything's fine."

The road was nearly empty beyond the checkpoint, and they were soon on a broad avenue with three lanes of traffic in each direction. The zelkova trees on either side seemed to watch them, long limbs reaching out toward the car like bony fingers. Haruko pulled over to the side of the road and switched on the hazard signal.

"Are we there now?" Nanami said, craning around to see. Haruko scanned the blind of bushes. It must be somewhere around here, she thought, trying to make the empty lot in front of her match up with her memory.

She was so engrossed in this task that she didn't notice a car stopping right behind her, and if she hadn't been wearing a seatbelt she would have jumped out of her seat in surprise when someone tapped on the glass next to her. Letting out a little cry, she rolled down the window.

"Mrs. Higuchi," said the square-jawed man staring in at her. "We meet again." She realized almost immediately that it was the detective from the hospital. It took her a second more to retrieve his name: Mamoru Kondo. He must have been the man in the suit at the checkpoint.

She smiled up at him. "Something tells me this isn't a coincidence," she said.

"Where are you going?" he asked.

"Everyone seems to want to know where I'm going," she said, feeling her pulse quicken. "Do I really have to tell you?"

"I would appreciate it if you would."

"Well, if you must know, I'm going to visit a friend. Is there something suspicious about that?"

"Of course not," he said. "But Masaharu Aoyagi is still on the loose."

"And you think I'm on my way to meet him?"

"We need to rule out the possibility. I know it may seem a bit extreme to be following you around, but we have no choice."

"Sorry to be so much trouble," she drawled, but sarcasm seemed lost on him.

"You're a scary man!" Nanami piped up at that moment, apparently not wanting to be left out of the conversation and not liking the tone Kondo was taking with her mother.

Leaning closer to the window, he looked back at her. "But there's a scarier man than me somewhere around here," he said.

"He's my mommy's friend," she told him. Haruko panicked for a moment, but then remembered that Kondo knew this already. She looked at Nanami and scratched her nose.

"I know he is," Kondo said. "That's why we're worried about your mommy."

"Oh!" Nanami said suddenly. "I have to go potty. Right now!"

"Can't you wait a bit?" Haruko asked, checking the mirror.

"No, I have to go now!"

"No, sweetie, not here." But she looked up at Kondo who was still stationed outside the window. "Would you mind if I take her into the bushes for a moment?" she asked.

"I'm afraid it's not allowed," he told her.

"I know, and normally I wouldn't do it. But this is a 'state of emergency,' apparently."

"It's a state of 'mergency! It is! I've got to go!" Nanami cried.

Haruko thought she could feel Kondo's official shell soften slightly. He took a step away from the car. "Come right back," he said.

"And if Aoyagi gets in touch in the meantime, you'll be the first to know." She grabbed her phone, pulled the key from the ignition, and climbed out of the car. Then she got Nanami out of her seat and shouldered the bag that had been sitting next to her. Kondo was about to get back into his car when he noticed the bag.

"Mrs. Higuchi," he called after her. "What's in the bag?"

"If you really have to know, it's all the things girls need to go potty," Haruko said. Kondo turned and climbed into his car.

The battery was heavier than she thought, but she was careful not to let any strain show on her face. "Let's go," she said, dragging Nanami off into the bushes.

"Did I help, saying I had to go potty?" Nanami asked as they walked.

"You certainly did! I'm glad you remembered."

Haruko Higuchi

"What do we do with it?" Nanami whispered, looking down at the bag. But Haruko was staring, amazed it was still there, exactly as it had been all those years ago. It was almost funny, huddled in the weeds, unchanged despite everything that had happened. This nondescript yellow car was becalmed, sidelined in the stream of time, stuck here in this forgotten place. With all the time in the world, the weeds and grass had grown up to conceal it from all but the sharpest eyes. "What's it doing here?" Nanami asked, tugging at her sleeve. "It's really dirty."

It was, shockingly so. She had remembered it as being yellow, but in point of fact it was fossil brown now. But it was still here.

Bending down, she found the key hidden in the wheel well, exactly where it had been in the old days. She fitted it in the lock and opened the door, telling Nanami to get in on the passenger's side.

"What's it doing here?" Nanami repeated her question.

"It's always been here," Haruko told her, climbing into the driver's seat. She turned around to study the interior. It smelled of dust and mildew, but it had been like that even back then. She inserted the key and turned the ignition, and though she hadn't been expecting it to start, the desolate click and dead silence still disappointed her.

"Always? Since when?" Nanami persisted.

"Since before you were born."

"That's silly," she laughed. "Before I was born?"

"It's pretty old, isn't it? It's a good old car."

"But it doesn't go anywhere," she observed. She had wriggled closer to

Haruko until she was practically sitting in her lap, apparently trying to see what her mother was doing with the key.

"No, it doesn't," said Haruko, putting her back on the seat. She reached down beside her own seat and pulled on the little lever she found there. It gave easily, and she thought she could feel the hood release in front of her, though the windshield was completely obscured in a layer of dust and pollen. "Now, let's see if we can do it just the way the lady at the store taught us."

She was amazed how easily she managed to change the battery—she who was usually defeated by electrical gadgets. What's more, they had succeeded in getting exactly the same type. She felt a surge of gratitude to the girl at the store. A bit surly, but she knew her auto parts. When she had finished reconnecting the cables, she slammed the hood shut, sending up a puff of dust.

"Will it go now?" Nanami asked as she began to climb back inside. Haruko got behind the wheel. "Will it go?" Nanami repeated.

"I hope so."

She wasn't sure herself why she was so intent on getting the car running again. But it had something to do with fireworks, and the idea that an old friend could be seeing them at the same time from somewhere else. Was there a chance that Aoyagi would remember this old car the way she had? She didn't know where he was or what was happening to him, but she did know that he wasn't responsible for this terrible crime. "Okay, let's give it a try."

Masaharu Aoyagi

Aoyagi turned the key and then let it go; the engine was dead. Admittedly, he had no reason to expect anything different.

Still, he had been hopeful. When he had spotted the back of the empty lot as he walked along the river, he had made a little bargain with fate: if the car was still there and he could get it to run, he would escape. He knew it was an unlikely fantasy, but it was the best he could think of and it sent him plunging into the bushes.

But the engine was dead. That was a fact. He sat for a moment with his arms over his head. Then he brought them down hard on the steering wheel. And then again. The car shook. The battery had probably been dead even back then, and now many more years had passed and more grime had collected on the old yellow body. He'd been lucky just to find the key after all this time.

He tried turning it one more time. Just a dry click. He released the hand-brake and stepped on the accelerator. Then he stomped harder, mashing it to the floor. At last he let go and rested his head on the wheel. If only he'd been able to bring a battery with him. He had known he would probably need one, but he was afraid to show his face at a gas station. But at least it was sheltered here, cut off from the road and the river by the tall grass and thick bushes. He should probably try to rest, to get some much-needed sleep. Perhaps when he woke up, months and years would have passed and no one would remember him anymore. . . . More worthless fantasies.

He looked at his backpack on the seat next to him. Then he turned the key again—how many times had he tried it now? Nothing. He opened the glove compartment. He had heard it held a supply of condoms for this make-shift love hotel. Morita said he was afraid some joker would put a pinhole in one and had sworn he would never use them. The one time he had come here with Haruko, he had prayed she wouldn't find them.

Now it held nothing but a small note pad and a grubby pencil. He began to write before he realized what he was doing.

"I am innocent. Masaharu Aoyagi."

It was pathetic. Not even long enough to be a haiku. But it was the truth. Then why couldn't he get anyone to believe it? He folded the paper and slipped it under the sun visor. Someone would find it, someday. Would it make them wonder? Or sneer?

And what will have become of me by then?

"Don't settle for too little." For some reason the words popped into his head. The mantra of the creepy fish in that old computer game. Haruko had said it convinced her it was time for them to break up. "If we go on like this," she'd told him, "we're headed for a life of 'Good effort.'"

He had been slouched back in the seat, but now he sat up straight. Reaching out toward the window next to him, he traced a star on the glass and then tried to write "Excellent!" underneath. But the dirt was mostly on the outside and the smudges he left were illegible. He gave the key one final turn. Nothing.

Giving up on the car, he made his way out of the bushes and back to the river. He needed to get a battery.

A narrow dirt track next to a bridge took him into high grass again. It was an overgrown hiking trail following the course of the river, ignored by tourists and barely used even by the people living nearby. Away from prying eyes for a moment, he walked along lost in his thoughts—thoughts, hopefully, of finding a battery. But a part of him knew already how absurd this was, and this part had stopped hoping at all.

Did you really think you could get that car running? he asked himself.

Not really, he had to admit. It's just that I thought I might have a chance if I could. Clutching at straws, probably.

All of a sudden, there was an unfamiliar vibration on his back. The cell phone Miura had given him was ringing. He fumbled in his pack and managed to pull it out. The display told him the incoming number was blocked, but he pushed the answer button anyway.

"Too bad," said a voice. It was Miura. "It seemed like a good idea to get an old friend to drive you out of town in his truck."

"I'm glad you think so."

"But they found out. Did he cut a deal with them?"

"No." Iwasaki hadn't let him down.

"Would it surprise you if I told you I was the one who turned you in?" Miura said.

"What?"

"If—I said 'if.' But I didn't," he laughed. "The police and I don't see eye to eye, as you can imagine." Aoyagi found nothing to say in reply. "Are you still there? . . . Can't you take a joke?"

"Who'd be stupid enough to believe anything a serial killer says?"

"Ohhhh!" he wailed. "But I helped you, I rescued you. And I would never ever turn you in." It was true: he had removed the handcuffs and let him stay in his apartment. But he might have done it on a whim. And if he had helped him on a whim, he might just as easily sell him out on another. Apparently, more than any sense of sympathy or justice, it was gut reaction that counted with him. "But I don't care whether you believe me or not," he said. "I just have two things I wanted to tell you."

"Good news?" He didn't want to hear any other kind.

"I suppose you could say that. Or at least some good advice."

"What kind of advice?"

"About a way out."

"I'm all ears."

"The TV was just showing the tape of you buying the helicopter. And the one of a practice flight in a field."

"That wasn't me."

"Obviously," said Miura. Aoyagi was almost disappointed to hear how quickly he had worked it out. "I could tell right away. And that's when I realized you'd fallen into something big. This is no ordinary plot, nothing one man could have cooked up. This is major." At last, someone who seemed to understand. "These guys are big league, with resources to spare, able to come up with a double when they need one."

"At last, someone who understands," Aoyagi said, this time aloud.

Miura laughed. "But the fact that they're huge could work against them, give you an edge."

"How so?"

"What you have to do is get your hands on this double. If you can find him, and expose him—on TV would be best—you'd be on the way to clearing your name. Just the sight of a second you would convince most people that something fishy was going on. You'd get them thinking about it, plant a seed of doubt in the minds of all those people who've already pegged you as the killer. Doubt—that's your tactic."

"I think they must have used plastic surgery," Aoyagi said.

"Naturally. One of the best surgeons is right here in Sendai."

"How do you know about him?" Rinka was one thing, but why should a serial killer follow the ratings for cosmetic surgeons?

"You think I really look like this? I used to be a lot better looking! But the point is, there's a double of you out there somewhere, and your best bet is to smoke him out into the open."

"But how do I do that?" Aoyagi was beginning to see the merit in his suggestion. "How do I find him?"

"I'll ask around," Miura said.

"You?"

"Set a thief to catch a thief, as they say. Anyway, I've got some contacts. But the first thing to realize is that they're not going to leave a guy who looks exactly like you wandering loose in the city. If somebody caught him, it'd be pretty awkward. On the other hand, they may still have a use for him at some point, so I doubt they've moved him too far out of town. I'd say chances are good he's cooling his heels somewhere nearby."

"Like a pinch hitter waiting to get in the game."

"Exactly. So I'll ask around, see if I can find out where they've stashed your twin. I'll get in touch when I know more."

"And I'll try to stay out of harm's way while you're looking."

"I've got another suggestion: find a big parking lot—at a shopping mall or a game center—drop the seat back, and get some rest. It's easy and fairly safe."

"Except for one small problem. I don't have a car."

"I think I can help you there, too—that's the other thing I wanted to tell you. About that car you were trying to start in the vacant lot."

Aoyagi gulped. "How do you know about that?"

"Well, you might say I've been shadowing you."

"Shadowing me?"

"Sorry, another shock," Miura said. "But I just had to see whether you were going to be able to mail yourself out of town. It was a nice idea. So I've been keeping an eye on you."

"From where?" he blurted out, looking around frantically. He'd been as careful as possible the whole time, and it gave him a creepy feeling to realize someone had been able to follow him anyway.

He craned his neck above the grass and scanned the area, convinced Miura was still watching him. On this side of the river was the gentle slope of the man-made embankment he had walked along after leaving the cover of the bridge. On the other, a rougher cliff dropping to the water. But no one in sight on either bank.

"Now keep your head down. Don't get all jumpy," Miura laughed. It was impossible to tell whether he was actually watching or just guessing how Aoyagi would react. "The way you dodged all those police back there was pretty cool," he went on. "So naturally I wanted to see where you'd go next.

I have to admit you surprised me when you ducked into those bushes. How'd you know there was a car in there?" Aoyagi glanced around again. "Relax," Miura said almost immediately. "Anyway, I was sorry to see you get out and trudge off back to the river like a disappointed kid."

"The battery's dead," Aoyagi said.

"But that's where you're wrong," he told him. "After you left, someone else came along." This seemed so improbable to Aoyagi that he said nothing for a moment. "Someone else found the car and did a few repairs—changed the battery, in fact. So I'm guessing it should run now."

"Changed the battery?" he repeated. "Who?"

"I assumed it was a friend of yours."

"Of mine? Who?"

"I'd like to know myself. I can imagine how you must feel right now—enemies everywhere you look, like you're playing an endless Away Game. But you should realize that anyone who puts themselves on your team is taking a helluva risk."

"On my team?"

"Maybe we're just cheerleaders," Miura laughed. "Still, I don't like the idea of involving a little girl, not one as cute as that."

"What little girl?" Aoyagi said, but at that moment the call ended.

A large brown bird—a kite perhaps—was circling over the opposite bank of the river. It flew in a lazy arc, watching silently from overhead. After looking up at it for a moment, he spun around and headed back the way he had come. He walked for a few steps but soon was almost running.

Though he knew it was unlikely that the car had miraculously been repaired in the time it had taken him to walk to the river and back, he had no other plans, nothing more pressing to do. The narrow path at the back of the lot sloped gently upward, but to him it felt like a climb. In the dense grass the yellow paint was barely visible. Clutching his pack, he forced his way in and reached his hand into the wheel well. The key was still there. Settled in the driver's seat, he put the key in the ignition.

Then he sat up and took a deep breath. Would it work?

With his foot still on the brake, he willed it to start. He may have even said it aloud. "Start!"

At first he wasn't sure what was happening. Something shook beneath his foot, followed by a deep growling sound. The engine had come to life, groaning as if about to turn over. It hadn't started, but it was no longer dead. The gas in the tank was old—might even have gone bad or was at least less volatile. But it might start with a little coaxing. He took a deep breath and turned the key again. This time the groaning lasted longer, like the grumbling of someone unwilling to get out of bed. "Start, damn it!" he muttered, and as he did so there was a trembling under his legs and the steering wheel in his hands began to vibrate. His mind went blank with excitement. In the rearview mirror, he could see a cloud of exhaust.

He sat there for a moment, gripping the wheel, his foot hard on the brake. Then he reached out to adjust the mirror, but froze at the sight of his own reflection. It wasn't the look of exhaustion that startled him—he could have expected that—as much as the streaks of tears on his cheeks. He suddenly wondered what Morita would have thought of a man who could cry over a car starting.

The face in the mirror was so completely miserable it was almost funny: he felt he was about to watch himself dissolve into a puddle. So he stepped on the clutch and started to put the car in first, but then remembered the note he'd left behind the visor, which had outlived its purpose if he was going to drive away. As he was about to stuff it in his pocket, something made him stop and smooth it out again. His heart skipped a beat. On the wrinkled paper, next to his note—*I am innocent. Masaharu Aoyagi*—someone had written one more line: *I thought so.*

He looked down at it for some time, then closed his eyes. He wasn't trying to figure out whether he recognized the handwriting or what the line really meant. He was overwhelmed. The engine purred in front of him, as if reminding him it was time to go. "I thought so," he said aloud, savoring the words.

He put the car in gear, released the handbrake, and plowed his way out of the weeds—only to find himself brushing close by an old man, bent almost double, who was apparently out for a walk when the car came hurtling out of the undergrowth. The man backed away in horror, then fell awkwardly onto the grass behind him. Aoyagi felt bad about giving him such a fright, but it didn't stop him from making a hard turn onto the street and stomping on the gas. The car rattled and groaned but failed to pick up speed. The tires were badly underinflated and wobbly from years of neglect, which made him worry that it was bound to attract attention.

He found it difficult to steer, and was afraid of hitting someone as he weaved along. The side windows were clouded over, the windshield only slightly better. A shadow appeared at the edge of his vision and he veered away—an RV passing. Straightening up in his lane, he drove on.

He remembered a self-service gas station he had noticed in his driving days. He could fill the tank there and add air to the tires, and he wouldn't have to talk to anyone. The dim prospect he'd had as he wandered along the bank of the river had been replaced by a much more vivid picture now.

Haruko Higuchi

"We did it, Mommy!" Nanami bounced on the seat next to her as the engine turned over and a cloud of exhaust belched from the tailpipe.

"We certainly did!" said Haruko, gripping the wheel. Then she cut the engine.

"Aren't we going anywhere?" said Nanami. "Why did we make it go?"

"That's a good question. I'm not sure myself."

"Is someone coming to drive it?"

Haruko laughed. She had no idea whether Aoyagi would remember this old car, much less whether he would be able to get here if he did. "I don't know," she said. "But if someone did come, it would be sad if it didn't work."

She took the key out of the ignition. She couldn't imagine the police officer was still waiting for them, but if he was, the last thing she wanted was to have him come poking around in the bushes and find the car. "Let's go," she told Nanami. Just then she noticed a slip of paper sticking out of the visor above her. She pulled it down and unfolded it. *I am innocent. Masaharu Aoyagi.* The handwriting was so familiar. She fished around in her bag for a pen. *I thought so*, she added. When had he written this? She was worried now that they had come too late.

With Nanami in tow, she made her way back to her car. She half expected to see a police car waiting there, but other than a little traffic passing by, the road was empty. The sky was still flat and cloudless, as though a sheet of blue paper had been pasted overhead.

"Excuse me," said a voice behind her, making her nearly jump out of her skin. She turned to find—a boy or a youth or a small man?—she couldn't tell. He had a high forehead and was wearing a black parka, and smiling tentatively. His hands gripped the handlebars of a fancy-looking bike with narrow tires.

"Yes?" she said. As she answered, she felt almost certain that there was no connection between the police and this fellow; in fact, he seemed the exact opposite of anything she associated with people in authority.

"I'm sorry, I was just wondering . . ." He pursed his lips and fiddled with his glasses.

"What?"

"What you were doing just now . . . in there?" He pointed toward the bushes.

"My daughter needed to go to the bathroom," she said, stroking Nanami's head. "It was a bit of an emergency."

"Oh, I'm sorry. I didn't mean to pry," he said.

Haruko smiled and started walking toward her car. "Come on, Nanami," she said.

"Is that your bike?" Nanami asked, looking up at the little man.

"Sort of," he said.

Haruko felt there was something odd about him. "Come on, Nanami," she said again, a little more urgently. She opened the rear door. Her daughter waved goodbye.

On the way home she realized she no longer had any doubt at all about Aoyagi's innocence. It was enough to see the note in his handwriting.

"The car has to be our little secret," she said. But when she glanced in the mirror, she could see that Nanami was already asleep.

As she drove up to their building, she noticed a car parked near the entrance—just a normal sedan, but she had a bad feeling the moment she saw it. She parked in the lot next to the building and was heading for the door with Nanami asleep in her arms when a man in a suit approached her.

"Not another coincidence," she said, as she searched in her bag for her keys.

"I've been waiting for you," Mamoru Kondo said, bowing slightly. The sun was behind him and she couldn't see the expression on his face. He took a step closer and glanced down at Nanami.

"You could have called if you had more questions."

"I wasn't sure you'd answer," he said. Kondo's range of emotions was obviously quite narrow, but she could tell he seemed more stern than he had when he'd found her at the side of the road. "I need you to tell me the truth," he said. "Has Masaharu Aoyagi contacted you?"

"No, he hasn't. I'm afraid you're wasting your time following me around." They stared at each other for several seconds, as if waiting to see who would blink first. He studied her face, observing every detail, and she looked right back, standing her ground as best she could. She was worried he would sense how nervous she felt—a feeling that seemed to grow the longer she looked at his expressionless face.

Eventually he broke the silence, though there was no hint he had backed down. "Please contact me whenever you make a move," he said.

Make a move? Could he be more vague? But in her eagerness to get away, she promised him she would, like a girl scout taking an oath. Then she went inside, sensing his eyes on her back until she disappeared into the elevator. As she was opening the door to their apartment, Nanami jumped down from her arms. She had apparently been awake for some time. "That man is creepy," she said.

Haruko turned and looked beyond the railing at the blue sky, thinking about Aoyagi. He was somewhere out there, and he was in a lot of trouble.

Masaharu Aoyagi

This thing's in a lot of trouble, Aoyagi thought as he gripped the wheel. Still, it was moving—not bad for a car that hadn't been driven for years.

He found the self-service gas station right where he thought it would be.

There was an attendant there, but if you didn't need any specialized service, you were left to fill the tank on your own. And in one corner was an air pump, just as he had remembered. Given the long period of neglect in the weeds, the tires seemed to be in relatively good shape, and once he had attached the nozzle, they reinflated in no time. Aoyagi topped off the gas tank and then used a hose to spray the worst of the dirt off the car. Even so, it could hardly be called clean, but it was in better shape than when he had barreled out of the bushes. Soon he was back on the road again.

He knew the engine could give out at any point. It seemed to run well enough when he had his foot on the gas, but every time he had to slow down or downshift or stop for a red light, he was afraid it would quit on him altogether. If he stalled in the middle of traffic, that would be the end of him.

He pulled into the parking lot of a shopping mall just off the beltway in Izumi Ward. A dirty old yellow car was not exactly common in Sendai, where most cars were the latest model and spotless, but neither would it automatically attract attention. Furthermore, for the time being at least, the chances were good that the police were not aware that he had taken to the road.

A man with signal flags was waving drivers into the vast lot. Aoyagi kept his face down as he took his ticket, then wove his way through the rows of cars to an open space in Section 3. He sat back and turned off the engine—not knowing if it would ever start again. So he tested it by switching it on, then turned it off a second time.

Unfastening his seatbelt, he let the seat drop back. He was much less visible now. His hand reached into the backpack and found one of the energy bars. He ripped open the wrapper and started chewing, though he didn't feel particularly hungry.

After pulling up the antenna on the game unit cum miniature TV, he turned it on, fiddled with the sound for a moment, and then watched the screen, more or less resigned to seeing himself appear on it. You again? he thought. Yes, again. Two-year-old pictures from his adventure with Rinka, and the footage by the river with his look-alike flying the helicopter.

"A man resembling Masaharu Aoyagi has been spotted fleeing from a convenience store in Wakabayashi Ward after stealing a loaf of bread."

"A man thought to be Masaharu Aoyagi was spotted in front of the pier for tourist boats to Matsushima Beach."

"A number of witnesses report seeing a man resembling Masaharu Aoyagi running near the beach at Nobiru."

Neat trick, he thought—I seem to be everywhere at once. He wanted to laugh, not because he felt relieved but because he'd grown numb to all feeling. It occurred to him that all these sightings might actually be helpful in concealing his real location, like a smoke screen of sorts. But then he wondered whether this disinformation might be part of a larger strategy the police were developing. Maybe they were trying to lull him into a sense of security, to encourage him to drop his guard by putting out a stream of false reports. It wasn't out of the question—but was anything beyond question anymore, except perhaps the possibility of resuming a normal life without coming to harm?

He felt the urge to pee, but at first he decided to ignore it. Eventually, however, this proved impossible as his bladder seemed to swell from minute to minute. Still, now that he was settled in the reassuring shelter of the car, the idea of venturing outside was pretty unattractive. So why not just take care of things right here? It was an old heap anyway, the year and owner long since forgotten. So what would prevent him from slipping into the back seat and quietly solving the problem? Okay, it would stink, but it would hardly stop him from driving the car when the time came to leave.

But when his hand reached for his zipper he stopped. It wasn't so much that he couldn't piss in a car as knowing that as soon as he started he wouldn't be able to stand the sight of himself doing something like that. He glanced around to make sure no one was coming, shouldered his pack, opened the door, and headed for the mall.

As he stood at the urinal, a young man appeared to his right. At the same time, a man in a suit came up to his left. The one on the right glanced at Aoyagi, while the man on the left took a quick look in his direction, too. The looks were casual enough, but Aoyagi tensed up. He wanted to get away, but his bladder seemed bottomless.

He peered down intently, feeling his heart beat quickly. When he was done at last, he moved over to the sink, ran the water for a few seconds, then left the bathroom as quickly as he could, flicking drops off his hands.

His car seemed impossibly far away, but he scurried along at a half run.

Moving through the parking lot felt like crossing a stage under a spotlight. Ahead and to the right, he noticed a group of kids squatting next to a van—dyed hair, cigarettes, gaudy shirts, neck chains. Some with designer shades. He envied them the freedom to hang out here like this. They made him think of his own days at the cafeteria or a burger joint in the company of the Friends of Fast Food; and one time in particular when they'd been enjoying themselves innocently enough, and a man in a suit appeared out of nowhere and practically yelled at them: "Enjoy it while you can, punks. Life is hard!" As he was trying to remember if they had said anything back, one of the kids by the van looked up and pointed in his direction. The other four stood up, and before he knew it they had surrounded him.

"Look who it is," said one of them.

"The guy on TV," said another. Their hair and clothes were so similar they seemed to blur into a single kid. With them leering at him, he swiveled around, unsure what to do. They weren't particularly tough-looking, but it didn't seem likely that his judo move would work against all five at once. Nor did he want to attract attention by getting into a fight.

"Would you mind getting out of the way?" he said. He knew they wouldn't do it—what self-respecting juvenile delinquent would get out of the way just because you asked him nicely?—but still it couldn't hurt to ask.

And, in fact, it didn't hurt. The bleach-blond kid in front stepped aside. "Sorry, guess you're in a hurry," he said. Aoyagi stared at him in shock.

"Must be a shitload of cops looking for you," said another. "Keep the faith, Pops."

"We just wanted to say 'Hi.'"

"Don't suppose you have time for a picture?"

For a moment, he wasn't sure what he was hearing. Then the boy in front stuck out his hand. "Good luck," he said. Aoyagi started to reach out to shake it but stopped, afraid they would grab him and pin him down. "Good luck, Pops," the kid said again. "Anyway, you didn't do it, right?" Aoyagi was speechless.

"We know exactly how you feel, man. They're always trying to pin stuff on us that we didn't do."

"Nothing sucks like being framed for somebody else's gig."

"We're like America, man. Anytime bad shit happens, we get blamed."

Then, like dancers in a chorus line, they made two neat rows and waved him through. He shuffled past them, heading for his car. Maybe there was something he should have said to them, but nothing came to mind.

It was probably just a coincidence, but all the other cars in this section of the parking lot had left, and the dirty yellow one stuck out like a sore thumb. As he was reaching into his backpack for the key, though, the cell phone began to vibrate. A number he didn't recognize flashed on the display.

"You okay?" he heard Miura say.

"More or less." He looked around, but the boys had vanished.

"It took a bit of doing, but I found out," Miura told him.

"Found out what?"

"Where they've got your double parked."

Haruko Higuchi

Though she was back home, Haruko found it impossible to relax. Nearly every channel on the TV was running a special on the assassination.

"Mommy, are you in trouble?" Nanami asked as they watched one of them.

"No, not at all," she said. "But my friend is."

"Mr. Aoyagi? They'll never catch him!" The footage seemed to be from a surveillance camera, and the man in the picture did look a lot like Aoyagi.

Witnesses were coming forward one after another, but their accounts contradicted each other in obvious ways. Still, the networks passed along this contradictory information without comment or, apparently, verification, perhaps comforting themselves with the thought that it was Aoyagi's fault as well for causing so much confusion. The announcer summed up the situation: "The police have obtained visual and voice data from the Security Pods around the city and are analyzing this information as we speak." The pods again, thought Haruko as she lowered herself onto the couch. She knew they were monitoring her phone and relaying the information to the police. And the knowledge made her sympathy for Aoyagi all the stronger as they stalked him with all this equipment of theirs.

She suddenly remembered something Morita had once said. "The fat cats sit around with their legs crossed, sipping their tea, looking down on us like we're some kind of sideshow. Makes you kind of mad, doesn't it?" The thread of her memory unraveled from the words to the scene. It must have been while they were cleaning the city pool, a job Kazu had found for the four of them. Though it would have been early in the summer, she remembered they were barefoot as they scrubbed the pool with deck brushes. Morita, who avoided hard work whenever he could, had started grumbling right away about how big the pool was, how he liked his pools a little grubby anyway. Then abruptly he had looked up at the security camera on a pole above the pool and said his line.

"I doubt the fat cats are wasting their time watching us scrub this pool," Aoyagi had pointed out. "And I doubt it's tea they're sipping."

"Don't you doubt it," Morita told him. "People like us, the little people, we're just playthings to them. We act out our lousy little parts, do our jobs, make love, live our lives, put up with all sorts of shit—and they sit behind those cameras and sneer at us."

She had laughed at his ranting that day along with the rest of them, but one thing he said had stayed with her: "When the shit hits the fan, when the big boys come for you, the only thing us little people can do is run; find someplace they'll never think of and hunker down."

"What the hell are you talking about?" Aoyagi had asked.

"What would you do if you were floating around in the sea and a whale attacked you?" Morita said.

"Do whales attack people?"

"Probably. Everything out there hates us human beings, so a whale would probably want to beat the shit out of you if it found you floating around. But what would you do? Would you fight it? Not likely! Would you want to go a few rounds with a sperm whale? It would eat you for supper, like Pinocchio."

"You, too."

"Which is why the only smart thing to do is run away. Swim away. Get away any way you can. There are no points for style—just swim like hell."

"And it might still catch you. . . ."

Haruko glanced down at Nanami, who had come to sit with her on the couch. Her eyes closed slowly and then popped open, closed and then opened, as though she was playing tug-of-war with sleep. The scene at the pool came to an end in Haruko's head, but the trail of memories led to another moment in the past.

They had been gathered at a fast-food restaurant as usual. Kazu showed up late, with his junior-college girlfriend in tow. She turned out to be a cheerful girl who warmed to the group in no time. The conversation had been typical—a ramble through a collective brainstorm—but this time Morita had taken to punctuating it with an occasional loud "Kaboom!" Each time they had looked at him with uncomprehending stares, until he finally explained—inexplicably: "I just thought some ideas needed sound effects." As they moved on from topic to topic, he kept up the odd interjection when someone made a point. "True? False? Which is it?" They asked him again what he was up to. "It's the new fashion," he said. "Full frontal reaction!"

Aoyagi had tried to calm him down, but it had only escalated until he seemed to be having minor fits—which were completely inexplicable until Kazu's girlfriend left for the restroom. As soon as she was gone, Morita turned to Kazu. "Did that do it?" he asked.

"I'm not sure," Kazu said, his hand under the table.

"What are you doing?" Aoyagi said.

"Kazu said he wanted to check the calls on his girlfriend's phone, so we were supposed to distract her while he got his hand in her bag."

"That's so shitty!" Haruko sputtered. Kazu looked up and blushed.

"Not at all," said Morita. "If she's running around on him, that would be shitty."

"Well is she?"

"That's what we're trying to find out."

"It's still shitty," Haruko said. "And what was all that stupid shouting about?"

"You really want to know?"

"On second thought, not really."

"Animals are hardwired to react to sudden, loud noises. They have to look, to find out whether the noise means danger."

"Not if there are so many loud noises they get used to them."

"Oh. Maybe you're right," said Morita. "But it worked. Kazu got the phone while she was distracted."

"Or because she had to go to the bathroom, more likely," said Aoyagi.

"I still say it's shitty to snoop around in somebody's phone," said Haruko.

In the end, Kazu couldn't handle the guilt, and when she got back, he told her he'd tried to check up on her phone. Naturally, she was furious, and Aoyagi and Haruko did what they could to cool her down. Meanwhile, Morita, suddenly on the side of the righteous, had begun to give Kazu hell. "That's the shittiest thing I've ever seen. Don't think you're going to wriggle out of this one."

Haruko smiled at the memory, but it made her wonder again whether it was true about Morita and the second bomb. Was he alive or dead? She wanted to call the TV station or a hospital to find out, but at the same time she was afraid of what she might be told. Her misgivings prevailed. I don't want to think about it, she thought.

A few minutes later, she picked up her phone.

"Hi," said Akira Hirano's cheerful voice. "What's up?"

"Can you talk?" Haruko asked.

"Of course, I'm at work but it's fine," she said, then corrected herself. "I'm at work *so* it's fine." She made no attempt to lower her voice. "Oh, I made the copy," she told someone, and Haruko could hear the sound of rustling papers. It brought back her own days at the office, and Akira's brusque manner, which hadn't changed in the least. "So what's up?" she said, back with Haruko. "An emergency? Lunch?"

"Boyfriend," said Haruko, the word sounding more provocative than she'd intended.

"But you're married, dear," Akira laughed. "You want me to find you a little action on the side?"

"Not mine, yours. I want to meet Lord Taira no Masakado." She spoke quickly, intent on keeping the call under thirty seconds.

"Masakado? What do you want with him all of a sudden?"

"Hold on, I'll call you right back," Haruko told her, and hung up. She waited a moment, then hit "redial."

"What's this all about?" Akira said almost before the phone rang.

"Could you introduce us? I know it's kind of out of the blue, but I need to ask him a favor."

"No, it's fine," said Akira. "Why don't we have lunch or something this weekend? That might work better with your little girl."

"I meant right away," Haruko said. It wasn't like her to be so blunt, but this was no time for niceties. Keeping one eye on the clock on the sideboard, she proposed meeting at the coffee shop near Akira's office.

"Maybe I forgot to mention it," Akira laughed, "but I'm at work."

"It's about the guy on TV. The one the police are chasing."

"The cute deliveryman?"

"I used to go out with him."

"You're joking! . . . Aren't you?"

"I need to ask Masakado something." The second hand was just coming around to thirty seconds. She heard Akira yelling, away from the phone:

"I'm taking some time off!"

Masaharu Aoyagi

"You found him?" Aoyagi said, sitting in the car with the phone to his ear. He had never really believed in the existence of a double, let alone Miura's ability to locate him.

"Why would I lie about something like that?" Miura said. It occurred to Aoyagi that the question of where was just the beginning; it would now be necessary to think about what could be done with this information. "Frankly, I was stumped about how to go about it." Miura had a habit of putting a dramatic spin on his activities. "Then I remembered that your double must be the product of plastic surgery, so the easiest way to find him would be to talk to the guy who'd done the deed."

"The same one who did your surgery?"

He ignored the question. "Luckily, I knew the good doctor's number, and when I called, he was able to tell me what I wanted to know. Turns out that they have your unfortunate look-alike stashed away in a ward at the Sendai Hospital Center."

"But why would the doctor tell you something like that?" Just then, a car began backing into the parking space directly to his right. With so few cars in the lot, why would someone be parking next to him? He slouched further down in the seat but craned his neck up to look out the window. A young woman was driving the car, checking her mirrors obsessively as though inexperienced behind the wheel—or was she just pretending when she was actually another piece of the great plot to capture him?

"A doctor who makes his living changing people's identities doesn't set up shop in one of the big hospitals. He isn't some glamour plastic surgeon. He works in the shadows, out of sight of the police and the media—meaning, he's on our side."

"I'm not sure I like being on the same side you're on," said Aoyagi, noting that the car had stopped next to him. The woman got out.

"That's cold," said Miura.

"But he said he operated on my double?"

"Not exactly. This thing they've got going is huge, not the work of some small-time crook."

Aoyagi pictured himself dodging the footsteps of a giant. "No surprise there," he said. "Like the Kennedy assassination."

"And the people behind it are powerful, and arrogant. So my friend the doctor refused the project. He didn't want to get involved in some big drama. Still, it's a small field, and they asked someone he knew who did accept."

"Who asked? The police? The government?"

"I doubt they exchanged business cards, but it had to be something like that, by a process of elimination. At any rate, my friend tells me that his friend said the double is in a room at the Hospital Center."

"Was he hurt?" He knew it was odd, but he somehow felt protective of this other self.

"He's probably just waiting in the wings for his cue. A hospital room is the perfect place since they can supervise who gets in and out; bed and board and no prying eyes. Not a bad hideout. Hey! You might try that yourself!"

"I doubt the hospital would agree," said Aoyagi.

"Still, there might be a way."

"I don't see how."

"What if you could substitute yourself for this double? That's the beauty of it—no one could tell you apart!"

Aoyagi imagined himself replacing the man in the doppelganger ward. How long could you lie there, pretending to be someone who looked like you but wasn't? You'd be trapped, even if relatively safe. But the fantasy came apart in his head almost immediately. "What would happen to this other guy?" he said. "I don't think he'd be willing to start running in my place."

"That could be a bit of a problem," Miura admitted, as though this was the punchline of a joke he'd been telling all along. "Still, I think you should meet me at the hospital. If you can get to the parking lot in back, I can get you inside."

"Won't they have a few guards around the place if they're hiding a key player in there?"

"It's good to see your brain's still working," he said.

"I don't know for how much longer, though."

"But I'm happy to report that I'm calling from the Hospital Center itself, and the security is not all that tight. I'm sure they never thought you would find out where the double was being kept—they underestimated you." Though he would never have made the discovery if he hadn't met Miura. "So just pull into the parking lot like any other prospective patient and we should be able to get you inside. Trust me on this."

"Do I have a choice?"

"Do you know what man's greatest strength is?" And this time Aoyagi did know—Morita had told him, clearly if painfully: trust and habit. "Resolve," said Miura, naturally giving his own answer. "Call me when you get here. Do you know the way?"

"Do you know who you're talking to?" Aoyagi said.

"The man who assassinated the prime minister?"

"A former delivery driver," he said. After they'd hung up, he got out. His door nearly hit the blue car in the next space, and he had to turn sideways to get past as he headed back toward the mall. He looked around, wondering whether the kids could still be there—or even whether he'd imagined them in the first place, odd as the encounter had been.

"Hey, Pops. You think it's smart hanging around here? Shouldn't you get going?" There they were, all five, still squatting next to the van.

"You're right," Aoyagi said, nodding. "But could I ask you a favor first?"

The boys looked skeptical for a moment, but then curiosity apparently got the better of them. "Sure, what?" said one of them.

"Could I switch clothes with one of you?" He didn't think a disguise would be of much use in helping him sneak into the hospital, but he felt he should do what he could to improve his chances. The boys burst out laughing. He had expected them to get the wrong idea, to take offense, but they seemed to understand right away.

"You mean it?" another kid asked. "Sure, why not." Then all five began undressing.

"There's only one of me," Aoyagi said, laughing now, too.

One of them passed him an expensive-looking padded jacket. "No, take it," he said when Aoyagi tried to refuse. He put it on reluctantly, but when he felt how warm it was he was grateful for the change.

"You sure?" he asked.

"No problem," said the boy, while the others stuffed some cookies, a CD, and a watch in his backpack. "And I'll wear yours," he said, pulling on Aoyagi's jacket. Someone laughed and said it could become a collector's item.

"Keep the faith, Pops," another kid said, holding up his hand.

Aoyagi wanted to thank them, to leave them with a bit of wisdom maybe, but all he could come up with was "Life's tough." He laughed at his own cliché.

"You're telling us!" they laughed along with him. As he walked toward his car, he turned to look back one more time, but they had already disappeared.

As he climbed behind the wheel, he said a little prayer and turned the key. The car shook to life; he threw it in reverse, released the clutch, and stepped on the accelerator—and a moment later he was at the exit.

Masaharu Aoyagi

While he drove, he felt as though a haze had descended in front of him—or, more accurately, as though he saw his surroundings through the filter of a nightmare. The oddness of it was compounded by the relative security he felt inside the car.

At any rate, he knew the way to Sendai Hospital Center. It wasn't quite like seeing a map in his head, but he could trace the various directions and turns in his mind's eye and follow them without hesitation. The area around the Center was not part of his old route, but he had made deliveries there any number of times when other drivers were out sick. He knew there was a large parking lot, with an automated ticket machine.

His main problem was to avoid being stopped between here and there. The car wasn't that conspicuous, but it was dirtier than almost anything else on the road. It occurred to him that he and the car had much in common: they were both the worse for wear but still running; squeaking through, if only by the skin of their teeth.

There was a fair amount of congestion on the roads but he was impressed that things were generally smooth and orderly only a day after the prime minister had been killed. Cars passed him, sending bits of litter fluttering up—who knows, perhaps blowing evidence of the crime away. But maybe that was exactly what they wanted—for all the evidence to disappear and everything to return to normal? The thought crossed his mind.

The hospital was located in a quiet district to the northeast of town, at the bottom of a long slope on the loop road. The valley seemed tight and he felt a bit trapped in it, maybe because the traffic had thinned but the car ahead of him was slowing down. He realized they were coming to a checkpoint. He knew it would be suspicious to turn off right before being stopped for the inspection, so if possible he wanted a new route well in advance.

He pulled a pair of gaudy designer sunglasses out of his backpack as he sat waiting at a stoplight and put them on—something one of the boys at the mall had given him. They were perfect for a juvenile delinquent, but he wasn't sure if they were the right fashion statement for a suspected assassin. Feeling self-conscious, he took them off.

Next, he pulled out the CD they had shoved in his pack. He had never heard of the band, but from the cover he could tell it was a hip-hop group. He smiled, remembering Rock Iwasaki's injunction to avoid the genre at all costs. Odd that he would get the gift of hip-hop now. He took the disk out of the case and put it in the changer.

The stereo was filthy from years of disuse, and he thought the disk might get stuck and never come out again. But the music started almost immediately—and he found he liked it. He liked driving along, bouncing to the beat, to the jaunty tune and the insistent voices. There was something good about this cheerful response to a bad time, these bright rhymes that seemed to lash out at anyone who tried to put a stop to them. The more he listened, the more he liked it.

When he reached the hospital, he drove around to the parking lot and took a ticket from the machine at the gate. Then he found a sunny space. As he was turning off the engine, he realized someone was standing right outside the door. Someone in a white hospital jacket. What business could the hospital have with him before he was even out of the car? He rolled down his window.

"Nice duds," said Miura. "But I thought this would be better camouflage," he said, pointing at his coat. Aoyagi looked up at him. The small frame and boyish face made him look like a kid playing doctor. He grabbed his backpack and climbed out of the car. As always, the young doctor's manner seemed a strange mixture of diffidence and daring.

"Have you lost weight?" The words slipped out before Aoyagi realized what he was saying. Miura looked almost frail.

"You mean since yesterday? If I knew how to lose weight overnight, I'd write a diet book. You're late," he added.

"I thought I was doing well just to get here."

"I suppose. Anyway, you made it in time."

"In time for what?"

"For me. I can't wait around here all day. A bit later and I'd have gone."

"Gone where?"

"Here and there. I'm afraid I'm in a bit of a hurry," he said, turning on his heel and striding off toward the back of the hospital. Aoyagi fell in step behind him.

"Do you have to march along like that?" he murmured, staring down at his toes as he shuffled to keep up.

"It's a big place," said Miura, ignoring the question. "But I know my way around. Your double is in the ward at the far end of the fifth floor." They walked in by a rear door and Miura pressed the button at the bank of elevators. "Hardly anyone uses this except the staff."

The elevator doors opened to reveal a young man and woman in white coats like Miura's. Aoyagi felt an urge to bolt. Miura nodded and they nodded back as they passed on their way out. But as Aoyagi hurried into a back corner, they turned to look at him.

"They recognized me," he said when the doors had closed.

"Something caught their attention, but they didn't know it was you." Miura pressed the button for the fifth floor.

"How do you know?"

"They saw you with me—the wanted man is on his own, all the news reports say so. How could he be walking around a hospital with a doctor?" Made sense—so if those two had seen him alone, they would have known immediately. The doors opened and Miura turned right as though he'd been doing the rounds here for years. Despite a fresh coat of paint in a cheerful color, the corridor gave off that unmistakable hospital chill. "The last door on the right," he said.

"In a regular ward like this?" Aoyagi had imagined his double hidden away in a closely watched room, somewhere difficult to find and even more difficult to access.

"Check that out," said Miura, nodding down the passage at a familiar object.

"Security Pod," Aoyagi hissed. Even in disguise, he felt exposed before these wide-angle data hogs.

"Relax," Miura told him, tugging on his elbow with unexpected strength. "I made a few 'repairs' when I was up here earlier. It can't see or hear for the moment."

"How did you manage that?"

"Don't forget, these things were originally designed to catch me—or at least that's what the politicians said when they started scattering them around. In fact, they just wanted to keep tabs on people in general."

"Spying on us?" Aoyagi said.

"What else? Knowledge is power, it's what keeps the elite elite. If they don't know what we're up to, how will they keep us down? At any rate, I made it my business to find out about these pods—my pods, so to speak—and I know enough to fool them now, at least for a while."

"The battery?" he asked.

"No, that doesn't work. If the power goes off the police get notified automatically. No, you have to cross the wiring, switch the input and output terminals. The pods record visuals and sound on an internal hard disk. If you reverse the terminals, it just runs in a loop, recycling the old data."

"As simple as that?"

"You have to know what you're doing, but it's not too hard."

"But you had to get up here beforehand." Aoyagi stole a glance at him. There had been a hint of impatience or irritation in Miura's voice—nothing too threatening, but he somehow felt uneasy walking next to him.

"I had to be sure your double was really here before I got you to come all the way to the hospital," Miura said. "That's the room, at the end of the hall."

"Odd that there's no one around," said Aoyagi. Even for a normal ward, there should be a nurses' station nearby. They had passed a counter on their way from the elevator, but there was no one in sight.

"That's quite sharp of you," said Miura. "Seems they haven't opened this floor yet—it doesn't go into service until next year."

"This isn't a real floor?"

"No."

"Then it's a . . ." Aoyagi finally said the word that had been welling up inside him since the moment they had stepped off the elevator. "Trap?"

"Hey!" said Miura. "You're good."

Aoyagi turned to look at him again. If it was a trap, why were they still walking into it? Or was it a trap Miura had set? He stopped, suddenly frightened, but Miura grabbed his arm and pulled him along. The corridor, which had felt endless, seemed to contract and they were soon standing in front of Room 502. Miura opened the door. With the room there before him, Aoyagi had to fight the urge to turn and run. A draft from somewhere seemed to flow over him and he flinched. The room was large and bright—apparently destined to be an expensive private facility—and in the foreground was a bed, which was occupied, to judge from the lumps under the quilt.

Miura spoke up behind him. "What were the odds you'd make it here? I just happened to show up and provide you with the information."

"I owe you one," said Aoyagi.

"I doubt you'd have found this place if I hadn't come along."

"You're right," Aoyagi said, trying to sound as sincere. "It's all thanks to you."

They took a step into the room. "But even if there was almost no chance of your coming, they still must've taken some precautions." Aoyagi wasn't sure what he was getting at. "The guys who are after you must've made some provisions for the unlikely event that you'd show up here. They might have put out the story about the double themselves."

Aoyagi could feel the floor under his feet turn to sponge. "The story about the double?"

"The story that your double was in this hospital, here in this room. They may have made sure that information got out to the right sort of people.

Then, if by some accident you did make your way to the hospital, they could grab you. Not a bad backup plan."

"But there's no one here to do that," Aoyagi said. Unless you're planning to, he thought to himself.

"There's a Security Pod outside. Maybe they assumed it'd see you when you showed up and they could send in the troops. Since it was so unlikely you'd come, they might have thought that was enough." Miura went to the window and looked out. "But they never counted on someone tampering with the pod before you arrived."

"Where's this heading?"

"Unfortunately," he went on, "my information seems to have been doctored."

"Doctored?"

"My friend the surgeon did tell me your double was here, but it seems he'd got hold of the story your boys had planted." They must have known that information about a double would spread through the world of plastic surgery like a new type of Botox. They seemed to have time and money for just about anything. "These guys are good," said Miura, as if reading his thoughts.

Aoyagi moved to the bed. "Then this is a doll, or pillows?" he said, taking hold of the cover and pulling it back. There was a burst of laughter from behind him. And in front of him—a body. Prone on the bed, knees bent. At first he hoped it was a very realistic doll, but then he noticed the bloodstain spreading out into the sheet.

"He must have been the clincher." Miura had come to stand beside him. "When the Security Pod saw you outside, he'd be waiting in the bed to nab you. Probably seemed like a good training assignment—never see any real action otherwise." The man on the bed was tall and, from the look of the arms and feet protruding from the pajamas, well built.

"Did you do this?" Aoyagi asked, nodding at the blood.

"As a reflex," he said, staring down at the man. "When I pulled back the cover like you did just now, he jumped me."

"Well, we'd better get out of here." He was having enough trouble understanding any of this, but it was obviously just a matter of time before the hospital staff—or the police—showed up.

"What's the hurry?" said Miura. "It'll be a while before they figure out what's happened." His eyes moved from the body to the far end of the room, and it was then that Aoyagi noticed a second Security Pod. "They put too much faith in those things." Presumably he had fixed that one, too. "If we lie low, I think it's safe here for a while yet. After all, no one bothered me when I went out to meet you."

Aoyagi looked at the face of the man on the bed—who looked nothing like him at all. "The double's double."

"I'm afraid my little plan backfired. When I phoned you, I still thought this was the real deal."

"Well, it sucks," Aoyagi muttered. The man probably had a family—but now was just a pawn toppled over on the board. "Who did this?"

"That would be me," Miura said, raising his hand. "I stabbed him, but don't bother explaining why it's wrong—it'd be wasted on me."

"No, I mean who did all of this? Who's after me? Who's hurting my friends? Who made you kill him? Everything."

"I can only speak for myself," he said. "But it's just the way I am. I'm a murderer . . . with a touch of psychopath thrown in. And nobody made me stab him."

Aoyagi looked at Miura, and for the first time in a while he faced the fact that he was dealing with a serial killer. But somehow the thought no longer bothered him much.

"No, that's not right. You're responsible for the things you've done up to this point, but this time is different. This time someone else made you do it, for reasons that have nothing to do with you."

"Someone with very long arms and big plans."

"Who stays well out of sight."

Miura sighed—or tried to laugh, perhaps—then walked over to the window and sank back against the wall. "I'm pooped," he murmured.

"You okay?"

"Yeah, but this enemy of yours—I can't get a grip on him. You might as well be fighting 'the government' or 'authority' itself."

"That's what I've been telling you all along."

"While we stand around in a daze, they make laws and rearrange taxes and health care, start a war somewhere—and all we can do is go with the flow, follow their lead. That's the way the game's rigged. Everything happens while guys like us are half asleep. I read somewhere that the state's main interest is to protect itself, not the people—now I see what that meant."

Aoyagi wasn't sure what to say when Miura got going like this. "Which means there's no way for someone like me to win against them, right?"

"I'm not sure what it would look like to 'win' this kind of fight. If you asked me . . ." As Miura spoke, Aoyagi suddenly remembered a conversation long ago, under a clear sky, with friends. Someone—Morita—was talking seriously about something, but since it was Morita, the actual content was probably less than serious. Someone else—Aoyagi himself—was listening. "What would you do if you were floating around in the sea and a whale attacked you?" Morita's solution had been the same as the one Miura was suggesting now.

" . . . I'd say you should run."

"Run." Everyone had been telling him that since yesterday.

"Until no one's following you anymore. I guess that's about all you can do. When you've got the authorities after you, you run."

"Okay, but how?"

"There, I'm sorry to say, I can't help you. I gave it some thought, but I'm afraid I won't have time to help you work it out." Aoyagi remembered that he had said he was in a hurry. As they stood facing one another, Miura's white surgical coat fell open, and Aoyagi noticed a stain on his shirt under his breastbone—a big one. "You see, the guy in the bed had a gun. Small caliber, with a silencer—the kind they'd give an officer in training. He wasn't bad, that guy. Shot me at the same moment I stabbed him." Miura frowned, but he seemed cheerful enough. "At first I didn't think he'd hit anything vital, but now I'm not so sure. That's a lot of blood—I should know."

"We've got to get you to a hospital!" Aoyagi blurted out.

"I thought this was one."

Sunlight flooded the room through the crack in the curtains, bleaching and drying everything damp and dark.

"It's all your fault," Miura laughed. "I thought it'd be interesting to help you get away, but I guess I was pushing my luck."

"I'd say you've been pushing it all along."

"Point taken."

"But why didn't you tell me as soon as I got here?" He couldn't bring himself to cross the room to him. Instead, suddenly dizzy, he leaned against the bed. "I didn't realize," he said.

There had been no sign that Miura was wounded as they made their way here from the parking lot, no hint as they had discussed Aoyagi's problem. He had thought he looked somehow thinner. Now he realized it wasn't weight he'd been losing.

"Surprise . . . ," Miura murmured.

Masaharu Aoyagi

He felt as though he had been staring at Miura's still body for a long time. At last he looked up and checked the clock. Then he turned toward the young policeman.

What seemed like a vibration made him feel in his pocket for his cell phone. When he realized it wasn't the phone, he thought it might be a small earthquake or nearby construction that was shaking the building. But there was no sign that the room was actually moving. He had just decided he was imagining things when he figured out what it was. Pulling open Miura's white coat, he could see something vibrating in his pocket, as though a small animal was hiding there.

The display gave the number of the incoming call—from another cell phone—but there was no name. He considered the risk in talking on the phone, but then pressed the button anyway and said hello.

"Who is this?" said a man's voice. The tone was neutral. "You're not Miura."

"He can't talk right now," Aoyagi said. Which was true enough.

"And who are you?"

"Me?"

"You're the suspect," said the voice.

"And you are?"

"I'm the doctor," said the voice, which was, in fact, cold and clinical. He was in a hospital, so it occurred to Aoyagi that they might have tracked him down, that this might be one of the doctors here in the building. But then he realized the call had been for Miura, not him, and that this doctor was the one on "their" side. "The plastic surgeon?" he asked.

"I called to apologize to Miura, but I suppose this concerns you as well, so I'll just say that the information I gave him was inaccurate."

"In other words, my double is not at the hospital."

"You know already?"

"I'm just figuring it out."

"Are you there now?" The tone was polite but the voice dry, almost mechanical. "Has something happened to Miura?"

"He can't come to the phone," Aoyagi said as he began moving toward the door. It was time to get going.

"Anyway, I wanted to apologize." The doctor seemed to have understood the situation.

"No need," Aoyagi said quietly. "These things happen. It's not easy confirming a story like that." It occurred to him that he himself should understand better than almost anyone how misinformation can come to be taken for the truth.

"So what will you do now?" the doctor asked.

"I guess the only thing I can do is run."

"But where will you go? How will you get there?"

He hung up without answering. Why should he answer, when he had no idea? He grasped the doorknob and turned it, expecting again to find a row of men with guns trained on him. But the passage was empty and he retraced his steps to the elevator and pressed the button. His heart was pounding. When the doors opened, a woman in a white coat stood there and he nearly panicked, but he forced himself to get on and move to the back. The woman was next to the doors, in front of the buttons. "What floor?" she asked.

"First," he said, the word barely audible. A bead of sweat ran down his spine. A man in street clothes calling an elevator from a floor that wasn't being used was bound to arouse suspicion.

When the doors opened again he got off, but then hesitated. He didn't know the way back to the parking lot, but he set off to the right anyway, realizing it would seem even more suspicious to stand in the corridor looking lost. Just as he was about to emerge into a larger hall, he had an odd feeling and turned around. He knew it wasn't wise to look back, but he couldn't help it. And there, still in front of the elevator, was the woman he rode down with, talking into a miniature walkie-talkie.

He didn't really think she had seen through his disguise, but it was likely she was reporting a suspicious person wandering around the hospital. As she talked into the handset, she looked up, noticed Aoyagi staring at her, and looked away. He turned and hurried on, though too much haste would make him even more conspicuous.

Every patient in pajamas he passed gave him a start. Every old man with an intravenous drip scared him. He was as nervous here as he had been out on the streets of the city. The long, window-lined corridor seemed sterile and cold. The floor seemed to suck at his feet.

"There he is," said a voice behind him. He glanced back to find the woman from the elevator pointing him out to a guard. Should he run? He could hear the sound of the guard's footsteps coming closer. He went rigid, as though a flood were about to sweep over him. He felt sick and wanted to fall to his knees. Instead, his eye caught sight of a sign that said "Emergency Exit," and he dodged through it.

Cold, damp air met his face. A spiral staircase led upward. Having made it to the ground floor, it was against his better instincts to head back up, but with no other choice, he bounded up the stairs.

"Hey, kid! Watch where you're going," a voice said from above. When Aoyagi looked up, he saw an old man sitting cross-legged on a landing, pointing at him with a long toothpick. "Hey," the man said again, lowering the toothpick. "Aren't you the kid on TV?" Aoyagi tried to think what he could say to this. "I've been watching you," the man laughed. "You don't give up easy, but for this man's money you're just about out of options."

Haruko Higuchi

"So what's this all about?" said Akira, facing Haruko eagerly across a table at the back of the coffee shop. She had gathered her brown hair in an attractive knot on top of her head, like the tip of some exotic fruit.

"It's good to meet you at last," said the man next to her. "I'm Masakado Kikuchi." He sat with his back straight, hands on his knees, and he seemed all arms as he looked expectantly at her. His hair was shaggy and he had a short beard—generally, not as much like the jack in a deck of cards as Akira had led her to believe.

"Thanks for coming on such short notice," Haruko said.

"Don't worry about it," Akira laughed. "You just rub the lamp and we appear."

It hadn't been possible in Haruko's day to suddenly announce that you wanted to take time off and walk out of the office—at least not for anyone but Akira. Evening was deepening outside the window.

At first glance, Masakado looked like the sort of person teenage girls would find attractive, but sitting next to Akira sipping an orange juice, he came across as more of a well-trained pet than a pop star.

Haruko told them about Aoyagi—that the man running from the police had been her boyfriend, that she hadn't seen him since they'd broken up, but that the person she knew was incapable of that sort of crime.

"Still, people change," said Akira, a bit skeptically.

"I know."

"But you believe he didn't do it," said Masakado.

"I do. Or, I guess I should say I trust him."

"You still trust a man you broke up with?" Akira smiled. "I have half a mind to tell your husband."

"For all the good it would do you," Haruko laughed. "He couldn't care less."

"So why are we here?" Akira said. "What have you got in mind? And for that matter, where is that little girl of yours?"

"I left her with a neighbor." The woman in the apartment next door was a housewife in her fifties. Her two sons were grown up and off on their own, but she loved children and offered to babysit Nanami from time to time.

"So, you're worked up enough to park your kid while you chase around after the old boyfriend?"

"I wouldn't put it exactly like that. But yes, I'm worked up." Haruko realized her behavior was a bit out of character. And what *was* she planning to do? She had no idea. "First, I was hoping Masakado could tell me about the Security Pods."

"The pods?" he echoed.

"What kind of problem are they for someone trying to stay hidden in the city?"

"Well, to be honest, I've never thought of them as a problem—they're supposed to be working for the good guys. What you're saying is kind of scary."

"She always did say scary things," said Akira. "Like suddenly 'I'm quitting my job' or 'I'm getting married.'"

Haruko didn't have a clear plan, nor did she think there was much she could do, but if there was a chance of helping Aoyagi even without actually finding him, she wanted to try—and the only thing that had come to mind was to disable or fool the Security Pods in some way. They sat there—somewhere—watching everything from behind their little cameras. She wanted to hit them where they lived.

"What do you want to know?" said Masakado.

"I want to know if there's a way to disable them, even for a short time. If we could take them off line for a while, it might give him some breathing room."

"Which ones did you have in mind?" he asked.

"I was thinking all of them."

Masakado shook his head like a dog trying to dry itself. "No way," he said. "Do you have any idea how many of them there are in the city?"

"Don't give up so easily," Akira told him. "Give it some thought."

"Well, since you mention it, there might be a way." His immediate about-face was appealing.

"I was hoping we could somehow cut the power, maybe," said Haruko.

"If the power gets cut off, there's a backup system to automatically notify the police. So that's pretty much out. But there is a way to fool the camera and audio mike."

"Fool them how?"

"You switch the input and output terminals. You'd have to have adapters, but if you could manage it, the old data would just be recycled and you'd have them out of operation for twelve hours or so."

"Sounds like a plan," said Haruko.

"No way, I'm afraid. We'd never be able to switch all the terminals."

"'No way,'" Akira parroted. "You say that a lot."

"You could disable a certain number, if you wanted to get into some building unnoticed, for instance. But to knock out every pod in the city . . ."

"What would happen if you made a lot of noise near one of the pods?" Haruko asked. This had been her idea from the start. "Could you use a noise as a diversion or cover, to mask a voice or prevent the pod from processing it?"

"What good would that do?" Akira looked puzzled, but Masakado seemed interested.

"You know how you turn to look when you hear a loud noise?" said Haruko. "Well, I'm wondering whether you could distract the pods with a loud radio or something and make them focus on that instead of anything else that might be happening in the area."

She had expected them to laugh at the proposal, but after a moment's thought Masakado replied. "You might have something there. The pods supposedly keep tabs on everything within fifty meters or so, but in practice it's hard to record sound and images in all directions at once—there's a limit to their capacity. So a sudden noise in the vicinity would attract the pod's attention and tie up its recording mechanism. I've also heard that the picture quality drops off when the pod's busy with other functions."

"Well, that kind of sucks," said Akira. "They use a huge chunk of my taxes to put these things all over the city and boast about how great they are, but then any little noise from a boom box or a jackhammer can put them on the fritz?"

"And how would that be different from all the other things they've spent your tax money on and boasted about?" said Masakado.

"So can we find some way to create a diversion?" Haruko asked. "Right away?"

Masakado thought for a second. "I'm not sure what we could do to generate that much noise," he said.

"Did you have something in mind?" Akira asked.

"Afraid not."

"Well, I've got another idea," said Akira. "Do these things have a blind spot or something?"

"They do," said Masakado. "If you stay on the back side of the pod and up close, there's an area where the camera can't see you. If you're quiet, you'd be almost invisible."

"But you'd stick out a mile away to the rest of the world if you were curled up behind a pod," Haruko said, laughing.

"Not to mention the fact that anything you'd do to these things would be discovered within a day by Masakado and his fellow pod people," said Akira.

"I'm afraid so," he agreed. "My district covers about a third of the pods in the city, so the guys who look after the rest would realize you'd been tampering with their stuff pretty quickly."

"Do you get around to all of them every day?"

"No, we usually try to look in on each pod once every three days or so. Except that the police have been on our backs since the assassination, and they want us to check every one of them twice a day, morning and evening."

"Twice a day," Haruko murmured. She thought for a moment, hand to her mouth, but nothing came to mind.

"I know you want to try to help him," Akira said, "but there's not much we can do."

"I don't suppose you'd settle for a nice gesture," said Masakado.

"You have an idea?" Akira turned to peer at him.

"No, it's too crazy. It would never work," he said.

Disappointed, Haruko was looking around for the waitress when she recognized a familiar figure sitting at a table near the entrance. He was reading a newspaper.

"Well, if you think of anything, let me know," she said, turning back to them.

"I'm doing my rounds tonight. Call me if you need me," Masakado said, scribbling his number on a paper napkin and handing it over.

"I'm sorry to pull you out of work," Haruko told Akira.

"Don't be silly. Who wouldn't want to ditch the office to aid and abet an assassin?" She stood up and Masakado followed suit, but Haruko made no move to join them. "Are you staying?" Akira asked.

"Just for a minute," she said.

"What a coincidence." A few minutes later, two men were standing at her table.

"Somehow, I doubt it," said Haruko, looking up at Mamoru Kondo, now wearing a wrinkled suit and even a tie. Without asking, he dropped into the chair across from her. The man with him was well built, with a crew cut and chiseled features—the image of a martial arts enthusiast—and for some reason he had earphones on. He sat in the other chair, his face as blank and offputting as Kondo's.

"No, it really is," said Kondo. "But you don't seem too happy to see us."

"I can't say I'm wild about the idea of being followed everywhere." She wondered how they had found her and how much they had guessed. She had kept her call to Akira under thirty seconds. Perhaps they were just listening in on all her calls or had even bugged her apartment at this point.

"No one is following you around. We just noticed you as you came in."

At this, Haruko looked out the window. Across the street, partially hidden in a clump of azaleas, she could see the little dome and flashing eyes of a Security Pod. You bet they had "noticed" her as she entered the place—and sent Kondo on the double to find her.

"Do you get your kicks intimidating innocent people?" she said.

"I'm just doing my job," said Kondo. The other man sat staring at her, as impassive and scary as some temple guardian. "So can you tell me who those people were and what you were talking about?"

"I'm sure you could find out easily enough. She's a colleague from the office I used to work in, and her boyfriend. We were just getting together to talk about old times."

"How did you contact her?"

So it had worked. The brief call had gone under their radar, had avoided the pod recording mechanism, so they didn't know how the two of them were connected.

"We ran into each other a week or so ago and made a date for today." As they had only started shadowing her yesterday at the earliest, this seemed safe enough.

"I see," said Kondo. There was no way of telling whether he believed her.

"Is Aoyagi still leading you on a merry chase?" she asked.

"You think it's funny, do you? You want him to get away?" He stared at her, apparently gauging her reaction. In addition to everything else, it was galling that he seemed determined to force her to tell lies.

"Do you really believe Aoyagi did this?" she asked.

"I don't 'believe' anything. I know he did."

"You really think that one ordinary little guy like him could pull off something like this?"

"Most assassins are ordinary little guys."

"You could say the same about character assassins," she said, wondering whether she was going too far.

"Mrs. Higuchi, are you defending the man who killed our prime minister?" Haruko sucked on her straw to drain the last drops of her iced cocoa. The man next to Kondo watched her as she rattled the cubes in the glass. She was afraid the fingers holding the straw would start shaking. "I understand your reluctance to accept the fact that your old friend has done something like this. . . ."

Haruko interrupted him before he could finish. "Thank you," she said, smiling at him. "I appreciate your understanding."

He paused for a moment, and she couldn't tell whether he was annoyed or amused. "Fine," he said, getting up. "If you hear anything, please let us know right away."

There was something gruesome about the two of them, Kondo and the other one who had all the animation of a stone carving. She had no doubt whatsoever that they would have happily beaten or even killed her right here in the coffee shop if the order had come down to do so.

Masaharu Aoyagi

"I'm Hodogaya," said the old man. "Yasushi Hodogaya." They walked up from the landing in the emergency stairwell and came out in a corridor. Hodogaya led Aoyagi to a door at the far end on the west side.

"Is this your room?" he asked, but as they entered he could see that the beds were unmade and the curtains closed.

"It wasn't safe talking on the stairs," Hodogaya said, closing the door. "I'm in another ward. This room is empty because the air-conditioning's broken down. I use it when I want to rest my legs."

"You broke them?" Aoyagi asked. With casts on both legs, it should have been difficult for him to walk, but to watch the way he handled his crutches like little sticks he'd found on the roadside, it was hard to see him as a cripple.

"Yep, both of them," he said. "They're just about mended, but I kind of like it here, so I'm giving myself a little holiday. The casts come right off, anyway." He demonstrated the release catches on them.

Aoyagi looked around the dimly lit room. The way the dust moats danced in the ribbon of light from between the curtains was almost graceful. It occurred to him that it seemed odd to be able to prolong a hospital stay at will, but when he asked Hodogaya how this was possible, he explained that he had "underworld connections" who arranged it for him.

"Underworld connections?" Aoyagi repeated.

"You have a problem with that?" he said.

"No, but it's kind of funny, don't you think? A guy with 'underworld connections' in here enjoying free bed and board, while I'm out there running for my life, even though I've never been anywhere near your underworld. Doesn't seem fair somehow."

"I see what you mean," Hodogaya said. "It has been a bit cushy in here. But to tell the truth, I was just getting bored with the whole thing when your little incident broke on the TV and things got interesting again."

"And you're not planning to turn me in?"

"Is that what you want me to do?"

"I'm something of a catch—the king of the 'underworld,' at the moment."

"For one thing," Hodogaya said, holding up a bony finger. "I'm underworld myself, so I don't feel like it's my 'civic duty' to turn you in. And two." He held up a second finger. "I'm not convinced you did it." Aoyagi felt as though the curtains had just parted and Hodogaya was illuminated in a spotlight. "So," he continued. "They've got just about every cop in Japan after you. I'm not sure why you're here in our little hospital, but you sure seem to be running all over the place."

"That's about all I can do," said Aoyagi.

"You're outnumbered, to say the least, so it didn't seem fair for me to pile on, too." Hodogaya produced an ear pick from somewhere and began scratching. Aoyagi thought the pick looked like something that had recently held a skewer of grilled meat. He realized he didn't have time to listen to this strange old man much longer.

"I appreciate that," was all he said.

"It's a shame, though."

"What is?"

"That they'll be catching you soon. Even I can see you can't keep this up much longer."

"Maybe. But they haven't got me yet."

"You're tougher than you seem," said Hodogaya.

"Not really," he replied, backing toward one of the beds. "I've just been running as hard as I can since yesterday, and I've had a few people helping me—I feel like I'm on a mission or something."

Hodogaya took the pick from his ear and pointed it at him. "How are you getting around?"

"Any way I can. At the moment, I've got a car that I'm hoping will get me out of the city."

"And the roadblocks?"

"I'm not sure, but I used to be a delivery driver, so I'm good behind the wheel." He had no idea how many roadblocks they would have set up around the city, but he thought there was a chance of getting away if he was willing to risk a crash, an injury. He would line up with the other cars, get all the way to the point where he was supposed to show his papers—and then take off. A car driven by a determined driver was a useful weapon.

"For all the good it'll do you," Hodogaya said. "They've got these big-shit barriers all around the place."

"It's got to be better than yesterday," said Aoyagi.

"Still, if you try busting your way out, you're a dead man." Hodogaya was smiling, but his face abruptly turned serious. "You're not planning to get killed in that car, are you?" Aoyagi looked at him and said nothing. "Get killed rather than get caught?" Still no answer. "That makes no sense," said Hodogaya. "That's no way out of all this."

"But it would leave a bad taste in their mouths," Aoyagi said at last.

"In whose mouths?"

"The people watching TV."

"That's who you're worried about?" he said, waving his pick like a conductor's baton. "Well, don't bother. But if you're out of ideas, I've got a suggestion for you." Aoyagi looked up at him, but he had retreated into the shadows. "Why don't you try the sewers?"

Masaharu Aoyagi

The tale Hodogaya began telling him was so patently unbelievable that Aoyagi was worried that a whiff of bullshit might somehow leak out of the room and give them away.

"It was a while back. They had this huge sucker of a jewel at the Sendai museum, and some associates and I were planning a heist."

"Did you pull it off?" He remembered that one of the drivers at work had boasted about being asked to deliver it to the museum.

"No, no," said Hodogaya, lowering himself onto one of the beds and propping up his casts in a practiced way. "It was just a plan. But somebody said if they put up roadblocks, we could use the sewers."

"An interesting idea," said Aoyagi, though in his mind he pictured an enormous pipe filled to capacity with filth.

"I know what you're thinking," the old man said—apparently he did. "But they're not all the same. Some pipes carry household waste—sinks, toilets, showers—and those are running fast and impossible to walk in. But others were designed to cope with overflow rainwater—storm drains, really, rather than sewers. As long as the weather holds, those are fine to walk through. Some of them are huge. They used to have the same pipes for both systems in Sendai, but a few years ago they divided them up—must have been somebody's pet pork-barrel project."

"That's the way the game's rigged," Aoyagi said, quoting Miura.

"Exactly. Textbook case."

"Are you saying I should use the pipes to get away? How would I get in? And where would they take me? How far do they go?"

"They're usually about two meters in diameter, but the ones that big, that you can get through, don't go everywhere. The storm drains end up at the river, or a pumping station. They won't take you out of the city, or to another prefecture."

"So what's the point if I can't get out of here?" he said.

"Fair enough," said Hodogaya, "but they might come in handy at some point. You could do some flimflam—distract them over here while the real deal's over there. It's not a bad strategy. Duck down a manhole somewhere and pop up somewhere else. There are plenty of good routes here in town—I've figured them all out."

"Do manholes open that easily?"

"They're heavy, but if you can lift them, you can usually get in. It helps if you've got the special hook they use." Hodogaya flipped his hands to demonstrate using one of these openers. "The bigger trick is getting out—lifting a sixty-kilo weight, standing in a vertical shaft."

Aoyagi tried to picture himself stopping on some street, producing the tool, and uncorking a manhole cover. "No, I don't think it would work," he said. "Too conspicuous."

Hodogaya smiled, and there was something in the mischievous look that reminded him of Morita. "When we were making our plans, we got the idea of using fakes," he said.

"Fake whats?"

"Manhole covers," Hodogaya said. For a moment, Aoyagi had an image of tiny plastic manholes in a scale-model city. "They'd look just like the real thing, but much lighter. You could pop them right off. We thought we'd replace all the covers around the museum with fakes. That way, we could dive right in if we needed to."

"You were going to switch them before you did the job?"

"It would have attracted too much attention to spend time fooling with them in the middle of the getaway. It pays to do a little legwork beforehand, when no one would notice."

"But I'm afraid I don't see how any of this is going to help with my situation."

"Just, if you think you might want to go underground for a while, you could give me a call." He might have been inviting him to go drinking. From somewhere, he produced the paper in which the grilled meat had been wrapped, turned it over, and wrote down his phone number. Then he folded it and handed it to Aoyagi. "Unless it's raining. You don't want to be down there when a storm comes through. . . . So, what are you going to do now?" he said after a moment.

"The first thing is to get out of here. I've got the car I came in." Then he remembered the scene he'd left a short while ago in room 502: a lifeless man in a pool of blood on the bed and Miura, eyes half open, slumped by the window. He considered telling Hodogaya about the bodies, but decided it might hold him up.

"Okay, then," said Hodogaya, dropping his cast-encased legs to the floor. "I'll see you as far as the parking lot."

"Broken legs and all?" said Aoyagi.

"Hurts like hell." He made a mock grimace. Outside the door, he stopped. "I'll show you the route I use when I need to get out for a breather." He set off, and Aoyagi saw little choice but to follow him. They took a freight elevator to the ground floor and made their way down a narrow service corridor. There was no sign of the people who had been after him before he ran into Hodogaya—maybe they'd given up and moved on.

The sleepy-looking woman behind the security desk peered at them as they passed, but when Hodogaya nodded politely, she waved them on like a health-room nurse indulging two naughty boys. As they emerged from the building, Aoyagi realized it was already evening.

"Listen," said Hodogaya, his tone serious for almost the first time since they'd met. "If you're going to get yourself arrested, make sure it happens with lots of TV cameras and witnesses around."

"So you can watch?"

"So the police can't shoot you while nobody's looking." There was something unreal about the idea—even though they had tried more than once already. "I believe you when you say you didn't do it, but they're after you and they'd like to nail you for the assassination. And the easiest way to do that is to have you gunned down in the confusion of an arrest." He held out one of his crutches and pretended to fire it. "Dead men don't testify. Case closed. So when you show yourself, do it in front of the whole country—they can't start shooting on live TV without some sort of consequences."

Aoyagi recalled the moment at the apartment complex with Iwasaki as his bogus hostage. The police had hesitated to open fire—perhaps because of the crowd gathered on the balconies. If they hadn't been there, Aoyagi thought, they would have shot him, even if it had meant killing Iwasaki, too.

The car came into sight. "I'm fucked, aren't I?" he said.

"Looks that way," said Hodogaya, leaning on his crutches and scratching his head.

Haruko Higuchi

Haruko decided to walk home from the café where she had met Akira and Masakado—and Mamoru Kondo and company. The shopping arcades in the center of town were crowded, as though no one remembered what had happened in Sendai the day before; but the crime scene had been cordoned off and stern-faced policemen were standing guard. A closer look at the crowd revealed a number of men hurrying here and there—reporters and cameramen who had been hastily dispatched by the national media—and quite a few shops were shuttered, perhaps to avoid the confusion.

She made her way north, keeping off the biggest streets. When she came to a pedestrian underpass, she would have gone down if she hadn't noticed a crowd of kids hanging out on the stairs. They had on gaudy jackets or baggy suits with shiny shirts open at the chest, and they seemed to be leering at her.

Telling herself she was imagining things, she forced herself to walk past the group and down the stairs, but as she went through the tunnel, the sound of her own footsteps seemed to follow her and she quickened her pace until she was almost running. She flew up the stairs on the other side and then stopped for a moment, hands on her hips, to catch her breath. It was getting dark, and she had the strange feeling the sky was growing blacker with every breath she took.

"What? The police just came to get her." Her neighbor, Yaeko Mochizuki, was uncharacteristically agitated when Haruko arrived to retrieve Nanami. As she stood in the doorway, she could feel the color draining from her face, and in response, Yaeko, too, went pale, perhaps realizing she'd made a mistake. "They showed their badges. Surely . . . ," her voice trailed off.

"I'm sure it was the police," Haruko said, casting a glance down the passage. That was the problem. "How long ago did they leave?"

"Just a minute ago. You might have passed them."

"I didn't see anyone."

"But they just left. There were two of them, they said you'd been injured." Yaeko was clearly mortified, and was making no excuses for herself.

Haruko turned without another word and ran back down the way she'd come. She could see that the elevator was on the ground floor, so she sprinted down the spiral staircase that served as a fire escape. It was only two flights, but she nearly fell several times as she charged down, hands clutching the railing. If anything happens to Nanami . . . , she repeated to herself—not sure what came next. She missed the edge of a stair and slipped, landing on her bottom. Her hip hurt and her head was spinning. When she reached the ground floor, she ran out to the building entrance and there in front was the black-and-white shape of a police cruiser and several officers in uniform. A telephone pole and a fence obstructed her view as she looked frantically for Nanami.

She ran out to the car and found two officers facing a woman with short hair in a ratty pink jacket—Kazu's girlfriend, Ami Tsuruta, she realized after a moment. Hiding behind her legs was her little boy, Tatsumi. Nanami was standing next to him.

She called her daughter's name and ran to her. The policemen turned to look at her, and Ami's expression relaxed visibly. "Mrs. Higuchi!"

"Haruko Higuchi?" one of the officers said.

"Who gave you permission to take my daughter?" Her breath was ragged and the question came out louder than she'd intended. "How dare you tell her I was injured! Who do you think you are?"

"We never said you were injured," she was told. Liar! Haruko thought to herself. "But we believe there is a good possibility that Aoyagi will try to contact you."

"What are you talking about?"

"And we were concerned for your daughter's safety if he did show up here."

"How can you stand there and just lie through your teeth?" she hissed. Her back and ankles throbbed from the fall on the stairs. "I don't know where Aoyagi is or what he's doing, but I'm more afraid of you than I am of him." The policemen stared, their faces expressionless, as Nanami slipped over and stood next to her.

"We were coming to see you," said Ami, speaking more quickly than usual. "And then these men came out with Nanami. I asked them what they were doing, but they wouldn't tell me."

"Scary men!" said Tatsumi, pointing at them. He seemed frightened but angry at the same time. Nanami was clutching Haruko's belt.

"Were you just planning to walk off with her?" she said.

"We were protecting her from Aoyagi," one of them informed her, completely unperturbed.

"Taking her into protective custody," said the other. "Which we would like to do for you, too."

Haruko could feel a sick rage welling up inside her, but she knew it wasn't wise to take on the police.

"No thank you," she said, as calmly as she could.

"You don't seem to understand. We're not asking you."

"I haven't seen Aoyagi in years," Haruko said. "This has nothing to do with me."

"You say that now, but if he comes to find you and you've rejected our offer, there would be nothing we could do for you." This sounded like a veiled threat.

"I'll call if I need you," she told them.

"I want to go," said Tatsumi, tugging at his mother's skirt. "Scary men!"

"I agree," said Ami. "Let's go." Haruko nodded.

"Hold on," said one of the policemen. His tone was sharp, more "You're under arrest" than "We serve and protect."

"Why were they trying to take her?" Ami's eyes met Haruko's in the rearview mirror as she gripped the wheel of her station wagon. The back seat was roomy, even with Tatsumi in his car seat and Nanami next to him. The children were already playing quietly, as though the exchange with the policemen had never happened.

"They seem to think I'm going to do something stupid, so they want to lock me away where they can keep an eye on me." If they could get Nanami, they knew her mother would be close behind.

"Something stupid?"

"Try to help Aoyagi."

"But how would you do that?"

"I've been trying any way I can." Ami laughed as she drove on down the street. Each time they turned a corner, Haruko looked back to see whether anyone was following. "Thanks for stopping them from taking Nanami," she said. It must have cost Ami some effort to stand up to the police, a source of authority she would have accepted unquestioningly under normal circumstances.

"He said you can't trust them," Ami said.

"Who did?"

"Kazu."

"Really?" It was only then she thought of asking where they were going.

"To the hospital. He woke up a little while ago. That's why I came to get you."

The hospital was quieter than it had been in the morning, with fewer outpatients wandering about, like a school after it had let out for the day. They used the rear door and got on the elevator. "They called to tell me he'd come to, so I came right over," said Ami. "I think his parents should be getting here soon."

When they reached Kazu's floor, they got off and went straight to his room. As Ami was about to open the door, a doctor appeared from inside. His hair was gray and thinning, and for some reason he had almost no eyebrows at all. His nose was delicate, with lines around his mouth. Haruko couldn't tell whether he struck her as competent or not.

"How is he?" Ami asked him.

"Stable," the doctor answered. His tone wasn't exactly warm, but compared to Kondo or the two men back at her apartment, he seemed at least to have blood flowing in his veins. "He's still weak, so you shouldn't tire him. We'll do more tests tomorrow." Haruko was standing behind Ami. She wanted to warn them that the police would show up to question Kazu as soon as they knew he was conscious.

His head was still bandaged, and the swelling around his eyes had not gone down, but as soon as he caught sight of Haruko, he murmured her name.

"It's good to see you," she said.

"Good to see you," Nanami echoed.

"Do you remember me?" he asked her.

"No," said Nanami cheerfully.

Haruko bent over the bed and brought her face close to Kazu's. She had to keep herself from gasping at the cuts and bruises. "What did they do to you?" she whispered.

"Don't worry about me. What are they doing to Aoyagi?"

"They told me *he* did this to you."

"That's what they're saying? It's scary how they can lie about things," he said. "Ami told me they haven't caught him yet."

"Not yet."

"Do you think he did it?" Kazu asked.

"I know he didn't. I got a note."

"I don't follow you."

"There was a note tucked in the visor of an abandoned car I happen to know about, and it spelled it out: 'I am innocent. Masaharu Aoyagi,' it said."

Kazu frowned, thinking she was making a joke.

"Did he really rescue you?" she asked.

"I was a little groggy, but I remember clearly that when the police were beating me he came in and stopped them."

"Are you sure it was the police?"

"I never saw their badges, but they said they were—and I think one of them was a guy who's been on TV today."

"You mean Sasaki?"

"That's the one. I'm pretty sure he was there." Kazu looked up at the ceiling and smiled ruefully. "Actually," he said, "I was planning to turn Aoyagi in at first. They called just after the assassination and told me I should let them know if he contacted me. I didn't take it seriously then, but they said he was a 'person of interest' to them."

"They called you yesterday? But how did they know? That was before he was even identified as a suspect." The news had said that it wasn't until this morning that he'd been named.

"I thought it sounded funny, too. Besides, I hadn't seen him in years and I told them I thought there was no chance he'd get in touch. They said they wanted to monitor my calls—just in case. They were polite enough, but I didn't feel like I had a choice."

"You didn't, and 'monitor' meant tapping your phone, eavesdropping on every word you said. They told me the same thing, and Ami, too. It can't be legal."

"But I'm afraid it didn't seem to matter much when they first asked me. I never thought Aoyagi would actually call me." The memory seemed to revive his physical pain. "So I didn't think it was such a big deal. But right after that he did call, and left a message on my cell phone—just said it was Aoyagi."

"He's never had much luck, has he?" said Haruko.

"No, that he hasn't. Anyway, I called him back. I assumed the police were listening. I didn't know what to say to him, what to do. I wasn't sure whether I should call the police. I wanted to warn him that something was up, but I couldn't even do that. And then he showed up at my place—and the police called. I was confused, so I told him to wait at a restaurant down the street." Kazu's remorse grew visibly as he spoke.

"You didn't do anything wrong," Haruko said. "Aoyagi trusted you. That's why he came to you when he needed help."

"He didn't call you?"

"No, and the police didn't ask me for help, either."

"I guess they didn't think he was likely to get in touch with an old girl-friend."

"I guess not," she agreed, trying to sound lighthearted.

"But I'm afraid I didn't deserve his trust," Kazu murmured.

Haruko Higuchi

"I had a dream while I was unconscious," Kazu said. His arm twitched as though he had tried to snap his fingers but was held back by the bandages.

"What sort of dream?" Haruko asked.

"You remember that trip we took to a hot spring in Yamagata when we were in school?"

"I remember," she said. In their junior year they had gone off with the usual group and a few other close friends. In theory and in practice, the Friends of Fast Food was never meant to be anything more than a bunch of people sitting around in burger joints shooting the bull. So, in keeping with the spirit of the organization, this road trip had been an aimless affair, a mere change of venue, with lots of time spent shooting the bull—but in a hot spring pool. "I remember we were all hoping for an inn with some atmosphere, so it was disappointing to wind up in a regular hotel."

"'Regular' is generous. The place was a dump, and Morita was the one who picked it." Kazu's expression changed visibly as he mentioned Morita's name, and Haruko realized he must have heard from Ami that something had happened to him. She decided to avoid the subject. "I was dreaming about that trip. We stayed three nights, and spent most of the time in the bath."

"Except that we began to wonder whether it was the real thing or if they'd hidden a boiler somewhere." She had completely forgotten about the trip, but as Kazu spoke the details came back to her.

"The third night in the bath, everyone suddenly started yelling."

"I don't remember that."

"They had mixed up the bottles of washing stuff." Haruko looked at him, wondering whether his injury and the long time he had been unconscious had somehow prompted this pointless story. "There were three bottles at each sink—shampoo, conditioner, and soap—and by the third day everyone had learned what order they left them in. So that evening, they switched the bottles."

"Who did?"

"Morita and Aoyagi," Kazu laughed.

"But why would they do that?"

"It was their idea of a practical joke. Dumb, I know, but they realized everyone was using them without checking which was which, and they wanted to see what would happen when they got them wrong. But I think Morita must have forgotten and ended up pouring conditioner all over himself."

"Typical," said Haruko, looking up at the ceiling and sighing.

"Completely dumb," he agreed. "I wonder what made me remember it?"

Tatsumi came over to the bed and reached up to brush his hand over Kazu's cheek, which was wet with tears. Kazu smiled at him and began to sing quietly in English.

"The Beatles?" Haruko asked. The tune was familiar.

"'Golden Slumbers,'" he said, pausing for a moment. Then he repeated the phrase: *Once there was a way to get back homeward.* "I can see that now. We

can't get back there anymore. There might have been a way once, but somehow we've all . . . grown older."

So we have, thought Haruko. At some stage we graduated from those lazy
days at school, we put on suits or uniforms, stopped phoning each other, got
on with our own separate lives. Not that we've grown up exactly, but gradually something changed. "I guess that happens," she said. "But it doesn't
explain what's happening to Aoyagi. It's too strange."

The door opened at this point and, as expected, a detective stood facing
them. "Mr. Ono," he said, "I have a few questions I'd like to ask you, if that's
okay."

"I'm not sure you're going to like the answers," Kazu told him, his eyes
fixed on the ceiling. It was the police who had beaten him before, so he was
bound to see this as a further attempt to choke him off.

"Can't this wait?" said Ami, getting to her feet. "He's barely regained
consciousness."

"No, it's fine," Kazu interrupted. "If he has questions, let him ask."

Kondo and another detective crossed the room to the bed. "Could I ask
you to wait outside?" Kondo said to Haruko.

"Kazu, be nice to these people," she suggested. "I know the police didn't
treat you very well the last time around, but you've got to watch your step. If
you cross these two, they could turn nasty on you, too."

There was no sarcasm intended. She simply spoke the truth. The police
had shown that they were willing to ignore the law in their pursuit of Aoyagi.
She wanted to defend Kazu, to take on these bastards, but she was worried it
might put him in more danger if she was too direct. There was no way of telling—the whole situation was so weird—but they may even have intended to
silence him permanently earlier and, when he recovered unexpectedly, had
sent these two to finish the job.

So this was no time for righteous indignation. Kazu needed to think about
his future, about Ami and the boy. He needed to survive—something hopefully he realized, lying there flat on his back. "Don't worry," he assured her.
"I'll be nice."

Kondo gave her a chilly look as she left the room.

Masaharu Aoyagi

It was unclear whether the police knew that he had a car. They probably assumed he had no way of getting one. So there was some satisfaction in the fact that he did. It was a minor victory, a token of resistance, but it was something at least.

The game unit lay on the seat next to him, tuned to the news, and it was all still about him. He had been seen walking along a highway, or holding hands with some kindergartners, or coming out of a restaurant, or driving a truck. But they were all wrong. There were even reports that he was seen driving a car, but the make and model and even the color the witness reported seeing had nothing to do with his little dirty yellow machine.

So where to go? With Miura gone and his double's whereabouts unknown, his options were wide open again—or nonexistent. He drove along trying to avoid making any decisions, and when he came to an intersection, he turned at random and drove on in the new direction. He knew he would run into a checkpoint sooner or later, and he wasn't sure he cared anymore—but each time he caught himself losing hope, he would hear that voice, those voices, urging him to keep running, and he would force himself to concentrate, to go on. He had no plan and every expectation of getting caught, but somehow he couldn't bring himself to give up.

He'd been back on the road for some time when it occurred to him that he could use Inai's empty apartment again. It wasn't a brilliant idea, but something told him that the police might have a blind spot for places they'd already searched. Why, their reasoning would go, should he go back where he'd nearly been caught? Even he wasn't that dumb. Or was he?

A short while later, he turned into the parking lot in front of the building and pulled into a space next to the main entrance—one he had often used when he was making deliveries here. He switched off the engine and got out. Looking up at the building, he could see light seeping from behind closed curtains in several windows and felt a surge of regret and envy at the normal life going on in those rooms. Looking down and covering his face as best he could, he went in. He bent double to slip past the building manager's office and got in the elevator. The note telling deliverymen to leave their packages downstairs was still on Inai's door.

He tried the knob and found that the door was unlocked. No shoes had been left inside, so he closed and locked the door behind him. "I'm back," he whispered. Sliding his backpack off his shoulders onto his arm, he removed his shoes and headed down the corridor.

As he was nearing the room at the far end, he realized that the door was ajar and a man was looking out at him. White hair, a round face, with an expression that said he'd thought he heard something and had come to check just in case. He blinked in astonishment as he came face to face with Aoyagi.

Aoyagi was just as startled—probably more so since he had been more tense to begin with—but without an instant's hesitation he covered the short distance between them while the man was still taking in the situation. Tossing down his pack, he planted his left leg next to the man's right, grabbed him by the collar of his police uniform, and pulled in while his leg swept out. The move worked again. The man fell on the boxes that still littered Inai's living room. He lay gasping, with Aoyagi's hand pressed to the base of his throat.

Then things got a little hectic. He began flapping his arms and pawing at his waist, apparently trying to reach his revolver. But Aoyagi held him down. He put his foot on the man's arm and fumbled for the gun with his free hand. The first thing he felt was a pair of handcuffs, which he pulled free. He managed to get them on one of the man's wrists, but he struggled even harder. They were both frantic, bodies twisting, spittle flying. He didn't like fighting someone so much older, but if he was pinned now, it was all over. At last he snapped the cuffs shut on the other wrist, bound his ankles with some duct tape he found, and put another strip over his mouth.

"Can you breathe okay?" he asked after propping him against a wall. The man's eyes were bloodshot and his breath was ragged, and presumably he was feeling enraged and humiliated. But if he hadn't been so worked up, Aoyagi thought the slack cheeks and wrinkled skin around his eyes suggested a placid, middle-aged man; and when they had fought a moment earlier, he had felt mostly flab instead of muscle. No doubt he had worked hard at his job and was about to begin a peaceful retirement on his government pension. At the moment, however, he was staring at him with open hatred. "I'm sorry," Aoyagi said. "I'm not going to hurt you. I just can't let myself get caught."

He slid the officer's wallet out of the pocket of his uniform and checked the name on his ID: Yasuo Kojima. When he said the name, the man gave him a sullen look. "You know who I am, don't you?" Aoyagi said. He mumbled something Aoyagi took to be "assassin," but the tape made it unintelligible. "I'm not," he told him, looking him in the eye. "I'm being framed." He thought he might have a chance of getting through to him if he was completely direct. Kojima writhed and struggled, as though goaded by a sense of duty, by the need to get out of the handcuffs, tear off the tape, and arrest Aoyagi on the spot. "It's the truth," he said. "I didn't do it. But for some reason they're trying to make it look like I did, and that's why I'm on the run." Kojima sneered from behind the tape. "Let me know if you're hungry," Aoyagi said, pulling an energy bar from his pack. "I've got more of these. . . . Actually, I stole them from here. Or if you need to go to the toilet, just say so. I'm afraid I'm going to have to keep you here, at least till I'm ready to move on."

He wasn't sure how long he wanted to stay in Inai's apartment, but the real question was probably how long he could safely hang around.

Less than twenty minutes had passed when Kojima slumped against the wall and closed his eyes, either from resignation or exhaustion. Perhaps he had decided that he wouldn't survive the encounter. Feeling guilty, Aoyagi leaned closer. "I really won't hurt you," he said. But there was no response, so he sat down near him and buried his face in his knees. As he did so, he thought that Kojima looked over at him for a moment, but he didn't look up.

He woke up, sensing Kojima squirming near him.

"The toilet?" he asked. Kojima nodded. "Okay," Aoyagi said, getting up and peeling the tape off his legs. "I'm afraid I'll have to leave the cuffs," he said. "But I'm sure you can manage." He helped him to his feet and led him to the bathroom. Closing the door behind him, Aoyagi waited outside. The whole situation felt awkward, but he had no choice.

After a few minutes, he heard the toilet flush and he knocked on the door. He was ready for Kojima to try to jump him the minute the door opened, but the man simply walked meekly back to the living room. Aoyagi wrapped the same piece of tape around his ankles. It was less sticky now but should still do the trick.

"I'm really sorry about all this," he said. "But I'll be moving on in the morning." Was that true? Did he really mean to leave here with nothing else up his sleeve? Kojima looked at him quizzically, as if to ask where he would be going. "I know I can't just leave you like this," he added. Then he picked up the remote next to him on the floor and punched the power button. The TV, mounted on the wall across from them, made a low noise and the picture came on. He looked at the clock on the desk: 7:30. He had been asleep a long time.

"Still me, all the time," he said, flipping from channel to channel, news special to news special. One lone channel had apparently decided it would buck the trend and show a sitcom starring a number of young actors. Aoyagi watched this for a while but was soon bored. Glancing over at Kojima, it was clear he felt the same way, so he hit the button and moved on. This time, a close-up of his own face appeared on the screen, followed by a map of Sendai on which all the Aoyagi sightings had been marked.

In the studio, another panel of experts had been assembled to comment. "If Aoyagi is still hiding somewhere in the city, that would seem to indi-cate that he has accomplices," said a man who had been a detective. "They should be doing door-to-door searches in the older apartment blocks and the neighborhood where he lived as a student." A psychologist was more worried about the suspect's mental state. "He's probably sleep-deprived and exhausted. If he isn't located soon, there's no telling what might happen."

No telling what might happen. Aoyagi thought about this for a moment. He wasn't sure whether the psychologist was worried that he would hurt himself or that he would take hostages or do someone else harm. At any rate, they all felt free to speculate wildly about him without any reference to the facts. He looked over at Kojima. "You may not believe me," he said, pointing at the TV, "but they're all a bunch of puffed-up liars."

He expected Kojima to glare back at him, but there was no particular anger in his eyes. Maybe he was tired, or had just given up. Or maybe he wanted to keep Aoyagi calm, to reassure him until he got his own chance. "I'm sorry you got dragged into this," Aoyagi said. There was no response.

He felt a vibration in his backpack—a call coming in to the phone he had taken from Miura's pocket. He took it out and checked the display. The number was familiar. "Sorry," he said to Kojima, "I've got to answer this."

"Aoyagi?" said the voice of the plastic surgeon. "I have some new information."

"About the double?" he asked. Miura's small, lifeless form came briefly to mind.

"It seems he was being hidden at a private clinic run by one of my colleagues."

"The last time it was the Hospital Center, but we both know that was a lie." How could he be calling with the same story, with nothing more than a change of venue?

"The police took him away about two hours ago. The doctor at the clinic called to tell me."

"Why would he do that?" Aoyagi asked. The whole situation seemed highly improbable.

"He resented the way it was done—by force, without a word of explanation. They didn't say why they were taking him or where; they weren't even civil. They broke the frame of a picture on the wall by the back door and didn't even apologize."

"He was worried about his frame?"

"He was angry. He knew I was looking for your double, and news travels fast in our little circle. I guess you could say he called me out of spite."

"Spite? When the stakes are this high?"

"Castro took up with the Soviets and caused the Cuban Missile Crisis because he felt he was badly treated when he visited the U.S. He had nothing against America before that trip, but when he got back he was ready to crawl into bed with the Russians. People do a lot of things out of spite." The point was shrewd enough, but the man's flat tone made Aoyagi feel he was more interested in people's skin and bones than in their feelings.

"So where did they take him?" he asked.

"I don't know. But I'm fairly sure that if you keep hiding, they'll dispose of him soon enough." The lack of emotion in his voice left Aoyagi at a loss for a moment. "If they can't catch you, they'll use him. They'll probably just issue a report and produce a body. They're quite capable of that kind of thing. Do you find that shocking?"

He pictured his double lying faceup in a field somewhere. Shot through the heart. Or wrists slit. And the headline: "Aoyagi Found Dead."

"They think the whole thing'd be over if they could convince people I was dead?"

"Dead men tell no tales, as they like to say."

"But I'm not dead. What if I resurfaced and started talking? If I said it was a double that died?"

"I suspect they're confident they've seen the last of you."

"So they'd just be tying up loose ends," Aoyagi said, feeling a bit queasy. "But why are you telling me all this?"

"The information came to me, and I just felt I should pass it on. I wanted to make up for the trouble I caused."

"I've had a good bit of trouble since yesterday," said Aoyagi. "A false lead and a trip to the hospital are hardly the worst of it."

"I have one more bit of news, though I'm not sure if it's relevant."

"At this point, I'd prefer irrelevant."

"This friend of mine, the plastic surgeon who runs the clinic, told me that he'd been asked to do another operation, to create another double of someone else."

"I don't know what to say," said Aoyagi. "That's quite a racket you guys have going for you."

"You don't understand," said the doctor. "The request seemed to come from the police, or their surrogates. But the man who had the operation was taken away the other day, too."

"I don't follow."

"Well, it's just speculation, but I think they were planning to frame someone else. Not you."

"Not me?"

"They originally meant to pin the assassination on another person, and they had a double made of him, too. I think they couldn't use him at the last minute, and that's why they settled on you."

"You mean he was otherwise engaged?" Aoyagi wasn't sure what the doctor was trying to say but he played along. "So I got the job?"

"It just seems possible that you were a kind of backup plan," said the voice on the phone.

Aoyagi thought about this for a moment. Given how powerful these people seemed to be, how carefully they had worked out every last detail, it was certainly possible he was only part of their scheme. "But even if it's true, that doesn't change anything. Whether I was the star or an understudy, I'm just as screwed."

"Yes, but at least you know that the people chasing you might have weaknesses, soft spots. I'm sure they prepared carefully, even for the backup plan, but you were only for use in an emergency, not their favorite option, and that might give you room to maneuver, to outflank them."

"So this is your way of telling me I should keep the faith, keep trying?"

"I suppose you could say that."

Aoyagi hung up without another word. He could feel Kojima watching him as he stared at the floor and sighed.

"You're not going to believe this either," he said, looking up at the TV screen, where some pundit was holding forth. "But hear me out. I did not do this. They . . . ." He paused, realizing he had no idea who "they" were, chilled by the thought that an enemy he couldn't even name was crushing the life out of him. "They made a body double of me, or rather, they had a plastic surgeon make one. The pictures of me on TV are actually him."

Kojima looked as wary as ever, but now there were signs of bewilderment in his expression. His eyes seemed to plead with Aoyagi to leave him alone, to let him wait in peace for his pending retirement without being caught up in this mess.

"Now I think they're planning to get rid of the double sometime soon instead of me. Since they haven't caught me, they're going to produce his body and claim that I'm dead." He had managed to stay calm up to this point, but he was suddenly overwhelmed by anger and frustration. "I just thought you should know," he muttered.

The tape on Kojima's mouth had worked loose and he was apparently trying to speak. Aoyagi was just about to ask him what he wanted to say when a familiar face came on the TV.

Masaharu Aoyagi

"Mr. Aoyagi! Mr. Aoyagi!" a reporter with a microphone was yelling, and Mr. Aoyagi, his father, stood frowning in front of a familiar house. Beside him on the gatepost was a plaque reading "Aoyagi," and in the background, the front door. He had not been home since the end of last year, but here was his father, on national TV, shaking his fist at the camera. "You have no right to force your way in here!" he was shouting.

"But we're still outside," giggled a reporter whom Aoyagi remembered seeing on one of the popular news shows.

"How dare you invade my home and accuse my son of being a criminal!"

"The police have identified him as the prime suspect, and there are witnesses. Do you have anything to say about what your son is accused of doing?" This reporter was a middle-aged woman who also had a mike to thrust in his face.

"What do you know about him?" his father shouted at her. "You don't know the first thing about my son!" The reporters were silent for a moment, apparently considering their next line of attack. "I've known him since the day he was born! And his mother even longer than that, since he was in her belly. I saw his first steps, heard his first words. I've known him forever. You've been snooping around since yesterday. What can you know about him?"

"Mr. Aoyagi, we understand that you'd like to believe in your son's innocence. . . . ," said the woman.

"You don't understand anything! 'I'd like to believe'? I *know*! I *know* he's innocent." Aoyagi couldn't take his eyes off the screen. He was shaking and his pulse had quickened, as though his blood was racing around in search of a way to escape. "Something like this happened when Masaharu was in middle school. A shopkeeper accused him of stealing some CDs. That time, too, I knew for a fact that he didn't do it. Just like now. I don't know how many times I have to tell you, he could never do something like that."

Reporters continued to call his name from here and there in the crowd, but he waved them off as though they were flies. "Who wants to bet me?" he said now. "Who wants to bet that he did it? I'll bet anything you want that he didn't! Who'll bet me?" He pointed at each one of them in turn. "If you're so sure he did it, bet me. It doesn't have to be money. Bet something that matters to you. At the moment *this* seems to be the only thing that matters to you—to take it out on my family. I realize it's your job; that's the way it is. But if your job is to destroy other people's lives, you need to be damn careful about how you do it. We all take our jobs seriously—bus drivers, builders, cooks—they all do their best, because they know people's lives depend on it. Can you all say the same?"

His listeners started complaining audibly. They were furious that the old man could speak to them this way; he should remember how many people had been injured or killed in the explosions; he should use his common sense. Or maybe they weren't really furious but only pretending to be. At any rate, no one was willing to take his father's bet.

"Just as I thought. A bunch of bullshitters." His father smiled, and Aoyagi felt as though he was watching a comic sketch unreel behind the tube in front of him. A moment later, his father pointed to his right. "Is that the camera?" He turned to face it. "Masaharu. This gets uglier and uglier the longer you stay in hiding."

Aoyagi laughed. "You can't imagine," he said to the TV.

"But don't worry about us. Your mother's fine. I'm fine. You just keep doing whatever you have to." The reporters took this as tantamount to aiding and abetting a wanted criminal, and they began to shout again and wave their microphones. But Aoyagi's father was unfazed. "Just keep running, boy."

Aoyagi could feel a lump rising in his throat. He knew what would happen if he wasn't careful. The lump would become a knot, his eyes would start to water, and soon he would be bawling. He clenched his teeth. The minute he started crying, his anger and his will to go on would drain away. If he began to blubber, it was all over. If he broke down, the fuel that kept him going would disappear.

He sensed a slight movement in the room, a vague crumpling in the air, as though a sheet of paper had been wadded up. When he looked over at Kojima, he realized he was shaking slightly, and that tears were running down his cheeks. The tape over his mouth was damp.

He continued to cry for some time even after Aoyagi had removed the tape. His shoulders heaved and he wiped his eyes with his handcuffed hands—but he made no attempt to shout and give him away.

Aoyagi turned off the TV, but the silence made him uncomfortable so he switched on the CD player. *Abbey Road* was still loaded in the tray. He skipped to the medley at the end and listened to the cheerful tune.

"The Beatles made masterpieces right to the end, right to the moment they split up." It had been Kazu up on the soapbox at some fast-food place back when they were in school.

"Even though they couldn't stand each other," Morita had added. Then someone—he no longer knew who—had wondered how Paul had felt as he stitched the songs together. He must have felt that he was trying to stitch the band together again.

Aoyagi leaned back against the wall and hugged his knees. He closed his eyes, wanting to absorb the music rather than just listen to it. Paul's solitude seemed to wash over him. "Golden slumbers . . . ," he sang with an intensity that echoed inside Aoyagi for a long while. The curtains were closed so he had no idea whether it was fully dark outside, but he felt oddly sure that the sound of Paul's voice wouldn't carry beyond the room.

"The End" began to play, the last song on *Abbey Road*. Paul and John on vocals, then John's guitar solo. While they'd listened all those years ago, Kazu had spoken up again like some music critic, pointing out how the song showcased their individual talents. "Can you even tell the difference?" Morita had teased him.

When the CD ended, Aoyagi started it again, this time from the beginning: "Come Together."

"You really didn't do it?" Kojima murmured. Aoyagi glanced up at him. His eyes were closed and he had stopped crying.

"Do I look like I could pull off something like that?"

"But everyone's convinced you did. I believed it myself."

"I can see why. Someone did a great job of framing me. But you're a cop; you've got a job to do. That's just the way it is."

"They don't expect much when you reach my age. I'm going to retire soon, which is why they put me here. They thought there was virtually no chance you'd come back."

"I guess you just got lucky," Aoyagi said. The Beatles continued to play in the background. He could see his reflection next to Kojima's in the dark screen of the TV. "Do you have a son?" he asked.

"A little older than you," Kojima told him. "And I suppose I'd be on his side, too. I'd want to believe him unless it was something too terrible."

"Like killing the prime minister?" This made the man smile for the first time since they'd met up. "But what my dad said about shoplifting the CDs? I actually did that." Kojima stopped smiling. "I was with a buddy. We got carried away. Nobody framed us—I guess my dad's instincts were off."

Aoyagi closed his eyes, and the lyrics to "Golden Slumbers" drifted through his head again. *Once there was a way to get back homeward.* He thought of that place from his past—that was gone now.

Golden slumbers fill your eyes. Smiles awake you when you rise.

He wished he could find that warm, golden sunlight, let it embrace him. He wanted to fall asleep drenched in golden light. Little by little, his anger left him. Slowly, he felt himself accepting his situation. He clenched his fists, recalling the scene of his father letting fly at the TV reporter. It occurred to him that his father was a much likelier choice for the role of a hit man. He pictured him again, and the memory began to warm him like sunlight.

"Human beings don't act on impulse. They do things deliberately, consider the consequences." He had said something like this once. "Act deliberately, consider the consequences."

But what good would thinking do him now? What weapons did he have at his disposal? He tried to be calm, to think about what he knew and stitch it together the way McCartney had stitched together his medley. Then, for some reason, he remembered noticing a piece of thin cord next to a stack of Inai's boxes—a pin mike, the kind that connects to a cell phone. The gears began to turn in his head.

. . . *When you rise.* Just as Paul sang the words, Aoyagi opened his eyes. Kojima watched him as he got up and took out his phone. Next, he brought his wrist close to his face and studied it carefully. "It's still there," he murmured.

"What is?"

Aoyagi pointed to the spot where he had written down a telephone number. "I'll take it as a good omen that it didn't get washed away," he said as he punched the number into the phone. He counted the rings, telling himself he would give up if no one answered.

"Yaji Yaji Yajima," a man's voice chirped. It sounded like a TV jingle, but it was music to Aoyagi's ears.

"Who'd have thought anyone in TV could be so happy," he said, only half joking.

"Who is this?"

"Masaharu Aoyagi."

The man screamed and there was a loud clatter followed by silence. "I'm sorry, I dropped the phone," said the voice when it came back on, all business this time. "Yajima here."

"As in Yaji Yaji Yajima?"

"That's just a little ritual, my trademark, you might say." He didn't sound in the least embarrassed.

"Because there are so many other Yajimas?" Aoyagi asked. He resisted the urge to laugh, but he noted not unhappily that he was still capable of laughing. Morita had once said that our greatest strengths were trust and habit—he would have liked to tell him that laughter should be added to the list.

"There are three Yajimas in our office; I'm Yaji Yaji Yajima."

"I'm Ao Ao Aoyagi. I called before."

"I remember. You wanted me to promise I wouldn't call the police."

"Do you believe I'm the real Aoyagi?"

"I'm afraid I do, strange as it may seem." For some reason Yajima sounded younger now than he'd imagined him the time before, and more positive, perhaps.

"I have a favor to ask," he said.

"Who doesn't?"

"I'd like you to put me on the air, as I said earlier. I want to explain my side of things—that I'm being framed, that a lot of people are getting hurt because they've been drawn into all this. . . ."

"And will you be telling us the name of the real culprit?"

"No, I don't know who actually did it. But it doesn't matter. No one person killed the prime minister."

"Are we talking about some sort of secret society?"

"Society is right, but it's not secret." He glanced over at Kojima, who was watching him with a troubled look on his face. He seemed puzzled by this new turn of events. "Can you put me on?"

"Of course we can—that's what we do."

"I might even be good for ratings," Aoyagi said.

"You might at that, but the question is how we can pull it off. If you come in to the studio, we'll have to let the police know you're here. We could pretend you just showed up, but the people upstairs are a little antsy and the police are leaning on everyone. . . ."

Impatient, he cut short Yajima's list of obstacles. "I'm going to resurface tomorrow, somewhere in the city. Do you think you could arrange for some cameras to be there? The police will know ahead of time as well, so it should be quite a show."

Yajima was quiet for a moment, probably considering Aoyagi's request. "Where?" he said at last.

"I haven't decided yet. Downtown, but someplace wide open. I'm guessing the police will try to keep any cameras at a distance, so a place with good visibility."

"And you're just going to show up?"

"The police will have the place surrounded."

"And you want us to film the arrest?"

"I want to call you while it's happening. Do you think you could arrange to talk to me live?"

"On the phone? While you're being arrested?" Yajima's voice rose with excitement. Aoyagi suddenly worried that the conversation had gone on too long, but there was no reason to think the police had this number. Still, there was always the chance they would catch them in their random eavesdropping. At this point, anything seemed possible.

"What do you think? When people hear me on the phone, with the police all around me, no one's going to think I'm a fake, right? There's something convincing about hearing somebody on TV, live." He wanted to speak directly to a large number of people without any interference or filter, and this is what he had come up with. Going to a studio was dangerous and left open the possibility that someone would edit him; a live, open-air broadcast was his only hope. "I'll call you before it happens, and I'll be wearing a pin mike when I surrender. You should be able to broadcast the whole thing."

"You want us to broadcast what you say just as it comes in to my phone?"

"Can you do it? Technically speaking?"

"We should be able to. But what happens after you have your say?"

"They arrest me. I'm just hoping I can plant some doubt in a few people's heads. If I can get that far, if there are just a few people out there who start wondering whether I really did it, then things could change after I'm arrested. They won't be able to convict me and execute me without someone asking questions. That's why I need to get my story out to as many people as possible, to attract attention to my little show. Plus, if you can get the whole thing on camera, the police won't be able to shoot first and ask questions later." This was his other motive in asking for Yajima's help. If he was really an Oswald, then there was a strong likelihood that they would gun him down the moment he showed himself. The people behind the assassination had no interest in hearing what he had to say. Like Ruby with Oswald, they would turn some killer loose on him and put an end to the whole thing. "So it needs to be a spot where everyone can see what's happening."

Yajima was quiet again for a moment, presumably trying to decide whether to agree to this proposal, but the outcome was pretty certain. There was little risk for the TV station—except the risk that Aoyagi would take the scoop of the century and peddle it elsewhere. "You're on," Kojima said.

"Thanks."

"So what time tomorrow is this going to happen? And where should I send the cameras?"

"Early, before dawn most likely. I'll call you later tonight to let you know."

"Okay. I guess you know there's no downside for us in this. But I'd hate to be in your shoes."

An honest man, thought Aoyagi.

Kojima was still staring at him as he finished the call. "What are you going to do?" he asked.

"You just heard. I'm going to give myself up tomorrow morning—hopefully without getting shot."

"The police don't just go shooting people."

"That hasn't been my experience," he said. "I don't want to discredit anybody, you being a policeman and all, but you guys have been doing a whole lot of shooting, at least in this case. I should know. So I'm pretty sure I know what I'm talking about when I say they're planning to shut me up for good."

"But why would they want to do that?"

"Because I'm innocent, and they don't want me shooting off my mouth once they've arrested me. I'm much more useful to them as a dead assassin than as a live suspect."

"Early tomorrow?" Kojima said. That left just a few hours.

"Once I'm ready, there's no point sitting around and waiting. I'd just start second-guessing myself." As they talked, Aoyagi was thinking of all the things he still had to do before morning.

Kojima watched him, a half scowl appearing on this face, as though Aoyagi were being uncooperative or even a bit dangerous. A moment ago he had been crying like a sentimental kid at the sight of Aoyagi's father on the TV, but now his sense of duty as a police officer seemed to have returned. Aoyagi noted the look.

"You won't have to put up with me much longer. I'll be leaving soon," he told him.

Kojima ignored this, but then unexpectedly a few minutes later he gave a little cry, like a schoolboy realizing he'd forgotten his homework. "I'll have to be checking in soon," he said.

"Checking in?"

"Somebody'll notice if I don't report in at the proper time. They'll phone here eventually, but to avoid anyone getting suspicious, I should probably call first. On the other hand, things are pretty crazy at headquarters, so maybe no one will remember I'm out here."

"Still, better safe than sorry, I suppose."

"I suppose. Actually, someone should be coming to relieve me in the middle of the night. But if I call, I can say that I'll stay until morning. They're having trouble coping with all the personnel on this case, so they'll probably be glad to let me stay."

Aoyagi agreed immediately. "Do you use your walkie-talkie?" he asked, looking at the device on Kojima's belt. Kojima nodded. "Sorry if I don't take off the handcuffs," he added.

"Just pull it off and put it here on the floor." He held his cuffed hands in front of him. "I can manage. And I can talk lying down. Just out of curiosity, though, what would you do if I told them you're here once I got on the phone? Not that I would, of course."

"I thought about that, but I'll have to risk it. You know what they say: trust is one of our strengths."

There was a look of amazement on Kojima's face, as though he couldn't decide whether he'd run into the world's biggest idiot or its last decent soul. "Well, if that's the case, you might want to take these off, too," he said, holding up his wrists.

"I was afraid you'd say that. But I have to draw the line somewhere."

"I suppose so."

"But while you're reporting in, I'll go make another call," Aoyagi said, heading outside.

"Don't you want to hear what I'm going to tell them?"

"No, I trust you," he said over his shoulder. When he looked back, Kojima was squirming on the floor to get his face close to the walkie-talkie. He looked ridiculous, and Aoyagi felt sorry for all the trouble he was causing him.

He went into the bathroom. The face in the mirror was grim and unfamiliar, with dark circles around the eyes and mouth. He tried forcing a smile, but the face just twisted into an ugly smirk. Nothing to smile about.

He reached into his pack and pulled out a slip of paper he had wadded into a pocket: the wrapper for the grilled meat—with a telephone number written on the back. The fingers of his left hand hurriedly dialed. It rang several times but no one answered, so he was just heading down the passage to check on Kojima when a voice came on.

"Hodogaya," it said.

"It's Aoyagi. Can we talk sewers?"

Haruko Higuchi

"What kind of guy was Aoyagi?" Ami Tsuruta asked. She and Haruko were sitting in a waiting area next to the elevator, down the corridor from Kazu's room. It was pitch dark outside the window, as though a black curtain had been hung over it.

"Pretty average," Haruko laughed. "The last person you'd imagine getting involved in something like this." She could picture Aoyagi and Morita facing each other across a table in the cafeteria. The two of them talking and enjoying themselves, and then other friends arriving and joining in, and then more, until there were a dozen people laughing and gesticulating around the long dining table they had made up. How often had she seen this happen?

"Kazu always lit up when he talked about them, and it made him sad that he couldn't keep the group going after they graduated," Ami said.

Six small tables with four chairs each had been lined up in the waiting area, almost like a miniature cafeteria. Against the back wall was a vending machine selling juice, and next to the window, a table with an electric kettle and a box of tea bags. A sign informed visitors that they should confine cell phone use to this area. Tatsumi and Nanami were on tiptoe in front of the vending machine fiddling with the buttons, at first gently and then more vigorously until at last they were pounding them with their fists and shouting with excitement.

"That's enough," said Haruko.

"But nobody's here," Nanami sulked, though as if on cue a man appeared. He was short with white hair, and he wore faded pajamas. But what made them take notice was the fact that he had casts on both legs—and he made his way toward them without the help of crutches. When he caught sight of Ami, he smiled and waved, and waved again when he saw Tatsumi by the vending machine. Tatsumi waved back.

"A friend of yours?" Haruko whispered.

"We just met him today. He's a patient here, a funny old man. He says he broke both legs, but he seems to get around well enough." When the hospital called to say that Kazu had regained consciousness, she had come running over, but they had kept her waiting outside his room. The man happened to pass in the corridor. He'd been eating something on a skewer and had offered Tatsumi a piece. In return, apparently, Tatsumi had offered him the cap from a pen he found somewhere.

At the moment, he was talking on his phone, but he produced the pen cap from his pocket and held it up for Tatsumi to see. Then he went over to the window and talked there quietly. Since he was obviously trying to avoid being overheard, Haruko signaled to Ami that they should go, and they called to the children as they stood up. The women left the waiting area and started down the passage toward Kazu's room, but then stopped, realizing that Nanami hadn't followed. Haruko turned and headed back, finding the girl in the corner behind the tables.

"Mommy, that man was talking about you on the phone," she said. When she looked, the man was smiling and scratching his head. Ami and her boy came up behind them.

"My name's Hodogaya," he said. "You're a friend of that guy they're looking for, aren't you?" Haruko felt as though someone had hit her in the chest.

"He was talking about you, Mommy," Nanami repeated. Hodogaya's eyes smiled. "At the end he said your name and Mr. Aoyagi's. I heard him."

"It's not polite to eavesdrop," Haruko said sharply. On numerous occasions she had found herself laughing at the girl's tendency to spill the beans, but she wasn't laughing now.

"Sorry, I forgot," Nanami said. "It's a secret." Then, pointing her finger at the man: "This is secret," she told him.

"Don't worry, I know," he said, smiling more broadly now and looking at Haruko. She wasn't really sure whether the look was meant to reassure or intimidate her.

"We went to school together," she said, feeling in spite of herself that she had to explain her connection with Aoyagi.

"I see," he said, before lowering himself into a chair with his rigid legs splayed out in front of him. He motioned for Haruko to join him and she sat down on the other side of the table. "Well, he's a friend of mine, too. After a fashion." Hodogaya seemed to take some pride in this admission. "You're his oldest friend, maybe, and I'm his newest. In fact, I was just speaking to him." He held up his phone.

Haruko was so startled she leaned forward, as if hoping to find some trace of Aoyagi in it.

"What did he want?" Ami said, taking the seat next to Haruko.

"Our friend is about to roll the dice," he told them.

Haruko Higuchi

As Hodogaya finished his story, which had been delivered with considerable enthusiasm, Haruko gave him a slightly reproachful look. "Do you really think you should be telling us all this? You'd be doing him a lot of harm if we weren't on his side."

Hodogaya seemed utterly unconcerned. "Oh, are you the enemy? Then forget everything I just said."

"We're not the enemy, are we, Mommy?" said Nanami, peeking around her.

"No, we're not. But it's not safe to talk so much."

"Relax!" said Hodogaya. It occurred to Haruko that he was the sort who made a habit of reassuring people without good cause.

"Why did Mr. Aoyagi call him?" Nanami said.

"I was just wondering the same thing," said her mother.

Hodogaya seemed unfazed. "Me, too," he said with a chuckle. "He must have been in a tight spot to come looking for somebody like me. I guess he ran out of options."

"But is it really possible?" Ami asked, lowering her voice. "Using the sewers."

"Actually, it would be the storm drains. And sure it's possible. But I'm going to have to run around a bit and lay the groundwork." And with that he popped off his casts, then clapped them back on.

From Hodogaya's excited account, they gathered that Aoyagi was planning to put in an appearance tomorrow at Central Park across from the city hall. He would let the police know ahead of time, and TV cameras would be there as well. He apparently thought it would be better to proclaim his innocence and turn himself in than to keep on running.

"He must have given up," Haruko said, but then realized how grim that sounded. "I mean, he must have decided he can't win—but that he's got his innocence on his side."

"On his side?" Hodogaya interrupted, like someone who had seen a lot more of life than her. "Where do you think that will get him? Nowhere, that's where. If he lets himself get caught, it'll land him in jail or in a shallow grave, that's where."

"He can't let them just catch him," Ami said, staring at her hands on the table in front of her.

"He says he wants the TV station to broadcast him live, let him explain directly to people. The TV has been making him into the villain all along, so he wants to use them to do a little damage control at the end," Hodogaya said.

"But why does he think anyone will believe him, no matter what he says on TV?" Haruko knew that nearly everyone ever arrested claimed he was innocent; and most people thought of these claims as more proof of guilt. Once an accusation was made, the impression of guilt clung to the suspect, and once someone appeared on TV as a suspect, all the denials in the world only made him seem guiltier. "If it weren't for the fact that I know Aoyagi, I'd think he was making too much fuss myself, that he didn't know when to quit. I doubt I'd believe him. Still, maybe there isn't anything else he can do."

Aoyagi had made his choice. He now seemed intent on avoiding arrest until he could surrender in a very public way. But if it became known that he was heading somewhere—his point of surrender, in this case—then the police would redouble their efforts to catch him along the way and arrest him out of the spotlight. So he had asked for Hodogaya's help in getting him close to the park without being caught.

"But isn't it next to impossible to open a manhole from underneath?" Ami asked, already spotting a flaw in the plan. "The covers look really heavy, and he can't take all day to push it off."

"You're right, they weigh a ton. But that's where I come in," Hodogaya said. He explained that he had a supply of fake manhole covers from a previous line of work, and that he would spend the night switching them with the real ones.

"But which ones?" Haruko asked, feeling for a moment as though she was back at work and in an important planning session. "There must be hundreds of them just in the center of town alone. Do you know where he's planning to go down and where he'll come up?"

Hodogaya gave her the thumbs-up sign. "Storm drains come in all different sizes, and they're at all different depths under the city. But there happens to be one that's nearly two meters in diameter that runs from the big parking lot near the station to Central Park."

"And Aoyagi could get through it."

"If he had some light—it's pitch dark down there. But fortunately I can supply that, too." Hodogaya was plainly rather pleased with himself. "I'll leave a flashlight at the bottom of the ladder, and a map to show him where to go. What more could he ask for?"

The waiting area was quiet again for a moment. Haruko looked out the window. Their reflections were mirrored in the glass over the darkness beyond. Tatsumi and Nanami had started pounding on the vending machine again.

"I can tell you've still got some questions," Hodogaya said. "Fire away."

"If he can get into the storm drains and move along under the city, why would he want to come out at all? Why doesn't he just keep going and get away?" Haruko asked.

"Well, there are practical considerations plus there's the matter of his feelings," Hodogaya said. On the practical side, he explained, the structure of the drain system presented some obstacles. When the water volume was low, the drains could be used for moving around under the city, but even then some stretches of pipe were so narrow you could barely crawl through them—and there was always the chance you'd be stopped short. What's more, even if you could wander freely under the center of the city, you would need to surface somewhere to get out of town. Depending on the route you took, there was also the possibility that you would end up being pulverized at a pumping station. "So we can arrange for him to move about a bit downtown, but getting him out of town altogether is a lot trickier. It's basically a free pass to Central Park."

"And his feelings?" asked Haruko.

"I think he wants to give himself up on his own terms and say his piece. He wants to be sure no one else gets hurt in the process."

"Is this really the time to be worrying about anyone else?" Ami asked.

"He said somebody's life was at stake," said Hodogaya.

"Whose?" Haruko asked, thinking of Kazu in his hospital bed—and Morita, who might already be dead.

"He said it was his double."

"He's got a double?"

"He didn't say much, but it seems there is one, someone who was supposed to stand in for him." Haruko had no idea what this was about, but she realized she had seen enough to know that nothing could surprise her anymore. "Anyway, I'm going home to get the dummy manhole covers, and then I'm heading out to get them in place. Looks like a busy night!" Seeming years younger and more energetic already, he rose from his chair and stretched his arms overhead as if working himself into the mood for the job.

"Wouldn't you attract attention?" Haruko asked.

"I doubt anyone's going to notice me prying open a few manholes in the middle of the night—and it only takes a second."

"But the police aren't stupid," Haruko pointed out. "If Aoyagi tells them ahead of time that he's going to give himself up in Central Park, they're going to be watching the whole area and checking any unusual activity—like someone casually switching some manhole covers."

"Aoyagi's not stupid, either. He's going to wait to call the TV station and the police until after I've had a chance to change the covers. That's just good planning. Besides, he'll probably tell them to meet him somewhere else, at least at first."

"What do you mean?"

"He'll arrange the meeting and then switch spots at the last second. He'll keep the park a secret. A little dodge, a little hocus-pocus. But that means I have to get the covers changed before it starts to get light, so he can get all this going while it's still hard to see, while they'll have trouble making out what's happening."

"But I still don't see why you're telling us," Haruko said. "How do you know we won't give away the whole thing?"

"Like I said, I thought you were on our side. If you aren't, just forget I said anything."

"But we are . . . on your side," Haruko said. And then she remembered something useful. "And I know someone who can get around the city at night without attracting suspicion."

"Who?"

"You'll need a truck to move the manhole covers. I know just the guy to drive you." She realized that there would be no tap on Hodogaya's phone and that she could use it to get in touch with Masakado.

Masaharu Aoyagi

Aoyagi glanced at his watch and saw that it was already close to midnight. He was sitting on the floor, back against the wall, staring up at the ceiling. His eyes had been closed until a moment ago, but he hadn't slept, even though he knew it would have helped calm his nerves. A few hours from now, he would be leaving this apartment and heading toward his date with the police and the mass media. He didn't know how well his plan to use the sewers would work, but at this point it was his only option.

Kojima had been sitting next to him. He had got up twice to go to the bathroom, but otherwise he had hardly moved. "Are you really going through with it?" he said now.

"I'll have to leave you here. I'm sorry, but I can't think of any other way. I've got a few arrangements to make and then . . ."

"And then?"

"It's up to fate."

A half hour or so ago, Hodogaya had called to say he would be able to manage the manhole covers. Aoyagi had been worried that the switch would be impossible in a city as closely watched as Sendai, but somehow they'd got the use of a maintenance truck, and several of the manholes were in Security Pod blind spots. When he asked how they'd come up with the truck, Hodogaya said cryptically that they "had help from various quarters"—which in turn made him worry that too many people had been let in on the plan. But Hodogaya assured him it would all work out, and he had little choice but to trust him.

Now it was almost time to make his calls.

"Aren't you going to sleep?" he murmured to Kojima, unlikely though it was in his current situation.

"No, I'm fine," Kojima said, and despite his age he actually seemed to be okay. Maybe his police training had kicked in, but he showed no signs of nerves or exhaustion.

Aoyagi picked up the remote and turned on the TV—perhaps for the last time, it suddenly occurred to him. As the uncanny blue light gradually filled the room, the box in front of him seemed almost like a mind-control device.

Sitting next to Kojima, facing the screen, he could half imagine that he was enjoying a movie at home, but the image that appeared gave him a jolt: it was his father's face talking to the camera, the same scene that had played live several hours earlier. They seemed to be recycling footage in tighter and tighter loops.

And his father was a big star now. Standing outside the house, facing the mikes with the same intensity, the same gruff gestures, and, at the end, the same line: "Just keep running, boy."

He didn't know how Kojima was reacting to the scene this time, and he didn't bother to check. Instead, he put his hands on the floor and got to his feet.

He picked up the phone Miura had given him and dialed the number Kojima had given him: a direct line to the unit responsible for the investigation. He had thought of dialing 911 and talking his way through to the people in charge, but then realized Kojima would know a way to cut through the explanations.

Kojima, too, had suggested he limit the conversation to thirty seconds. It had been a suggestion, but somehow Aoyagi knew he should follow it.

As he listened to the phone ring, he felt himself tensing. Then a man's voice grunted "Yes?" No greeting, no name, but that was probably normal police etiquette—or lack of it.

"I'd like to speak to Ichitaro Sasaki," Aoyagi said.

"Can I tell him who's calling?"

"Masaharu Aoyagi."

There was a moment of what Aoyagi took to be shocked silence while the man considered what to say. Finally he muttered that he should stay on the line, and Aoyagi suspected at that point the phone was being switched to a speaker.

"Sasaki here," a voice said. "Where are you?"

Haruko Higuchi

Haruko woke with numbness in her face. She had fallen asleep leaning on the dining room table, her head resting between her arms. Her phone was vibrating next to her. The clock on the display said it was 3:30 A.M.

When she sat up and looked over her shoulder at the tatami room, there were no futons and no sign of Nanami. For a moment she was confused, before she remembered that the girl had gone to spend the night with Ami and Tatsumi. Haruko had expected some resistance, since Nanami's experience of sleeping away from home was limited to one trip with her kindergarten class, but she was having fun playing with Tatsumi and had simply told her to "Help Mr. Aoyagi" and had gone off happily enough.

At ten o'clock, Haruko had met up with Hodogaya and Masakado to work on the manholes. She knew they probably didn't need her help, but she was the one who had got Masakado involved, so she could hardly have left them and gone home to bed. Besides, when she thought about what was happening to Aoyagi, she knew she had to do something herself.

They met on a narrow, one-way street near the hospital. Masakado told them the rounds for the Security Pods started at eleven, so they used the hour to collect the fake manhole covers from Hodogaya's place, which was a large house in an expensive neighborhood in Uesugi. Haruko was a bit surprised by the size of it, but when she asked him why he didn't get out of the hospital and come home, he had nothing to say.

Seeing him return to the van clutching an armload of realistic but featherlight manhole covers, they knew better than to ask any questions and simply loaded them in the back. Then they headed for the area where they planned to make the switch. On the way, they began to realize they were dealing with a professional. He had brought rubber gloves and made them put them on. "Wouldn't want to leave any messy prints," he said.

He had also brought a kind of crowbar with a hook on the end for hoisting the real covers. When they reached the first manhole, he attached the hook, bent his knees, and pried it open. "These weigh sixty kilos," he said. "It would take Aoyagi half the night to get one open from below." He dropped in the fake, then pulled it back out with one hand.

"Is this really where he's going to start?" Masakado asked. He seemed to be having trouble believing the whole scheme could work.

Haruko bent over and lifted the cover, then peered into the hole. It was dark, with no sign of the bottom. When Hodogaya reached over her shoulder and aimed a flashlight down the ladder, a patch of damp cement appeared about six meters below. She tried to imagine Aoyagi disappearing here tomorrow morning.

A chain was attached to the underside of the fake cover, with a hook at the end. "If he latches this onto the ladder after he climbs in, it'll be harder to open from the outside," Hodogaya explained. Then he seemed to remember something and climbed down into the hole for a moment—to leave an extra flashlight, apparently. "I also left a map of the drain system," he said with a note of satisfaction as he reappeared. "That should do it."

When they had finished and Haruko stood looking at the manhole, it struck her as weird that she might never see Aoyagi again and yet he wasn't far away and was heading in this direction. In the half-light before dawn, he would lift this cover and lower himself into this dark aperture. Was he all right? Would he make it? she wanted to ask the person who would soon be here in this strange place.

The whole job took less than thirty minutes. When they were done, Hodogaya insisted they celebrate, so they repaired to the parking lot of a nearby convenience store and drank some juice and beer from cans in the van. Masakado was still marveling at how well Hodogaya managed to get around with the casts on his legs, and also curious as to why the hospital let him stay on when he was so able-bodied.

Hodogaya's claim that it was due to his "connections in the underworld" might have sounded like so much bluster, but they were far less inclined to doubt him now that they had seen the skillfully faked manhole covers and the ease with which he organized the switching operation.

"We've done our bit," he said as he drained his beer. "Now we'll have to wait and see whether he can pull this off." He might have been talking about a pennant run by his favorite baseball team.

"What would that mean?" Haruko said. "Simply surviving the night?"

"It might at that," Hodogaya admitted. "The cops are basically cowards. If things get messy during a chase, they're quite happy to shoot first and ask questions later."

"Even when they're on live TV?" Masakado asked.

"No, but they might find someone else to do the job. They wouldn't need to do it themselves if they could say that some gung-ho citizen did it for them. A very likely scenario."

"I hope he'll know enough to run if things get bad," Haruko murmured. "He has to give it a try, but he shouldn't be afraid to retreat."

"It's hard to admit you've lost and turn around, but I suppose he could always go back the way he came, down the manhole," said Hodogaya.

"It's a long way out to the middle of the park from where he'll be coming up, and he'll be taking a risk getting there, won't he?"

"There're plenty of manholes closer in. Maybe we should fix them so he can use them, too. And you should be around to distract them if it looks like he's in trouble," Hodogaya said, pointing at Haruko. "You can yell 'I did it!' or something to get their attention while he makes his getaway. If you go yelling in the middle of that scene, I guarantee the cameras and the law will shift your way, at least for the few seconds it'll take for him to disappear."

"But why should I say I did something when I didn't?" she asked.

"Where's your spirit of romance?" said Hodogaya. "Isn't there any such thing as true love anymore?"

She had wanted to tell him that they'd broken up years ago, but something had stopped her. . . .

And now she realized again that her phone was ringing on the table next to her. The display told her it was her husband.

"Do you know what time it is?" she said.

"They said it would be on TV at 4:00, so I thought you'd be watching." She didn't understand what he was talking about at first, but then it hit her.

"They've announced it on TV?"

"A half hour ago. He's going to come out into the open. There's a huge crowd around the bus stand at the east exit of the station. Lights blazing, like a festival or something. Like the night before the World Cup."

"But why were *you* watching at this time of night?"

"We were working late, trying to finish some things for a meeting tomorrow."

"You poor thing." She had allowed herself to believe that he had it pretty easy when he was away on business.

"Save your sympathy for your friend," he laughed. "I'm afraid he needs it a lot more. We were checking figures in a conference room, but one of the guys who was looking at the news on his laptop hopped up to turn on the TV. Sendai seems to be the center of the universe tonight."

The cogs in Haruko's sleep-fogged brain began to turn. Someone was undoubtedly listening in on this call, which had already lasted more than thirty seconds. She picked up the remote and turned on the TV.

"How's Nanami?" he asked.

"Asleep at the moment," Haruko told him, neglecting to add that she was at Ami Tsuruta's house. "What do they say he's going to do?"

"Apparently he called the police and said he'd show up at the bus stand at the east exit. They plan to arrest him there. But he's claiming he'll have a hostage with him so they're supposed to keep their distance."

"A hostage?"

"I assume he wants to make sure the police don't get too close—that they don't clap him in irons or shoot him dead the minute he shows his face. He may be bluffing, but it should keep them back for a while at least."

"Pretty good." The words slipped out before she knew what she was saying. He'd come surprisingly close to guessing what Aoyagi had in mind. "You should get a job as a profiler."

"Looks like the police have guessed that much without my help. But there's also a rumor that one of the stations is going to be broadcasting his voice live as he makes his entrance."

"Where did you hear that?" she said. She couldn't imagine Aoyagi had wanted that information to get out.

"It's making the rounds on the blogs. He'll be talking live to some reporter as he surrenders."

"No doubt 'some reporter' posted it himself."

"Probably," he said.

"And they're probably sorry they couldn't convince him to surrender in prime time," said Haruko. Aoyagi may well have chosen the early hour just to put them out.

"There's more," said Nobuyuki. "The police are planning to use these new dart guns they've just brought on line." Dart guns? The new information was more than Haruko's brain could take in. "The cops must have realized they couldn't shoot him in cold blood on live TV, so they came up with an alternative that lets them 'shoot' him—with an asterisk. He shows up and at the least sign of suspicious behavior they bring him down with a tranquilizer dart and hog-tie him. You have to remember: they're desperate, too."

But would Aoyagi know about this development? Haruko felt a sudden rush of panic. If he was checking the TV, he might find out, but he might already be on his way down the storm drain via the manhole near the bicycle parking lot at Kakyo-in. And this was important information, the kind he would need to make his decision at the end.

"What are you going to do?" Nobuyuki asked suddenly.

"I'm going to watch," she said calmly. "It could be the performance of a lifetime." The scene on TV was brilliantly illuminated in the foreground. The sky beyond was dark. The camera panned back and forth between the elevated pedestrian bridges leading to the station and the row of buses below. Forced to keep their distance, the networks had apparently found spots for their film crews in the surrounding hotels and on the roofs of nearby buildings. The trains were still out of service for the night, so the tracks at the edge of the shot were silent and gray. In the foreground was the roof and parking lot of a large electronics discount store.

Spotlights played across the plaza, flitting one way and the other. Haruko realized that Hodogaya had been right: everyone was convinced that Aoyagi was about to appear there in front of their eyes, and the park on the other side of the station would be virtually unguarded.

"You should go home and watch on TV," Hodogaya had told her several hours earlier. "I'm going back to the hospital myself for the show. It would be awkward if someone there or one of my old business associates caught sight of me loitering in the park."

"So I don't need to call from near the park?"

"If you hang around there, the police are bound to notice. You should go home and wait."

"And call when I see what's happening on TV?"

"No, the call still needs to come from somewhere near the park," Hodogaya said. "If things aren't going according to plan, there's nothing much we can do about it anyway, so it's probably better that you aren't the one to do it."

"So who's going there to make the call?" Haruko asked, and Hodogaya's eyes shifted to Masakado, who had been busy checking the mail on his phone.

"Me?" he said, looking up.

After she hung up, Haruko looked back at the TV, where things were beginning to get out of hand. The camera was apparently positioned on top of a hotel so it could look down on the bus pool, but the staff and technicians for the TV channel were moving frantically in and out of the shot, evidently unconcerned about being visible. The scene cut back to the studio.

Despite the early hour, the announcer was freshly pressed and highly animated. "We have a report just coming in that Masaharu Aoyagi will be surrendering in Central Park, and not at the east exit as had originally been reported. A man identifying himself as Aoyagi called this station approximately ten minutes ago with this information. When we contacted the authorities to pass this news along, we were told that the police had received a similar call. We are moving a crew to the park now, and we've learned that the police have begun to seal off the area."

The change of plans had apparently thrown the television station into chaos. Confused shouts could be heard in the background, and the screen suddenly went blank. Then a smudge of light flooded in from the right—a camera mounted on a car was trained on the city lights, the image grainy like a low-budget film. "We are heading toward Central Park," a woman's voice said.

The fact that they felt compelled to keep filming while in transit was evidence either that they were enterprising or that they were just going through the motions. The city lights streamed out behind the car as it sped throught the empty, early morning streets. From time to time, red brake lights flashed ahead, perhaps vehicles from other TV stations racing to the scene. Soon the car stopped and the shot came to a rest.

"What's happening?" the studio announcer's voice could be heard asking.

"A red light," the woman said. She sounded exasperated at being forced to obey a traffic signal at four in the morning in an empty city, and no doubt they would have run the light if the camera had not been rolling. They started up again and at last the reporter said they were nearing the park. "The police have cordoned off the area," she said as the car pulled to a stop.

It took them a moment to set up, but when the scene came into focus again, the camera panned down a gently curving street lined with vans and police cars. As Haruko stared at the screen, one of the vans caught her attention—Masakado's work truck, the one she had been riding in just a few hours ago. She even caught a glimpse of Masakado himself jumping out of it, with another man who had been in the passenger seat.

Haruko got up and grabbed her jacket from the back of the sofa.

Masaharu Aoyagi

The storm drain was less than two meters in diameter, so he had to move along exactly in the middle of it. He could walk easily enough, but to run he had to bend over to avoid hitting his head. So he ran now, back bent, splashing in the shallow pools at his feet.

The flashlight in his right hand illuminated the pipe in front of him. His backpack had been left in Inai's apartment, and he had traded the padded jacket from the boy in the parking lot for a black sweater that would be easier to move in. He was too tense to feel the cold anyway.

"Once you go down at Kakyo-in, just follow the large drain to the west. Several other pipes connect to the main one, but if you keep heading downstream you can't go wrong. The water left over in the drain flows toward the Hirose River; on the way you'll find the passage that leads to the park." Hodogaya's instructions had been explicit. "I'll keep my fingers crossed there's enough air down there—and that it doesn't rain."

It hadn't rained. And there was air. Things to be grateful for. He ran on through the darkness. The water splashed noisily under his feet; the air was cool on his face.

The map Hodogaya had left for him showed the route to the plaza in Central Park with rough distances penciled in. He hurried along, now counting his steps, and then stopped when he felt he had come to the right spot.

He looked up and ran the beam to either side. A ladder. He reached for the bottom rung and began climbing. Hand over hand through the dark. His hand touched the manhole cover. He pushed, stretching up, and the cover rose above him.

Hodogaya had kept his promise. Ever so cautiously, he pushed the cover off and peered over the rim. The image of a circle of policemen was registered in his brain, their shoes right before his eyes. And countless guns pointed at his head. At least that was what he might have seen if Hodogaya had sold him out.

Stretching further above the rim, he took a deep breath but choked on a waft of dust scudding across the ground. There were no policemen in sight, no one at all. He replaced the lid above him and climbed down the ladder. Then he took the cell phone from his pocket, attached a miniature microphone to his lapel, and climbed back up. He popped the cover off the hole, slipped out, and replaced it all in one motion. Hodogaya's fakes were impressive—almost indistinguishable from the real thing.

Central Park was on the north side of a wide street where it crossed Higashi Nibancho Avenue, the site of the bombing. It was a flat, open area, some forty by seventy meters in size, with no fountains or other features except some trees at the border, selected because it should give the TV cameras a clear view . . . of him. A view that might prevent the police from shooting him, or so he was hoping. The manhole from which he had just emerged was on the south side, sandwiched between a large public restroom decorated with geometric tiles and a long, narrow commercial building.

He could see the trunks of the Himalayan cedars at the edge of the park, so thick around that two people could barely circle them with outstretched arms. The branches draped almost to the ground like dark cascades.

Aoyagi leaned against the wall of the restroom and looked at some smaller trees planted among the cedars, another evergreen known as *tabunoki*. They stood in the half-light like silent guards. To one side, he could make out a small pavilion housing an elevator and escalator leading down to the subway. Having been alerted that he would be meeting them in the park, the police would presumably keep a watch there as well.

There was a clear path from here to the spot where he would make his appearance, his final stage. The area was deep in shadow, except for one patch off to the right that was flooded with light. "You're on! That's your cue!" He could hear Morita laughing and whispering in his ear. "Presenting Masaharu Aoyagi!"

Fishing the phone out of his pocket, he hit "redial." Would one of the concealed TV cameras pick him up standing here beside the restroom? Fine. Let them film everything.

After several rings a voice said "Yajima speaking."

"As in Yaji Yaji Yajima?" he said, realizing it felt good still to be able to make a joke.

"Mr. Aoyagi? Where are you now?"

"Are your cameras in place?" he asked.

"We've got a clear shot of the whole park from the roof of the Prefectural Building. The place is wide open thanks to your last-minute change of venue." The Prefectural Building was still some way from the park, but they should be able to get a decent close-up with the right lens.

"Sounds good," said Aoyagi. "I'm on then. But I want you to broadcast my voice as we agreed." He fingered the mike. "I won't have the phone to my ear from now on, so I won't be able to hear you."

"Well, good luck then," said Yajima, like a section chief sending a new recruit off to a meeting.

Aoyagi was about to put the phone away when he suddenly realized that the line had gone dead. He tried hitting "redial," but there was no service, not even a busy signal. What was happening? His mind went blank for a moment. Then he tried the phone again, with the same result. He tried removing the battery and reinstalling it. Nothing. His connection to Yajima had been cut. Were they onto him?

The branches of the cedars swayed ominously. There was no reason to think the police knew this number. Still, they were probably capable of checking all the calls made from the vicinity of the park, and something may have alerted them to a call to a TV station. Perhaps they had listened in and figured out what he was up to and had somehow jammed his phone.

He tried punching in the number for the third time to see if it was working, but there was still no signal. The thing was useless. Could they really do something like that at a moment's notice? He realized he had no choice but to believe they could.

He pulled the mike from his lapel and threw it away. Closing the phone, he slipped it back in his pocket. He knew he was completely outmatched, but somehow the knowledge made him feel more exhausted than frightened. Who could expect to defeat a giant? The lord of the giants at that? Miura's advice came back to him. Run.

He spread his arms and took a deep breath. Okay, then. He stood still until the trembling in his legs stopped. His father's voice on TV the night before echoed in his head. I'm going, he murmured.

Haruko Higuchi

Haruko found her husband's bike in the rack behind the building, but she fumbled for a long time with the complicated lock. The more she hurried, the longer it took and the more she felt the need for speed.

When she finally got it unlocked, she raised the kickstand and swung her leg over the bar. It was a mountain bike and, counting the time she'd tried it just after Nobuyuki bought it, this was her second time riding it. Bending over to grip the handlebars, she stepped on the pedals and shot forward. The speed frightened her, especially in the dark, but this was no time to be timid. As she sped along, she felt the cold night air even through her jacket.

Her head cleared and she was suddenly wide awake, despite the ridiculously early hour. Images from the television came back to her as she rode—the line of police cars, Masakado's van—and with them a nagging dread.

The lights from the TV trucks surrounding the park were bright enough to steer by. Go west, right at the intersection. She sketched out the map in her head as her legs pumped the pedals.

At 4:00 A.M., the streets were empty of people and cars. Everything around her, the sky and sidewalks and buildings, was a deep indigo blur. Shades of blue, some darker, some a bit lighter. The streetlights streamed by on each side. It felt strange to be riding alone, since she almost always had Nanami on the back when she went out on her own bike. Yet it wasn't freedom she felt but anxiety. Her breath came hard and her legs were getting weary. Taking advantage of the lack of traffic, she cut diagonally across the wide avenue and stopped pedaling, letting the thing coast. As the front tire hit the curb on the other side, the bike bucked softly under her.

Masaharu Aoyagi

He walked on stage, out into the open where he knew countless eyes would be looking at him. As he raised his hands above his head and stepped forward, he could almost feel the TV cameras panning across the plaza, coming rapidly into focus. They could all see him, yet these reporters and policemen, aiming their lights and guns, were invisible in the darkness beyond the edge of the bright circle.

One step. Then another. The park felt vast to him at that moment. He knew they were out there—cameras, lights, and guns—but he had no idea which was which. Walk straight ahead into the brilliant circle—that was the only thing left now.

When he had called Ichitaro Sasaki a little earlier to change the place for his surrender, he said he would have a hostage with him, so they were to stay out of the park and the surrounding streets. He had told the TV station the same thing. He had tried to make it sound convincing, saying that the hostage would die on live TV if he saw anyone making a move in their direction. He had no idea whether the police had bought any of this, but at least the plaza was empty. And the media must have taken up positions on the surrounding rooftops and across the street.

"I won't make trouble if you come alone to meet me in the park," he had told Sasaki, and the latter had agreed.

"Can I wait for you on the plaza?" Sasaki asked, but he had insisted that Sasaki stay back until he appeared in the park. He wanted to avoid a struggle during the surrender. But he thought he would be talking to the TV station and that his words would be broadcast live while all this was happening.

"I'll come out into the plaza with the hostage. When we get to the center, I'll wave a handkerchief and you can move in by yourself. I'll release the hostage and surrender."

"I don't understand what you're trying to prove with all this," Sasaki said.

"I want to be on camera for as long as possible," he had told him. He needed a long moment of live action.

"Why do you need a hostage?" Sasaki asked.

"If I'm alone, what's to stop you from shooting me the minute I show myself?"

Right about now the police were realizing there was no hostage. They were probably surprised, maybe even a little disappointed. He may have succeeded in convincing them he had some hidden agenda, that they should hold their fire, at least for the moment. But only for the moment. He had thought all along that the odds were in his favor, that they wouldn't shoot him in such a public place, with the nation watching on TV. But odds could be tricky. Maybe he would realize he'd been wrong a few seconds from now as the bullets ripped into his body. At each step he told himself, half incredulously, that he still hadn't been shot. A wave of dizziness came over him but he fought it off.

Somewhere beyond this ring of light—everywhere, perhaps—people were staring at TV screens, trying to get a glimpse of the man who had killed the prime minister. How many of them had any doubt he was guilty? How many of them had even considered the possibility he wasn't? The question itself was beside the point—they were watching a spectacle, a drama as compelling as any soccer match, live on TV.

He could hear a motorcycle somewhere in the distance. Someone was delivering the morning papers. But of course they were, he thought to himself. I may be here, caught up in this disaster, but they still have to deliver the papers. The paper would arrive on the doorstep, dawn would come, a new day would begin. The citizens of Sendai would head off to work or school. They would complain about the sleep they'd lost watching the drama in the middle of the night, and then they would go on with their lives.

Would the events unfolding around him now be the sole proof he could offer of his own existence? There was a double out there somewhere, but this was the real Masaharu Aoyagi, here in this park. Masaharu Aoyagi, who was innocent. He hoped that someone watching would understand at least that much.

The motorcycle was still buzzing along a few streets away. Where was it headed? He would have liked to wish the rider well. Where were his mother and father? He had been unable to produce the proof of his innocence, but he could still wave to them.

Haruko Higuchi

The signal at the crosswalk was red. She would have ignored it, but then caught sight of a police car parked on the far side and pulled on the brakes. A short screech echoed through the empty streets. She suddenly felt as though the windows in the walls above were staring down at her. The night was dark and cold; wisps of cloud were smudges in the black sky. A red light flashed silently on the roof of the police car.

A bank building towered on one corner. It was closed and shuttered, but a man stood in front. It was Masakado, but his hands were against the shutter and two policemen were bent over behind him, frisking his arms and legs.

Haruko hesitated for a moment, then jammed her feet on the pedals and raced across the street against the signal. As her tire hit the curb, she put on the brakes and came screeching to a stop on the sidewalk. She jumped off the bike and ran forward, calling Masakado's name.

Masakado craned around, his hands still against the shutter. He shouted her name. The policemen straightened up and turned toward her.

"Stop right there!" one of them warned.

Haruko tried to slip between them, but before she knew what was happening, she was lying on her back. She wondered which one of them had tripped her. It had been too easy. She rolled to her knees and struggled to stand. "I know him," she managed to say. "What has he done?"

She sensed someone looming behind her, then felt a sharp pain in her shoulder and found herself down on the sidewalk again. Her jeans scraped on the concrete and her tennis shoes came half off. When she could look up, she was staring into the face of a large man with a crew cut and wearing earphones—the man who had been with Kondo when he'd followed her to the coffee shop where she'd met Akira and Masakado. His broad face looked down at her now, the nose so straight and prominent it might have been stuck on. It took Haruko a moment to realize that the thing in his left hand was a gun. Her first thought was that it was some sort of tool, or perhaps a toy. But she had seen something like it before—in foreign gangster movies. She knew he could hurt her badly even without firing it, just by clubbing her over the head.

"We were patrolling the area and spotted that van. We ran a check on the license," said one of the policemen as he held out his hand to help her up. She ignored him and got to her feet, grimacing from the pain in her shoulder.

"We confirmed that it's a Security Pod maintenance vehicle driven by Masakado Kikuchi. But while we were checking, a man jumped out of the passenger side and ran away. Naturally, we were suspicious," said the other officer.

They spoke mechanically, their faces almost indistinguishable. Haruko knew who had been in the van with Masakado, but she had no intention of telling them. If they found out, the whole game was over. She only hoped that Masakado had also refused to talk.

"I'm sorry about this," Masakado said. He had turned to face her now. "I'd stopped and was watching that screen over there, when they came and pulled me out of the van." He was pointing back the way Haruko had come, at a large video screen high up on one of the buildings, which showed a picture of a park flooded with spotlights.

Haruko stared up at the screen, and the policemen's gaze followed hers. In the very center of the picture, she could make out a lone figure wandering into a pool of light, while off to the west she heard a cheer, as though a star had just made his entrance on the stage.

She tensed up. It had been a long time since she had seen Aoyagi, but she knew him immediately. When the camera pulled in for a close-up, she could see the dirt and exhaustion on his face—but no sign of despair or defeat. If anything, he looked defiant.

Her heart beat faster. The talking heads on TV were probably scandalized by his attitude.

"Seems to me they might need you there." Masakado had turned to face the policemen.

"Shut up," said one of them, before shouting: "Hey, what are you doing?!"

In a flash, Masakado was knocked to the ground and his arms pinned behind his back. A cell phone lay next to him. "Who were you calling?" the cop shouted.

"My girlfriend," Masakado gasped, grimacing from the pain of the grip on his arm. Abruptly, the big man with the gun walked over to him. Haruko wasn't sure what he was going to do, but she had a bad feeling about it.

"Wait," she said, hurrying after him. She was almost on him when he stopped and swung his palm around, catching her in the side of the head. She didn't actually feel the blow land, but for an instant everything went white, along with the sensation of being lifted off the ground, before her body collapsed in a heap and her face banged on the sidewalk. It took her a moment to realize what had happened. She thought he might have hit her with his gun, but she didn't feel much pain, just a hot sensation near her right temple.

Then confusion, as though she'd been covered in a sort of glaze that made it difficult to react to what was going on around her. She wasn't sure how, but she had apparently managed to get to her feet. And her head had started to hurt; when she reached up to touch it, she could tell she'd been cut, with some skin scraped off.

"Mrs. Higuchi?" Masakado murmured. The policemen had dragged him upright. She looked over at him, then craned around, following his eyes up to the screen on the building.

Aoyagi was standing in the middle of the plaza—an utterly defenseless target for all the marksmen in the world. Haruko was sure that a tranquilizer dart would sink into him at any moment. He spread his arms, waving them as though in surrender, or perhaps as a signal to someone looking down from somewhere.

"We're too late," said Masakado. In one movement, he lurched forward, broke free from the policeman, and scooped up his cell phone. Running back toward the shuttered building, he put it to his ear. A second later, the big man with the earphones had dumped his firearm on the pavement and reached toward the hip of the officer next to him—and there was a gunshot, as Haruko realized that he'd taken the officer's service revolver from his holster and fired it. Masakado looked back at them, his eyes blank. He clutched his hip and his leg crumpled, as if in slow motion.

The big man lumbered the few meters' distance to Masakado and stood over him. Had he opted for the revolver out of restraint? Or was it just handier? Haruko now charged at him again, but he sensed a movement and spun around to face her. A wave of fear swept over her—was he going to shoot both of them?—but she couldn't stop herself.

Her body moved almost automatically, remembering how her college friends had taught her to do it. Step in with the left leg, plant it next to the opponent's right. Grab him at the waist, then pull with all your might as you swing with the other leg. And don't underestimate the strength of someone who has to carry a child around all day.

The leg moved, but it was Haruko herself who was thrown. She didn't quite get the physics of what happened, but as she launched the judo move, she found herself flying through the air and rolling on the ground, pain shooting through her whole body. Her arms and legs were scraped, her knee throbbed, and there was blood on her hands, though she couldn't have said from where.

The man was immovable. And was now aiming the revolver at her. But just as she was closing her eyes, thinking it was all over, she saw him rock forward slightly. Masakado had tackled him from behind. Dragging his leg, he bulled into the big man and made him turn. Akira hadn't been kidding about rubbing the lamp, and this genie was sturdily built, like his namesake, Lord Masakado. But the results were the same. He let out a cry when he, too, was thrown to the ground. The big man's earphones had come off, yet he seemed otherwise unfazed as he turned the gun on Masakado.

But in the scuffle the cell phone had come sliding toward Haruko—Masakado had tossed it in her direction as he rolled across the pavement. She picked it up. "Hit 'redial,'" Masakado said, his voice nearly gone.

Haruko pushed herself up on her knees and then managed to stand. She looked back over her shoulder at the screen. Aoyagi was still waving. No one had shot him yet.

She suddenly recalled a night years ago when she had forgotten a date they'd made to go to the movies and had shown up after the film had started. Aoyagi had been annoyed, but in the end had forgiven her with the warning not to be late next time. It seemed like forever ago. But she wouldn't be late again.

She fumbled with the phone and pressed "redial," even though she could feel them watching her. Then she stood with the phone held over her head. "All together now," she said, her voice barely a whisper. The big man rushed her, but she had heard the sound of the call connecting. "Go, Aoyagi!" she said.

In the next instant, at several places around the city, the shushing sound of rockets could be heard one after another. *Psssst. Psssst. Psssst.* Then long, shrill whistles overhead as streaks of light rose high in the night sky. And finally, as the whistles ended in deep booms, the darkness was lit up with great explosive blossoms, which in turn slowly fell apart and drifted to earth. Flowers of light a hundred meters and more across, exploding in the sky.

In the shadow of a tall building, a great chrysanthemum. Since fireworks were never launched in the middle of town, the scene was utterly strange, as though the office towers themselves were sending out ribbons of fire. The night was no longer black, as the sparks lingered endlessly, floating ever so slowly down to the streets of Sendai. Finishing at last with a satisfying fizzle.

As the three men stood transfixed, looking up at the fireworks, Haruko got a running start and landed a kick between the legs of the big one.

Masaharu Aoyagi

His footsteps echoed from the sides of the drain, amplifying to a deafening boom. He was running along the tunnel again, as fast as he could go, though in the dim beam of the flashlight it seemed less a tunnel than a short tube that ended just up ahead. As he flung himself forward, the tube went with him into the dark. There was no way of knowing how far it went, how long it would go with him, and no time to wonder. He could only run, expecting sooner or later to bang into a wall.

Had they been fired by remote control? They had come from a number of places around the city, but it was hard to imagine someone had been at each spot to light the fuses at exactly the same moment. It must have been done from a remote site. And then he remembered that Todoroki had once told them that the day would come when a whole show could be done by punching in a number on a cell phone. "But the fireworks will always be the same," he'd added. Professional pride.

When Hodogaya had called him earlier that night to tell him the manhole covers had been switched, he'd said he had another proposal for him. Aoyagi had moved to Inai's bathroom so that Kojima couldn't hear before continuing the conversation.

"What kind of proposal?"

"Don't get me wrong; I like your plan. This whole thing about telling them you're innocent on live TV is a great idea, and if it works, you're golden. All I'm saying is, you might want a backup. If it doesn't work, you'll need a way out."

"If it doesn't work, I'm through," said Aoyagi. He was too weary to think beyond the park.

"I understand how you feel, but you might like to know that there's another manhole right there in the middle of the plaza. It's too dangerous to come out that way—you're better off walking out from where you've planned—but it might be just the thing for a getaway. Anyhow, I put a fake cover there, too, just in case. Just a thought we had."

"We?" It seemed the longer Hodogaya was involved, the more people knew about his plans.

"Just a few of us who've been brainstorming on your behalf."

"When I get out on that plaza, it's going to be surrounded by police aiming guns in my direction. You think they're going to just stand back and watch while I dodge down a manhole?" It didn't matter how light the cover was. "If I so much as flinch, they'll shoot—manhole or no manhole."

"Not if we can distract them for a few seconds. Listen, if you decide you want out, just wave your arms. As soon as we get the signal . . . kaboom!"

"What d'you mean?" But as he said it, Aoyagi suddenly thought of Todoroki. "Fireworks?" he asked.

"When I found out you used to work at that factory, I put in a call. I explained the situation, and they said they'd be happy to help."

"But the police must be watching them, too." And they were probably tapping the phones at Pyrotechnics. If anybody was planning a display on his behalf, someone had probably found out.

"Fortunately, the boss's son can't stand the media any more than the rest of us. When I tracked him down, he jumped at the chance to help."

"Todoroki's son?" So he'd come home from Aomori to take over the family business.

"He's going out now to do the setup; then later, if you give the high sign, he'll do the rest. And I don't care who they are, cops or secret agents or the goddamn Pope, when those fireworks go off, they're going to look—at least long enough for you to get down that hole." When Aoyagi asked where he would put the launchers, Hodogaya had laughed. "You'll have to wait and see," he said. "But if you end up back underground, you should head west. The drain passes under Nishi Park and empties into the Hirose River. Comes right out of the bank."

"And I just jump into the river?"

"There's a kind of gate at the end, like a big flap. It opens from the water pressure when the drain's running. They've got it fixed up to look like a rock, sort of like camouflage so it doesn't spoil the view. But you should be able to push it open from inside. The river's pretty shallow right there, so you can just walk across. There's a way up the far bank, near a driving school."

"And after that?"

"After that, you're on your own."

He went on running as fast as he could, not stopping to look back. The tunnel seemed to roar. He could feel the walls closing around him.

They must have realized by now that he'd gone down the manhole. The fireworks might have distracted everyone for a moment, but the TV cameras would have caught him as he disappeared underground. Still, it would take them some time to seal off the drains, and at the moment they were probably desperately trying to figure out where he would come up. And there was also the chain holding down the cover in the park—that should slow them down a little.

He had to keep going. His head was practically empty, his brain past thought, but he knew one thing—his life was over. His footsteps echoed down the tunnel. The flashlight let him see a short way ahead, but beyond that was darkness. Behind him, too. And that was his life now in a nutshell. His past and his future were black, and even the present, the ground under his feet, was vanishing fast.

"If they could make a double of me, could you make *me* into someone else?" After Hodogaya had told him about the fireworks, Aoyagi had called the plastic surgeon. Though it was the middle of the night, he hadn't seemed particularly surprised. "It's just an idea. But if things don't go well, maybe I could get rid of this face, live as someone else. Could you hide me at your clinic while it was being done?"

"As someone completely different?" said the doctor.

"Not if I can help it. But I don't have a lot of options left." He would prefer to stay as he was and prove he was innocent.

"No, I suppose you don't."

"It's my last move," he said, feeling for the first time that it really was the end. And yet it was one more thing he could do, one last choice he had available. If you went to war with a giant, that was the kind of sacrifice you had to make. When the earth moved, all you could do was survive, even if it meant abandoning everything you had. At least you would still have your life.

"How would you get here?" the doctor asked. "Do you know the way?" Aoyagi had asked him for the address, though he doubted he would ever need it. "It's a little difficult to find. Shall I send someone to meet you?"

"Who?"

"A friend. She was worried about you and called to see if I knew what was happening. I'll ask her to show you the way." Aoyagi asked again whom he had in mind, and when he was told he agreed.

"If you see fireworks early tomorrow morning, you can expect me," he said. "Have her wait near the driving school on the west bank of the Hirose River."

"I hope we won't be seeing you," the doctor said.

"I hope so, too," said Aoyagi. Last night, he had been counting on the TV station to broadcast his version of things, on the cameras to protect him while he surrendered and started the process of convincing the police of his innocence.

But it had come to this.

He was on his way to a place where he would cease to be himself. But he would still be alive.

"Run!" Morita's voice echoed around him, here in the darkness of the tunnel. "There are no points for style. Just run! Live! That's what being human means."

"Morita," he muttered, gasping for breath. "Is that the voice of the forest again?"

No, it's me saying it this time, he thought he could hear Morita say.

Then suddenly something seemed different up ahead. He could see something. He remembered what Hodogaya had told him and slowed. Bending his shoulder, he pressed against the wall and felt the panel slowly give way. As he did this, he could hear the sound of the river, like the snuffling of some beast at the bottom of the bank.

He pushed harder and the floodgate swung open. His legs slid out from under him and he rolled face down into the river. Splashing wildly, he managed to get to his feet—the water came barely to his knees. He wiped his face; the water had a rank, organic smell. But there were no police cars with flashing red lights. No cameras. He set off for the far bank, his legs struggling in the current.

As he pulled himself onto the rocks on the west side of the river, he could see someone approaching through the dark: a slightly built woman with a baseball cap pulled down around her ears. Aoyagi took a deep breath.

"I can't believe you're here," the woman said.

"I can't believe you came," said Aoyagi.

"You're soaked."

"It's a long story."

"I can imagine. But we should get moving. My car isn't far away." She reached out her hand to pull him the rest of the way up the bank.

"Are you back in Sendai?" he asked. She had written a few months ago to tell him that she was going to give up acting and come home.

"Sort of," she laughed. "But you've been making something of a spectacle of yourself again." After a moment she added: "I think we're even now."

"But I didn't exactly choose any of this."

Struggling to keep up as she marched through the field, he said: "Can I ask you one thing?"

"Of course."

"Did our doctor friend ever do any work on you?"

"Don't worry," Rinka laughed, ignoring the question. "He has some great computer games. We'll have a marathon while you're waiting for the swelling to go down."

Aoyagi hurried after her, the water sloshing in his shoes.

PART

FIVE

THREE MONTHS LATER

"We were being threatened, and you guys didn't help with all the pressure you put on us." Todoroki sat across the table from Mamoru Kondo and an older detective who was picking his nose.

The snow that had fallen two days earlier still covered the ground outside the window. A string of clear days after the New Year had convinced the staff at the factory that it would be a light winter—and then this storm. It was said that the total snowfall in Sendai was exactly the same every year, regardless of when it fell, as though the weather gods were keeping a balance sheet.

After it became known that the fireworks on the morning of Aoyagi's escape were Todoroki-made, the police had paid repeated visits to the factory. The boss's response was always the same. The day before, Aoyagi had shown up at a pachinko parlor where Todoroki's son, Ichiro, was playing, had put a gun to his back, and told him to set up the fireworks or he'd kill him.

"But we've checked the security tapes from the pachinko place. There's no sign of Aoyagi or your son."

"Of course not. I was playing a machine that was out of sight of the camera." Ichiro Todoroki was leaning against the desk by the entrance, scratching his ear. "Just because they have a lousy security system, doesn't mean I wasn't there or that Aoyagi didn't threaten me. I thought he was going to kill me. Are you saying the police won't protect you unless they get the whole thing on video?"

Not bad, thought the older Todoroki. "Anyway, I didn't think we had any choice, so we did what he told us to do. I set up the launchers and rigged them to go off by remote control. Ichiro didn't want to go, but I made him."

"You've told us all that, and the reporters who were outside that day confirm that a van left the factory late that evening," said Kondo. He had heard the story any number of times.

"Reporters have one-track minds. They were so focused on Aoyagi they ignored the van once they'd decided he wasn't inside." Ichiro laughed at the memory. It was their tunnel vision that had allowed them to get away with staging the diversion.

The older detective took a turn at the questioning. "But if they were right there at the factory, why didn't you tell them that the fireworks in the van had been ordered by Aoyagi?"

"No one asked," snorted Ichiro.

"So you maintain that Aoyagi threatened you and that you set up the fireworks at his insistence," Kondo repeated, though by this stage he seemed to be merely going through the motions.

"He had put the screws on the Security Pod guy, too, and he drove the van that night. We did it because Aoyagi said he would kill us if we didn't."

"Your story matches testimony from Masakado Kikuchi. And from Haruko Higuchi, who was also involved in the events of that evening. But why did you set up the fireworks in Security Pod blind spots?"

"Because he told us to, with a gun to make it more persuasive."

Kondo sighed. "Mrs. Higuchi has testified that Aoyagi threatened to take her child's life," he said. "And that she was willing to do whatever he said in order to save her."

"Can you blame her?" Ichiro said. "We're just average, law-abiding citizens. We would never have done any of this if we hadn't been forced into it."

"So you say you were waiting at that intersection near the park for Aoyagi to contact you, but when a patrol car stopped you, you got out and fled. At that point, why didn't you just ask the police for protection?"

"Like I told you, I didn't know whether they were really cops or not. I was terrified. Just wanted to get away." Ichiro's story had been completely consistent from the morning after the event, even if it didn't seem completely logical. For all his father knew, perhaps he had been frightened.

As he listened to the back-and-forth between his son and Kondo, the older Todoroki wondered how long the questioning would go on and how many more times they'd come back. The fireworks had provided Aoyagi with the chance to escape, but the details surrounding their preparation and launching had all been explained and weren't really central to the case. Most likely, the police were just looking for a scapegoat, someone to blame for their failures. He looked from his son to Kondo and the other detective, their faces expressionless as they repeated the same questions and answers.

Kondo turned to him this time. "If you don't tell us what we want to know, I can't guarantee you'll be able to keep this place open," he said.

Todoroki wanted to point out that he was being threatened now for the second time in three months. But instead he said that Sendai would be heartbroken if its famous Tanabata fireworks weren't available. "But if you think you can close us down, go ahead and try," he said. The other detective yawned. "I realize you guys don't get a kick out of this anymore," he went on. "So can I ask you something, just between us?"

"Such as?"

"Do you think he really did it or not?"

Kondo closed his eyes and sat for a moment. "Definitely," he said at last.

Shota Kamata pulled into the parking lot of his apartment building. He looked over at his son, sleeping in the seat next to him. The boy would be starting elementary school next year and he sometimes marveled at how much he had grown, but as he watched him sleeping, he realized he was still a baby. He called to him softly and touched his face, but the boy's eyes didn't open. He would be heavy to carry inside.

They were returning after a year and a half, and Shota was worried about the condition of the apartment. It had been such a windfall, he had been unable to resist, but had it really been wise to sublet to a stranger for all these months? Before she had left him, his wife had told him he was too impulsive—though before they were married she used to say she loved him for being so spontaneous.

Loosening his seatbelt, he reached for the newspaper he had thrown in the back. He would read while he waited for his son to wake up. It would be cold until he got the heat running in the apartment, so the kid might as well sleep here.

An article about the assassination caught his eye. It mentioned that a body had been found in Sendai harbor a few days after Masaharu Aoyagi disappeared. The police said it was Aoyagi's, but the article insisted there was no credible evidence to support this claim. Somebody in the know had pointed out that no DNA testing had been done, and concluded that the authorities had fabricated the story in an effort to close the books on the case. The whole thing seemed fishy to Shota—the bungled investigation and the over-the-top journalism. How could you know what was true when you were dealing with something that big? He stared for a moment at the photograph of Aoyagi. Handsome sucker, he thought. Probably had it coming.

Then there was a knock on the window next to him. The man peering in had sleepy eyes and a weak jaw. It was difficult to tell how old he was, but Shota could see there was something odd about him. Warily, he lowered the window. A blast of cold air came in.

"Can I help you?" he said.

"Sorry to bother you," said the man. He smiled, revealing a mouth full of crooked teeth. "I recognized the red convertible."

"I'm afraid you're mistaken," said Shota. "We've been out of town for months."

"Driving around the country?" the man asked. It wasn't really a question.

"How did you know that?"

"On the money you made subletting your apartment?"

Shota was feeling more and more uncomfortable. "Who are you? Who told you all that?" he said, opening the door and getting out. The man was slighter than he had imagined, younger perhaps, and there was something hard about his face. He wasn't ugly exactly, but his appearance was rough and a bit unsavory. "What do you want?" Shota said.

"Don't get me wrong. I'm just happy to see you back. You see, I thought you were dead. You live here, don't you?" The man pointed at the building. "I spent a little time in your place a while ago."

"Thought we were dead? What makes you think you can go around saying things like that?" Suddenly nervous, he glanced in the car at his son.

"Sorry, I'm just glad you're okay," he heard the strange man say, but when he looked back he was gone.

As Eijiro Iwasaki unlocked the door and stepped into his apartment, he felt something heavy in the air. His daughter's shoes were missing; she must have gone out to play with her friends. Probably to make a snow fort in the park.

He checked the clock. A little past four. It was his day off and he had been out wandering around town.

"It's freezing out there," he announced as he made his way from the entrance hall into the living room. He could hear his wife chopping something in the kitchen, but there was no answer. From long years of experience, he knew this was not a good sign. She was mad about something. But what?

It wasn't the first time he had gone out on his day off. So what had he done today? Left the seat up on the toilet? Left his clothes all over the bedroom? He ran the possibilities over in his head, but there was no way of knowing. Muttering something that sounded vaguely apologetic, he sat down and turned on the TV.

Before long his wife emerged from the kitchen and went to straighten the magazines on the coffee table. From the way she avoided making eye contact, he could tell she was angry. He had a queasy feeling in the pit of his stomach.

"You had an odd visitor," she said at last, making no attempt to hide her temper.

"Odd how?"

"I left the chain on, but as soon as I opened the door, he told me you'd been playing around with a girl from a club." When she finally turned toward him, he could see the anger and suspicion in her eyes. But he had no idea what this was all about. "I was scared, and started to close the door, but just before I did he bowed and told me to tell you how grateful he was."

"Aoyagi," he murmured, feeling goose bumps rise on his arms.

"No, I would have recognized him," she said. "This one looked a bit grim, with droopy eyes. Besides, Aoyagi's dead, isn't he?"

No longer listening to his wife, Iwasaki planted his hands on the floor behind him, looked up at the ceiling, and took a deep breath. "So that's it," he said.

"What is?"

"So that's it," he said again more quietly. "He got away."

"Are you listening to me? What did he mean about the girl?" Iwasaki got up. He needed a beer. "Are you cheating on me?" his wife said, pummeling him on the shoulder.

Ignoring her, he said, "That guy *rocks!*"

Heiichi Aoyagi was seated at a low table, watching TV and eating clementines. He stared at the screen as he pulled off the peel, glancing from time to time at the snow in the garden outside the window.

"We should get a dog," he had said to his wife, Akiyo, about an hour earlier. Her response had been noncommittal. "The yard's just going to waste."

"I suppose so," she said.

Three months had passed since the period when their son, Masaharu, had been on TV day and night. When they'd announced that his body had been found in Sendai harbor, Heiichi had insisted it wasn't Masaharu. But as he saw the forlorn look on his wife's face now, he realized that she assumed his sudden desire for a dog was in some way an admission that he had finally accepted that their boy was dead.

The phone calls from the media had nearly stopped, though the occasional reporter would get in touch even now to ask for an interview. The police, on the other hand, were still camped out across the street. It occurred to Heiichi that the continued surveillance meant they couldn't confirm that Masaharu was dead. So every time he caught sight of a detective outside, his annoyance was tempered by a sense of relief.

As he bit into the clementine, the juice splashed across the table. He wiped it with the side of his hand and called to his wife in the kitchen: "Do we have any more of these?" There was no answer, and it worried him. Akiyo had collapsed a month earlier with abdominal pain, probably brought on by stress. Then, too, he had called her and had no answer, and when he'd gone to find her she was doubled over in the kitchen. "Everything okay?" he called again, getting up from the table. But at that moment his wife appeared through the door leading to the front entrance. "There you are," he said.

"I just went to get the mail."

"Well, don't scare me like that." Padding out to the kitchen, he grabbed a clementine in each hand and went back to sit at the table.

Akiyo was kneeling next to him, sorting through a stack of letters. "There's no return address on this," she said, holding up an envelope.

"More hate mail, I suppose. Kind of makes you mad that everybody seems to want you dead," he laughed. "But I guess I should thank them. I'm getting pretty thick-skinned."

"Getting?" Akiyo murmured.

"You're pretty tough yourself these days," he said. He had always thought of her as sensitive, but she had held up remarkably well under the pressure of the last few months. There had been moments when she'd been upset, but underneath he had recognized a quiet strength.

"Knots in my stomach is more like it," she said. She started to tear open the envelope but then stopped and got out a pair of scissors. "At least I've learned enough to know you have to check these. You can never be sure they haven't slipped in something funny, like a razorblade," she said, carefully cutting along the flap.

Heiichi dug his thumb into the rind of the clementine and tore away the peel. He was just about to say how sweet they were in winter when his wife burst out laughing. "What?" he said, turning to look at her. She was holding out the letter, her face beaming but threatening at any minute to dissolve in tears. He took it gingerly.

The thin rice paper felt strange to the touch. The brush-written characters were large and crude. "Perverts Must Die" it read.

Heiichi stared at the paper, his mouth gaping open. "Oh!" he muttered, but that was all.

At that moment the doorbell rang. Since Akiyo was sobbing, he went to answer it himself and found a familiar detective standing outside. "Could I have a look at the mail that just arrived?" he said. They came every day to ask. Part of the investigation.

Heiichi handed over everything, just as he always did, and the officer went through the letters one by one, with the same embarrassed look he always had. When he came to the brush-written one, he studied it for a moment. "Still getting these threats?" he said, a note of sympathy in his voice.

"Pain in the ass," Heiichi said, scratching his head with apparent indifference.

He had been away from Sendai for two and a half months. After the surgery, he had recuperated at the doctor's private clinic for a couple of weeks and then taken the bus to Niigata. Nights in cheap hotels and Internet cafés, days searching for work. Not that there was much to be had, and what he found was backbreaking and poorly paid. Still, beggars can't be choosers, and for the most part he was just happy to be able to move freely through a city again instead of sneaking around everywhere.

He was back now in Sendai because he wanted to pay his respects at Morita's grave. He hadn't learned for certain what had happened after the explosion until he got to Niigata. Up to that point he had tried to avoid looking at the news online or in the weeklies, but finally he'd caught sight of a headline on the magazine rack at a convenience store—"The Secret Life of Aoyagi's Closest Friend"—and he had stopped to read the article. It confirmed that Morita had died in the car after Aoyagi had run off, then gave a gossipy account of his debts and the problems with his family.

Morita dead and him still here. Lots of people had been harmed in all this, including the double, whose body was found in the harbor. He'd been unable to help any of them, and now here he was, still alive, with someone else's face.

After the Kennedy assassination, too, any number of people had died, presumably to make sure they never talked. Oswald, of course, but others as well. And it was the same now. He took no pleasure in having escaped with his life. On the contrary, he felt guilty, and a profound sense of impotence.

Almost before he finished reading the article, standing there in the store, he decided to visit Morita's grave.

The cemetery was on a hilltop an hour's walk from downtown and had a fine view of the surrounding area. Morita was about halfway up the slope. "Morita Family" had been carved into an upright slab of black stone. Aoyagi thought of asking the stone whether it could hear the "voice of the forest," but at just that moment a breeze blew through the leaves overhead. He checked to make sure there was no one else around, then yelled Morita's name one last time. There would be no more smart answers.

He made his way back to Sendai Station and went into a shopping center nearby. It was brand new, perhaps no more than a month old, and surprisingly empty. On the top floor was a restaurant where he had lunch. As he looked down at the patches of snow still melting here and there in the city, he searched for the site of the explosion. What had happened to him? To everyone? He had run for his life through the landscape spread out before him, barely keeping his panic at bay, and in the end he had been willing to lose his own face to put an end to it.

The prime minister was dead. He had become a different man. And the man who looked like him had been found floating in the harbor. But what had really changed?

He left the restaurant and walked out into the lobby just as an elevator was arriving. The car was empty, but he froze for a moment as he caught sight of his reflection in the window at the back. He wasn't sure he would ever get used to this new self.

He had asked the doctor to give him a face that would allow him to blend in. Something plain that would be unlikely to attract attention.

"Understood. But I'm leaving you with your old fingerprints, so you should paint the tips with this when you're out and about." He had given him a bottle of clear liquid that looked like nail polish.

The elevator stopped at the fifth floor and a couple got on with their little girl. Aoyagi nearly let out a shout when he recognized the woman, then stared straight ahead at the buttons. The family moved to the back of the car and peered out the window at the city. "Where are we going now?" asked the girl. She was waving what seemed to be an ink stamp, the sort of thing children press on notes or cards.

"You shouldn't play with that here," Haruko Higuchi said, trying to take the toy from her.

"No!" the girl objected. She turned to her father for support, but he just laughed.

Of course, none of them recognized the man standing by the door. Why should they? Why should Haruko, even after all the time they had spent together?

A number of people had helped him escape, he knew, and Haruko was almost certainly among them. "Thank you," he whispered to himself. When the elevator came to a stop at the ground floor, he moved to one side and pressed the button to hold the door, signaling for them to get off first.

They moved past him, the little girl, her father, and finally Haruko. At the last moment, he realized he was pressing the button with his thumb and tried to switch to his index finger. There was no way of knowing whether she had noticed. If he was going to live life as someone else, he would have to get rid of the old Aoyagi habits.

After they had walked away, he got off the elevator and went in the opposite direction. But he had gone only a few steps when he heard a soft voice behind him. "Mister?" He turned to find the girl; her parents were nowhere in sight.

"Yes?" he said, looking down at her.

"Mommy said I should give you this." She took his hand, hanging limp at his side, and pressed the stamp she had been playing with into the skin on the back. Too startled to react, Aoyagi stood looking down at her as she turned. "Bye," she said, and ran off into the crowd. He looked down at his hand. There, in the center of a pretty flower, was a single word: "Excellent!"

People pushed past him as he stood there, lost in thought. Then he glanced once again after the girl and held his hand up to his lips to blow it dry.

（英文版）ゴールデンスランバー
Remote Control

2010 年 10 月 25 日　第 1 刷発行

著　者　　　伊坂幸太郎

訳　者　　　スティーブン・スナイダー

発行者　　　廣田浩二

発行所　　　講談社インターナショナル株式会社
　　　　　　〒112-8652　東京都文京区音羽 1-17-14
　　　　　　電話　03-3944-6493（編集部）
　　　　　　　　　03-3944-6492（マーケティング部・業務部）
　　　　　　ホームページ　www.kodansha-intl.com

印刷・製本所　　大日本印刷株式会社

落丁本、乱丁本は購入書店名を明記のうえ、講談社インターナショナル業務部宛
にお送りください。送料小社負担にてお取替えいたします。なお、この本につい
てのお問い合わせは、編集部宛にお願いいたします。本書の無断複写（コピー）
は著作権法上での例外を除き、禁じられています。

定価はカバーに表示してあります。